Love's Journey™
in Sugarcreek
Rachel's Rescue

BY SERENA B. MILLER

LJ EMORY
PUBLISHING

LJ EMORY
PUBLISHING

Published by L. J. Emory Publishing

First L. J. Emory Publishing trade paperback edition February 2017

For information about special discounts for bulk purchases, please contact L. J. Emory Publishing, sales@ljemorypublishing.com

Printed in the United States of America
10 9 8 7 6 5 4 3 2 1
ISBN 978-1-940283-24-1
ISBN 978-1-940283-25-8 (ebook)

To Steven

"To forgive is to set a prisoner free and discover that the prisoner was you."
Lewis B. Smedes

Prologue

....

Fifteen minutes before the organist began the traditional "Bridal Chorus," Aunt Bertha asked Rachel point-blank whether she was carrying a concealed weapon.

Rachel couldn't lie. She lifted the skirt of her white floor-length gown and revealed the leg holster and .38 Glock she had hoped to keep hidden. If there was one thing in which Rachel believed, it was to be prepared to defend herself and those around her at all times.

"Rachel Troyer!" Bertha clucked her tongue in disapproval. "Wearing a gun to your own wedding! You should be ashamed!"

To an outsider, Bertha, with her sensible black tennis shoes, homemade navy blue dress, and gray hair peeping out from beneath her black bonnet, would seem to be just one of the many elderly Old Order Amish women who lived in the Sugarcreek, Ohio, area. An outsider might assume that Bertha spent her days quietly baking pies, sewing quilts, and having gentle conversations.

Anyone who assumed that would be sadly mistaken. Having recovered from the broken leg she had sustained last year after falling down the stairs of the bed-and-breakfast she and her sisters ran, Bertha still did most of the outside physical labor around the family farm. She seldom baked pies or quilted, if she could get out of it, and she was not necessarily gentle in her speech. The old woman had a will of iron and bossed people around if she felt they needed it. Rachel often thought that in another place and time, Bertha might have made an excellent general.

"I'm a cop, Aunt Bertha," Rachel said. "That's what cops do. We carry weapons. Sometimes we even shoot them."

It was an old argument never completely settled. Her aunt had been disappointed when Rachel chose not to join the Old Order Amish church, but she was truly appalled at Rachel's choice of profession. Pacifism had been deeply embedded in the Amish psyche for over five hundred years. Bertha had no problem giving someone a tongue-lashing if they needed it, but she would rather die than raise a hand against another human being. From Bertha's point of view, having a handgun strapped to one's person was on par with wearing a rattlesnake.

Rachel, on the other hand, made her living by wearing a gun and chasing bad guys.

Well, actually, there weren't a whole lot of "bad guys" in Sugarcreek, a small village that sat at the edge of Ohio's Amish Country. Her job as a policewoman tended more toward giving a stern lecture to an intoxicated Amish teenager poorly driving the family buggy. However, if a bad guy ever showed up, she was ready for him.

Still, even *she* had to concede that being armed during her own wedding might be a bit much.

That was the reason, as Rachel held Cousin Eli's arm at the end of the church aisle, that she felt a little naked even though she was wearing a gown that consisted of approximately seven yards of white satin.

Joe waited for her at the end of the aisle. He was a handsome man with dark hair, still built like the world-class athlete he had once been. Beside him was his little son Bobby with his sweet face, curly blond hair, and big blue eyes. She loved both of them more than life, and in a few moments, she intended to say the words that would make them her own.

As the beginning strains of the wedding march began, she vowed that she would protect her new little family with every breath, every prayer, and every ounce of strength for the rest of her life. She would be the *best* mother and wife. With adorable Bobby and his amazing father for her to love, how could she possibly be anything less?

Chapter One

....

One year later...

Joe Mattias's car, a silver S8 Audi with the ability to go from zero to one hundred miles per hour in 8.5 seconds flat, was presently crawling along at the blinding speed of four miles an hour. The black Amish buggy directly in front of him swayed from side to side as the horse labored up the steep hill.

He had carefully chosen this vehicle three years earlier while his first wife was still alive. It had been the perfect car for taking Grace to one of her red-carpet events, stopping by McDonald's with Bobby, or outrunning paparazzi.

It would take only a second to pass the slow-moving buggy, but he couldn't risk doing so. The chances of meeting another car were too great. The roads in Tuscarawas County, Ohio, were hilly, curvy, and increasingly unsafe for the Amish buggies that stubbornly shared them with their impatient non-Amish neighbors as well as the sometimes-careless tourists who flooded the countryside each spring and continued to crowd the area until the snow flew.

Although he had lived here for nearly two years, Joe still marveled at a belief system so strong that it caused people to put themselves and their children at risk rather than succumb to the temptation of owning a motorized vehicle.

He just didn't get it. A car would have protective air bags and seat belts and a steel frame. A buggy had nothing to protect its occupants except too-easily-crushed wood. To him, the choice was a no-brainer. To them, it was a matter of faith. If it was God's will that they made it home safely, they would. If it was God's will that they endured a tragic accident, then that was to be accepted as well.

It was a fatalistic mentality, but one the Amish had clung to for generations. Joe respected his wife's relatives, but he did not understand them. All he knew was that he had determined to never be a cause of the pitiful wreckage that sometimes occurred in an area where cars, trucks, and Amish buggies shared the road. He loved these gentile people and would not allow his desire for speed to cause such a tragedy.

It took a lot of patience to live in Amish Country, but it was worth it. He would gladly trade time plodding behind a buggy in this beautiful countryside versus getting stuck in LA traffic, an experience which had been a daily routine when he'd played for the Dodgers. Therefore, he fidgeted, eager to see his family but forcing himself to follow the sedate black buggy until they topped the hill and he could pass safely.

He rolled down the window to enjoy the mild spring weather and then passed the time by communicating with the three adorable children peeking out at him. Joe waved, and a ruddy-cheeked boy about his son's age shyly waved back. The boy's two smaller sisters, both with white-blonde curls escaping from black bonnets, followed their big brother's example.

Joe made the peace sign, which they copied—the little girls putting hands over their mouths and giggling. Then he waggled his fingers on the steering wheel and they waggled their fingers back, enjoying the game of mimicking the silly *Englischman* in the car behind them.

He gave them the "live long and prosper" Vulcan hand sign from *Star Trek*, which was a momentary challenge to them before they mastered and exhibited it along with reserved smiles. The children each appeared to be about a year apart from the next in age. Stairstep children, common among the Amish.

The exchange made him miss his son. It wouldn't be long now. The four-hour flight to Columbus from LA and the two-hour drive from the airport to Sugarcreek was almost at an end. He was almost home. He couldn't wait to find out what wonders had happened while he was gone. It seemed as if there was constantly something new and exciting for Bobby to share with him. New piglets...new kittens...pears ripe for picking, found in the old orchard behind the Sugar Haus barn. Life was a constant source of wonder to a small boy who now spent a great deal of time on a farm.

Not only did Bobby have Rachel's Amish aunts' farm to explore, but he was also welcome at Eli's, their cousin who owned the small dairy farm next door. Eli had raised several fine sons and did not seem to mind answering a six-year-old's stream of questions. Eli, a widower who now lived alone, seemed to welcome Bobby's constant chatter.

There were many things Joe regretted in his life, but choosing to raise his boy within the loving circle of Rachel and her Amish relatives was not one of them. During his recent stay in LA, his longing to get back to Ohio was so strong that it surprised even him. His West Coast friends could tease him about living in flyover country all they wanted, but he didn't care. He knew where he belonged and, best of all, he knew to *whom* he belonged. Despite the personal troubles he had discovered in California, the feeling of getting closer to the people he loved most in the world was intoxicating.

The horse and buggy topped the hill and Joe saw a straight stretch with no other cars coming. He carefully pulled around the buggy, giving it a wide berth so as not to frighten the horse, and then he sped up as much as was safe on this road. It was hard to hold back. He had been gone for two weeks, and those two weeks had felt like an eternity.

Memories washed over him as he entered Sugarcreek and drove past the giant cuckoo clock in the middle of town. The waiting tourists snapped pictures as the wooden doors opened and a small band of wooden characters come out of the clock playing polka music to celebrate the fact that it was noon.

Had his truck not chosen to blow a head gasket here two years ago, he would have passed through without ever facing the flinty-eyed stare of Rachel, the beautiful Sugarcreek cop who had *not* been pleased to discover that a penniless stranger and his son were staying with her three elderly Old Order Amish aunts in their farmhouse bed-and-breakfast.

Nope, he had definitely not impressed her. He'd been a rough-looking stranger deliberately dressed as if he had crawled out of a Dumpster. No ID. No money. She had not bought his truthful tale that his wallet had been stolen. He had been as determined to hide his real name from her as she was to discover it. They'd had quite a clash of wills until Rachel learned his true identity...and became his greatest ally.

Those weeks of hiding from the media after his first wife's murder—unable to access his bank account or cash in on his fame while struggling to keep his little son safe from the nation's prying eyes—had taught him a great deal about priorities.

Many people spent their lives wishing for fame and fortune. Too many of them believed that the only thing standing between them and a perfect life was to have plenty of money and admiration. He had experienced both in abundance and knew firsthand that it wasn't all it was cracked up to be. His own experience showed that fame and fortune did little except put a target on a person's back...and on the backs of their loved ones.

Yes, it took patience and grace to live in Ohio's Amish Country, especially when sharing the road with horses and buggies, but that patience and grace was always returned. He loved Tuscarawas County and the eccentric and loving Amish people who lived here. If Joe had his way, he would never leave again. The only problem now, after what he had discovered in LA, was finding a way to stay.

Chapter Two

Carl Bateman was a bad man.

He knew this because his mother had told him so each time she'd locked him out of the house when he was a child.

"Don't, Mama, please," he'd begged the first time she shoved him outside. It was January, he was eight, and his clothes were not warm enough to withstand the freezing cold blowing through the inner-city streets of Columbus, Ohio. "Why're you doing this?"

"Because you're a bad boy!" she'd shouted as she slammed the door shut. He heard the lock snap into place.

For several minutes, he'd stood shivering on the rickety doorstep, alternately pounding on the door and begging to be let back in. He was desperate. There was no place to go. No one to take him in. And though he was a child, he knew instinctively that it would not be smart to go to the neighbors. At least not *their* neighbors. There was no telling what might happen to him if he tried knocking on someone else's door in this neighborhood.

The wind whistled around the corners of the small house, chilling him to the bone.

"Please, Mama! I'm cold!"

The door didn't open. Instead, seeping through the cracks, he could hear her voice and one of her male visitors. They were laughing, and loud music was playing on the radio.

Just then, a dog darted beneath the wooden porch steps. Carl had noticed the shaggy old thing skulking around the neighborhood. It didn't seem to belong to anyone. He'd seen it eating out of an overturned garbage can, bolting down part of a discarded pizza so old that even *he* wouldn't have touched it, and Carl loved pizza.

With nowhere else to go and no better ideas coming to him, he too crawled beneath the porch—where it was still cold, but where the wind wasn't quite as bad. The dog didn't seem to mind sharing its space with a small boy. It even licked his face a couple of times that night as though to comfort Carl, which was more tenderness than his own mother had ever shown him. He never forgot that bit of canine kindness. They didn't exactly keep each other warm, but they did keep each other from freezing to death. Together, they survived the night.

His mother had money the next day when the man left. She seemed surprised to see her son crawl out from beneath the porch but smiled brightly and let him back inside the house. That morning she took him to a warm diner and they ate their fill of ham and eggs as though nothing had happened.

That was the first he suspected that his mother wasn't entirely right in the head. He was too young to put words to it, but he began to expect of her a certain pattern of cruelty countered by an effusive, giddy, forthcoming kindness. It was part of his world, and since she blamed his "badness" for the cruelty she inflicted—and because he was only a child with no other template against which to compare his experience—he accepted her reasoning.

He was a bad boy…and he had grown up to be a bad man.

After that first night, he was careful to keep a couple of ratty old blankets tucked under the steps. He never could tell when she would take it into her head to kick him out. Stray cats and dogs became his salvation as a heat source in the dead of winter. They appreciated the bits of food he gathered in hopes of keeping the animals loyal to his cave-like sanctuary beneath the porch.

The counselor they'd forced him to talk to in prison seemed to be appalled at the idea of a child being locked out of a house in the wintertime. Carl supposed it was a terrible thing for his mother to do, but he'd sometimes been grateful for the safety and privacy he'd found there as a child. Worse things happened to small boys in his neighborhood when men came to visit single mothers. Much worse things than shivering beneath a porch and hugging a stray dog or cat.

Carl accepted the fact that he was a bad man. He was a murderer and a thief. But he wasn't *quite* as bad of a man as some who shared this prison with him. Carl didn't hurt children, and he didn't hurt animals. That was his code. He had never broken it, and he despised people who did.

Chapter Three

"Bobby!" Rachel paused in the act of setting one of Aunt Lydia's apple pies on the long makeshift table. "Get down from there!"

Her six-year-old stepson was an adventurous little guy whom she loved dearly, but the skeleton of the new one-room schoolhouse her Amish friends were building today was entirely too enticing to a small boy. Bobby needed to realize that the new structure was not a playground for him.

Compared to the obedient Amish boys pounding nails beside their fathers or the little Amish girls helping their mothers put lunch on the table, Bobby was entirely out of control, which was embarrassing. The child had more energy than he knew what to do with. Joe could usually keep him in check, but her…not so much.

Her husband had been gone for two weeks, which felt like forever—not only because she was entirely responsible for Bobby while her Joe was away, but because she missed him so badly. Their marriage was all she had hoped for and more, but she was worried about his trip to California. He had seemed preoccupied and worried before he left, but when she had asked whether anything was wrong, he smiled and reassured her that everything was fine.

Their phone calls since then had been unsatisfactory. He'd said they would talk in depth when he got home. She hoped that was not as ominous as it sounded.

***

Joe drove around the curve in the road and up the long driveway of the Sugar Haus bed-and-breakfast and was surprised with the most remarkable sight one could see in Tuscarawas County. Amish carpenters were swarming over the new frame of a building.

Rachel had recently informed him over the phone that her aunts had donated an acre of their farm for the new Amish school building. Apparently, the men of their church had decided not to waste any time.

He parked his car near a line of black buggies in the pasture behind the aunts' house. There was no reason to lock it. A theft within this group was not something he worried about.

Joe knew many of the Amish carpenters now, and he was familiar with how the Amish parochial school system worked. Most of the materials for the school would be donated. The rest would come straight out of the Amish settlement's pocket. Some would come from fund-raising dinners.

Even though they paid public school taxes like all other property owners, the Amish also built, furnished, and staffed their own schools with no help from the government. That meant they also had no interference from the government, which was exactly the way they wanted it. They were free to choose their own books and set their own curriculum.

The Amish were the first to admit that they were a flawed people, but Joe had found much to admire in them. He was grateful to live in a community where the bonds of family and community were valued and supported.

As he got out of the car and approached the group, he saw Rachel pulling Bobby off one of the roughed-in windowsills. Typical. His son could grow up to be a mountain climber or a circus performer if his recent behavior was any indication.

Dozens of barefoot Amish women bustled about not far from the construction, setting up a potluck dinner on long tables made of boards and sawhorses. Some worked while carrying a baby astride their hip. He wondered if they ever worried about stepping on a nail in the soft spring grass while so near a construction site, but they seemed unconcerned.

Aunt Bertha was at the center of it all, directing where to set the plates and desserts. She reminded him of a traffic cop, as she gestured here and there. As one of the oldest women of her church, she was respected...and obeyed. He was too far away from her to hear what she was saying over the general buzz of conversation and occasional shouts from the men, all accompanied by the pounding of nails and the sound of handsaws rasping through lumber, but he knew it would be said in her usual no-nonsense way.

Aunt Anna, Rachel's third aunt, helped also, by lending her excitement and joy to the gathering. At the moment, she was standing in the middle of the food preparations, smiling and nodding happily. Born with Down syndrome, Anna was cherished among the Amish as one of "God's special children." She had always been loved and gently cared for by her family at home. It had resulted in a sunny disposition in which she simply expected the best of everyone...and was rarely disappointed. He always found it hard to be unhappy while in the presence of Anna and her appreciation of life.

The loss of the aunts' original farmhouse B & B at the hands of an arsonist had been the hardest on Anna. For a long time, she could not wrap her mind around the fact that the familiarity of her home and possessions was gone. It was impossible for someone so tenderhearted to understand the kind of evil that would cause someone to deliberately try to hurt them.

Being Amish, the sisters had no insurance on their ruined house. That would be considered a lack of faith in God's ability to provide. Instead, whenever there was a fire in the Amish community, the family paid what they could, the rest of the money was then contributed by other church members, and the labor was donated. So there had been a similar scene here a couple of years ago when Joe helped Amish carpenters rebuild the sisters' home.

There were a few areas in which the Amish excelled, and taking care of one another in an uncertain world was one of those ways.

"Joe's here!" Anna trilled happily. With no responsibilities to tend to, she was the first to spot him.

Rachel stopped trying to coax Bobby out from under a table and stood straight and still, waiting. Instead of her Sugarcreek police uniform, she wore a long, flowing blue dress. Her dark hair was unbound, and she was barefoot like the rest of her Amish relatives and friends. She was a beautiful woman in any circumstance, but today she looked especially lovely. His heart ached with love and gratitude the moment he saw her.

She did not come running toward him as many *Englisch* women might do when their husbands came back from a long journey. Nor did she embrace him when he reached her. The Amish seldom displayed affection in public, and despite having chosen not to join the church, Rachel still had absorbed many of their culture's traits.

He often enjoyed a private chuckle over the polite physical distance Amish couples kept from one another while in public. Were it not for the multitude of children running about, one would never suspect them of being the romantic and passionate people they were.

"Hello, Rachel," he said. "Are you and Bobby doing okay?"

"Never better," she said. "It is good to have you home."

The only physical sign of affection she gave him was to reach out and squeeze his hand. But her eyes danced with the light of welcome, and he saw knowing smiles on the faces of the women working beside her. His and Rachel's great love for one another was no secret—especially since it had developed under the watchful and amused eyes of the entire community.

"You must be hungry," Aunt Lydia said as she placed a masterpiece in the form of a cherry pie on the table. "You will eat with us, *jah*?"

Joe blinked back tired tears of relief and gratitude. It was so *good* to be home. How lucky could a man be?

He knew the answer his Amish friends would give him. They would tell him that there was no such thing as luck. That having his truck break down outside Sugarcreek two years ago was no accident. They would say it was God's will.

Considering all that had transpired since then, he was inclined to agree with them.

"I would love to join you, Lydia. That pie looks amazing."

Lydia's smile of pure joy at having him back went straight to his heart.

"Daddy!" Bobby crawled out from under the table and came running. There was no holding back for Bobby. His son nearly knocked him over with his enthusiasm. Joe scooped him up and closed his eyes while he savored the feel of his little boy's arms around his neck.

"Have you been a good boy while I've been away?" Joe asked.

Bobby glanced around at the other adults with a worried expression, as though he were afraid someone would tell on him.

Rachel smiled. "A few bumps along the way, but he tried hard to be a good boy."

"A few bumps along the way?" Joe tickled Bobby's belly, making him giggle. "Knowing this little guy, I'll just bet there were."

He wished he could put an arm around Rachel and draw her to him, but he knew it would embarrass her. He ached for a kiss—and he knew she did too—but there would be time for that later.

Just then, Bertha began ringing the dinner bell to signal that it was time to put down the hammers and saws and come to the table. The men left their work and began to wash up at the old-fashioned outdoor water pump, some sticking their entire heads beneath it and then shaking off the water from their beards and hair.

After everyone had assembled and quieted, one of the bishops, Samuel Yost, called for silent prayer. The moment he nodded and said "Amen," the eating and passing of food began in earnest along with the hum of talk. The Amish were devoted to food, conversation, and one another. They especially loved learning details about each other's lives.

"Bertha says you went west to finalize the sale of the house you left behind in California when you came here?" In addition to being a bishop, Samuel was one of the community's more experienced builders. He shoveled a large forkful of food into his mouth upon asking the question.

It seemed strange to Joe for a bishop to be nearly his own age. But godly behavior counted more in the selection process of Amish bishops than the number of years one had lived on the earth.

"I did."

"And did you get a good price for it?"

He could depend on the Amish to have no problem asking for details. There were few secrets between them.

"No," Joe said. "When the negotiations were over, I barely broke even."

Samuel looked at him, head tilted, concerned. "There is something wrong with the house?"

"No. It is a good house."

"Explain, please."

"People tend to shy away from homes where murder has occurred."

"*Ach!*" the bishop exclaimed. "I am so sorry for my words, Joe. I did not heed my own counsel to think ten times before speaking. My curiosity was that of a carpenter's. I thought there might have been some repairs needing to be made."

"There is no need to apologize. I understand your interest, and I had a caretaker who kept the house in good repair."

"In spite of the earthquakes and fires we hear about, making living in that country dangerous?"

"Yes, in spite of those." Joe was not surprised at the question. California must, indeed, seem like an entirely different "country" to this Ohio carpenter. And a frightening one.

The bishop changed the subject. "The Englisch schools will be letting out for the summer before too long. You will be without work?"

"For awhile."

"This coaching you do, it pays well?"

Joe smiled and shrugged.

Actually, the part-time job he held of coaching at the local high school didn't pay well at all. In fact, it was somewhat embarrassing how little he was making. Money hadn't been a problem when he had first accepted the position. He coached for the love of the game and for whatever he could accomplish with the kids. And he was grateful for the chance.

However, now he most certainly was not a rich man, and there weren't a lot of good-paying jobs available for an almost-over-the-hill ballplayer. At least not in Sugarcreek.

A bite of fried chicken so tender it nearly melted in his mouth made him feel infinitely better. The financial sacrifice of living here had payoffs that were impossible to put a price on. Rachel and Bobby were happy here. Being part of a community that truly cared about *him*, instead of the baseball legend he used to be, mattered to him. And then there was the food!

Jeremiah Miller, a man always ready with a joke, joined in on Joe's conversation with Samuel. "Perhaps you should become a farmer, now that you are out of work!"

"I've been thinking about buying a farm," Joe said with a straight face. "After all, if *you* make a living at it, Jeremiah, how hard can it be?"

"This Englischman makes a good point." The bishop slapped his knee and laughed. Then he sobered and nodded toward Rachel, who was fixing a plate for Bobby now that the men had gone through the line. "I hear Rachel is still working at the police station. You should find a steady job so she can stay home and train up Bobby in the way he should go. It is not wise to allow your wife to continue working a job better suited to men."

And that was one of the downsides of being part of an Amish community.

The idea of a wife who continued to work outside the home after marriage and children was an alien concept. A husband who allowed it could easily lose the respect of the others, no matter how far and fast he might have once been able to throw a baseball. The fact that Rachel was working as a cop made it even harder for them to accept.

They weren't particularly impressed with his former job, either. The Amish loved to play baseball, and they were good at it. Girls and boys alike played hard during recess at school, and there were often pickup games after a picnic or during youth outings. But the idea of a grown man making a living at playing a game struck most of them as exceedingly odd.

"I agree. You should tell your wife to quit her job," Peter Hochstetler, sitting next to the bishop, apparently felt no reluctance to offer his opinion. "Rachel is not so young anymore, but I think you can still get many children off her."

The comment sounded crude even to Joe's ears, which had heard the worst that the locker room had to offer. But this earthiness was also a part of the Amish psyche. These were not a people who pretended that sex did not exist, except for the caution of keeping their young children from too much knowledge. The Amish were a practical people, and the mating of farm animals and people were an accepted and acknowledged part of their world.

Joe deflected the comment with a joke. "I think I'll let one of *you* tell Rachel what she can and can't do—especially while she's wearing a gun."

This, as he had intended, brought on hoots of laughter. They knew and loved Rachel despite often shaking their heads over her choice of profession. On the other hand, on the rare occasions when they needed to talk to a police officer, Rachel was the one they preferred. Her ability to speak and understand Pennsylvania Deutsch, their mother tongue, had been a great boon to the relationship between the Amish community and Sugarcreek's small police force.

"Her skill with a weapon might come in handy when you buy that farm," Jeremiah joked. "She can shoot the animals that come to steal the prized hens from the henhouse you will no doubt build."

"He should become a dairy farmer instead, I think," Samuel suggested. "After a few months of getting up at four in the morning to milk, he might run back to his baseball playing real quick."

"No, he should raise chickens," Peter insisted. "Lots and lots of chickens. Shoveling chicken manure would strengthen that bad shoulder he got by pitching too many baseballs."

"Come over to my farm," Jeremiah said. "I will teach you how to plow your fields with my team of six horses. It is not hard." He flexed massive shoulders that Joe knew had been hardened by long hours in the field. "Not hard at all."

"Whatever you do"—Jeremiah chuckled—"don't invest in sheep."

"That is a true statement," Peter said sadly. "Whatever you do, don't raise sheep."

"Why?" Joe asked curiously.

"Someone spray-painted Peter's in the middle of the night," Samuel said.

"Why on earth would they think *that* was a good idea?" Joe responded.

"I think some Englisch people got bored," Peter said. "My sheep did not mind looking like a rainbow, but it ruined much of the wool. Yes, you should definitely not raise sheep."

The good-natured ribbing continued, and Joe enjoyed the camaraderie. Being teased meant that he was accepted by these good people. Had they not liked and trusted him, they would have eaten in silence while he, an Englischman, tried to make awkward conversation in their midst.

Then, over Samuel's shoulder, he saw Rachel glance up from where she was tucking a napkin beneath Bobby's chin. Their eyes met and held, transfixed, as the men's voices faded into the background and Joe's heart leapt at the sheer wonder of being married to this woman.

He had loved his deceased wife, Grace, and always would, but there was room in his heart to spare for Rachel. In fact, his longing for her was so great at this moment that it stole his appetite. He forced himself to swallow the last bites of food and then rose and took his empty plate to the team of women who were chatting and washing dishes at a mobile sink. Most of the women chose to eat only after the men and children had gotten their fill. Bobby sat at a table with many other children. With his son happily engaged and everyone else busily eating and talking, he and Rachel could have a few moments of relative privacy. He walked toward her and she met him halfway.

"I missed you," he said in a low voice.

"And I you."

Leaning close so that only she could hear, he commented, "Peter seems to think that though you are no longer young, I can still get several children off you."

"What?" Rachel's head whipped around to look at Peter, who was oblivious to their conversation.

Joe chuckled. "And the bishop believes that having a wife who can shoot straight and kill the animals with evil plans for the henhouse might be a great help to a novice farmer."

"Farmer?"

"They are planning my future for me."

"Oh! My father's people love doing that." Rachel's cheeks had grown pink with embarrassment. "But I am astonished that the men have been discussing the length of my childbearing years."

"Men are men, Amish or not. I'm not at all surprised that there have been some manly speculations about you. I think it was a good idea to take you off the market as soon as I did. You might have found yourself being courted by someone wearing suspenders and driving a buggy."

"After hearing about that comment of Peter's, I believe you're right."

The high color of her face subsided. She turned her back to the men and Joe saw that her eyes were troubled. He knew it had nothing to do with the banter of his male Amish friends. Despite her surprise over Peter's comment, Rachel was tougher than that.

"I know you're happy to be home, Joe, but…is something wrong? You seem to be worried."

Rachel didn't miss much. His wife could read body language as well as other people could read the newspaper.

"We'll talk tonight," Joe said. "After Bobby goes to sleep."

"I already made arrangements for Bobby to spend the night at Ezra's house."

"That's even better."

"Something bad happened in LA?" Her brow was furrowed with worry. "What was it?"

"Things were not as I had hoped." Joe glanced around at the crowd. "Like I said, we'll talk tonight."

Chapter Four

"Got a new friend for you, Carl." The dog handler walked into the common room of the prison where Carl had been waiting. This was where the exchange between dog handlers and prisoners took place. "She's going to need a lot of care. This is a bad case."

The dog the handler brought to Carl was not the worst example of animal abuse he had ever worked with, but it was close. She was a black Labrador retriever mix, one of the sweetest breeds of all, and she was a mess of nerves. As he stooped down to get a better look at her, she tried to hide behind the handler's legs. When he reached out to pet her, she made a puddle on the floor from the sheer fear of the touch of a man's hands.

He felt his anger rise and immediately tamped it down. Being angry at the dog's previous owner could transfer to her, in her mind, and she would not be able to distinguish the difference.

"Thanks, Sarah," he said. "I'll take good care of her."

The middle-aged, heavy-set blonde who handed the dog's leash to him had devoted her life to rescuing animals. Carl respected her for that. He also respected her for having the courage to deliver the dogs to the prison.

It was not as dangerous as some would think. The prisoners who had been given the privilege of working with the dogs did not want to put their hard-earned positions at risk. But, still, even driving up to the prison was intimidating to most outsiders. He gave Sarah points for being willing to do so.

"I know she's in good hands now." The volunteer wiped her eyes with the backs of her hands. Sarah was tenderhearted and a crier. "I don't understand what's wrong with some people."

"I don't either." Carl hated to see Sarah cry, so he tried to distract her. "Hey, what was the weather like when you were coming in?"

"Oh, you know what March is like." She sniffled a little. "In like a lion, out like a lamb."

"So it's nice outside?"

"It's perfect—warm with clear blue skies."

"Then go home and enjoy it, Sarah," he said. "I can take it from here."

"Thanks, Carl."

It was hard work getting the Lab back to the cell. She skittered around on the surface of the shiny concrete floor, trying to get away. He was finally forced to simply pick her up and carry her, her terror exhibiting itself by the dog going stone-still.

As soon as he closed his jail-cell door, Carl put her down and tried to get a better look at her as she ran, shivering from fear, to the nearest corner.

"It's okay, girl. You're safe now." He crouched and put out his hand for her to smell.

Instead of sniffing him and beginning to make friends, the dog cowered with its backside pressed hard against the cement wall. The whites of her eyes showed as she searched for a way of escape.

"I know you don't trust me," Carl spoke gently, staying where he was and letting his hands dangle between his knees. Dogs this frightened could become dangerous—even a sweet-tempered breed like the Lab. He knew better than to make any sudden moves around her. "I don't blame you, girl. I wouldn't trust me either, if I were you. Not after what you've been through."

With her tail tucked tight between her legs, the dog sidled along the perimeter of the cell until she was directly behind him. At sixty-two years of age, Carl didn't move as easily as he used to, but when he turned around, he saw the dog exactly where he expected her to be—curled up tightly in the furthest, deepest corner, beneath the metal bunk where he slept.

"You feeling safer now?" He might be angry at the unknown person who had hurt this beautiful, gentle creature, but he felt proud to be given the opportunity to heal her.

When he had first asked to be included in the prison's dog-training program, it was entirely for selfish reasons. The prisoners who trained dogs were to keep them at their side seven days a week, twenty-four hours per day. The best part, in Carl's mind, was that they shared their cells with the dogs alone. As long as he was a dog trainer, he would not be assigned a human roommate. Now, working with the dogs consumed most of his waking thoughts and gave him a reason to live.

He filled the frightened dog's water dish from the stainless steel lavatory in his cell and sat it at the foot of his cot beside her food bowl. He sat quietly and thought awhile. His new roommate needed a name, and he prided himself on coming up with good ones.

Blackie was an obvious one, but everyone used it. Carl remembered seeing a movie once by the name of *Black Beauty*. He didn't remember much about the movie except that there was a beautiful black horse in it.

Black Beauty sounded a little pretentious, though. Maybe he would shorten it to *Beauty*. That suited the pretty young animal still cowering in the corner of his cell. He leaned down and looked beneath the cot.

"Do you like the name *Beauty*, girl? I believe it fits you. At least it will when those scars get all healed up."

It would take six weeks of careful work to bring this dog out of her terror. At least six weeks. Maybe more. At the end of his time with her, she would be housebroken, able to obey simple commands, and trained to walk quietly at the end of a leash—and she would have gotten her heart and her dignity back. Carl intended to use every method he knew to make her whole again.

At the end of his time with her, someone from the outside would come to the prison, pay one hundred and fifty dollars to help cover the prison's expense of food, and take possession of the animal Carl had lived with and trained and loved. There was a long waiting list for prisoner-trained dogs.

He would be allowed to meet the new owners and give them special instructions about the personality of the dog. He would also take stock of the people taking his animal home with them. Usually, he was pleased. Sometimes he wasn't. There was nothing he could do about it either way.

Each time, it felt empty in his cell after his charge had been taken to what some of the visiting civilians called a "forever home."

His feelings were ambiguous about that term. Nothing was forever. Homes could be destroyed by any number of things, some from without, some from within. Some quietly rotted away from neglect.

The only "forever home" he knew was the one here where he could not leave of his own free will. The one with metal bars and guards. The one where he was serving a life sentence for a murder he had not intended to commit.

Carl had killed a man. Some said it was in cold blood. At least a dozen people saw him do it, so he could not deny it. But it had not been in cold blood. It had been a knee-jerk reaction to what he saw as a threat. Unfortunately, he had been at the wrong place at the wrong time and had reacted in the worst way possible.

Carl understood how a man could accidentally kill another man. The one thing he would never understand was why anyone would deliberately hurt a defenseless animal.

Without a dog for a roommate, he always felt lonesome in his "forever home." But he was seldom alone for long. There was always another damaged dog to take in, and he was very good at healing them. It was the only thing he *was* good at. He understood the psyche of abused dogs.

After all, he had grown up feeling like one of them.

Chapter Five

"Jock-itch cream?" Rachel paused in forking up her salad and stared at him.

"I only have to memorize a couple of sentences," Joe said. "It shouldn't take more than a day in California for me to film the commercial."

"Wearing nothing but your *underwear*?"

"Well...yes."

"On *television*?"

Joe felt a little sick to his stomach at hearing the shock in her voice. It hadn't sounded quite as bad when an agent in LA contacted him and said that the owner of the company was a big fan of his.

"It pays well, Rachel." Joe took a bite of spaghetti and noted that the noodles could have used a few more minutes in boiling water. He chose not to point out this fact to her. "And a lot of other athletes would jump at the chance."

"Are you teasing me?"

"No. I'm serious."

"Are we really that bad off financially?"

"Yes, actually, we are."

He had not wanted to give her the bad news on his first night back, but it was not easy to keep anything from her. This was one of the drawbacks of being married to a cop. He had thought he could cushion things by first telling her about the money he would make with the commercial. Obviously, that was a mistake.

"I know you were disappointed that you didn't get a better price on the house," she said, "but did something else happen in LA?"

"I'm afraid so."

"Okay." She shoved her plate away. "I want details."

He took a deep breath. Dinner had lost its appeal to him as well, and his lack of appetite had nothing to do with undercooked spaghetti.

"Do you remember how we divided up the household chores when we first got married? We decided that I would take on the job of banking and paying the bills?"

"I remember. Was that a mistake?"

"No," he said. "I'm actually pretty good at it. I only wish I'd figured that out a lot sooner."

She leaned against the back of her chair and crossed her arms. "What do you mean?"

"Back when I was playing ball and Grace's acting career was sky-rocketing, we had no idea how to handle our money. Grace came from nothing, and my parents subsisted on a missionary's pay while my brother and I were growing up. I was signing million-dollar contracts and so was Grace. We didn't trust ourselves to know how to deal with all that money. The busier we got, the more we allowed Henrietta, as our agent and manager, to handle things."

"Oh no." Rachel groaned. "Henrietta is part of this story?"

"I'm afraid so."

"It's truly amazing how much damage one toxic individual can do."

"*Tell* me about it." He sighed. "The more she took care of us, the more we let her. It was easy to turn over our lives to such a competent woman. At heart, we were still just a couple of kids who wanted the grown-ups to take care of things. Before long, Henrietta was managing everything, including our finances. We thought eliminating so many business decisions would make us more productive in our jobs."

"Considering what that woman did to my aunts and to Grace, that was a mistake."

"It was a terrible mistake. Henrietta was a disaster," Joe said. "But Grace and I didn't know that at the time. We were impressed with the fact that we were at a point in our careers where we needed someone to be a business manager and take care of all the PR. Henrietta hired an investment broker to look after our finances. It seemed like a great idea as long as we didn't have to do anything about it."

"I'm assuming it was *not* such a great idea."

"No. But we thought we were being wise. Compared to other careers, an athlete's is a short one. I had seen other ballplayers blow everything on crazy investments or high living. Grace knew that actresses could be the hottest thing in Hollywood one year and unemployable the next. We were determined to be smarter than that."

"So what went wrong?"

"Henrietta chose the wrong man to handle our finances."

"Did he simply make some unwise investment choices, or was it worse?"

"Much worse. I recently noticed my investments trending down, but I figured that was to be expected with all the fluctuations in the stock market. It was slow at first. A trickle. But the trickle got more aggressive. The reports I received started to get confusing. Numbers were not adding up. Finally, I called and questioned him. He was vague and did not give me solid answers. I told him I was coming out and wanted to personally go over my investments with him."

"I'm guessing that was a mistake too," Rachel said.

"You're right. I shouldn't have given him any warning. When I arrived, the office was closed and it stayed closed. I got the police involved. It turns out I wasn't the only client he had been stealing from, but I was the biggest. When he knew I was coming—that was the final straw. He's probably enjoying a nice retirement now, some place from which we can't extradite him even if we can manage to find him."

"Aren't investment brokers backed by their companies?"

"Not all of them. This guy ran his own company. The bottom line is that the police aren't holding out a lot of hope that we'll get any of it back."

Rachel was quiet. She stared down at her hands and toyed with her wedding ring.

"I'm so sorry." He reached over and grasped her hand. "I should have paid more attention."

"I thought the only reason you flew out to California was to take care of some paperwork involved with selling the house." Rachel glanced up at him. "At least that's what you told me."

"I didn't want to worry you until I knew for sure that my hunch was right," Joe said. "He cleaned us out. That's why I need to make this commercial—and several others, if I can get them. I can also do baseball signings, some personal appearances…"

"All the things you hate," Rachel said.

"I won't be the first man to do things he hates in order to support his family."

"I'm sure that's true." Rachel blew out the candles and began to clear the table. She had created a romantic dinner and he regretted the fact that he had managed to ruin it.

"I'll work extra hours," Rachel said finally.

"Sweetheart, what you can make working a few more hours isn't a drop in the bucket compared to the money I can make in an afternoon of telling the camera how well the jock-itch cream works."

She covered the salad bowl with plastic wrap. "You've actually used the stuff?"

"No," he admitted.

"Then how can you tell people how good it is?"

There it was again. That basic rock-hard honesty to which she and her Amish relatives held fast.

"The people who make commercials don't necessarily use the product. The public knows that."

She poured the leftover spaghetti sauce into a jar and stored it in the refrigerator. "They deliberately lie?"

"It's not exactly lying," Joe said. "It's a gimmick, like an actor playing a part. It's advertising. Everybody does it."

"But you aren't just anyone, are you?" she said. "You're Bobby's father. You're my husband. For years, you were considered one of the finest athletes in the world. People trust you. How can you consider standing there in your underwear and lying to people on camera?"

"What if I wear a towel?" he asked. "I could try to talk the company into letting me wear a towel. It pays a quarter of a million dollars, Rachel."

"That much?" She gave it some thought and then shook her head. "I don't like you having to lie, and I don't want other women looking at you while you're wearing nothing but a towel."

"Rachel, it's just one commercial." He was losing this argument and he knew it, but he was also surprised to discover relief and gratefulness that she felt this way. He'd had enough public attention to last him two lifetimes. The last thing he wanted to do was to appear in a commercial, but if that's what he had to do to support his family...

He gave it one more try.

"Rachel, one of the biblical principles I learned at my father's knee was Romans 13:8."

"What does that have to do with advertising jock-itch cream?"

"It says to owe nothing to anyone."

"Does that mean we're in debt?"

"Not yet, but we will be soon if I don't find a real job."

"You have a real job. You love coaching those kids, and you're good at it."

"I also love the idea of being able to keep a roof over our head. I don't want you to have to put on a uniform and a gun because I can't support you. Samuel was already telling me that I should make you quit, now that you're a mother."

"But we're okay for now, financially?" she insisted.

"If we continue to live in this house," he said. "But I wanted to build you a new and bigger house. I wanted to give you nice vacations, like taking you and Bobby to Hawaii or Europe."

"I have no desire to go to Hawaii or Europe."

"Okay, Disney World, then. For Bobby."

"Bobby won't be scarred if he doesn't go to Disney World."

"That's not the point, Rachel. You thought you were marrying a rich man. Instead, you are married to a man who allowed someone to steal everything he'd ever earned."

She rinsed and loaded their few dishes into the dishwasher. Then she faced him, crossed her arms again, and leaned against the sink.

"Joe, look at me," she said.

He did. Big brown eyes. Lovely hair. Perfect skin. A face and a figure that could make a man forget his own name…but compliments were not what she was after.

"Do you trust me?" she asked.

"Absolutely."

If there was one person on the earth in whose hands he would place his life and the life of his son, it was this woman.

"When you came to Sugarcreek, you were searching for two things. Do you remember what they were?"

"Privacy and a normal life for Bobby."

"I remember the exact words you used. You said you were sick of being in the spotlight. You said you wanted to go to a grocery store for a carton of milk without having to sign autographs in the checkout line. You said you wanted to be an ordinary guy with an ordinary life."

"I did," Joe agreed.

"Well, here it is—exactly what you asked for. A normal, ordinary life. You have a wife and a son and friends, and you're living in a small town where both of us work ordinary jobs, earning just enough to pay our bills, and staying in a cramped house that's hardly big enough for the three of us. This is what an ordinary life looks like, Joe. Congratulations. You're finally living your dream."

"But I want more for you than just getting by."

" 'Getting by' is enough for me if I get to live it with you. I can be happy with what we have. What worries me is whether it's enough for you. Has living an ordinary life lost its appeal?"

"That's not fair."

"It's not fair *or* unfair. Is wanting to do that commercial really about the money? Or are you, deep down, tired of being ordinary and want to feel like the great 'Miracle Micah' again?"

Her accusation stung.

"I'm going for a walk," he said.

"That's probably a good idea." She turned and put the hardened candles into the cupboard.

At first, he simply strode the darkened streets of Sugarcreek, burning off hurt feelings and nervous energy. How could she accuse him of wanting to go back to the invasion of privacy he had endured for so many years? It was a relief to live below the radar of constant public interest. Hadn't she noticed that he had *chosen* to live with her in this small Ohio town that rolled up the sidewalks at five o'clock each evening—when he could have lived anywhere?

Yet he was honest enough with himself to ponder her question. She knew him almost better than he knew himself. Did he miss all the attention he'd once had? *Did* he miss being the athlete known as Miracle Micah?

His missionary parents had optimistically named him after two minor biblical prophets as they lay side by side in a hut in Africa, holding

41

hands and dreaming dreams for their newborn son, Micah Joel Mattias. None of those dreams had come true.

Instead, he had been given the gift of extraordinary athletic ability. He'd been recruited for the LA Dodgers during his junior year of college in the States and shot up through the farm teams. With two of his main pitchers sidelined by injuries during an important game, the coach stunned much of the ball-playing world by putting Joe, a rookie, on the mound. He'd seen enough of Joe's skill and steady nerves under pressure to take a gamble. Neither the coach nor the fans had been disappointed.

Joe coolly threw a no-hitter under conditions that would have shaken the most confident of players and sent everyone in the sporting world into a frenzy. It was the kind of story baseball fans loved. The people in the press box had called it a "miracle," and soon people were calling him "Miracle Micah." It was a heady time.

He had strayed from his parents' religious teachings for a while, but more and more Joe saw the validity of those principles and realized how deeply their teachings were imbedded within him.

One of the principles he saw played out was that pride could ruin a man.

This, he knew firsthand to be true. Too many top athletes had been destroyed by being treated like young gods. Too many broken marriages because of inflated egos. Too many bankruptcies by those who refused to acknowledge that prowess as a ballplayer was not a permanent state.

That's why he despised the nickname "Miracle Micah." He was a skilled ballplayer—perhaps even a great one—but he was also aware of his limitations. He reminded himself of that whenever fans acted awestruck over meeting him.

When his first wife was murdered and the press wouldn't stop hounding him at a time when he most needed to be left alone, he started calling himself "Joe" and tried to disappear from the scrutiny until both he and his little son could begin to recover from Grace's death.

Discovering the Village of Sugarcreek and the gentle people within it had been a gift from God.

No, he did not have some deep-seated wish to ever become Miracle Micah again. He did not need the adoration of fans to feel whole. The only miracle in his life, in addition to Bobby, was finding himself married to a woman who could absorb such devastating financial news and not fall apart or want to leave him. He'd seen too many of his ball-playing buddies deserted by spouses and significant others when they could no longer bring home multimillion-dollar contracts—to not value Rachel's reaction.

If she would rather live on a reduced income than allow him to advertise jock-itch cream on TV...then so be it. His steps turned toward home—where the woman he loved most in this world waited.

Rachel was wiping down the kitchen counters when he came through the door. She glanced up, and her gaze was steady as she waited for his answer.

"No." He continued the conversation as if there had been no break in it. "I have no desire to be 'Miracle Micah' again, but you and Bobby deserve better than what I can provide on my part-time coaching salary alone."

"We'll be okay." Rachel folded the dish towel and laid it on the counter. "We're young and strong. We won't go hungry, and we won't be homeless. We'll figure things out...and we'll make a good life for our son."

Joe felt the quarter-of-a-million-dollar contract fade from his future as he pulled his wife close. His woman had beauty, brains, *and* heart. He had definitely won the wife lottery. Although he was pretty much broke, he had never felt richer.

Chapter Six

George Milo was a Mennonite minister who visited the Mansfield Correctional Institution on a routine basis. The first time Carl saw him, he wondered what on earth had possessed the man to come here. After a few conversations, he realized that George's motivation had nothing at all to do with earth. He came solely because he believed in obeying the scripture about visiting those in prison—even when it was not much fun to do so.

At first glance, George looked like the kind of person who, were he a prisoner here, would get eaten alive on his first day. With his kind face, humble attitude, and thick glasses, Carl judged him to be the kind of man who would spend his first night at the prison sobbing into his pillow. The more Carl got to know him, however, the more he realized that not only would George *not* be sobbing into his pillow, he would probably spend the evening trying to encourage the man in the cell next to him.

Over the years, George and Carl had developed a careful relationship—careful because George had been around a lot of inmates over the years and was not easily fooled. He knew how skilled some prisoners were at manipulation. And Carl was careful because he had yet to meet a person he could trust.

But as much as Carl ever trusted anyone, he trusted George. Over the years, the murderer and the minister had come as close to becoming friends as Carl had ever experienced.

And as Carl's spiritual advisor, George had been allowed by the prison to be the first to break the news.

"You're up for parole in a couple of weeks," George said.

"What?"

"You're up for parole."

"If this is an April Fool's joke, it's a bad one."

"April Fools' Day was three weeks ago, Carl. I'm telling you the truth."

"I'm a lifer. You know that." Carl was not amused. "Don't mess with my head."

"Yes, I know. But you've served twenty years, and you could have been considered for parole as early as fifteen years. There are some who think you've been rehabilitated enough. They asked me what I thought... and I told them that I agree."

Rehabilitated. That was the word the dog handlers used when they talked about the abused dogs they brought.

"Oh."

"You don't seem excited."

"I won't be finished working with Beauty by then."

"You would rather stay in prison and work with your dog?"

"No, but it took three weeks to get her to trust me. I don't know what will happen to her if someone else takes over her training.

"There are no guarantees," George said. "Most prisoners don't make it out their first time at parole, anyway."

"That's true." Carl immediately felt better.

"Seriously," George prodded, "don't you *want* to be free?"

In order to emotionally survive the past two decades, Carl had trained himself to never think in terms of "getting out" or "freedom." That kind of thinking could drive a man crazy. It would be foolish to get his hopes up now, after all this time.

"I'm a sixty-two-year-old con," Carl said with disgust. "What do you think I'd do on the outside?"

One of the things he valued about George was the man's honesty. Once again, George didn't disappoint him.

"I have no idea," he answered.

Chapter Seven

Aunt Lydia poured whole coffee beans into the old cast-iron grinder and turned the handle. The aroma of freshly ground coffee soon permeated the kitchen. The Sugar Haus Inn's reputation for the freshest coffee and the best breakfasts in Ohio's Amish Country would not be tarnished today, not as long as Lydia was in charge!

Rachel stifled a yawn. After Joe had broken the news to her last night about their financial difficulties, they had stayed up until after midnight discussing job possibilities and what they should do. Now, it was four thirty in the morning and she was kneading dough for cinnamon rolls in the dim gas-lit kitchen of her aunts' Old Order Amish bed-and-breakfast. They had guests this weekend and she knew Lydia needed the help.

She did not *want* to be kneading dough in what felt like the middle of the night. She wanted to go home, burrow beneath her soft quilts, and get some more sleep before she had to go on duty. Her and Joe's late-night talk hadn't brought them any closer to a resolution—it had just made her sleep-deprived.

"And how is Bobby doing today?" Lydia asked.

"He had a sleepover with his friend, Ezra, last night. He's probably still sound asleep."

"Ezra Yoder?"

"Yes."

"Luke and Naomi's son?"

"Yes." Rachel stifled another yawn.

"Ach. Such a fine Amish family. He will be well cared for there. Naomi is a *goot* mother."

"And as a bonus, with no television in the house, he won't be asking to watch Saturday morning cartoons while he's there. Ezra has a pony and pony cart now, and Bobby is enthralled."

"A pony cart!" Lydia nodded knowingly. "He will have much fun. Remember the pony cart your father bought you when you were a little girl?"

Rachel smiled at the memory. "I do."

"Let's see, what was that pony's name?" Lydia said. "My memory is not what it was, but I do remember the look on your face when we gave him to you."

"I named him Fireball."

"Ah yes. He was a good pony but not nearly as fast as his name would suggest."

"I was seven," Rachel said. "The name could have been worse."

Lydia started to pick up the heavy cast-iron skillet in which she liked to fry bacon for her guests, and Rachel saw her face settle into the stoic expression she wore whenever she was in pain and trying to hide it.

"Here, Aunt Lydia." Rachel quickly wiped her hands on a dish towel. "Let me." She grabbed the skillet from the shelf where Lydia kept it, setting it on the stove.

"*Danke,*" Lydia said. "But I could have gotten it."

"Of course you could have," Rachel said. "But I don't mind helping."

It was getting harder and harder for Lydia to fix breakfast for their guests every morning. She never complained, but her arthritis was getting worse. Rachel ached when she saw her aunt grimace over the pain from some small task or noticed how swollen Lydia's knuckles were after a day of baking.

Which was why Rachel found herself kneading bread at four thirty in the morning—and it was one of the reasons she had talked her aunts into closing the inn two years ago in spite of their great reluctance to do so. They had finally agreed, but only after Rachel conceded that they could still take in someone occasionally if they felt God was sending them an "angel unaware."

The inn hadn't been closed for more than a day before Joe and Bobby showed up and Bertha decreed that not only could they stay but even offered Joe a job! There had been a small trickle of guests ever since. All of them, of course—if one listened to Bertha—sent to them straight from God.

Rachel had given up trying to protect her aunts from themselves. They were old, but they were women who had worked hard all their lives and could imagine no other way. The Amish work ethic was apparently too deeply ingrained for them to ever retire as long as they could put one foot in front of the other and had the use of their minds and hands. To her Amish relatives, work was a gift from God.

Her aunts' Sugar Haus Inn was authentically Old Order Amish, and because of that, it tended to draw a different type of guest than most B & B's. It appealed to those who longed for simpler times and an atmosphere of peace. It was a house in which quietness was not considered an enemy to be slayed by television and electronics.

Sometimes older guests, who had memories of bringing firewood into their own mother's kitchens, would carry in an armload for the inn's wood cookstove, acting as though it was an honor to do so. During certain times of the year, some visitors also helped Lydia when she was canning produce from the garden.

Then there were the gentle old books that her aunts had gathered over the years, dog-eared and well-thumbed, which comprised most of the reading literature within the inn.

Rachel had seen the stress and worry drain from people's faces when they stayed at the Sugar Haus Inn. Perhaps it was the simplicity of the furnishings or the lack of ambient noises of electricity-driven appliances. Or maybe it was the unfinished quilt and quilt frame Lydia kept in the living room, available to anyone who wanted to try their hand. Many women and a few men enjoyed plying a needle and thread once they knew they were welcome to do so. Some spent hours in the quiet act of rhythmic sewing as they healed from the various cares they had brought with them.

The aunts loved company—and they especially loved hearing about the lives of their guests. Sometimes retirees who could afford it stayed for weeks and became close friends with the three sisters. Aunt Bertha's handwritten correspondence with former guests was a major hobby for her.

"It's as good as having television," Bertha had once said. "We hear so many stories from our guests. Some sad, some happy, but everyone has something interesting to tell us."

Rachel was certain that having listeners like Lydia, Bertha, and Anna was a blessing to some of their guests as well. She often wondered if her aunts had any idea what a sanctuary they provided to so many—including her.

On the other hand, it *was* a business. All the quilts hanging on the walls or draped over the couches and beds had small price tags pinned to them, and it was rare for one of the quilts to stay around longer than a few days during tourist season.

As Bertha often quoted, "Whatever your hands find to do, do it with all your might."

And in their practical, Amish mind-set, it did not hurt if one made a little extra cash while doing so!

The turnover of quilts had been so great that they were presently supplementing their stash with surplus from their other Amish friends' quilts. There was no danger of running out of quilts in the Sugarcreek area. If there was one thing the Amish women loved to do, it was to have quilting "frolics." Or "gossip frolics," as Eli enjoyed calling them, teasing his cousins.

Rachel was technically not Amish, but she wasn't exactly an outsider, either. Her father had been raised Amish along with his three sisters, but he had chosen not to join the church long before Rachel was born. She often wondered if he would have become Amish had he not fallen in love with a local Englisch girl.

She would never know, of course.

"We need to hurry," Lydia said happily, jolting Rachel into the present. "Both rooms are filled this morning. We have two couples with us. One of them has traveled to China! They promised to tell us all about it after breakfast."

Rachel yawned again.

"Did you not sleep well, Rachel? You seem a little sleepy headed."

"It's not even five o'clock yet, Aunt Lydia. It is still pitch-dark outside. My body thinks it should still be in bed."

"Ach! It is goot to get a head start on the day."

Most B & B's in the area took at least a few shortcuts in their breakfast preparations by freezing breakfast pastries to be warmed up in the morning or ordering goodies from one of the many excellent bakeries in the area.

Not Lydia.

Rachel never stopped hoping that her aunt would see reason someday.

"There's a new bakery in downtown Sugarcreek," Rachel said. "An Amish woman from your church owns it. If you purchased your baked goods from her, it would give you at least an extra hour's sleep in the morning. I've heard her products are very good and she opens early."

"You think Esther's pastry tastes better than mine?" Lydia sounded hurt.

Rachel was quick to reassure her. "No one is a better cook than you. But there is so much work to do in running this inn. I thought the breakfast pastries might be at least one thing you could hire out."

"Hard work is from *Gott*, and it is good for the soul." Lydia nodded for emphasis. "And our *grossdaddi* always said that it brings health to the body to get up early. He lived to be a hundred and two, he did."

Rachel couldn't argue with her. This tiny Amish woman in her white prayer *kapp*, long gray dress, and sensible black tennis shoes could work rings around most women half her age in spite of her arthritis, and she most definitely loved getting up early. Lydia was so bright-eyed and chirpy this morning, she reminded Rachel of a happy little sparrow hopping around the dimly lit kitchen.

Maybe Lydia had a point. Maybe work helped keep a person healthy—but so did sleep, and right now Rachel could have used a couple more hours. Or twenty. Before she got married, even though she was working a job that rotated shifts and she often helped her aunts as well, she could at least get enough sleep the rest of the time. Now that she had a small son to care for, it seemed like most of what used to be sleep or free time was taken up by Bobby's need to be entertained. His latest favorite was Candy Land, which he found utterly entrancing and she did not.

She glanced at the windowsill above the sink where she had placed her engagement and wedding rings for safekeeping. Bread dough was not a friend to fancy diamond rings—a fact she'd discovered the hard way when she'd had to spend a good five minutes detailing the rings with a toothbrush after she'd forgotten to take it off first.

Her engagement ring was lovely but wearing it bothered her. Joe did not know this. He had surprised her with a proposal and a small box wrapped in silver paper the Christmas after they met. Inside was the biggest, most beautiful diamond ring she had ever seen. She'd been thrilled with the proposal but had mixed feelings about the ring. Had he asked her preference before selecting it, she would have reminded him that she came from people who never wore simple wedding bands or wristwatches, let alone diamond engagement rings. In fact, it embarrassed Rachel to wear it around her Amish relatives.

She was no judge of diamonds, but it didn't take an expert to know that Joe had paid a lot of money for it. Her first thought was that it was something his first wife, Grace, would have chosen, which lessened Rachel's enthusiasm for it even more. It wasn't that she was jealous of his deceased wife, but Grace had been a beautiful and glamorous actress, which was a little intimidating to a small-town cop who had never quite mastered the art of using a mascara wand.

"You need to go to bed earlier, Rachel," Lydia chirped, bringing her out of her woolgathering. "You were up late watching that television you Englisch people love so much, weren't you?"

"I wasn't watching television last night, Aunt Lydia," Rachel said. "I was talking with Joe."

At that moment, Bertha, who had been out feeding the chickens, entered the kitchen through the back door. She was wearing a dark navy dress that came to her ankles, thick black stockings, black tennis shoes, and an ancient black sweater with moth holes in it.

Bertha walked over to the sink and washed her hands beneath the sink's gravity-fed faucet. "Now, Lydia, what would you have me to do?"

As bossy as Bertha could be, she always deferred to Lydia's expertise when it came to preparing food. The kitchen was Lydia's small kingdom, and no one questioned her about what to serve or how the cooking would be done.

"We used up the jar of applesauce yesterday morning," Lydia said.

"Could you get a new one from the cellar?"

"Of course." Bertha left to get the applesauce.

Cousin Eli had a small orchard that bore wonderful apples for the making of applesauce. The aunts always canned at least a hundred quart jars of it.

"It has been ten minutes." Lydia poked the dough with a finger. "I think it is ready."

Lydia believed that dough must be kneaded a full ten minutes to fully distribute the yeast. Rachel happily relinquished the wooden kneading trough and Lydia dumped the dough onto the flour-covered table. There, she began rolling it out with an equally-flour-covered rolling pin.

"I think it would be good to start the coffee now, Rachel," Lydia said. "We can serve that good, thick cream Eli brought us yesterday. His new Guernsey cow is giving in abundance."

"I thought she looked like a good milker when he got her." Bertha reappeared with the jar of applesauce and searched for the blue bowl in which they always served it.

"That sweater you are wearing is looking pretty worn, Aunt Bertha," Rachel noticed. "We'll need to go shopping for a new one for you."

"This is my choring sweater," Bertha said. "It keeps me plenty warm. I have no need for a new one."

"But…"

"When it no longer keeps me warm, then I will use my good one for chores and go shopping for new. Until then, I am fine. We do not waste things, Rachel. You know that."

"Whatever you say." Rachel decided she would keep quiet for now and simply buy her aunt a new one for her birthday. Frugality was one thing. Wearing a sweater that most homeless people would discard was another.

While Rachel filled the old-fashioned ceramic percolator with water and put it on the stove, Lydia ladled softened butter onto the spongy, flattened dough and then sprinkled it heavily with a mixture of sugar and cinnamon. Rolling the dough into one long, fluffy cylinder, Lydia made thick slices and arranged them onto the industrial-sized baking pan she favored for her cinnamon rolls.

"What else will you be serving, Aunt Lydia?" Rachel asked.

"Sausages and fresh eggs." Lydia's hands paused in their work as she considered. "Scrambled, I think. In lots of butter. Oh, and the individual custards I made last night. Those are in the refrigerator. Will you start the sausage frying, Bertha?"

"Of course."

"You spoil your guests," Rachel said.

"I hope so," Lydia said. "Some people have very hard lives. I want our guests to leave here with full stomachs, feeling hopeful and renewed. I want them to think that maybe this world is not such a bad place after all."

"And you can accomplish all that with sausage and cinnamon buns?" Rachel asked with a smile.

Lydia shrugged. "I can try."

"Lydia has always shown her love to people through her cooking, Rachel." Bertha said. "You know this. Did I say that right, Lydia?"

"Your words are true." Lydia lifted a blue ceramic pitcher from their propane-powered refrigerator and poured thick cream from it into a bright yellow creamer-and-sugar set that was older than Rachel.

"I know," Rachel said. "But you are in pain all the time, Aunt Lydia."

"Yes, but the happiness I see on people's faces when they sit at my breakfast table makes me feel the pain a little less, I think." Lydia shoved the tray of cinnamon rolls into the oven.

The coffee began to percolate, and Rachel desperately wanted a cup before she left. The Keurig coffeemaker she had in her home was handy, but it could not touch the taste of her aunt's coffee. Whether that was in fact reality, Rachel didn't know. Sometimes she suspected it had more to do with the aromas and good memories in her aunts' kitchen than the actual flavor of the coffee.

"Want me to start the eggs now?" Bertha asked.

"Please." Lydia stirred up her special caramel sauce from butter, brown sugar, cream, and vanilla.

"Pecans?" Rachel asked.

"Walnuts," Lydia said. "They are in the drawer next to the refrigerator."

Rachel started chopping walnuts into the small pieces that Lydia would sprinkle over the cinnamon rolls once the caramel sauce had been drizzled over them.

"Boo!" Anna said, as she wandered into the kitchen.

The three of them gave the requisite start.

"You scared me, Anna!" Rachel said.

This was Anna's little joke, and no one knew or remembered when it had started or where it had come from. They always reacted with feigned fright because it gave Anna so much enjoyment.

"I'm hungry." Anna rubbed sleep from her eyes. Her dark green dress was pinned crookedly and her white kapp was askew. She held her apron in her hand. Apron strings were hard for her to tie without help.

"Breakfast will be ready soon." Lydia repinned Anna's dress, straightened her kapp, and helped her put on the apron. "In the meantime, go see what gifts our hens have left us this morning. I heard Fanny boasting about her newest egg."

"That Fanny is a proud one, she is," Bertha said. "I think that chicken must be Englisch, the ways she struts about all *hochmut* and cackling every time she lays an egg."

Then Bertha realized what she had said and shot a guilty glance at Rachel. "I'm sorry, Rachel. I didn't mean..."

"That's okay, Aunt Bertha," Rachel said. "You're right. We Englisch can be a proud bunch."

Most of the Amish people she knew sometimes enjoyed poking quiet fun at the Englisch, many of whom they considered loud, arrogant, and often downright silly in their pretentiousness.

Anna picked up the egg-gathering basket and went outside. Bertha pushed the skillet of sausage to the back of the woodstove, settled herself in the rocking chair beside the kitchen stove, and folded her hands atop her lap.

That was not a good sign. Bertha was seldom still unless she was ill or preparing to have a serious conversation with someone.

Bertha cleared her throat. That was also not a good sign. Bertha always cleared her throat in preparation of broaching a difficult subject. Silence lay between the three of them as the kitchen clock ticked the seconds away and Rachel waited to hear what Bertha had to say.

"We need to talk about Anna," Bertha said.

"Anna?"

"Yes. I do not think she is well."

Rachel's heart plummeted. She would much rather receive another lecture on the evils of carrying a gun than hear that something was amiss with her sweetest aunt.

"What's wrong with Anna?"

"I think her heart might be worsening," Bertha said. "She seems to be having more difficulty doing the things she loves to do. She gets winded easily now. Sits down more often to rest. I was hoping you could take her to the doctor on this coming Tuesday. I made an appointment for three o'clock. I would use the buggy to take her, but..."

Bertha left the sentence dangling. They both knew it was getting harder for the aunts to hitch up the buggy. As they aged, the need for Rachel to drive them to doctor's appointments was becoming more frequent.

"I'm happy to take her."

She would need to trade shifts with Kim again, to free up the afternoon so she could take Anna. Her heart lurched as the reason behind rearranging her schedule hit Rachel afresh. Anna had to be okay. Nothing could happen to Anna.

"Anna's not all I wanted to talk to you about, Rachel. We need to discuss you and…"

Bertha's voice took on the same tone it always did right before she gave Rachel a good talking-to. This past year she had strongly advised Rachel to quit her job and stay home with Bobby at least a half-dozen times. Rachel argued that Bobby was in the first grade and did not need her all day, every day, but it fell on deaf ears. Rachel's other argument— that she actually *liked* her job and felt her training and skill contributed to the well-being of the community—didn't make a dent on Bertha's opinions, either.

This morning Rachel was in no mood to hear it, and she definitely wasn't ready to explain to Bertha that Joe had lost his fortune and hers was the only income they had now.

"Can this wait?" Rachel interrupted, glancing at her watch. "I *really* need to get back home."

Without waiting for an answer, she bustled out the door. She would let Bertha chastise her another time—preferably when she'd had more sleep. She loved her aunts deeply, but sometimes Bertha was just a little hard to take.

Chapter Eight

The parole-board hearing was supposed to happen directly after break-fast. Carl assumed it would not take long, but he was wrong. Carl and several others were kept under guard in a small waiting room while one prisoner after another was interviewed. Carl had no problem with wait-ing—he'd waited for twenty years.

But as the time dragged on, he began to worry about Beauty being stuck in her cage back at his cell. That was part of the training discipline, to leave a dog in their cage for housebreaking purposes. A dog would not foul its own nest—unlike a lot of people Carl had known—and to leave Beauty there for too long meant she would soon be in pain.

"Are we boring you?" a lady parole board member interrupted when it was finally his turn and he began to haltingly answer their questions. She wore glasses on the end of her nose, and with her hair pulled straight back, she looked as severe as his third-grade teacher, who had terrified him as a child. "You seem to be having trouble concentrating."

"No, ma'am," Carl answered. "You are not boring me."

"Then what is the issue?" the woman asked. "You seem to be quite distracted."

"I'm worried about my dog," Carl blurted out.

"Your dog?" She made a note on a pad in front of her. "Why?"

"She isn't used to being caged for such a long time. I didn't realize all this would take so long, and she needs to be let out."

The woman tilted her head to one side. "Why do you think she needs to be let out?"

"Because it's cruel to leave her for so long with no chance to relieve herself."

"You're worried about your dog's bladder?"

"She was badly abused when I got her, ma'am. She's starting to trust me. I don't want to break that trust by leaving her alone for too long."

"What if I told you that you could leave right now to care for your dog," she said, "but that you would be forfeiting your chances of parole if you chose to leave without taking the time to answer all our questions?"

"I apologize to the board," Carl said as he stood, "but that dog is my responsibility, and I can't bear to hurt her."

And then he left.

When he arrived at his cell, to his surprise, he found that one of the other inmates who had known of Carl's parole hearing had already gotten permission to let Beauty out. His sacrifice for his dog had been unnecessary, and he'd blown his chance of parole for no better reason than he was worried about his dog's need to pee.

The irony of it kept him awake long into the night. Unfortunately, he discovered that he had begun to allow himself to hope for freedom after all. Fool that he was, he'd destroyed that chance. Beauty sensed his unhappiness and quietly rested her nose on his hand until he began stroke her silky fur.

Maybe it was for the best. Someone like him had no business being on the outside anyway.

Chapter Nine

. . . .

"What did the doctor say?" A worried Bertha was waiting on the porch when Rachel pulled up with Anna after their visit with the doctor.

Anna pulled a lollypop out of her mouth and held it up. "I was goot. See?"

Bertha ignored Anna's announcement and looked to Rachel for answers.

"He changed her meds." Rachel handed over the new prescription she had filled at the pharmacy. "He said that her heart is not strong and she shouldn't overdo but she'll be okay if she takes her medication and rests more."

"How are we supposed to make that happen?" Bertha fussed. "You know how Anna likes to be part of everything, especially the cooking."

"I cook goot!" Anna offered.

"Yes, you do cook goot," Bertha said. "But you must rest more."

Anna seemed confused by the idea of resting.

Rachel wasn't surprised. "Now you know how I felt when I tried to get you and Lydia to shut down the inn a couple of years ago."

Bertha waved a dismissive hand. "That was different."

"It wasn't," Rachel argued. "You'll work until you drop regardless of what I say, so I've stopped talking about it."

"It is true that we are not idle like so many of the Englisch," Bertha said. "But we do not know what to do with ourselves if we do not work."

"I know, but don't expect me to tell you what to do with Anna. She comes by her inability to rest honestly."

"I'm a goot worker!" Anna took the sucker out of her mouth and beamed at them again.

Rachel sighed. "I need to get to work myself. Are you expecting any guests tonight, or will Aunt Lydia have just you and Anna to cook for tomorrow morning?"

"We have one couple from out of state and one woman traveling alone from Canada." Bertha glanced at the medication Rachel had handed her and then put it into her apron pocket. "The woman from Canada called and asked if it was dangerous to come to Sugarcreek."

"Dangerous?" Rachel said. "Sugarcreek?"

"She seemed quite worried about something she'd seen on television. Something about an Amish...mafia? I do not know exactly what that is supposed to be, but I told her I am pretty sure we don't have one."

Rachel had watched only part of one episode of that program before turning it off. The last thing she wanted to do was describe it to her aunt.

"Don't worry about it, Bertha. If she has any other questions, tell her to talk to me."

"I will be happy to do that," Bertha said. "By the way, are you taking any vitamins?"

"Why?"

"You look a little pale. Do you feel okay?"

"Yes."

"Because if you aren't, my cousin Martha is using some supplements that she says are wonderful."

"Does she also happen to be selling that product?"

"Well...yes. She offered to bring over some samples."

"Uh-huh." Rachel nodded. "Did she suggest that you start to sell the supplements here at the inn as well?"

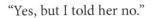

"Yes, but I told her no."

"Good for you. I think I'll pass too."

Many Amish women were interested in nontraditional products that promised to make them healthier. They were quick to use the alternative medicines and salves, many of which were homemade. Some worked; some didn't. Most didn't do any damage, at least. Unfortunately, their interest in nontraditional medicines made the Amish perfect targets for pyramid schemes involving miracle supplements and products. They also had an almost limitless number of relatives to sell to within the Amish "network."

"That is fine," Bertha said. "I am not so sure that Martha knows what she is talking about anyhow."

Bertha took off Anna's kapp and laid it on the porch swing. Then she smoothed back her little sister's hair and refastened the bobby pins that had come loose. It was a loving gesture Rachel had seen many times.

"Thank you for taking Anna to the doctor." Bertha positioned Anna's kapp back on her head.

"I want to feed my chickens," Anna announced, her lollypop finished. "And find the eggs."

"Maybe it would be best for you to lay down for a while, after the trip to the doctor," Bertha said.

"No," Anna said. "I will go feed my chickens. And find the eggs. And then I will peel potatoes with Lydia. I am a good potato peeler."

"I have to leave," Rachel said apologetically.

"But I need to talk to you, Rachel," Bertha said. "It's important."

"I'll be back sometime this week, Aunt Bertha. We'll have time for a good visit soon."

"So busy all the time!"

Rachel was grateful to see that Bertha had become distracted by Anna, who was walking toward the chicken coop. "Anna, I will give you another sucker if you will take a nap."

As Rachel walked to the car, she heard Anna's refusal. And in her rearview mirror, she saw Bertha trailing Anna to the chicken coop, still trying to talk her into having a rest.

Rachel loved her aunts so much it hurt—but sometimes she had no idea how to help them.

It also bothered her that Bertha had said she looked pale. Bertha paid attention to things like that and was seldom wrong. It was especially worrisome to Rachel because, when she had stopped at the pharmacy to get Anna's new prescription, she'd slipped a pregnancy kit in with the purchase. When she got home, she intended to quietly use it and then bury it deep in the trash regardless of what it showed. With Joe worried about finances, this was not a good time to tell him that she thought she might be pregnant.

Chapter Ten

. . . .

"I have to go to the bathroom," Bobby announced. "And Rachel is in there. Can I go outside?"

Bobby's voice was hopeful. He had learned the little-boy joys of going behind the barn or against a tree or into the bushes while they lived on the aunts' farm before Joe and Rachel had gotten married. The aunts had not minded. In fact, they seemed to take such behavior for granted. Unfortunately, living in town with neighbors on all sides did not deter Bobby from wishing for the outdoor freedom he had once enjoyed. With only one bathroom in Rachel's house, the subject came up a lot.

Joe suspected that Bobby sometimes timed his need based on the bathroom already being occupied. He loved the child dearly, but ever since he and Rachel had married, Bobby seemed more determined to push the limits of Joe's patience. Joe guessed that his son was still trying to figure out where the boundaries were in this new family they had created.

"No," Joe said, "you may not go outside. Do you see *me* going to the bathroom in the yard?"

"No."

"Okay, then." He knocked on the bathroom door. "Rachel? You about done in there? Bobby has to go."

He heard the commode flush and water in the sink.

"Just a minute," Rachel said. "I'm almost done."

She opened the door, and Joe was shocked to see that she had been crying. Her bangs were wet, as though she'd splashed water on her face to hide the evidence. As Bobby shot into the bathroom and closed the door, Joe leaned against the wall and said, "What's going on?"

"Nothing," she said. "I–I'm just upset over Anna's heart condition."

That made sense. Rachel wasn't a crier, but she loved her aunt, and he knew she'd taken Anna to the doctor's.

"Come here." He pulled her into a hug and patted her back. "Anna will be okay…"

He was interrupted by a puzzled little boy coming out of the bathroom with his pants unzipped.

"What's this?" Bobby asked, holding up a small, white plastic article.

For an instant, Joe wasn't sure what he was looking at.

Then Rachel gasped. "That was supposed to stay in the trash can."

"But what is it!" Bobby asked. "Is it a toy?"

Joe plucked it out of his son's hands. He knew exactly what it was.

"I don't know how to read this," he said. "Are you, or aren't you?"

Rachel hesitated. "I am."

Joe felt a little light-headed. "Then why are you crying?"

"Because it's lousy timing."

"Why didn't you tell me you suspected?"

"I—I needed time to get used to the idea."

Bobby zipped his pants, looking from one parent to the other. "What are you guys talking about?"

Joe glanced at Rachel and decided it would be best to wait to share the news with Bobby until after they'd had time to stabilize. They had wanted to have children together, but not yet—and definitely not when money was so tight. If Rachel was pregnant, he was concerned about her having to work when she didn't feel well. Plus, there was no room for a nursery in their current house.

"I think it might be a good idea for you to go outside and play," Joe said. "And don't pee in Mrs. Leach's bushes this time. I don't want another phone call like the last one I got from her ever again."

Bobby grumbled but grabbed his Nerf gun and took it outside to shoot.

"It will be okay." Joe tried to reassure both Rachel and himself, but he was thinking that what he needed was to find a good job—and fast.

The problem was finding one with his very narrow skill set in Sugarcreek, Ohio.

Chapter Eleven

May thirteenth was a bittersweet day for Carl.

He approved of the outdoorsy woman who came to take Beauty to her forever home. The woman seemed kind and was quite knowledgeable about dogs. She told Carl that she was retired from teaching and had recently lost her dog companion of fifteen years. She said her home felt empty without a dog in it. Her hobby, now that she was retired, was hiking, and Carl knew Beauty would love exploring with her new owner.

Beauty took to the woman immediately, which was some comfort, and the woman seemed thrilled with Beauty. The happy, confident dog that wagged her tail as the woman petted her bore no resemblance to the cowering animal Carl had been given. He felt proud to have been part of her healing.

It also helped that he'd been given seven weeks to work with her. Beauty had needed every minute, but he was certain she was ready—especially since she would be going to such an ideal situation.

It was the best possible scenario for a rescue dog. He was happy for Beauty and the woman, except for the pain that seared his heart.

He wondered if it would ever get any easier. It usually took about six weeks of round-the-clock training and attention to get a damaged dog ready for its forever home. Beauty had taken a little longer because of her trust issue with men.

Carl poured his heart into his dogs, helped them heal, and trained them with patience and much praise. In turn, they gave him uncondi-tional love...right up until the moment they walked out the door beside their new owners and he never saw them again.

What followed was always a period of deep grief, no matter how hard he tried to fight against it. He had learned it was better to simply give up and accept the darkness of his spirit for a while. He would lay on his bed in silence for hours, replaying every step of the training and trust he had accomplished.

After a few days, when he had convinced himself that he had done the most professional job possible, had given the dog the best he had within him, only then did the darkness begin to dissipate. Soon there would be another dog and another challenge.

Some of the volunteers had informed him that he was the most suc-cessful trainer in the program. That did not surprise him...but he knew it wasn't a matter of talent. It was because he identified so closely with the abused dogs that it often felt as though he read their minds.

One thing was for sure: he would never lack for an animal to love as long as the program continued. Nurturing the dogs back to health had become his sole purpose in life. They were a reason to keep breathing as his life drained away behind bars, one hopeless month after another.

Chapter Twelve

"Those two are a pair, are they not?" Naomi Yoder said with fondness.

Rachel sat on the Yoders' front porch swing, watching Bobby and Ezra hitch the pony to the small pony cart.

"Peas in a pod," Rachel said. "Like you and I were when we were little. We had some good days together."

"Do you ever wish for those days back?" Naomi asked. "Or wish that you had made a different decision about the church?"

Naomi wore a light blue Old Order Amish dress and was letting her blonde, waist-long hair dry in the sun. She had washed it earlier that afternoon in preparation for Sunday services. Their long-standing friendship made Naomi comfortable enough to allow it to dry freely in front of her. Rachel wore jeans and a T-shirt. Both wore flip-flops.

"Do you mean do I regret choosing not to be baptized into the Amish church like my aunts had hoped?"

"Yes. Do you?" Naomi wrung a few more drops of water out of her hair.

"It was the right decision for me. I was already starting to rebel against all the rules and restrictions, and I knew I wanted to become a cop like my dad."

"You went away for a long time," Naomi said. "I missed you. You were not the same person when you came home. You were so...Englisch. It seemed like there was no Amish left inside of you."

"I know," Rachel said. "And I'm sorry. Getting through the police academy was tough. Working in downtown Akron for those few years was even tougher. It felt like I had to become a different person in order to survive. The job burned all the Amish right out of me for a while."

"But some of it is coming back," Naomi said cheerfully.

"What do you mean?"

"You are...how do I say this...softer now. Kinder. Not so suspicious. You feel like my friend again."

"I am your friend," Rachel said. "I had to harden myself to do my job, but I never forgot our friendship."

"I'm glad." Naomi rested her hand on Rachel's for a moment and Rachel noted how callused and work-worn her friend's palm felt. Naomi's life was far from easy, and yet she never complained.

Rachel glanced over at her friend. "Do you ever wonder what your life would have become had you not chosen to stay Amish?"

"Of course!" Naomi chuckled. "I think about it every time I sit in my buggy in the dead of winter and a nice car drives by. I think about how soft the seats are in that car and how warm it is inside. But I also made the right decision for me. Luke would not have done well in the Englisch world...and I believe our people's way is the best way to raise children."

"I won't argue with you there," Rachel said. "I really appreciate your allowing Bobby to come and play with Ezra. School will be out soon. There will be days when Joe and I will need someone to watch him."

"I enjoy having your son here," Naomi said.

"Thank you. That makes me feel good. Many Amish mothers would be worried that having an Englisch child around might be a bad influence on their own children."

"Bobby is filled with much energy but he is kind and respectful of our culture. He is very bright and already speaks some of our language. If you are not careful, you might find yourself raising an Amish child,"

Naomi teased. "He seems quite taken with Ezra's suspenders and hat."

"I *know.*" Rachel laughed. "Do you remember how we dressed up in each other's clothing when we were very small?"

"I remember my father being surprised when he came for me and discovered that I had turned into a little Englisch girl," Naomi said. "And that you had turned into a little Amish girl."

"And I remember my father apologizing," Rachel said. "He hadn't even been aware of what we were doing."

"It was harmless fun," Naomi said. "My father laughed about it later when he told my mother."

"You had good parents."

"I did."

A comfortable silence settled upon them as they watched the two six-year-olds climb into the cart and start down the long driveway.

"What is in that gallon jar in the back?" Rachel asked.

"Milk," Naomi said. "I told Ezra he could drive the cart up and down the driveway until the milk turned into butter. Then he must come and do his other chores."

"That works?"

"It is a bumpy ride. It saves me from churning and gives purpose to their play." Naomi said. "I have bread dough rising in the kitchen. By the time the butter is finished, the bread will be ready to put into the oven and the pony will be ready for a rest. While the boys are taking care of him, I will work the sour milk out of the butter. Then I will thank the boys for helping provide food for our table and reward them with fresh bread and butter for their lunch. Would you like to stay?"

"I'd love to," Rachel said. "But I have to get going. I'll pick up Bobby after work, if that's okay."

"I always enjoy having your son. Ezra sometimes gets lonely with no brothers or sisters to play with."

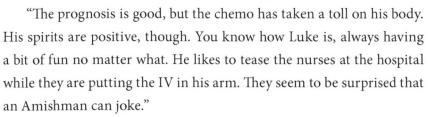

"Perhaps that will change."

Naomi looked away. "If God wills."

Rachel did not press. "How is Luke doing?"

"The prognosis is good, but the chemo has taken a toll on his body. His spirits are positive, though. You know how Luke is, always having a bit of fun no matter what. He likes to tease the nurses at the hospital while they are putting the IV in his arm. They seem to be surprised that an Amishman can joke."

"Luke is a good man."

"He is," Naomi said. "He was quite wild during his *rumschpringa*, but once he joined the church, he settled down and has been a wonderful husband."

"We have been lucky in the men we chose," Rachel said.

"We have been blessed," Naomi agreed.

"I'm sorry, but I need to get home," Rachel said. "How much do I owe you for yesterday?"

"I do not like to take money from a friend for merely looking after her child," Naomi said.

"I know, but I'm so grateful to be able to bring him here," Rachel said. "My aunts are willing to watch him, but Anna tries to keep up with him and her heart is not strong. It is a gift to know that he is here with you."

"If you wish to pay something, you can," Naomi said. "But I will not charge my friend. We are doing well enough. The men of our church are putting crops in for us while Luke is still weakened by his treatments, so we will have a harvest in the fall. I have my cow and garden and chickens, and I take in some sewing for my Englisch neighbors. I am content."

"Of course you are."

There were many subtle differences between the two cultures in which Rachel had lived her life. She had often noticed that her Englisch friends spoke of being happy or wishing they were happy. Her Amish friends rarely spoke of happiness as a condition to which they aspired. Instead, they often spoke of being content, as though that were the greater blessing of the two.

"There is one thing, though," Naomi said, hesitantly.

"Anything," Rachel said.

"I wasn't sure if I should tell you..."

Rachel went on instant alert. "What is it?"

"Someone took several bales of hay out of Samuel's field last night. They put them in the middle of the road and set them on fire."

"Why didn't anyone call me?"

"Luke and Samuel think it was probably just some silliness by Englisch teenagers who don't know what to do with themselves. You know that our people have always dealt with things like that by turning the other cheek. Usually when we don't retaliate, the person gets bored and leaves us alone."

"Is Samuel going to file a complaint?"

Naomi looked at Rachel as though she had said something stupid. "Samuel? Going to the police for a few bales of hay set on fire? It would take more than that for him to get the authorities involved. Besides, there wasn't any real damage; it was only a matter of raking ashes into the ditch afterward. But I thought you might want to know about it."

Rachel knew that Naomi was a great deal more concerned that she let on. Setting bales of hay afire in the middle of the road was only a couple of steps from setting a barn on fire—which all farmers feared and watched for. At the very least, it could have badly frightened a horse pulling a buggy if one had been traveling that road.

"Does Samuel have any enemies that you know of?" Rachel said.

"I don't think so," Naomi said. "Most people like him. He is new at his leadership role, but he is learning to be a good bishop. He and the church did have to shun that Hochstetler boy back a few months ago, but the boy moved to Kentucky and is living with some other relatives who chose to leave the church. No one has seen him around since."

"I don't like the sound of this," Rachel said. "I'll keep an ear out. In the meantime, if anything else like that happens in the community, please let me know."

Chapter Thirteen

An hour after Beauty left, Carl got a message that the warden wanted to talk with him. He had done nothing wrong that he knew of, so he assumed it had something to do with the dog-rehabilitation program. He was unprepared for the reason behind the summons.

"Your parole has been approved," the warden said.

He was an older man, about Carl's age. Both had put in about the same amount of time at that prison. There was one big difference, though. The warden had control over his environment and could come and go at will. Carl could barely imagine walking out those doors.

Carl sat there, blinking, unable to absorb the warden's words.

"Excuse me?" Carl said.

"You have been granted parole."

"But I didn't even finish my interview with the parole board. I got up and left."

The warden smiled. A decent man, Carl had decided years earlier, with a hard job.

"From what I understand, you were more interested in your dog's comfort than the possibility of your own parole."

"I was afraid Beauty was suffering."

"Well, for what it's worth, the board was on the fence about allowing you to get out. It could have gone either way. Fortunately for you, two of the board members are dog lovers. Your compassion for Beauty was the tipping point. They did ask that you not be told until you finished your dog's training."

Carl could hardly believe his ears.

"You mean I...get to leave?"

"There's some paperwork we have to do—and you'll need to check in with a parole officer for a year before you can leave the state—but you should be out within the week. I wanted to tell you now so you'd understand when the volunteers don't bring you another rescue. Obviously, we wouldn't want you to leave during another dog's rehabilitation."

"Obviously," Carl repeated, his head spinning.

"Any questions?"

"Where will I live? I have no family."

"That's being arranged. Most prisoners have to stay in a halfway house for a while, but your friend the preacher has found a place for you. I believe it has something to do with his church. He's coming in later to tell you about it. I wanted to be the one to tell you about your parole, though. It's one of the few parts of my job I actually enjoy."

"George has made arrangements for me?"

"That's what he says. It's good you have a friend like him on the outside. The halfway houses can be brutal places, and I have no control over that. Any other questions?"

"What—what will I do on the outside?"

"I suppose anything you want...as long as it's legal. If it were me, I'd probably go fishing for a month. At least that's my plan when I retire in three years."

The warden stood and offered his hand. It felt odd to Carl to do so, but he also stood and shook the warden's hand.

"Good luck," the warden said. "I'm hoping—for all our sakes—that we never see you again. I don't want to break our record."

"Thank you."

Carl knew exactly which record the warden was referring to. Approximately 50 percent of the men who received parole ended up back inside the prison walls, with the exception of those prisoners who entered the dog-rehabilitation program. The recidivism rate for the dog-training prisoners was about 11 percent. It was a win/win/win situation for the dogs, the prison staff, the families who received a well-trained dog, and the prisoners most of all.

The old dog that had kept Carl alive beneath the porch that winter night when he was a child had given him yet another chance at life as an adult through Carl's love and understanding of abandoned animals.

He had no idea what sort of living arrangement George had scraped together for him, but he knew one thing for certain—he was determined not to be the one who made that recidivism rate go up. Now that the miraculous had happened, he would make certain he never went back once he got out.

Chapter Fourteen

Filling out job applications definitely took a toll on a man's ego. At thirty-four, Joe had never had to look for a job. As a missionary kid, he had never worked what most people would consider a real job. When his father sent him to the States to get a college education, he'd had the grades and athletic skill to get scholarships.

Now he stared at yet another of the week's applications, wondering what to write. It had been a month since he'd flown back from LA, and he still didn't have a clue how to support his growing family without uprooting them and moving away or being gone from his wife and children for long stretches of time.

Everything in his life had revolved around baseball. Nothing he'd ever achieved fit into the little boxes of employment. He couldn't even list flipping burgers at McDonald's.

Plus, he'd quit college after his junior year. College had seemed unnecessary at the time. He'd been invited to join the Dodgers' farm teams, and knowing how short an athlete's career can be, he hadn't wanted to waste another year on college.

Joe filled out the application as best he could and handed it to a bald Amishman with a scraggly beard, who put it on a stack of other applications and thanked him politely. Coming here was probably a mistake since Joe knew next to nothing about lumber or lumber stores, but he had heard they were hiring and figured he'd give it a shot.

One of the problems of getting work in this area was that the few regular-type jobs he qualified for were already being taken care of by Amishmen who were probably doing a better job than he could.

Tomorrow he would put in an application at the feed store and then maybe one of the cheese factories. He had pretty much exhausted all possibilities this past month.

When Joe got home, he pulled three steaks out of the refrigerator to grill. He was good with steaks and burgers, and it didn't take a genius to throw some potatoes into the oven to bake. There was lettuce for a salad. Rachel would be pleased to have supper already started when she got home. She was picking up Bobby from Naomi's, and he was looking forward to having his family together again.

Hunting for work was a lot harder on a man's self-esteem than he'd realized. It would have been so much easier to have simply accepted that stupid TV commercial. He knew Rachel was right, but the toll for having integrity sometimes carried an awfully high price tag.

It occurred to him that he did have that friend who owned the car dealership, and who would probably be happy to give him a job selling cars. The only problem was, it was in Texas. It would just about kill Rachel's aunts if he moved his family all the way to Texas. Those three women had been too good to him. He couldn't hurt them like that.

And then suddenly Rachel and Bobby were home and Bobby came running to him. Joe scooped him up, gave him a hug, and sniffed the air.

"Did I just hug a horse? It sure smells like it."

"You smelled me, Daddy. I've been playing with Ezra's pony! And we made butter!"

While Bobby enjoyed his daddy's attention, Rachel went through her ritual of locking away her gun before she did anything else. He was grateful for her care. Bobby was way too curious to have an unlocked gun in the house.

Her gun secured, utility belt and jacket hung up, squad-car keys on a nail beside the door where she could grab them in an instant—only

SERENA B. MILLER

then did she come to the table where he was wrapping the potatoes in foil, to give him a kiss.

"How are you feeling?" he asked.

"The nausea seems to be letting up."

Joe finished wrapping the last potato and sat the pan in the oven. "I'm glad to hear that."

"Me, too," Rachel said. "I looked it up, and some women have it the whole nine months. I'm hoping I'm going to be one of the lucky ones. Thanks for starting dinner. I'm going to go put Bobby in the bathtub and then I'll come back and help. My stomach is better, but I'd still prefer not to eat steak next to sweaty-little-boy-and-horse smell."

"No problem."

A few minutes later, with the potatoes in the oven and the steak marinating in the refrigerator, Rachel and Joe had a moment to sit together on the couch. Rachel curled up beside him and snuggled beneath his arm while they listened to Bobby splashing in the tub above them.

"Sounds like Bobby had a great day at Luke and Naomi's," Joe said.

"He did, but Naomi told me something that concerns me."

"About what?"

"Someone set fire to some hay bales near Samuel's place. They took bales out of his field and burned them in the middle of the road."

"That's weird."

"It's probably just a teenage prank. Kids from town sometimes like to come out and bait the Amish in order to entertain their friends. Occasionally there are bad feelings because the Englisch boys tend to be overlooked for summer jobs if there are Amish boys available."

"Because the Amish boys are better workers?"

"Usually, and because most of them are more skilled at manual-labor jobs."

Joe felt immediate sympathy for the Englisch teens but chose not to share that with Rachel.

"Well, I'm sure you'll get to the bottom of it eventually," Joe said. "So what's this about him and Ezra churning butter?"

"Naomi is a resourceful woman." Rachel smiled. "She put milk from their cow in a gallon jar and let the boys turn it into butter by jostling it in the pony cart. She said it gave purpose to their play. It's the whole Amish work-ethic thing. She invited me to share her freshly baked bread and the strawberry jam she made today along with the butter the boys churned."

"And you didn't stay?"

"I didn't need the calories."

"Not sure I could have passed it up, although knowing the butter was churned by two little boys kinda takes away the appeal."

"Maybe you'll get lucky and be the one who is picking up Bobby the next time she bakes."

He fondled a strand of hair that had come undone from the tight bun she usually wore to work. It felt so good to have her home and at his side again. "I get the feeling you enjoy going over there almost as much as Bobby does."

"Naomi and I have been friends for as long as I can remember. I think we're something like third or fourth cousins too. I can't think of any home I'd rather Bobby spend time in."

"Did you tell her about the pregnancy?"

"I think I'd like to wait a bit longer. That kind of news travels like wildfire on the Amish grapevine. It would get to my aunts quickly, and I don't want Bertha clucking over me yet. The first thing she'll start in on is that I should quit my job."

"Of course she will, but they'll be so excited when you tell them."

"I'm only ten weeks along. The doctor says it will probably be a couple more before I start to show. I'd like to wait another week before I take on all that advice." She pulled several hairpins from her bun and shook out her hair. "That feels better!"

"What did you have planned for this evening?" Joe asked.

"Not Candy Land, if I can possibly get out of it." Rachel laughed. "Since you're fixing supper tonight, I thought I'd try to work my way through that stack of paperwork accumulating on my desk."

"Could we do something together tonight instead?"

"Like what?"

"I don't know...popcorn and board games at your aunts? A movie at the Quaker Cinema in New Philadelphia? There's an animation flick I saw playing over there that Bobby might enjoy. I'd just like to spend some time together as a family."

"What happened today, Joe?" Rachel asked with concern. "What's wrong?"

That was his Rachel. She could always recognize the slightest nuance in his voice. He mentioned wanting to spend time together tonight and instead of taking it at face-value, she heard his sadness. It made her a good cop and a great wife.

"I put in an application at Keim Lumber today."

"For what kind of job?"

"I don't know. I just heard they had some openings. I thought I'd put in an application at the feed store tomorrow. I figured I might be handy at lifting and stacking sacks of grain."

"Oh, Joe." Rachel put her arms around his waist. "Do we need to have a serious talk about moving to where there are better opportunities for you?"

"Not yet." Joe pulled her closer. "I'll find something eventually. The last thing I want to do is take you and Bobby away from here. Not only do your aunts depend on you for help, but our son has had to adjust to enough changes in his life already. I want to keep things stable for him. Where could Bobby ever be as happy or as safe as in Sugarcreek?"

Chapter Fifteen

Carl made up his bed with military precision, folding the sheets and blankets carefully and tucking in the corners.

This small utility room in the church basement had been intended to be used by the janitor to hang up brooms and mops, so Carl kept them there neatly where they belonged. A long shelf for supplies ran the length of the small room, and there was enough space left over for Carl's cot and the small trunk the preacher had scrounged up, in which Carl kept his few clothes. He stored his toothbrush, comb, bar of soap, and two washcloths on the shelf beside the cleansers and floor wax. He owned so little that he didn't need much room.

There was no window to the room. The floor was bare concrete. The walls were made up of gray concrete block. When Carl got his first paycheck from the church, he intended to buy some white paint for those walls. He'd had enough of gray to last him a lifetime. Being allowed to choose any color he wished felt quite luxurious.

As sparse and as cramped as his living quarters were, at least it was his own personal space for now, and he cherished the privacy.

He did not have to make sharp corners on his bed. No one would mind or be surprised if they looked in and saw the covers lying in a heap, but it pleased him to keep his few possessions nice and neat. He had always been that way. It gave him some control over all the disorder of his life that he *couldn't* control.

He took his toothbrush, comb, and one of the washcloths to the men's bathroom around the corner and locked the door behind him. Unlike the restroom upstairs on the main floor, this one had only one stall and one lavatory.

George, the preacher of the church, had apologized for the fact that there was no shower. Carl assured him that it did not matter. He was telling the truth. It didn't matter. Knowing that he could wash his body without fear of being attacked trumped the best shower Carl could imagine. Having a basin of warm water all to himself, with a lock on the door that he controlled, was another great luxury.

He stripped off and lathered up with one of the extra bars of sweet-smelling hand soap that some thoughtful woman had placed in the upstairs women's bathroom. It felt like a bath from heaven to Carl. Even his hair could be washed in the basin, not that there was much of it anymore.

Once finished, he went back to his room and rummaged in the trunk for his cleanest work clothes, also a gift from the preacher, who had purchased them from the Mennonite-run Save-and-Serve thrift store in Millersburg. George had taken Carl along with him so he could choose his own clothing, but it had been twenty years since Carl had any choice in what he wore. The task had proven to be daunting. In the end, George had to pick five work outfits for him.

Carl had now been out of prison a whole three weeks.

Today, he would repair a dripping faucet in the women's bathroom. Tomorrow he would give the wooden pews in the sanctuary a good polish. The day after that, he intended to wash the windows. He cherished the fact that he was free to make his own plans for each day.

First, however, he would make coffee in the church kitchen. George would arrive soon to put in his morning office hours before going on hospital visits and checking on shut-ins. George always appreciated a fresh cup of coffee.

The preacher had given him permission to use his office and read any of the books that lined the walls. It was a nice offer, but Carl wasn't much of a reader. Making sure her son went to school had not exactly been a priority to his mother.

What Carl hoped for was to save up for a small television to keep in his room. He liked watching ball games. When he was a kid, he loved playing baseball. He and the other neighborhood boys played pickup games in an abandoned lot nearby his home. They had almost always ended in a fight, but he had liked the feeling of running the makeshift bases and snatching the ball out of midair. Remembering those summertime games in detail had helped him use up a lot of hours, lying on his bunk and staring at the ceiling, during these past twenty years.

Carl had no idea what George had gone through to get permission for him to work and live here. He was afraid it had been a struggle. It was not a large church; they could not afford to pay much. He thought that perhaps the fact that he came cheaper than most janitors had helped get him the job.

All he knew was that he was grateful for a roof over his head and for the small paycheck. He was absolutely determined not to do anything that could put George's faith in him at risk. With the last third of his life lived behind bars, he was lucky to have any place to stay at all...even if it was a utility room in the basement of a church. It was warm and dry, which was all he really needed.

After starting the coffee, he took a box of cornflakes out of one of the kitchen cupboards and a quart of milk from the refrigerator. There were some mismatched bowls and spoons to choose from that had accumulated over the years. Carl preferred the yellow bowl with sunflowers painted on it. Yellow had become his favorite color. It was the color of sunlight.

He ate the cereal and then washed and dried his bowl and spoon and put them away. By then the coffee was finished, and he heard George's car pull up outside. He poured both himself and George cups of coffee then added a dollop of whole milk to George's. For himself, he'd long ago learned to drink his black. It was simpler. He walked to George's office with the cups, prepared to enjoy a short conversation. In the few weeks he'd been here, having morning coffee with George had become a routine and Carl's favorite part of the day.

Chapter Sixteen

Stripping the beds after their guests departed had always been Anna's job. She didn't have the dexterity to make up the beds with fresh linen, but she was able to pull the sheets off and trundle them down to the back porch for Bertha to wash in their gasoline-fueled wringer washer.

What would have been an easy task for someone else turned out to be quite laborious for Anna. Removing each sheet and pillowcase took a great deal of her concentration and involved walking around the bed several times, but if it took her a lot of time, then so be it. Anna would finish in her own fashion.

She was so proud of being a helpful part of running the inn that no one had ever imagined trying to take it away from her. Until now. Now, allowing her to continue with her heart condition was a worry to them all...except Anna. She was so determined to do this by herself that Lydia finally called Rachel to come help reason with Anna.

Even with Rachel there, things were not going well.

"No!" Anna insisted, tugging the sheet out of Lydia's hands. "This is *my* job."

Lydia looked at Rachel helplessly.

"Do you enjoy helping us with our jobs, Anna?" Rachel asked.

"Yes." Anna's voice was suspicious.

"We like helping you too," Rachel said. "Let Lydia undo one side and you undo the other. That way you won't have to walk all the way around each bed. It is better to work together."

"Oh! Okay." Anna capitulated and helped Lydia remove the sheets, which Rachel grabbed and quickly bundled up before Anna could get hold of them.

"I'll just toss these down the stairs," Rachel said. "We'll pick them up at the bottom after we're finished with the other rooms. Together."

"Okay," Anna said. "I am a goot worker?"

"You are a wonderful worker," Rachel said.

"Have you had lunch?" Lydia asked Rachel as they finished stripping the beds in the other rooms. "I'm frying chicken livers with fried apples."

Rachel shuddered involuntarily. Lydia had learned to make that dish from a relative who had embraced some of the local dishes after her Amish settlement moved to Kentucky. The aunts loved it. Although it wasn't her favorite, Rachel normally didn't have a problem eating it, but today the thoughts of it made her gag. Although her nausea had diminished greatly, it had not left her entirely. The right foods could still trigger a quick trip to the bathroom. Fried chicken livers was evidently one of the right foods. She tried to hide her gag reflex, but she wasn't quick enough.

"You don't like my chicken livers and fried apples?" Lydia sounded hurt. "You want to throw up even thinking about them?"

The one thing that could dim Lydia's normally happy disposition was the thought of someone not liking what she cooked or baked.

"I'm just not hungry right now, Aunt Lydia. Big breakfast."

"Oh?" Lydia said. "What did you have for this big breakfast you say you ate?"

Rachel was tempted to make something up to keep from hurting Lydia's feelings again, but lies did not come easily to her. Not even little white ones, if there was such a thing.

"Um." Her voice sounded sheepish, even to her. "A container of yogurt."

Lydia stared at her. Then her eyes fell to Rachel's stomach, which had started to push out her T-shirt just slightly. The light dawned.

"Bertha!" Lydia shouted. "Come quick! I think Rachel's pregnant!"

She had never seen Bertha take the stairs so fast. Anna, who understood the notion that pregnancies ended with babies, was dancing in place on her tiptoes.

Next to God, babies were everything to those raised in the Amish culture.

"Why didn't you tell us?" Bertha demanded after she had caught her breath. "Are you sleeping enough? Eating well?"

Rachel laughed. "Yes, I'm taking good care of myself."

"When is it due?" Lydia asked eagerly.

"Sometime in December."

"Oh, I cannot wait!" Lydia said. "Maybe it will be a Christmas baby!"

"Can I hold the baby?" Anna asked.

"Yes, of course, but it will be several more months. You will have to be patient."

"You've seen the doctor?" Bertha asked.

"Of course."

"Are you taking vitamins? Because if you aren't, our cousin Martha has special ones for pregnant women from her health food company."

"Thanks, but I'll stick with what the doctor prescribed."

"Probably for the best," Bertha agreed. "I think Martha might be getting overly interested in counting her *geld* since she started selling for this company. She is so enthusiastic, some of our people are starting to avoid her."

"Thanks for the warning," Rachel said.

"Have you told Bobby yet?"

"Not yet. We were planning on telling him tonight."

"I know that is the Englisch way," Bertha said. "But there is wisdom in waiting awhile."

"True," Lydia said. "Sometimes it is best."

"Why?"

"Time feels so much longer for a child than it does for us," Bertha said. "Waiting so many months for a little brother or sister can seem like forever to the child who is waiting."

"I know that many Amish mothers choose not to tell the younger children they are pregnant so the baby can show up and be a surprise," Rachel said. "But Joe and I feel differently about it. We want Bobby to experience the pregnancy with us."

"But what if..." Lydia sounded worried. "What if something happens?"

"What do you mean?" Rachel asked. "What if *what* happens?"

Bertha glanced at Lydia, who was suddenly fighting back tears.

"I think what Lydia is trying to say is..." Bertha hesitated, as though trying to choose her words carefully. "Not all pregnancies go as the mother hopes. If anything happened...well, it might be best for Bobby if you wait until a little longer before you tell him about the pregnancy. Things usually settle out after the third month and the chance of a miscarriage lessens."

Miscarriage. Of course. Rachel had forgotten. Lydia had endured the grief of not being able to carry a child full-term. Of course that would be the first place Lydia's mind would go.

Rachel put her arm around her aunt's shoulders. "I'm sorry, Aunt Lydia, and I think you are right. I'll talk to Joe and we'll wait awhile to tell Bobby."

Bertha nodded approvingly. "Now, if I could just have that talk I've been wanting to have with you?"

Rachel glanced at the clock. She really did have to leave. "I'm so sorry, Aunt Bertha. I have to go to work now. Can it wait?"

"Yes." Bertha sounded resigned. "What I need to say can wait."

As Rachel went downstairs, Lydia called after her. "We will have a full house tonight. If you would like to come tomorrow morning to help with the baking, I would not mind...and we can talk about the baby!"

Chapter Seventeen

A man could only spend so much time polishing pews, floors, and windows.

The church at night was a lonely place. Apart from fixing himself a sandwich in the church kitchen or walking to the local IGA to pick up a few groceries, there was little to occupy Carl's time after he quit work in the late afternoon. The only events happening at the church were on Sunday evenings when there was a worship service or on Wednesday evenings when there was a Bible study.

There were a couple of bars in town, though. In his isolation, he had considered going in and watching TV—most bars had at least one mounted on a wall—but Carl had months to go before he would feel free enough to do something that risky.

Drinking had once been a problem to him. It brought out the anger he tried to keep buried. He didn't want to risk getting into a bar fight. Someone fresh out of prison had to be on high alert at all times. One ill-advised decision under the influence could make the difference between freedom and prison. He may not be currently living his dream life, but it surely beat the past twenty years.

The need to be careful sometimes made his freedom feel almost as restrictive as his incarceration. But he did have a larger area in which to live, and he could listen to the comforting sounds of the old church settling at night instead of men cursing, screaming, or crying themselves to sleep.

The respite from that was a great blessing.

George had invited him home for dinner one evening, but it had not been a success. George's wife, a faded but still-pretty woman with a kind face, had tried to be cordial, but making conversation was uncomfortable for both of them. The poor woman had no idea what to talk with Carl about and his previous life was so alien to her that they were both tongue-tied as they tried to work their way through dinner.

He did enjoy the good food she had prepared and the ball game he watched with George later, but neither had suggested a repeat of the evening. That was fine with Carl. Trying to socialize with respectable people was a strain. He felt like he had to carefully measure every word he uttered.

Some evenings, now that it was June and the weather was getting warmer, he would go out on the front steps and sit there. He liked watching people go by on the sidewalk, and sometimes he caught interesting snatches of conversation. Millersburg attracted quite a few tourists in the spring, and Carl amused himself by trying to place the various accents he overheard.

Sometimes the people would nod at him in friendly greeting, and he liked the way that made him feel—as though he were a normal part of the human race. Evenings when George and his congregation had church were okay. Some of the people went out of their way to try to talk to him, but he knew that they knew who he was and what he had done and where he had been for the past two decades. That knowledge made getting to know them an uncomfortable proposition. He much preferred being an observer to trying to make small talk, no matter how well-meaning.

Besides coffee with George most mornings, a friendly nod from a fellow human being was about as much social interaction he could handle right now. There was a lot to get used to, and he was taking it one step at a time.

The one bad thing about sitting outside on the church steps was that people sometimes gave him funny looks, as though wondering whether he was homeless or lurking.

After some thought, Carl solved this problem by purchasing a package of cigarettes. He had never developed the habit, but sitting on the church steps while holding a lit cigarette in his hand made him look like a man just having a smoke. With all the bans against smoking inside public buildings, this was an understandable reason for someone to sit on the steps. He no longer looked like someone who had nothing to do and nowhere to go.

One evening, an elderly woman stopped and gave him a short lecture on the evils of smoking. She was very intent on her mission because a loved one had recently died of lung cancer. He found her unexpected involvement in his life heartwarming, and he promised her that he would try to quit. He chose not to break it to her that he had never started.

Her earnest lecture made him smile every time he remembered it. The old lady had been quite the mother hen as she scolded him. He envied whatever kids she might have had. She was so impassioned about a stranger's health that he could only imagine how carefully she had looked after her own children's.

Of course it was not George's plan, nor Carl's, for him to live the rest of his life inside the church. It was nothing more than a safe place to stay with a small salary to care for his basic needs while he waited to fulfill his parole obligations. He would live here for a year, proving that he could be trusted to be a law-abiding citizen.

Eventually he would find some sort of a job, perhaps another custodial position, and rent a small apartment. At that point he would be allowed to leave the state if he wanted to. Carl had given this some thought, and there wasn't any place he particularly wanted to go. Nor did he have anyone out of state that he wanted to see. His mom had died years ago from a drug overdose, and he'd never known his father. Morality had not been a strong point in his home.

There was one person he wanted to visit, though—someone he needed to thank. He alternated between savoring the thought of visiting this person and nervousness over how he would be received. One thing he knew was that he was not yet ready for that meeting.

Yes, a man could only spend so much time polishing pews, floors, and windows. Carl had gone over everything twice and yet he'd run out of things to do by noon on Friday. Without a wedding, a funeral, or a scout meeting to tidy up after, the afternoon had felt dull and endless.

Being lonely was a great fear to many, but Carl did not fear being lonely—he endured it. After all, he had lived with it most of his life.

Chapter Eighteen

"They did what?" Ed said.

"Someone deliberately cut the fence at Naomi and Luke Yoder's last night," Rachel told the police chief. "Their cattle got out, and Luke has cancer. He's dealing with a lot of weakness and nausea from the chemo treatments. The neighbors had to help Naomi repair the fence and get the animals back in."

"I'm sorry to hear that about Luke," Ed grabbed a notepad and a pencil and began scribbling down the information she had just given him. A computer would have been faster, but Ed was old school.

"Last week we talked about those hay bales that were set on fire at Samuel Yost's place." Ed tore the page off the notebook, rose, and thumb-tacked it onto the cork bulletin board he kept on the wall behind him. "Have you heard any more about that?"

"I've asked around," Rachel said. "No one seems to have heard or seen anything. There are also the sheep that were spray-painted out at Peter Hochstetler's a couple of months back. Peter had to trash much of his wool crop."

"Sounds like we're having an epidemic of pranks aimed at the Amish community. Any ideas who might be doing this?"

"Who knows?" Her hands in her front pants pockets, Rachel leaned against the door. "It always happens at night, and it's always at a different place. There's no pattern to it, no particular time or day of the week. I've talked to some of the town kids I know, but they seem to be as clueless as I am."

"You can add to the list the fact that John Yoder discovered the metal teeth in his mower blade bent and ruined before he went to cut hay." Ed tapped another page stuck to the bulletin board. "He lives next door to me and called yesterday to see if I could help him find some new parts. He's nearly eighty and doesn't know how he'll repair it. Those old horse-drawn mowers are hard to find these days, and it's even harder to find parts."

"Why would anyone want to vandalize an old mower?" Rachel said.

"Your guess is as good as mine. But you know that even if we discover who is doing this, the Amish will probably refuse to press charges," Ed said.

"But if we could find out who's doing it, maybe we could convince them to stop."

"Scare them into stopping?" Ed said.

"If we have to," Rachel said. "I'm guessing it's some local Englisch teenagers."

"It could also be Amish kids. They do some strange things during their 'running around' time," Ed said.

"But Amish teenage pranks tend to run along the lines of dismantling someone's buggy and rebuilding it on top of their barn. They don't usually do real damage."

"I know. These pranks aren't funny. If anything, they are particularly mean-spirited. You're our expert on the Amish. Can you see any connection between the families who are being hit? Could there be some sort of weird vendetta going on?"

"It's spread out between families, but they are all from the same church as my aunts. I wonder if the church itself is being targeted," Rachel said.

"That would be something I've not dealt with before," Ed said. "People who are only from a particular Amish congregation being targeted for harassment. Tell your friends and relatives from that church to let us know the minute anything else happens. Maybe we can get there in time to discover something."

"I'll try," Rachel said. "But I can't guarantee they'll do it."

Chapter Nineteen

....

Thursday morning was one of the two days Carl carried out the trash. The church had Bible study every Wednesday night, and that involved doughnuts and coffee. George had recently started a twelve-step addiction group on Friday nights, and a great deal of doughnuts and coffee was consumed then, too.

Carl attended that last group. Sometimes he even participated. He often went to Wednesday night Bible study as well; it broke up the week and made him feel as if he was somewhat part of things even though he sat in the back row in silence.

He continued to wish he could have a television in his room. Watching an occasional baseball or basketball game would have been an excellent way to pass the time, but he hadn't been able to save enough yet and he didn't want to mention it to George, who would probably try to get one for him. George had already done more than anyone had a right to expect.

In fact, George's interest in Carl had been a mystery in the beginning. He did not know why this minister, whom he had never met, would come into the prison and ask for him by name. At first, all George told him was that he was coming at the request of a friend. This made Carl suspicious. He didn't have any friends—at least none who would know a Mennonite preacher. Nor did he have any friends who would care whether he received a visit. But since Carl had no place else to go or anything better to do, he had tolerated George's occasional visits. He didn't expect to look forward to them, but George was different from the people Carl had known in the past. There was a rugged peace about the man that intrigued him.

There was seldom anything Carl wanted to contribute to the conversation in the beginning of their relationship, so George began telling him about his own life—and the people to whom he ministered and the small struggles many of them were having.

At first it was simply entertainment for Carl, to sit and listen to this preacher ruminate about what was going on in his church. And then, gradually, to his great surprise, Carl actually began to...*care*.

It was obvious to him that George genuinely loved the people he worked with. He talked about them with such sympathy and understanding that Carl found himself being drawn into their lives each time George came to visit, and he thought about them long after George left. It was almost like those television soap operas his mother had watched so long ago.

Carl began to care whether old Mrs. Smith's milk cow got over its bad case of mastitis or if the boy with leukemia at George's church survived. He listened to George tell about a couple who finally received the baby they had been praying for and how proud and happy they were the first time they brought that baby to church. It was an education to hear about someone who wanted a child that desperately. In his world, children had been a bother that brought in a small income from the government.

George told him about the trip where he and four other members of his church had gone to the orphanage in Haiti and how the church had spent time gathering school and medical supplies for the children. George told him about the street kids he'd seen there and how they had broken his heart. Carl did not tell him that he identified more with the street children than he did the adults who had traveled there to help.

Every time George visited, it was like looking through a window into a world that Carl had never experienced or knew existed.

He found himself wondering about these people he had never met and asked about specific ones when George came. He knew he would never meet any of them, of course, but in a small way, George's church became a sort of surrogate family.

Then the unthinkable happened. After months of George's visits, he brought a letter with him...from a person Carl had never heard of.

One of the Amish sisters of the man he'd killed had written to him. It turned out that she was a cousin of George's, a woman named Bertha Troyer, and she was the "friend" who had asked George to come to the prison and see him.

Bertha said in the letter that it had been a long, hard struggle for her, requiring much prayer, but she had finally been able to forgive Carl for his part in her brother's death and she wanted him to know.

It was a short letter, penned on old-fashioned stationery with pictures of strawberries across the top. There was no return address on it—which was wise in a prison where inmates liked to grasp hold of tenderhearted people on the outside and turn a situation to their advantage.

It was the first handwritten letter Carl had ever received. He took it back to the cell with him. It was not exactly scented, but it smelled differently than the institution where he lived. More...wholesome. He studied the pictures of strawberries. It was pretty stationery, and there wasn't much in prison that was pretty. He laid the letter on the pillow of his bunk and liked the way it looked there, so bright and cheerful against all the grayness. Bertha's handwriting was firm and flowing. He thought it was pretty also.

It took him a long time to absorb the fact that she had forgiven him. He wasn't sure what that meant, exactly. Forgiveness. But it felt good to think about it.

It was another year before George brought him a second letter. It was then Carl realized that she had written him both times on the anniversary of her brother's death.

The second letter was also on nice stationery. This time it was some kind of purple flower on a vine. George said it was called a morning glory. Carl liked the name, and he liked the flower. This letter included a story about her brother as a child. Her brother had gotten a beagle puppy when he was only six. He and that dog had grown up together and been inseparable. The dog had slept for years at the foot of his bed.

The letter wasn't meant to harm Carl in any way. It sounded more like the musings of someone who had simply loved and grieved that little boy. She said she had been thinking a lot about her brother today and that story had come to mind. She ended the letter by telling him once again that she forgave him.

Carl wasn't sure how he felt about the letter. Having the man he killed become real to him did not feel good, and yet he was intrigued by the story. He saved this letter too.

When he got back to his cell, he folded up the first letter with the strawberries and put it away. For the past year, it had lain open on the metal shelf where he kept his things, so he could see it. The letter with the pretty morning glories took its place. The only difference was that this time he put the last page on top so he could make out the words "I forgive you," which were printed in large block letters at the bottom.

Every night before he went to sleep, Carl glanced at those words.

Over the years, in a place where one did not accumulate many material possessions, he religiously protected the small but growing stack of letters.

Although he was a quiet loner who kept to himself, the men with whom he was incarcerated learned that, if provoked, Carl could be a

SERENA B. MILLER

vicious and merciless fighter who gave no quarter. It earned him the reputation of being a little bit crazy. Crazy was not a bad thing to be in a prison. The other men tended to leave alone those who were unpredictable. And as Carl moved from cell to cell, his roommates soon learned that the small stack of envelopes he kept bundled together was something that could not be touched.

With nothing else to do or think about, there was some speculation among the men over who had sent the letters to Carl. A mother? A sweetheart? A sister? When asked, all Carl would tell them was that they were from a friend.

He learned from the continuing letters that the little girl in the pink party dress who had haunted his sleep for years had graduated from the police academy. He learned about the beating she had received the day she tried to break up a domestic dispute—and how Bertha and her sisters had nursed her back to health.

Carl burned with rage when he read that letter. How dare someone hurt that brave little girl! Even though Carl was aware that she was a grown woman now, the only image he had of her was the one where she had taken a wide-legged stance and pointed a gun straight at him. That tiny little thing was determined to protect her daddy. The thought of someone hurting her became an obsession with him.

After she sustained that beating, Carl asked about her every time George came to visit. He wanted to know if she was better, if her broken bones were mending. It wasn't until George was able to tell him that she was healed and back to work that Carl began to calm down. The little girl wasn't hurting anymore. That was good. He could relax.

The fact that he could worry so much about another person's welfare would have been an impossibility years earlier—but Carl had changed. Helping heal so many broken dogs over the years had slowly given him the ability to care about people as well. At least he cared about George

103

and the old Amish woman who wrote him those letters. He also cared about the courageous little girl who had tried to protect her daddy.

Carl had only been incarcerated for two years when a deputy warden at the Mansfield prison started the Tender Loving Care program. Carl thought the new program was a bad joke when he first heard the name. There was nothing tender or loving within the walls of that institution.

Then he found out it involved working with abandoned dogs and he suddenly knew what he wanted to do with his life—or at least for as long as the program lasted. Carl had never wanted to do anything as badly as be accepted into that program.

It wasn't easy to get into it. A prisoner had to have a good record. This was difficult because Carl had an anger issue that could flare up at any moment, and the prison staff knew it. With the goal of the program in mind, Carl taught himself the skill of having enough self discipline to keep from lashing out when he felt his rights or personal space had been violated.

He finally confessed to George about how badly he wanted to join the dog handlers and how hard he was trying to keep his anger under control. George said to keep working on his good behavior and he would see what he could do. It was the first time Carl had let his guard down with George and allowed him to see a heartfelt need. Carl was surprised when the first thing George did was bow his head and pray that God would cool Carl's anger and help him make it into the program.

Carl had never heard anyone pray for him before, at least not like George prayed. George talked to God like they were friends. Carl didn't know if it was the prayer or the memory of George praying for him that kept his temper in check—but a small miracle happened. He made it into the program and his life changed. Everything changed.

As he healed those abused dogs, he found something within himself healing as well. Every sentence of praise he gave his dogs, every affirming word, even the small rewards for good behavior, was as if he was giving something to himself. When those dogs responded by loving him with their whole hearts—that love washed over him like a warm, comforting bath.

As he learned dog-training skills, Carl began to have something of his own to contribute to his conversations with the preacher. George's wife had gotten a cocker spaniel puppy and was having trouble knowing how to housebreak it. Now it was Carl, with several months of training and experience, who had valuable advice to give, and it was George who was grateful to get it.

It was a high-octane feeling, one Carl had never experienced. For the first time in his life, he had something of value to give to someone else.

At first, it was incredibly hard to give up his dogs when they were ready, but his position also involved instructing an individual or family on how to care for the dog. This brought him into contact with outsiders who wanted an animal to love but didn't have the skills to train one. To be considered a dog-training expert by people outside the prison walls was mind-boggling. It almost made giving up his dogs worth it.

Besides, there was always the challenge of another hurt dog to heal. The cruelty of people against animals was something he had never understood. But the kindness of the families and volunteers he met balanced things out a little and helped him believe that there was some goodness in the world after all.

Many letters from Bertha later, George brought him a new one where the content was unthinkable. She said that since he had now served the requisite fifteen years after a felony murder, she and her sisters had begun to petition the parole board to release him.

Imagine. Such kindness. Who *were* these people, that they would even consider the possibility?

It was incredibly kind of her, but he had not allowed himself to hope, which was good because it had taken another five years of letters before he walked out of that prison and climbed into George's car.

He had brushed off George's apologies about having only the church's janitor's closet to give him. It was impossible to express his gratitude for all that George had done. It felt like an honor to keep the church clean and polished and bring his good friend that cup of fresh coffee every morning.

The only problem was wondering what to do with the rest of his time.

Chapter Twenty

Joe was trying to make a new list of ways he might be able to make a living. It was not going well. Nothing was coming to him. The area surrounding Sugarcreek was all well and good for those who owned shops or made cheese or raised cows. There was a flourishing brick company and some furniture manufacturing places too, but getting work of any kind was iffy in an area where there were always a half-dozen well-trained, hardworking Amish people willing to settle for modest wages.

Last night he'd suggested to Rachel that maybe he could go back to playing ball. He wasn't at the top of his game and never would be again, but he could still play well enough to be on one of the farm teams. Maybe.

"Even with a bum shoulder?" Rachel had asked.

"Well, there is that," he said. "But there's also the possibility of getting a coaching job with them."

"You'd be traveling or training how many months out of the year?"

"Nine."

"And how could this possibly affect Bobby in a good way?"

"It couldn't."

He hadn't really been serious, but the more Joe thought about what he could—or couldn't— do, the more worried he became. He felt that he had run out of options.

Then he remembered being a child and hearing his father's

comforting voice as their family faced a much worse situation than what he and Rachel were experiencing.

"We have done all that we can," his father had said. "Now we must wait upon the Lord."

And his parents had waited and prayed. Eventually, the Lord had given them the answer.

Joe had tried everything he could think of—short of uprooting his son and wife—to find a job that could support his family.

He had done everything except the one thing his dad would have counseled. It was past time to rely on the faith that he claimed to have. It was time to wait upon the Lord.

"Your will be done, Father," Joe prayed. "Just show me what it is you want me to do and I'll do it."

Chapter Twenty-One

Several weeks after Carl began working as the church's janitor, on a Sunday afternoon, as he was taking out the trash after a church potluck, one of the older deacons stopped him in the hallway and told him he was doing a good job and that the church had never looked better or smelled so clean. Carl treasured that compliment. It was one of the few he had ever received.

The graveled parking lot behind the church held a Dumpster. The company that owned the Dumpster usually arrived on Tuesday morning to empty it. Normally there was plenty of room for what little garbage the church produced, but this week there had been a large wedding shower on Saturday afternoon along with a teen party on Friday. Once everyone left and Carl finished cleaning up after the potluck, the Dumpster had filled to overflowing.

As he tossed the last bags on top of the heap, he saw that one bag had fallen off to the side and was ripped open. Some of the paper plates had been chewed nearly in two by some animal trying to find food.

He backed away and waited quietly. His wait was rewarded by a glimpse of a medium-sized dog as it slunk out from behind the Dumpster to finish its pitiful meal.

Carl felt his anger rise when he saw that the dog was emaciated, its ribs showing through the dull brown coat. The animal attacked another paper plate that had bits of food sticking to it, and the plate scooted around on the gravel as the forlorn creature tried to lick up a few molecules of nourishment.

The sight of this hunger-ravaged dog made Carl want to hurt the person who had abandoned it, but that was not an option. Instead, he clicked into his training mode. Totally focused on the dog, he sank into a crouch to get a better look. It was a mixed breed. He guessed it to be part German shepherd and part mountain cur. It was hard to tell in the dark.

"You hungry, boy?" he said.

The dog flinched violently at the sound of Carl's voice. It was a gesture of fear that was not warranted by the soft words he had spoken.

"I'm not going to hurt you," Carl promised.

The dog growled softly, unhappy about being interrupted from its meager meal. Fear of the stranger won out over hunger, and it fled behind the Dumpster.

"Wait right here," Carl said. "I've got something better than melted ice cream and cake for you to eat."

He went back into the church kitchen, where he knew there were hot dogs. The woman in charge of the youth group had a habit of storing leftovers from the kids' get-togethers and then forgetting about them. He nearly always had to be the one who disposed of them. Now, he was grateful to her. There was an entire package of hot dogs, and as far as he was concerned, feeding that poor, starving animal was a great use for them.

He cut the package open, went outside, and closed the door quietly behind him. He had an abandoned dog's trust to win, and he was good at it.

Chapter Twenty-Two

. . . .

"That's a funny-looking car." Bobby pointed to it from the backseat as he and Joe drove to the *daadi haus* that sat next door to Rachel's aunts'.

Joe's father had made arrangements to rent the *daadi haus* as a home base between mission assignments. Joe never knew when his dad might show up to stay a few weeks, so he went and aired the place out from time to time when the weather was good to make sure the place didn't get too musty between visits.

"It's a DeLorean," Joe answered. "They made those about the time I was born."

"There are a *lot* of funny-looking cars today," Bobby said.

"That's because there's an antique car show this weekend."

"What's 'antique' mean?"

"Anything that's old."

"Like you?"

At thirty-four, Joe didn't feel particularly old, but he knew going down *that* path would only start a deluge of new questions.

"Yes...like me."

"There's another funny-looking car," Bobby pointed.

"It's a '56 Chevy," Joe said. "It's the kind of car your grandpa owned when he was courting your grandmother."

"What does 'courting' mean?" Bobby asked.

Joe loved his son. He would cheerfully die for his son. But sometimes

Bobby's constant stream of questions drove him nuts. He was attempting to form a definition of courting when he realized that his son had already lost interest.

"What are all these cars doing here?" Bobby asked.

"This is the weekend that Sugarcreek has their Fabulous Fifties Fling," Joe said. "It's where people bring their old, 'funny-looking' cars and show them off."

"Can we go?"

"Sure," Joe said. "Rachel will probably be working here anyway. She said there will be about five hundred diffcrent cars here for her and the other cops to watch over."

"Will they have hot dogs there?"

"Of course." His son's infatuation with hot dogs was well-known. "They'll probably have some vegetables too, and I'll expect you to eat some."

His son didn't let out the groan of despair that Joe had expected. He glanced in the rearview mirror and saw that Bobby had loosened his seat belt and was turned around in his seat, half standing and waving to someone.

"Sit down, son. Put your seat belt on the way it's supposed to be. Who are you waving to?"

"Uncle Darren."

"Uncle Darren?" Joe hadn't seen his brother since the wedding two years ago. Darren tended to move around a lot, sometimes just because he felt like it. Other times, although Joe had no proof, he suspected that Darren was forced to move on by unsavory circumstances. He loved his brother, but he had bailed Darren out of so many scrapes and bad business deals that he tended to dread seeing him show up.

"Uncle Darren wants you to stop," Bobby said, still turned around in his seat.

Joe pulled over into a church parking lot and Darren drove in beside him. His brother loved nice cars, but this one was over the top. Joe was no car expert, but it looked like Darren was driving an early Lamborghini. Since Darren was usually broke, Joe began worrying about where his brother had gotten it.

Darren unfolded himself from the low-slung car and approached them. He wasn't as tall as Joe, but he was handsome in a showy sort of way. Wavy, dark brown hair. Sleepy eyes. Darren always carried himself with confidence, even if his shoes had holes in the soles and he didn't have a nickel to his name, but his slow strut to Joe's car said that he was feeling quite proud of himself at the moment.

"Hey, brother."

"Hello, Darren." It had been a long time since Joe had felt any pleasure in his brother's company. Mainly he just felt resigned whenever Darren showed up. Family was family.

"Hey," Darren said, "aren't you glad to see your only brother?"

"Sure. What's with the car?"

"I was hoping you'd notice." Darren's grin was huge. "This is my baby, Lulu. Isn't she gorgeous?"

"Yes. Gorgeous. Where did you get her?"

"My former business partner bought it from Jay Leno. It's a 1965 and is in mint condition, but Jay wanted to make room for an older model."

"Seriously? Is any of that even remotely true?"

"I don't know." Darren shrugged. "But that's my partner's story and I'm sticking to it."

"What do you mean, *his* story?"

"It's what he told our customers. I didn't personally knock on Jay's door and ask him if it was true."

"Leno or not, that's one expensive piece of machinery. Why are you driving it?"

"Craig and I had a disagreement about the future of the business. We had different visions. He finally bought out my half of the business by giving me a clear title to this beauty."

"What's this business?"

"Isn't it obvious? We bought exotic cars and rented them out."

"Other companies are already doing that."

"Yeah, but they didn't kick it up an extra notch like we did. It was all my idea. We only provided cars that had formerly been driven by celebrities—cars with a history. You have no idea how much money you can charge someone to sit in the same seat and hold the same steering wheel as a car that Kim Kardashian once drove."

Joe shook his head. "People are nuts."

"Absolutely," Darren happily agreed. "But it worked out well for us."

"So what are you doing here?"

"I'm a little short on cash right now, so I gave up the lease on my apartment and thought I'd crash at Dad's place for a while. I mean, he pays rent on it, and he's not using it."

"You do realize there's no electricity, right?"

"I've lived in worse." A shadow passed over Darren's face and Joe wondered how bad it could have been. There was much about his brother's life he did not know.

Darren brightened. "I also plan to exhibit Lulu at the antique car show. It'll be easy prize money."

"Does Dad know you're here?"

"Tried to get a message to him but couldn't. He's probably sleeping in some hut in Africa, doing good works, eating grubs, and feeling happier than a pig in slop."

"He's doing what he feels called to do." Joe loved and admired their dad. Darren's dismissive remarks about their distinguished father bothered him.

"He's doing what he *wants* to do," Darren said. "And that's okay with me, but I don't think he'll mind me using his place until I get back on my feet."

"Getting back on his feet" usually meant that Darren had come for another handout, and this time Joe didn't have any extra to give him. His new poverty was probably going to be an even bigger shock to Darren's system than it had been to his own.

"Hi, Uncle Darren!" Bobby had managed to extricate himself completely from his seat belt and now stuck his head out the window beside Joe's.

"Hi, buddy." Darren reached over and ruffled Bobby's hair. "How's my favorite nephew?"

And then the mask of bravado crumbled as Darren looked at Joe with the sensitive brown eyes that had worshipped him when they were growing up. "It's good to be home, brother," he said.

The simple statement went straight to Joe's heart. Their father had been so busy moving from place to place and involving them in good deeds that there had never been any real geological "home" for their family. Their stalwart mother packed and unpacked and made do and did the best she could regardless of their circumstances. It was she who had defined "home" and kept them together.

After she died it was difficult to keep the family stitched together, and the brothers and father had quickly drifted apart. Since Joe had moved to Sugarcreek, they were all slowly finding their way back to one another. Evidently Sugarcreek was starting to become "home" to more than just him and Bobby.

Darren had issues, but Joe loved him. He just hoped he wouldn't come to regret the fact that his brother was starting to think of Sugarcreek as home.

"With all the pranks that have been going on these past weeks, I'm worried about the Fifties Fling." Ed drummed his fingers on the top of his desk. "There is probably a couple million dollars' worth of cars driving in here tonight and I want to make sure those cars are safe. If some angry teenager out there is deliberately doing random damage, I don't want him deciding to key the perfect paint job on one of those classics. People have been killed for less."

"Are you calling in the auxiliary officers?"

"Yes. I've also asked Nick to bring Ranger."

"Our new police dog," Rachel nodded in agreement. "Are you expecting

drugs?"

"No, but it won't hurt to let Ranger and Nick be on view," Ed said. "If nothing else, that dog is great PR for the police department. He knows how to work a crowd, and if there are any drugs for him to find, so much the better."

Chapter Twenty-Three

"I see you there." Carl pulled a few sturdy weeds that had forced their way through the cracks in the sidewalk while the stray dog watched him from behind the corner of the church. "You think you're hiding from me, but I can see you."

They were on relatively friendly terms now, but the animal was still keeping a careful distance between them. Fortunately, the dog did not have a problem with eating the food Carl sat out for him as long as he kept several paces away. It had been gratifying to watch the dog filling out and seeing his coat become sleek and healthy. The next few weeks would be interesting. There was nothing that gave Carl more satisfaction than helping a rescue learn to trust again.

He was surprised when George and his wife drove up and stopped at the curb. It was Friday night—their "date" night—which was a concept Carl found mildly amusing.

"Hey, Carl," George called, "Sugarcreek's annual Fabulous Fifties Fling is starting up tonight. You're welcome to come with us if you want."

The dog disappeared behind the building.

George tossed the few weeds he had in his hand behind a rosebush. "What's a Fabulous Fifties Fling?"

"Some people come dressed like people dressed in the fifties, and there's an antique car contest. Sugarcreek holds it every year the second weekend in June. The food is good."

"You sure you don't mind?"

"Not at all," George said. "Come with us. You'll enjoy it."

"Give me a minute to lock up."

"No problem."

Carl not only locked up, but he hurriedly grabbed a clean shirt, washed his hands and ran a comb through his hair. He had stayed away from bars for fear he'd accidentally get into trouble, but a car show? Accompanied by a preacher and a preacher's wife? There certainly would be no harm or danger in that.

Five minutes later, he climbed into the backseat of George's old, green, four-door Ford and found himself looking forward to an evening for the first time in years.

***

Rachel stood near the entrance to the field where the antiquated cars were lining up and parking. The owners came in twos or threes—with plenty of lawn chairs and coolers—so that one person was with the automobile at all times. Owners met with other owners and admired one another's precious vehicles. Food venders sat up in the main area. To match the theme of the festival, fifties' rock-and-roll music filled the air.

At one point, she saw several young people huddled together behind the back of a car that had pretend bullet holes pasted to it. The group looked a little suspicious to her until she quietly walked over and saw that the only thing going on was a matronly woman passing out sandwiches and soft drinks to the kids and their friends from the boxy trunk.

Everyone seemed super-vigilant despite the fun fifties' music in the background. No one wanted to risk having a thief walk away with an expensive, hard-to-get hood ornament.

She watched Nick strolling around with Ranger on a leash and was pleased with the city's recent decision to add the specially trained dog to the police force. He was working out quite well.

Ranger was a handsome dog. With his healthy, glistening black coat and an official police badge attached to his harness, he had the confident air of a dog with a job to do. If given permission by Nick, he gracefully accepted a few extra pats and exclamations of "Good dog!" from passersby. As with any other police officer worth his pay, he was relaxed and friendly with the people of Sugarcreek but could go on full alert at the first whiff of trouble.

"You doing okay?" Joe asked Rachel when he caught up with her.

"I'm fine," she said. "Where's Bobby?"

"With my brother," Joe said. "Bobby is helping Darren watch over the car he's exhibiting. You know, the one I told you about last night."

"The classic Lamborghini his partner supposedly bought from Jay Leno?"

"That's the one," Joe said. "I'm afraid he's depending heavily on winning the prize money. He's been polishing the thing all morning."

"That man looks familiar to me," Rachel craned her neck to see something over Joe's shoulder. "But I can't place him."

"Where?" Joe turned to look.

"The guy standing beside that black Thunderbird."

"I don't know him," Joe said. "Where do think you might have seen him?"

"I have no idea, but he makes me feel uneasy. I don't know why."

"He's not doing anything except looking at the Thunderbird," Joe said. "Seems like a normal-enough person to me."

Joe was right. There was nothing at all remarkable or threatening about the guy. He was average in every way. Nondescript clothing. Medium height. Probably somewhere in his sixties. There were a hundred other men milling about the downtown area who looked just like him.

But she couldn't seem to pull her gaze away. There was just something about him. Something that was affecting her in a powerful way. Something in his stance. Something in the profile of his face.

This man gave her a bad feeling. A very bad feeling. She concentrated hard, focusing, trying to place him. It was extremely rare for her to forget a face. It was a gift she'd had since childhood, and it had served her well as a cop.

Then, just as the memory of this man began to emerge, everything began slamming shut in her brain. Her vision turned black, her mind went blank, and she crumbled to the ground.

***

George brought an apple fritter to Carl.

"My wife sent me over with this. She says you have to try one. It's kind of a specialty around here. Most of us look forward to the festivals in Sugarcreek all year so we can fill up on these things."

"Thanks." Carl took a bite of the warm, sweet pastry and closed his eyes in appreciation. When he opened them, he saw that George was watching an ambulance drive across the grass toward a knot of people.

"I wonder what that's all about," George said.

"I don't know," Carl said, "but it looks like it's being taken care of by the right people. I hope no one is hurt."

Chapter Twenty-Four

"Rachel?"

Dimly, she heard someone calling her name.

"Rachel, honey?"

She felt a mild annoyance when a hand touched her arm and shook her gently.

"Wake up, sweetheart."

She grimaced. The last thing she wanted to do was wake up. What she *wanted* to do was to burrow back into the comforting deep sleep where she had been.

"Rachel?" The man's voice was vaguely familiar, but she did not open her eyes. If she kept them closed, perhaps whoever was talking to her would go away.

"RACHEL!" A woman's commanding voice startled her. Her eyes snapped open to see Aunt Bertha standing over her.

"It is time to wake up," Bertha said with deep disapproval. "You have frightened everyone long enough."

Frightened? What was Aunt Bertha talking about? Was it time for school already? She often had trouble waking up in time for chores. Aunt Bertha seemed to think sleeping in was a spiritual weakness. But Aunt Lydia said she was growing so fast that her young body needed more rest than they did. Aunt Anna simply sneaked her another cookie, giggled, and left her alone no matter how early or late Rachel was in rising.

Her mind felt fuzzy, as though she'd been ill. And where was her daddy?

She glanced at the man standing near her bed. He seemed familiar, but she didn't know who he was. The room was not at all familiar. It was white, and there were lots of electric lights. Rachel frowned. The aunts did not have electric lights where they lived.

"Rachel!" Bertha took her face between her hands. "Look at me!"

Rachel looked and was surprised to see that Bertha had gotten old.

Her arm itched and she tried to scratch it, but her fingers encountered tape. When she lifted her head to see, she realized that there was a plastic tube running into her skin. Was there a needle in her arm? She *hated* needles.

"Say something," the man said. "Please tell me you're okay, sweetheart."

She did not understand why this strange Englischman was calling her love names. All she knew for sure was that she was thirsty.

"May I have some juice, Aunt Bertha?" she asked.

***

The blank look Rachel gave him made Joe take a step backward. It was as though she had never seen him before. The complete absence of recognition in her eyes was a little creepy. Where had the strong, confident woman he loved gone?

And that voice! She sounded like a small child. A very confused small child. Had she really asked for juice? Rachel never drank fruit juice. She was strict about keeping her body in shape. Part of her discipline, she had told him, was that she preferred to eat her calories instead of drink them. Rachel almost always drank water.

"I will go find some juice for you, Rachel." Bertha's face was creased with worry. "Joe, will you come help me?"

"Of course."

Out in the hallway, with the door shut behind them, he was so terrified by Rachel's behavior, he could hold back no longer. "What's *wrong* with her? She sounds like she's Bobby's age, and she never drinks juice."

"She drank juice when she was a child," Bertha said. "It was her favorite thing when she was upset."

"But she's no longer a child."

"I think she does not know that right now."

The impact of Bertha's words hit him like a physical blow. When Rachel collapsed at the car show, his first panicked thought was that she'd had a heart attack. She always tended to take on too much responsibility, as though the world sat squarely on her shoulders. She was young, but heart attacks didn't happen just to the old.

When he ascertained that she was still breathing and her pulse was strong, his second thought was for their baby. Had something gone wrong with the pregnancy?

His third thought was that perhaps collapsing was what happened to pregnant women who were working too hard.

The ambulance team assured him that they did not think it was her heart. By the time they got there, she was awake—or seemed to be. Her eyes stared into space, but she said nothing and responded to nothing—not even when the ambulance drivers questioned her.

The more hours they spent in the ER doing tests, the more she seemed to regress. They suspected a stroke until that, too, was ruled out.

His wife was physically as healthy as a horse, but her mind was… well, her behavior was one of the most bizarre things he had ever experienced.

"What's wrong with her, Bertha?"

"I am no doctor," she said.

"I want to see Rachel," Anna demanded as she and Lydia joined them.

"I don't know if that's wise." Joe feared what it might do to Anna if Rachel didn't recognize her, either.

"I want to see Rachel!" Anna grew more insistent. "I want to see Rachel!"

"If we don't let Anna go in, there will be trouble," Bertha said. "And it is not a good thing for Anna to get upset, with her own health issues."

"Go on in and see her, Anna," Joe said. "But don't stay long. We'll be here if you need us."

They stood at the door and watched.

Anna plopped herself onto the side of Rachel's bed and began to stroke her face and hair. It was as though Rachel were a kitten that Anna felt needed to be comforted.

As Anna sat there, Rachel looked up at her and whispered something. Anna nodded with understanding and whispered back, their faces close together.

"Should I go in?" he asked.

Bertha watched the interaction between Anna and Rachel with rapt attention.

"Not yet," Bertha said. "When Rachel was young, she would talk to Anna about things she would not speak of with Lydia and me. It was like one child talking to another. There was a great trust between them."

When Anna came out, her normally sunny face looked troubled.

"What did she say?" Joe asked her. "Did she give you any idea what's going on?"

"Uh-huh." Anna nodded.

They waited for Anna to say more, but she didn't volunteer anything else. Instead, she appeared to be deep in thought.

"What did Rachel say?" Bertha prompted.

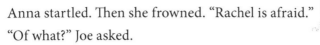

Anna startled. Then she frowned. "Rachel is afraid."

"Of what?" Joe asked.

Anna shrugged and twisted a handkerchief in her hands. She did not answer.

He glanced at Bertha. "What's going on?"

"Anna has trouble putting things into words," Bertha said. "Sometimes we have to wait awhile before she finds those words."

He left the sisters standing in the doorway and went back to Rachel's bedside. His wife was curled into as much of a fetal position as she could get at three months' pregnancy. He smoothed back her hair, tucked the thin blanket a little more firmly around her shoulders, and kissed her on the cheek, but Rachel never acknowledged him. She had gone away again.

Chapter Twenty-Five

"You should go home, Joe," Bertha said. "Get some rest. This has been a hard day for you. I'll stay with her tonight in case she awakens."

"I should be the one who stays," Joe insisted.

"No." Bertha shook her head. "She still might not know who you are, but she recognizes me and I can comfort her."

Bertha looked so tired. The woman was far from young and had carried so much responsibility for so long.

"I hate to leave you here," Joe said.

"Bobby needs you to be with him. He will be frightened that Rachel is in the hospital. Lydia and Anna need to go home, and their driver has left. Please take them with you, and I will stay."

When Bertha made a decision, there was little use in arguing with her. He went to take Lydia and Anna back to their house, but as they walked to his car, Anna seemed agitated and kept looking around as though searching for someone.

"What are you looking for, Anna?" he asked.

"Is the bad man here?"

"What bad man, Anna?" Lydia asked.

"*The* bad man." Anna stomped her foot, frustrated with trying to make them understand, and then she began to cry.

Anna rarely cried, but when she did, she didn't seem to know how to stop. He drove, grimly, while Lydia absorbed Anna's tears in the backseat—but they could get no more information out of her.

He could only hope that "*the* bad man" to whom Anna was referring was not himself. What was going on in Rachel's mind?

After dropping off Lydia and Anna, he went downtown to the car show to get Bobby. When he got there, he found his son bedded down in the backseat of Darren's fancy car. The festivities had ended for the evening and only a few people were left, but his brother was sitting in a lawn chair next to his car, keeping watch over his little nephew.

"I won," Darren said, without any real enthusiasm.

"Good for you." Joe couldn't have cared less.

"How is Rachel?" There was real concern in Darren's voice.

"No better." Joe settled in a lawn chair beside Darren. It was surprisingly comforting, having his brother beside him, especially after the day he'd had.

"I'm sorry to hear that," Darren said. "Any idea what happened?"

"The ER doctor ruled out everything he could of a physical nature. But one of the things he asked me was if she'd recently experienced anything particularly traumatic. He said that sometimes if a person is going through something traumatic or stressful, the body protects the brain with a form of temporary amnesia. He says it's rare but very real. The brain will be so emotionally traumatized that it will actually swell, temporarily wiping out their memory, because it simply cannot accept the terrible news. He says usually the person will simply awaken from the amnesia with no knowledge of what happened."

"Do you buy that?"

"I don't know." Joe lifted the lid of the cooler sitting between them. "You got anything to drink in here?"

"Water, soda, a couple of sandwiches... Help yourself."

Joe dug a foil-wrapped sandwich out of the cooler along with a bottle of water. He pulled the wrapper off, discovered a steak sandwich, took a bite—and realized that he wasn't just hungry, he was famished. Darren waited patiently while Joe bolted the food and drained the bottle of water.

"Feel better?" Darren asked.

"Yeah. Thanks." Joe leaned back in the lawn chair and stared up at the star-studded sky. "To answer your question, I'd rather it be that stress-related amnesia thing than finding out Rachel had had a stroke or heart attack...but if he's right, what is Rachel so stressed about? We have some challenges in our life but nothing traumatic enough to cause that. Rachel is a strong woman. It would take something truly horrible to have that kind of effect on her. She was standing there talking with me like everything was perfectly normal...and then suddenly she fell to the ground in some sort of catatonic state."

"She has a stressful job and has taken on the responsibility of a ready-made family. To someone as responsible as Rachel, it might be more pressure than you think."

"She's also pregnant," Joe said.

"You're going to have another kid?" Darren sounded envious. "You lucky dog! I hope he or she is as much fun as Bobby."

"I'll just be happy if the baby is healthy. I wondered if the pregnancy had anything to do with what happened, but the doctor said he didn't think so."

"Maybe there was a trigger of some kind that you didn't notice."

The two brothers sat in silence for a while, considering that possibility.

"Anna said something strange," Joe said.

"What was that?"

"Rachel and Anna talked privately at one point. Afterward, Anna said that Rachel was afraid of the bad man."

"Who is the bad man?" Darren asked.

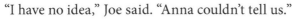

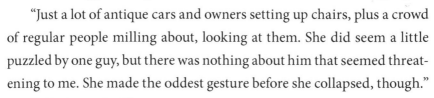

"I have no idea," Joe said. "Anna couldn't tell us."

"What happened right before Rachel fainted?"

"Just a lot of antique cars and owners setting up chairs, plus a crowd of regular people milling about, looking at them. She did seem a little puzzled by one guy, but there was nothing about him that seemed threatening to me. She made the oddest gesture before she collapsed, though."

"What was that?"

"It looked like she was starting to reach for her gun."

Chapter Twenty-Six

Rachel slept a lot, waking for short periods of time. As her body rested, her mind and memory began to come back in snatches. Each time she awakened, Bertha was sitting in the chair beside her bed, and Rachel felt comforted and knew it was safe to crawl back into the cocoon of sleep. Everything was safe as long as Bertha was keeping watch.

At one point, she remembered a nurse helping her dress, and then some man came and they got into a car. She dozed in the car and awoke only when they got back home. The Sugar Haus Inn did not look like what she remembered. They led her to a bedroom she did not recognize.

Bertha stripped back the quilt on her bed, helped her lay down, and then pulled the quilt up to Rachel's chin. It struck her again that Bertha was looking awfully old. She wondered if Bertha might be sick.

"Where am I?" she asked.

"You are back home with us," Bertha said. "This is Sugar Haus."

"No, it isn't," Rachel complained. "Where is *my* room?"

"There was a bad fire, Rachel." Bertha's voice was weary. "Our people rebuilt the inn for us after it burned."

"I'll stay with her now," said the strange man who kept coming in and out of her room. "You've done enough."

"No!" Rachel felt a stab of alarm at that statement. She grabbed Bertha's arm.

She did not want this man to stay with her. She wanted her aunts, and she wanted her daddy. It seemed odd that her daddy hadn't come to see her, but there was a darkness in her mind whenever she tried too hard to think about her daddy. There was also a darkness in her mind when she realized that her belly was bigger—that was scary.

"Anna and Lydia and I will take turns," Bertha said. "It will be all right."

Rachel was surprised when she saw tears on the stranger's face. Why was he crying? Who was he?

"It will be okay," Bertha told the man. "The Englisch are fond of their computers, but those computers are nothing compared to the human mind. Our Father created our brains to have the ability to heal... with time."

Rachel did not understand what Bertha was talking about. What was a computer?

"I feel so helpless," the man said.

"We are all helpless right now," Bertha said. "I believe she will come back to us. Gott will lead her out of the darkness, but I cannot predict when."

Something niggled at Rachel's mind as the two grownups talked. Something bad had happened. Something very bad. It crouched in the corner of her mind, lying in wait to pounce, but her mind refused to acknowledge it. She thought she remembered talking about something bad with Anna, but now she couldn't remember what they had talked about. The harder she tried to think, the sleepier she got. Aunt Bertha's quilt smelled of sunshine and soap and safety. The grownup voices receded as she fell back into the safe cocoon of sleep.

***

"Any change?" Darren turned off the TV when Joe came home. His brother had taken over the care of Bobby while he dealt with Rachel.

"None. It's like she's a child." Joe threw his keys onto a side table. "A very sleepy child."

"Is she regressing even further?"

"It seems that way," Joe said. "She's afraid of me now. Doesn't want me in the same room."

"I'm sorry to hear that. Would she be better off in some sort of treatment facility?"

"Some doctors would probably say so, but the ones around here tend to be a little more holistic in their approaches to medicine. The one at the ER said he believed a treatment facility for adults could traumatize her further. He thinks we should at least try allowing her to rest for a few days at her aunts' and see what happens before we talk about other options. Rachel has a strong will. I have to believe she'll fight her way back to us."

"Bobby wants to see her."

"Where is he?"

"Playing in his room. I told him you'd be back soon."

"Thanks, Darren. I'll go talk with him."

Joe was more grateful to his brother than he had ever expected to be. The rocky relationship between them had smoothed somewhat the past couple of days, and he was glad. He didn't want to dislike his only brother. Losing Grace had made him see everything through different eyes. People he loved didn't always stay alive. People he loved could be lost in an instant.

Bobby's door was open as the little boy played with action figures on his floor. Usually his son was quite animated as he spoke in different voices for the various toys, but Joe could tell that his son's heart wasn't in it this time.

"Hi, buddy."

Bobby glanced up, his small face alight with hope. "Is Rachel all better?"

"Not yet."

Bobby didn't say any more. Tears welled in his eyes and he looked down at the action figure he held in his hands.

"Don't be sad," Joe said. "She'll get better."

"Mommy didn't get better," Bobby said. "Mommy died."

So *that* was what Bobby was thinking. He had lost one mother and now he was afraid he would lose Rachel.

"Rachel will be okay," Joe said. "It's just taking some time."

"Can I go see her?" Bobby asked.

"I don't know if that's a good idea, son."

"If I was sick, Rachel would come see me," Bobby said. "Even if I was really, really sick. She wouldn't leave me."

He made this statement with such utter conviction that Joe's heart squeezed with pain from the truth of it. If she were well, Rachel would turn heaven and earth to get to Bobby if he needed her. In fact, it would tear her apart to know that she was causing the child any pain.

"We'll go see her in the morning," Joe said. "Right now it's time for bed and prayers."

He did not think Bobby's presence would have any effect on her when his own had not, but at least tomorrow his son could see that she was still alive.

"Can I pray for Rachel?" Bobby asked.

"Absolutely," Joe answered.

He welcomed Bobby's prayers. If God was going to listen to anyone, it would be his tenderhearted little son.

Chapter Twenty-Seven

In the end, it was the smell of bacon and coffee that awakened her. Rachel opened her eyes and was surprised to see the plain white walls and wooden furniture of her aunts' inn. Why on earth would she be here instead of at her own house? She didn't remember having come here last night.

In fact, she couldn't remember last night at all.

And she was wearing a nightgown. She didn't own a nightgown. She preferred to sleep in a tank top and underpants. That way, in an emergency, she could pull on her uniform and be out the door at a moment's notice. The nightgown had become all twisted and uncomfortable as she slept.

Everything felt so odd. Her mind was fuzzy, and that wasn't normal for her. As a cop, she had always been grateful for her ability to think clearly.

She threw back the covers and set her feet on the floor, but when she tried to stand up, she swayed and had to grab hold of the oak bedstead. It took a few moments to get her balance. Once she did, she went to get a robe that was hanging on a hook behind the door. As she passed the window, it surprised her to see that there were blossoms outside. She had somehow had the feeling that it was fall.

All this was very disturbing.

As she wrapped herself in the robe and tied its sash, she heard footsteps on the stairs and then a knock on the door.

"Come in."

Bobby came hurtling at her.

"You're not sick anymore!" The little boy encircled her waist with his small arms and hugged her hard. She hugged him back and then saw Joe standing in the hallway. There was an odd expression on his face that she couldn't read.

"What's going on, Joe?" she said. "What's happened? Have I been ill?"

A look of immense relief passed over his face the moment she said his name.

"Bobby wanted to see you and make sure you were okay."

"Okay from what?"

"There's a lot to explain. Maybe it would be best if you came downstairs first. Your aunts have fixed breakfast. They'll be thrilled to see that you're up. They don't have any guests this morning, so you don't have to dress."

"Come on!" Bobby grabbed Rachel's hand and tugged her down the stairs behind him.

The silence in the kitchen bothered her as she entered. The aunts were usually bubbling with conversation and laughter early in the morning as they planned their day.

"Rachel!" Bertha said. "How are you feeling?"

"I'm fine." Rachel was still puzzled. She sat down, and Bobby scrambled to sit beside her.

"I think she's back," Joe said. "Although I can't be sure."

"Back?" Rachel asked. "Back from what?"

"Let us give thanks for our food first," Bertha said. "And then we will explain."

Obediently, Rachel bowed her head for the silent prayer, but her mind was whirling, trying to figure out why everyone was acting so strangely. And why couldn't she remember yesterday?

When Bertha said "Amen," Rachel lifted her head and glanced at the wall calendar. Anna had a habit of crossing off each day right after supper. It was one of her little rituals. She enjoyed counting things, and crossing off each day's number helped her keep track of what day it was. She had done it religiously for as long as Rachel could remember.

So it startled her to discover that it was June thirteenth.

But it *couldn't* be June thirteenth. Had Anna started crossing off days that hadn't happened?

"What day is it?" she asked.

"June thirteenth," Lydia answered softly. "Monday."

"That can't be." Rachel glanced around at each face. All of them were still wearing a look of concern for her, even little Bobby.

Suddenly she remembered what was supposed to have happened over the weekend she had apparently missed.

"The Fifties Fling!" she said. "Anna and Lydia were going to be helping with the food booth...but I don't remember any of it!"

Rachel could feel her mind starting to cloud over again, and she knew she had to fight against the dark mist that suddenly threatened to consume her. She jumped up and rushed out the door, barefoot. She needed to walk. She needed to breathe. She almost made it to the barn before Joe caught up with her.

"Rachel!"

She turned and confronted him. "Tell me exactly what happened, Joe. I need to know."

"Okay." He leaned against the fence and described everything to her. Then he said, "The doctor told us there is something called 'stress-induced amnesia.' He said there might be something going on that your brain needed to shut out in order to protect itself. Do you have any idea what it might be?"

"No...I wasn't particularly stressed. Things were going well with the Fling. Why would I collapse like that? I'm no fainter. I never have been."

"I've been thinking...," Joe said. "When you were working in Akron, weren't you in the hospital for a while? A domestic-violence altercation that you tried to deal with?"

"I got beat up," she said. "What does that have to do with now?"

"You were unconscious for a few days then, as well. Maybe something happened to trigger that response again."

"But why?" she said. "That's in the past. My body healed."

"Rachel, you were reaching for your gun as you fainted, but there was no threat."

"I don't remember."

"When we were at the hospital, Anna went in to visit you. When she came out, she said you told her you were afraid of the bad man."

"The bad man? Who was I talking about?"

"We don't know. We hoped you could tell us."

"It doesn't make sense. I'm trained to deal with bad men. I've had to deal with bad men, and sometimes bad women, for the past ten years of my life. It's my job. Why on earth would I faint during a perfectly normal festival?"

"Beats me." Joe shrugged. "But it definitely made for a memorable weekend."

She bit her lip, thinking. What Joe was describing sounded like someone else, not her. If there was one thing she had always been certain of, it was having a strong mind. It was part of her identity as a cop.

"You didn't recognize me," Joe said. "The only people you knew were your aunts. You were afraid of me. It was as though you had to regress into childhood to escape the fact that I was your husband."

"I'm sure that's not true. I would never want to escape from you."

Rachel's legs felt weak, which was unusual for her. "I need to sit down, Joe."

"You were in bed for a long time." He helped her to a bale of hay inside the barn and sat close beside her, his arm steadying her. "You're still weak from it."

"Whatever happened to me, it had nothing to do with you."

Joe intertwined his fingers with hers. "We'll figure things out, sweetheart."

Rachel held onto Joe's hand, a life preserver in a turbulent sea. Clinging to his hand, she allowed herself to concentrate hard now, trying to remember what might have triggered this anomaly.

There was nothing but blankness. Her analytical and common-sense mind, which she had always thought she could depend on, had failed her, and she had no idea why.

Chapter Twenty-Eight

Ed informed her that she would not be needed for a few days; she was to rest. Rachel felt she had already had enough rest, but her boss was adamant. In Rachel's opinion, Ed was overreacting.

With nothing else pending, she tried to surfeit Bobby with Candy Land. Perhaps, if she played it long enough, he would finally tire of the game. Instead, all she accomplished was making her stepson very happy and nearly driving herself up the wall with boredom. She loved the little guy to pieces, but he needed an awful lot of attention. It was tempting to sit him in front of the TV to watch cartoons, but she and Joe had vowed to limit his television time. They had discussed the fact that going without television seemed to do good things for all the bright, well-behaved Amish children they knew.

Today, though, Bobby was hanging out with Joe for a few hours. Their church was involved in a repair project on an elderly veteran's home, and Joe had wanted to take Bobby along so he could participate in helping others.

Her foggy-minded feeling had finally, completely, lifted, and with Bobby gone, Rachel decided there was no good excuse for not digging her way through the paperwork that had continued to pile up on her roll top desk. She was afraid they'd ignored the stack for so long that there were some overdue bills in it. The problem was, she had so much paperwork to do while at work that she tended to drag her feet about the stuff coming into her house.

Rachel fixed a cup of tea and sat down in front of the desk, determined not to stop until the surface was pristine and envelope-free. She slit open the first envelope: the electric bill. Few people could appreciate electricity more. After growing up in her aunts' Old Order home, she cherished being able to have light at the flick of a switch. She set the bill aside to be paid later.

All fliers and advertisements got tossed into the trash can. She fed several credit-card applications into the small shredder she kept beside the desk. None were things she had wanted or asked for. For a full hour, she automatically opened and discarded or filed and dealt with each piece of mail in the pile, feeling lighter by the minute.

With an enormous feeling of accomplishment, she picked up a sporting-equipment catalog of Joe's that had been on the very bottom of the pile. Every now and then he would pick up a pile of the junk mail that began arriving during the months he and Bobby lived at the daadi haus. Lydia had a basket in the kitchen where she'd place anything that came addressed to him. There wasn't a lot, so they didn't check it often.

As she started to toss the catalog in the trash, she felt something on the back and turned it over. An envelope addressed to her—with her aunts' street address—had somehow gotten stuck to it. Worry blossomed in the pit of her stomach when she read the words Ohio Parole Department, Victims Notification Division.

Fearful of what might be inside, she started to read. It took a moment for the words on the page to fully register.

Carl Bateman, the man who had murdered her father, was up for parole. The cold-blooded killer who had given her nightmares and caused her to devote her life to protecting the weak and helpless was being considered for release because of his good behavior.

Even though murder while committing a felony, like the bank

robbery her father had interrupted, meant a mandatory life sentence, she had known this day might come. That was why she had registered for the victim-notification program when she was only nineteen and had just entering the police academy. Family members of victims had rights, and she wanted them!

Even as she read, she was starting to make plans. She would write letters. The aunts would write letters. She would get other people to write letters. She would bury Carl Bateman with letters to the parole board. She would personally appear at the hearing, where she would be allowed to speak against him getting out.

A calendar hung near her desk, so she grabbed a pen. Glancing at the letter, she started to write in the all-important date of the parole hearing: May second.

May second?

Today was June fifteenth. She stared at the date on the letter, unable to believe her eyes. The parole date had already come and gone? And she had done...nothing?

Her heart sank. Preoccupation with spinning all the plates in her life had caused her to miss one of the most important things she could have done—keep Carl Bateman where he belonged.

Of course, there was always the chance that the parole board had turned down his request. With hope rising, she made a quick call to the number listed on the letterhead. The woman on the other end of the line did not have good news. The parole board had released him. He was still answering to a parole officer—and would be for the next year—but her father's killer was walking around free.

"Where is he living?" she asked. "Are you allowed to tell me that?"

"A church in Millersburg is sponsoring him," the woman on the phone said. "Looks like he's living and working there. Is that close to you?"

"Eighteen miles." Rachel was devastated. "Only eighteen miles."

"I'm sorry," the woman said, "but there is nothing we can do about that. It does say that he was released for good behavior, and it appears that he had some sort of religious conversion while in prison."

"Thanks." Rachel disconnected.

She jumped up from the desk and started pacing the living-room floor. Of *course* her father's killer had experienced a religious conversion while in prison. Didn't they all?

Even though she believed in redemption, as a cop she was highly suspicious of prisoners who suddenly embraced God. Often it was done solely to manipulate people on the outside. It was also done to impress parole boards.

Apparently it had worked.

The man was a drug user, a thief, a bank robber, and a killer. She had memorized his rap sheet long ago when she had first joined the police force. There was no doubt in her mind that Carl Bateman was evil. He belonged in prison.

Her mother had died early enough that Rachel didn't remember her, but the scene of her father being shot on her eleventh birthday was so burned into her conscience that there was rarely a day she didn't remember the shock of hearing the gunfire, the feel of her father's arm in front of her as though trying to protect her as he went down, the acrid smell of gunpowder permeating the bank, the screams of the people as they dived to the floor, or the realization that her father had stopped breathing while she sobbed on his chest.

And then there was the feel of cold gunmetal in her hands as she hefted her father's revolver and pointed it at the man who had made her father die.

Right or wrong, by the time she was eleven, her dad had already taught her how to handle a gun. When he was off duty and there was no school, Rachel was his constant shadow. As a peace officer, he often practiced target-shooting with her behind their home.

Although she could push aside the bad memory and go on with her life, she knew it was impossible for her to ever forgive the man who had taken away her kind and loving father.

What she wouldn't give to have her dad alive today. He had been a relatively young man when he died. Today he would only be in his late fifties. How he would have loved Bobby and Joe and this new baby she was carrying!

She often wondered what would have happened had she pulled the trigger as her father's murderer stared into her eyes. She still believed that if he had been given a few more seconds, she would be dead now too. It had only been the shock of seeing a little girl in a pink party dress holding a gun on him that made him hesitate. There had been a wildness in his eyes that she later realized was from being hopped up on drugs— she had seen that look so many times as a cop in the years since.

Years had come and gone, but the memory of that day was lodged in her brain forever. It was the day she left childhood behind. No more dolls. No more pink party dresses. No more days of growing up with a father who loved her.

It was the day she determined that, no matter what, she would become a cop just like her daddy. She would learn how to pull the trigger on the bad guys if she had to. She would protect herself and the people she loved.

Her determination for her future life never wavered from that moment. It was probably the reason her actions seemed a little unnatural to those who expected her to wail and cry like a normal child who lost a parent. But after those few wild sobs on her daddy's chest, after she'd held his gun aimed at the murderer, after courageous bank customers took Bateman down as he'd stood there undecided about what to do with the little girl pointing the gun, her eyes had remained dry.

She remembered the aftermath of the funeral when both Amish and Englisch had tried to comfort her with hugs and pats and words of condolence. She had thanked them, mechanically and politely, wishing they would go away so she could continue to plot out her life and how she would never again allow a bad guy to hurt someone she loved.

What none of them understood, and what she had not understood until many years later, was that what she was feeling was not grief. It was fury. It was an anger so deep that she somehow knew—even at the young age of eleven—that if she let down her guard for just an instant, she might start screaming and never stop.

That was the kind of cold fury she felt at this moment upon knowing that Carl Bateman was out on the streets—and apparently only eighteen miles away. Her fury was so intense that she was shaking. So intense that she felt her mind starting to shut down again.

"Stop it!" she said aloud to herself. "Pull yourself together."

Chapter Twenty-Nine

"Looks like you've been busy."

Still in shock, Rachel turned in the swivel wooden desk chair and looked up at him.

"What?"

"I see you've worked your way through that pile of mail." He nodded at the overflowing trash can. "The desk looks nice."

Then he looked directly at her and touched her face. "Why are you crying?"

She silently handed him the notice. Her throat was so swollen with emotion that she couldn't speak.

He read it, dropped it onto the desk, and opened his arms. "Come here."

As he held her against his chest, she found her own racing pulse slowing down as she listened to the steady beat of his heart. In a turbulent world where murderers were released from prison willy-nilly, Joe's arms felt like an oasis.

"Where is he now?" Joe asked.

"Millersburg."

"Millersburg!" Joe tightened his grip on her. "So close? Is Ohio big enough to hold the both of you?"

"The universe isn't big enough to hold both of us. I don't know if I can handle this, Joe."

"Maybe, maybe not—but you won't have to face it alone." He stroked her hair. "I'm here. We'll figure out how to get through this together."

"People are going to say that it happened twenty years ago," Rachel said. "They'll tell me that it is time to let it go—but time doesn't heal all wounds, Joe. It just doesn't."

"I know, baby. I know."

"What I dread most is having to break it to my aunts. Dad was their little brother. They loved him so much."

"Come with me." He took her over to the couch, pulled her onto his lap, and settled her against his chest.

"I'm afraid the aunts will blame me. I'm the law-enforcement person in the family. I should have been more vigilant. I should have seen this coming and headed it off. If I'd only seen that notice sooner... If I hadn't allowed myself to get too busy to sort the mail..."

"This isn't your fault," Joe said. "I should have gone through that stack as well."

"This is going to devastate Bertha. She practically raised my dad."

"Shh," Joe tried to soothe her. "It will be okay. Maybe you and your aunts will hardly know he's been released. If I were him, I know I would steer clear of you."

"I hope you're right. His was the face of every monster I ever feared as a child."

"Is there anything you can do?"

"I intend to get in touch with his parole officer. Then I'll find out exactly which church is sponsoring him and where he's living. I'll check in with the Millersburg police and ask them to keep an eye on him. If he so much as drops a gum wrapper, I want them to arrest him for littering." She heard the coldness in her voice, but she didn't care. "It isn't easy for an ex-con to follow all the restrictions put on them when they get out. About fifty percent of them end up being arrested again. With any luck, he'll be put back in prison before the year is up."

"I'm glad you're my friend," Joe joked. "I would hate to have you for an enemy."

The back door suddenly slammed. Rachel heard Bobby's footsteps pattering against the linoleum kitchen floor.

"We're in here!" Joe called.

Bobby ran into the living room and looked longingly at them snuggled up on the couch. Rachel held out her arms and he ran into them.

Joe groaned with mock pain at the addition of his son's little body.

"You are getting so heavy, son. I'm going to have to start making you eat lettuce for dinner," he said. "Like a rabbit."

This immediately triggered Bobby's making faces and squeaky noises that Rachel presumed was his attempt to mimic a rabbit. She slid off the couch so Joe could wrestle with his son without her getting an elbow or a knee in the face. She wasn't in the mood for play at the moment.

As Joe tussled with his son, and with Bobby's giggles in her ears, Rachel went back to her desk, grabbed some notebook paper, and began drafting a scalding letter to the parole board. Considering the fact that Carl had been in prison for murder, more attempts should have been made to contact her. She might have only been eleven at the time of the killing, but she *had* pulled a gun on that man—and who knows what sort of twisted mind he might have. Victims of violent crimes and their families should not be left unaware—even if it was their own fault for not going through their mail in time to contact the parole board.

As she penned the letter, she remembered how Carl's craggy face had given her nightmares as a child—from which she would awake, screaming, with one of her aunts holding her and trying to reassure her. The nightmares had not completely stopped until she was in her twenties.

In spite of her years in law enforcement and all the anomalies she had experienced with the courts, when it came to what Carl Bateman had done to her family, it felt inconceivable that he could already be out of prison after serving only twenty years of a life sentence. Inconceivable and unacceptable.

***

Bertha appeared to be a gentle, elderly Amish woman, but looks could be deceiving. Bertha was the strongest person, spiritually and emotionally, that Rachel had ever known. Lydia looked frail and fragile, but she could work circles around most women half her age, managing to be cheerful and positive despite her arthritic pain. Anna, a woman with special-needs, was often overlooked by people who thought their notions of Down syndrome defined her—but it didn't. Anna often surprised all of them with an unsuspected reserve of understanding and strength. Rachel hoped her aunts could somehow manage to deal with the terrible news she had to deliver. She had been cared for by these decent, loving, godly woman for most of her life and could not bear to think of the trauma she was about to cause by telling them the news.

When Rachel entered the kitchen, she found Bertha alone, peeling potatoes at the table.

"Oh, hello, Rachel. Anna wants mashed potatoes for supper tonight," Bertha said. "Would you like to grab a knife and help?"

Rachel was not interested in potatoes. "Where is Aunt Lydia? I thought she would be here."

"She is helping Anna change sheets in the northwest guest room. We have been blessed by a full house tonight. We even have guests coming to us all the way from London, England."

"London?" Rachel was surprised. Florida, yes. California, okay. But from across the ocean? "How on earth did they hear of the Sugar Haus

Inn way over there?"

"The Internet, of course." Bertha's voice was matter-of-fact. "The message they left on our answering machine said they read about us in a travel blog."

"Oh." It sounded strange to hear the words "Internet" and "blog" coming out of Bertha's mouth, but her aunt tried to stay well-informed.

"I do not understand what is wrong with people"—Bertha plopped another peeled potato into the bowl—"for someone to be willing to fly across the ocean to watch our men plow with horses and sleep in this house that does not have electricity or telephones." Bertha chuckled. "Lydia's cooking is good, but it isn't *that* good!"

It was a common source of conversation among the local Amish— this strange phenomenon of nearly 3 million tourists per year swarming into their bucolic countryside to gawk at them as they went about everyday life. The newcomers usually tried to sneak photos too, which was a great annoyance to the Amish. They patiently endured it like so much else in their lives.

Rachel was upset and wanted to get the business of Carl out in the open so she could apologize for having missed the parole date.

"I'm so sorry to have to tell you this." Rachel laid the letter from the parole office on the kitchen table where Bertha could read it. "But they have released Dad's killer."

Bertha adjusted her glasses, and leaned over so she could read the letter without touching it with her wet hands.

"Yes," Bertha said calmly. "I know."

Chapter Thirty

"I don't understand." Rachel was shocked at her aunt's reaction. "When did you find this out?"

"George called me, oh, I think it was about the last part of April. About the same time the warden told him."

"And you knew Dad's killer was living in Millersburg?"

Bertha calmly peeled another potato. "I did."

Rachel was incredulous. "Why didn't you tell me?"

"I tried."

"When?" Rachel was so upset she almost shouted. "When did you try?"

"I told you I needed to talk with you at least three different times. Each time you had an excuse, so I stopped trying."

"I thought you just wanted to nag at me again about quitting my job," Rachel said bitterly.

"I do not nag," Bertha said, offended.

"That's not the point." Rachel felt herself becoming exasperated. "My father's killer is a free man. If I had known he was up for parole, I would have gone to the hearing and voiced my protests. I would have written letters telling them why he needed to stay in prison. You could have written letters!"

"I did write letters."

"Really?" Rachel felt relieved. "You wrote the parole people?"

"Yes," Bertha said. "I told them that I felt that he had been rehabilitated and needed to be released."

"Oh, Aunt Bertha," Rachel groaned. "How *could* you?"

"Twenty years is a long time, Rachel."

"You think that is long enough to be punished for killing my dad and destroying my life?"

"Oh?" Bertha cocked an eyebrow. "You had such a terrible childhood being loved and cared for by us every hour of every day? That is something I did not know."

"You were wonderful to me," Rachel said. "But you should not have had to raise me. That was my father's job."

"And if our brother had not chosen to leave our church and marry your mother, you would not have been born. And if you had not been born, he would not have been in the bank that day, getting money for your birthday. And if he had never chosen to become a policeman carrying a gun, the robber might not have shot him. There are many 'ifs' in life, Rachel. It is not wise to dwell on them."

"My dad was a hero!" Rachel shot back. "He saved dozens of lives that day at the cost of his own."

"A hero?" Bertha mused. "Because he pulled his weapon?"

"Yes," Rachel insisted. "He was a hero."

"I know that in the Englisch world, pointing a gun at someone can be considered heroic, but I have often wondered what might have happened if Frank had not pulled that gun. What if he had allowed the robber to take the bank's money and walk away? What if he had not put himself and you at risk by taking that chance?"

Rachel didn't know whether it was pregnancy hormones or the accumulation of years of dealing with her aunt's stubborn Amish pacifism that made her want to scream in frustration. Of *course* her father was a hero for what he did. Of *course* Carl Bateman deserved to stay in jail for the rest of his life. If she could have gotten the death sentence for her father's killer right that minute, she would have done so.

It would have been smart for Bertha to keep silent just then, but the old woman had one more word to say—and it was the wrong word.

"*Gelassenheit*, Rachel."

"God's will?" Rachel fumed. "You are trying to tell me that my father's death was God's will?"

"Of course not," Bertha said. "God does not condone sin, and murder is a sin. But God has promised that all things will work together for good for those who love Him. We can't always see how and why, but we have to have faith that God will take a bad situation and bring about something good from it."

"You think it is God's will that my father's murderer has been released from jail?"

"I do not pretend to know the mind of God, but this I know, and I know it well," Bertha said. "If you continue to harbor such bitter hatred for this man, it will destroy you. You are not as strong as you think you are, Rachel. Remember what happened to you that night you were protecting the antique cars."

It was those words that somehow turned the key to opening up the recent period of amnesia Rachel had endured. It was as though a door had flown open and she clearly saw the man standing beside the Thunderbird at the Fabulous Fifties. There was no doubt in her mind that the man was Carl Bateman. She had not mentally recognized him at the time, but her subconscious had, and it had reacted to the shock of it by shutting her down.

Bile rose in the back of Rachel's throat and threatened to choke her. She had two choices: leave at this moment or throw up. She turned on her heel away from her aunt, walked through the kitchen and out the door, and didn't stop until she'd gotten into her car and driven a mile down the road. Then she pulled over and began to shake. She had never been so angry in her life.

Her hands were still trembling when she put the car back into gear and started driving. She reminded herself to drive slowly and carefully. If anger alone could impair a driver, she had no business being behind the wheel.

Chapter Thirty-One

With George due in soon, Carl made coffee and slowly walked with it toward the minister's office. It was raining hard outside, so he figured George might be a little late and he'd put the percolator on accordingly. He liked to make sure the coffee was very fresh when he brought it in to George.

His friend never failed to politely thank him for the convenience of not having to make his own coffee, and Carl never failed to appreciate the small, civilized ritual. Making morning coffee was a minor thing to do for a man who had helped him so much.

While in prison, Carl had learned to read men's body language about as well as he read dogs'. It was necessary to become adept at reading faces and bodies if one was to survive, especially as one grew older and less able to defend oneself. His conclusion about George was that he was quite possibly the most honest, kindest man he'd ever met.

Even more impressive was the fact that the minister seemed to have a real faith. George didn't have a lot of material possessions and wasn't particularly interested in driving a new car or having a large house or an expensive wardrobe. There was nothing George had ever had to gain by coming to the prison to meet with Carl. He had visited him in part because his cousin—the sister of the man Carl killed—had asked him to.

After Carl got out on parole, George asked whether he wanted to go see her, the cousin who had written him for so long. Carl said he was not

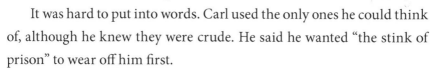

ready yet. He needed a little more time.

"Time for what?" George had asked.

It was hard to put into words. Carl used the only ones he could think of, although he knew they were crude. He said he wanted "the stink of prison" to wear off him first.

George told him to let him know when he was ready, and Carl said he would. The problem was that he wasn't sure he knew how to talk right or act right around the woman who had sent him those letters of forgiveness. How could he thank someone for giving him hope? He wished there was something he could say or do or give that adequately conveyed his gratitude, but he couldn't think of anything.

Focused on the coffee in his hands, he didn't realize someone had let themselves inside the church until he heard an unfamiliar voice.

"So they let you out," he heard a woman say.

He was so surprised that he stumbled and the liquid sloshed inside both cups. After he caught himself, he turned to see who had spoken. It was a woman in black slacks wearing a rain-slicked Windbreaker with the Sugarcreek Police insignia on the front. His heart nearly stopped beating from sheer fear. Had he done something wrong? Was there some law he had broken that he did not know about? Was he going back to prison?

"You don't know who I am, do you?" She pushed herself away from the wall where she'd been leaning.

"I'm sorry." The fear was so great and his heart was pounding in his chest so hard that it was all he could do not to run. He told himself sternly that running was out of the question. Whatever he had done wrong, he would try to face it.

Then he realized she somehow expected him to know who she was. His mind raced.

"Does the name Frank Troyer mean anything to you?"

"He was the man I killed."

She seemed a little taken aback at his words, as though she expected him to deny it. Then she pulled herself together and laid a hand on the gun that hung on her utility belt.

"Do you happen to remember his daughter?" she asked.

"The little girl in the pink dress. Yes, I remember."

"I've often wished I had pulled the trigger while I had the chance," she said.

He didn't know how to respond. Was she there to kill him? He noticed her hand was trembling as it lay on the butt of her revolver.

"I wish you had too," he said, and he meant it.

She seemed to want to say more, but instead she shook her head, turned, and walked woodenly out of the hallway and back out into the rain while he stood there holding two dripping coffee cups.

Shaken, he took both cups back to the kitchen, dumped out the coffee, washed the cups, and put them in the drainer to dry. He had lost the desire for coffee and conversation with George this morning. He had already had enough conversation for one day.

Chapter Thirty-Two

Rachel had somehow gotten through her work day, but she was furious with Bertha. She was furious with Carl. And she was furious with herself. There were so many bitter things she'd stored up to say to him. It was as though she had been having an ongoing conversation with him for most of her life and hadn't realized it.

She grabbed an apron and tied it over her uniform to keep it clean while she cooked.

As a cop, there had been so many criminals over the years. She'd managed to be calm and cool in dealing with most of them. But finding herself face-to-face with Carl had choked her voice and driven the words right out of her head.

How *dare* he tell her that he wished she had pulled the trigger! Ex-cons were so skilled at manipulation. That comment had been nothing but a ploy to make her feel sorry for him, but it hadn't worked.

She was busy slamming things around the kitchen, hating herself for her weakness, wishing she could go for a run to work the anger out of her system, and resenting the fact that she had to fix supper…when Joe and Bobby walked in.

"What are you making?" Joe asked.

"Supper." She was in the process of chopping carrots, wielding the knife with a lot more force than necessary. "Isn't that what *good* wives do?"

She hadn't expected her words to sound so sarcastic, but they did and she couldn't take them back. That upset her even more.

A small metal trash can was at her feet, the kind that opened when a lever was stepped on. Except, when she stomped on it to scrape some scraps into it, the lever broke.

"Stupid trash can!" She kicked it across the kitchen floor. It clanged against a lower cabinet, bounced off, and fell over on its side. She ignored it, grabbed a stalk of celery, and began chopping again.

"I like peanut butter," Bobby offered softly, his big eyes even rounder at her anger.

Joe set the trash can upright. Then he came over and laid his hand over hers to still the violent chopping. "What's wrong?"

She dropped the knife on the chopping block and turned to him. He put his arms around her waist.

"You went to see him, didn't you?"

She leaned into him and nodded against his chest.

"What did he say?" Joe asked.

"He said he remembered the little girl in the pink dress."

"And what did you say?"

"That I wished I had pulled the trigger."

"Oh, Rachel."

"I like peanut butter," Bobby said, bringing their attention back to him.

"Are you hungry, buddy?" Joe asked.

Bobby bobbed his head.

"I'll make you a sandwich," Joe said.

"I'll have supper ready in a half hour." Rachel pulled away from him. "I'm making stir-fry. The rice is already cooked."

"I want peanut butter," Bobby insisted. "With purple jelly."

"He needs to eat something besides peanut butter," Rachel said. "He can't live on peanut butter and hot dogs. He had peanut butter for lunch."

Joe looked at her. Then he looked at Bobby.

"A peanut-butter sandwich it is," Joe said. "With purple jelly."

"Joe…"

He gave her a nearly imperceptible shake of his head. She wasn't sure what that shake meant, but she wasn't happy that he intended to give into Bobby's demand. She had gone to a lot of trouble getting the ingredients for tonight's dinner, and she didn't appreciate him ruining Bobby's appetite with yet another peanut-butter sandwich. It wasn't good parenting. And besides that, it hurt her feelings.

She finished chopping the vegetables for the stir-fry while Joe set Bobby up with milk and a sandwich.

"Can I watch cartoons?" Bobby asked.

"Sure thing."

Joe turned on the DVD player with some old Bugs Bunny cartoons. Then, as the little boy ate his sandwich and giggled at the cartoons, Joe took Rachel by the elbow and led her into the living room.

"Is there something you wanted to say to me?" he said. "Something about not catering to Bobby's demands, for instance?"

"I think you're making a mistake."

"A peanut-butter-and-jelly sandwich is Bobby's comfort food."

"So?"

"So, when he starts asking for peanut butter morning, noon, and night—which he's been doing for the past couple of days—it's a pretty good sign that he's feeling stressed."

"He's six. Why would he be feeling stressed?" Rachel asked.

"When we walked through the door," Joe tried to explain, "what we saw was a woman attacking a handful of carrots like she was killing snakes. Your fury was noticeable. Bobby hasn't seen a whole lot of that kind of anger. It scared him. Heck, it scared me! He was hungry and frightened, and the child needed a peanut-butter-and-jelly sandwich."

The frustration and bitterness in her heart yet again spilled out of her mouth. "I don't suppose Grace ever got angry, did she?"

It was a snarky thing to say, and she hated herself for saying it. The moment she heard the words come out of her mouth, she wished she could take them back.

Joe was silent in response, and Rachel knew him well enough to know that his own anger was rising. His patience was not without limits.

"Grace got angry, but she was a much better actress than you," he said. "She made certain Bobby never, ever took the brunt of her anger."

That hurt.

"Okay. I'm sorry," she said. "But you have to understand, until I married you, I didn't have to monitor my actions or tone of voice. I could chop carrots any way I wanted."

The sound of Bobby's laughter floated back to them from the kitchen.

"It sounds like he's okay," Joe said. "I'm going to ignore what you just said because I know you didn't mean it. I know you love me and my son. Today is just a bad day. Now, tell me more about your confrontation with the ex-con."

"Carl is an old man, and he looks it," Rachel said. "He was holding two filled coffee cups when I startled him, and he spilled some. He looked scared. What hair he has left is gray. He wears glasses now."

"In other words, he no longer looks like the monster you remember?"

"He doesn't look like a monster," Rachel conceded. "What he looks like is someone's down-and-out grandfather. But he is recognizable. While I was at Bertha's, it suddenly came to me that I saw him at the Fab Fifties. He was the one standing there with his hands in his pockets, looking at that Thunderbird. He was the 'bad man' I must have been warning Anna about in the hospital. I guess that seeing him was more than my subconscious wanted to acknowledge."

"Well, at least *that* mystery is solved." Joe released a sigh of relief. "What are you planning to do now?"

"I don't know," Rachel said. "I don't want to live with the thought that I might run into him at any moment. What I wish is that he would go back to prison where he belongs and I could continue to pretend that he doesn't exist."

"From what I remember," Joe said, "you were never able to ignore his existence."

"I tried to," she said.

"You're going to have to find a way to get over this if we're going to feel like a family again," Joe said. "It isn't fair to Bobby to live with the kind of anger and emotional turmoil you're going through right now. It's toxic to all of us."

"It would be lovely if I could just flip a switch and forget all about it, but I don't know how to change my feelings," she said. "I'm a simple person. I feel what I feel. And as you just pointed out, I'm not very good at acting like everything is okay when I'm bleeding inside."

"Dad!" they heard Bobby call from the kitchen. "Dad! Can I have some more milk?"

"I'll go get it." Joe left the room to tend to his son.

Her behavior during the past half hour was not like her. It made her feel like an angry, miserable excuse of a mother. Having Joe upset with her too was just too much. It made her feel as if she were being punished even though she hadn't done anything wrong.

She hadn't robbed a bank. She hadn't killed anyone. And yet today she'd had an argument with Bertha so severe that she had almost thrown up. She'd also been chastised by her husband for frightening their son and had been pretty useless at work.

This was Carl's fault. Every last rotten thing that had happened today was Carl Bateman's fault.

Rachel didn't often get headaches, but when she did they were doozies...and she could feel one starting now. She went into the kitchen, pulled some ibuprofen out of the cabinet, and started to swallow two capsules with a glass of water. Then she stopped and spit them into the sink. Pregnant women weren't supposed to take painkillers.

Joe started cleaning up the crumbs from Bobby's snack and saw the bottle in her hand. "Headache?"

"A bad one," she said.

"Go lay down," he said. "I'll finish supper."

"Thank you."

The day and the war of emotion she had been through had exhausted her to the point that Rachel fell into a deep sleep that didn't end until about two o'clock in the morning. She awoke disoriented and thirsty. Joe was not with her. She wondered why he was still up at this time of night. Was he ill? Was he watching television? Reading? He still had the discipline of "early to bed and early to rise" that he had developed as an athlete. It was unlike him to stay up this late. She put on her robe and went to find her husband.

When she got to the kitchen, she found it clean. She glanced into the refrigerator and saw that Joe had been as good as his word. He had made the stir-fry, evidently eaten it alone, and then put it away.

Joe was not in the living room, but there were papers spread out on the coffee table where he'd been working. One was a handwritten list of their household expenses and a total. On another sheet were numbers involving their combined take-home pay. One thing was apparent: if she didn't keep her job, or if Joe didn't find one soon, they would be in serious financial trouble.

There was also a list of possible jobs. Some were in the area. Most involved the need to move away. Several involved commercial endorsements she knew he didn't want to do.

It appeared he had given serious consideration to an offer from Ohio State University. The letters OSU were written in big letters and circled. Below that were the words "Pitching coach!" Apparently OSU had the same idea as the Dodgers. Next to that was a number she assumed was the potential salary. Assuming their expenses didn't go up too significantly, it would be enough to live on. Underneath, he'd scribbled the words, "Small apartment during week?" Then he'd marked that out with a large *X*. Evidently he didn't consider it a viable option to live in Columbus two hours away and only come home on the weekend. She agreed. There would be weekend games and travel. She and Bobby would seldom see him unless they moved there.

She could handle it, but Bobby? Not so much.

It looked like Joe had gotten an offer from Allstate too. He'd mentioned that one to her earlier, but she had been so obsessed with Carl's release that she'd not listened closely. Now she read over the offer in its entirety. It would involve becoming an insurance broker and working as a front man for the office in Cleveland. It was more generous than the OSU salary. Obviously Allstate was banking on Joe's reputation to bring in new clients. Getting to sit across the desk from the great Micah Mattias as he took care of their insurance needs would be quite a draw for a lot of baseball fans. But not only would their family have to move to Cleveland, Joe would hate every minute of it.

It broke Rachel's heart.

She went back down the hallway and then to Bobby's room—the only room in the small house she had not yet looked for Joe. She found him asleep, fully clothed, on his son's bed, with his hand lying protectively on his little boy's shoulder.

Quietly closing Bobby's door, she went back to the bedroom she and Joe shared. It was the first time since they were married that Joe had chosen not to sleep by her side.

Chapter Thirty-Three

Things were awkward between them the next morning. She was hormonal and weepy—which she tried to hide behind a studied politeness. He was stiff and quiet. Normally, she would have fled to her aunts' for comfort, but she definitely was not ready to see Bertha yet.

It was a relief to go to work, but she struggled to get through the day.

When she got home that night, what she wanted to do was to lay down on the couch and sleep, but there was dinner to fix, and as a wife and mother, it was up to her to fix it. Or at least, that was how it felt.

She was deep into food prep when she heard a voice.

"Don't," Joe said.

Rachel turned away from the kitchen counter, where she had been getting ready to make hamburgers from a couple of pounds of fresh ground chuck.

"Why?"

"Because you've worked all day, you're pregnant, you're tired, and you don't need to try to cook dinner on top of everything else. Remember the meltdown from last night? I don't want to repeat that."

"But we need to eat." Rachel did not want to discuss her meltdown. "And I don't want to go out. I've been all over Tuscarawas County today, asking questions and trying to track down information."

"What happened?" Joe asked.

"Someone dug a six-foot-deep trench in the spillway of Henry Yoder's pond while he and his wife were visiting their daughter in Pennsylvania.

Drained the whole thing. Nothing but dead fish lying there in the mud when they got back."

"That was a lot of bother for someone to go to."

"Hours of digging just for meanness. It will take months for the pond to fill back up, and that was the main source of water for his cattle."

"Is Henry also part of your aunts' church?"

"Yes. I wish I could figure out a motivation, but nothing I come up with makes sense."

"Well, I've had an easy day compared to yours," Joe said. "All I've done is work on my car."

"Working on your car couldn't have been that easy."

"Why do you say that?"

"Well, Bobby was helping you, wasn't he?"

Joe laughed, and that made her feel better. "Okay, so I spent most of my time trying to keep him from killing himself with my tools, but let me fix dinner anyway."

"You don't have to ask me twice." Her feet hurt, and her back too. This business of having a little person growing inside her was taking a toll. She was feeling the effects, especially in her waistband that was becoming too tight. Even buying a larger size of slacks wasn't working anymore. She really needed to get a maternity uniform.

She sat on a stool at the kitchen counter and secretly unbuttoned her waistband.

Joe tucked a dish towel into his belt, washed his hands, and began a complicated business of whisking up sauces and spices and then folding it all into the meat.

"Where did you learn to do that?" she asked. "I just planned to fry the meat into patties for hamburgers, but you always do something special to make it taste better."

"I learned this at my mother's elbow," Joe said. "Darren did too."

"Darren can cook?"

"When he feels like it. The thing is, when we were boys and Mom and Dad were working in Africa, we didn't always have the best food to work with. Mom had to get inventive to make things taste good. We didn't have television or that many things to entertain us, so helping her in whatever kitchen we were using was about as entertaining as it got somedays."

"What kind of things did you cook?"

"We had to improvise a lot. I actually got pretty good at hunting small game by throwing rocks. Mom would clean whatever I brought home and figure out a way to make it edible. Learning to hunt like that might have helped my pitching accuracy later on. Who knows? It's amazing what you can get good at when you're hungry. Darren never developed the knack, but he was always tagging along. I made him carry my bag of rocks for me."

"Speaking of Darren…"

He followed her glance, looked out the window in the kitchen, and saw his brother walking up the driveway.

"Can you get the door?" He continued to knead the seasonings into the ground chuck. "My hands are messy."

She opened the door, without trying to force her waistband closed. Her shirt tail covered things enough for modesty.

"Hi, come on in, Darren. Your brother is making burgers."

"Are you using one of Mom's recipes?" Darren sounded hopeful.

"Yep," Joe said. "Want to stay and eat with us?"

"Sure would!"

After forming the burgers, Joe put them on a grill they kept on the small back patio. A pot of canned baked beans warmed beside them—to which he had added a dollop of honey and a half teaspoon of allspice. Rachel found some Vidalia onions, which she sliced, and Darren tossed a salad. Bobby brought out the potato chips, and soon the four of them were digging in.

"Nothing against Amish food," Darren said with his mouth full, "but every now and then a man needs a good burger. It's hard to find one around here. Lots of noodles, chicken, and pastry, but not much in the way of burgers. You should open a restaurant."

"Yeah, right," Joe said. "I've got about three things I can make well and that's it—burgers, baked beans, and sometimes I do a pretty good job of grilling a cheese sandwich."

"And peanut butter sandwiches, Daddy," Bobby said. "You make good ones of those."

"You should open a restaurant and call it Joe's Bar & Grill," Darren continued as if he hadn't heard Joe's objection.

Joe laughed. "Like nobody has ever used *that* name before."

"I'm afraid the aunts would have a problem with the 'bar' part of it. They're teetotalers," Rachel said.

"Can't you just picture Bertha coming in like Carrie Nation with an axe—smashing up all the liquor bottles?" Joe asked. "Now, there's a mental image."

"She might do it too," Rachel said. "Bertha's never been shy about expressing her opinion."

"Seriously, Micah," Darren said, "There might be a niche here in Amishland for a good hamburger joint. Maybe a sort of sports bar." He glanced at Rachel. "But without the bar."

"I know absolutely nothing about running a restaurant."

"A lot of athletes own them," Darren said. "They might not do the cooking, but they oversee them and lend their name to them. It could be a great business opportunity."

Rachel saw Joe freeze at the words "great business opportunity."

Joe's younger brother had sponged money off Joe for years, using it for one failed "great business opportunity" after another. Her husband had come to the sad conclusion that Darren didn't have the grit to stick to anything long enough to make it a success. His brother always seemed to think that his big break was right around the corner, if Joe would just lend him a little more money.

Their impromptu dinner had been going well until Darren started taking the idea of Joe starting a restaurant a little too seriously.

"You could have a baseball theme," Darren enthused. "You could name the hamburgers after baseball terms. Like Micah's Slider…or Joe's Grounder. Or…"

"Hate to burst your bubble, but restaurants need start-up money," Joe said. "And I don't have it."

Darren stopped mid-sentence. "What do you mean, you don't have it?"

"The financial guy Henrietta set me up with? He ruined me," Joe said. "Took off to parts unknown with my money and that of several others."

"But the house…?"

"Sold at a loss."

"You mean it's all gone?" Darren seemed dumbstruck. "Everything you made down through the years? All those big contracts!"

"Don't remind me."

"Any chance of getting it back?"

"Not much."

"Man, I'm sorry, bro. I hope someone gets hold of that guy and makes him swim with the fishes."

"Can we go swimming with the fishies, Daddy?" Bobby glanced up from his plate. "Can we?"

"Sure." Joe tousled his son's hair. "We'll take fishing poles along too, for good measure. Okay?"

" 'kay." Bobby went back to his meal.

"Be careful what you say in front of my son, Darren," Joe said in a low voice. "He's only six."

"Right. So. About that business opportunity we were discussing…"

Chapter Thirty-Four

The fish Bobby hoped to catch and cook had not materialized, so Joe was toasting a grilled-cheese sandwich. He was also worrying about Rachel. Her obsession with Carl Bateman was affecting everything.

He wondered whether things might have been different had she gotten professional help when she was a child. There were counselors who specialized in children who had seen traumatic events. It was a specific skill, one he knew neither Bertha nor her sisters possessed. They had done what they could, loving well the child they had been given. They had managed to raise up a woman with integrity, compassion, and a strong work ethic. Considering what he'd witnessed in the hospital, they had also raised a woman who had way more demons than he'd imagined.

He wished it were possible to go back and reach the child that she had been, but it was too late for that. All Joe could do was love her and try to be patient and sympathetic with what he saw as paranoid behavior. With Rachel, of course, her paranoia took the form of aggression. It wasn't in her nature to be passive. She had already asked the Millersburg police to keep a close eye on Carl and to let her know if there was any hint of illegal activity.

So far, the only thing they could report was that Carl sometimes smoked during the evenings on the steps of the church and had recently taken in an abandoned German shepherd mix.

Rachel had seen both of these activities in the light of suspicious behavior and mentioned it frequently to Joe. Smoking on the church steps? He was probably considering his next crime. A German shepherd mix? She had discovered he had trained dogs in prison. Perhaps Carl was training this one to be an attack dog. He would certainly have the skills.

It seemed to Joe that Carl had become the main focus of Rachel's life instead of him and Bobby. He was sick to death of hearing the man's name. At least she had sense enough not to talk about it in front of their son. But when they were alone in bed at night, he often fell asleep with her still musing aloud about what Carl might be doing.

At least she hadn't tried to go back to the church and confront him. That she did so even once worried him, because he really didn't know who Carl was or what he was capable of. It felt to him as though Rachel was poking a hornet's nest. If she pushed this man too far, bad things could happen.

How Joe wished she would get over it and be able to relax and enjoy the process of nurturing a new life. It was such a miraculous time, and he wanted to enjoy it with her—not fret and fume together over an old ex-convict.

He loved her more than anyone or anything on this planet—with the exception of Bobby. He had felt as if their souls were knit together. Therefore, it was especially annoying to him that he experienced so much impatience with her inability to let go of the anger.

He had always tried to fix the things that went wrong—at least those things within his power—and he was now frustrated by his inability to change this situation. All he could do was hope and pray that his brilliant and beautiful wife would soon figure out a way to live on the same planet as Carl Bateman. And hopefully she could do so without another emergency trip to the hospital.

That was one of his greatest concerns. He feared she would simply "go away" again. Stress-induced amnesia… It was so antithetical to

Rachel's strength of character that it was hard to imagine the depth of trauma still within her.

The ER doctor wanted Joe to make sure she saw a counselor. Rachel tossed that idea aside the minute he mentioned it. No need to see a shrink, she said, when she felt fine. There was way too much to do to bother with that sort of thing.

He'd not brought it up again, but it continually niggled at the back of his mind that she was making a mistake in not going. As he waited for Bobby's grilled cheese to finish browning, he glanced out the window... and was surprised to see his brother coming up the sidewalk. The last thing he'd expected was Darren showing up again so soon.

Joe loved his little brother, but he didn't enjoy him. There seemed to be a hole inside Darren that couldn't be filled, no matter how much he attempted to impress people with boasts about his accomplishments.

As Darren entered the house, he was swaggering with confidence and wearing an expensive dark suit and a colorful tie. It was not a good sign. Darren had probably just made another "great business deal" he wanted to tell Joe about. Of course whatever it was would soon fall flat. That was how Darren lived. He would then expect his big brother to bail him out of whatever difficulties he'd gotten himself into. Evidently Darren had not remembered that Joe no longer had the financial where-withal to pick up the pieces.

"I thought you might have gone back to Atlanta," Joe said. "Isn't that where you've been living recently?"

"Not anymore," Darren said. "I've moved for good."

Joe wasn't surprised or even particularly interested. His little brother had always been a nomad. Months would pass when Joe wouldn't hear from him, and then Darren would pop up in some new city. There was a restlessness to Darren's lifestyle. He would stay in a place until a deal fell through or the cops began to suspect that his latest dealings were a little shady or a girlfriend started pushing for marriage or maybe because he simply wanted a change of scenery. Joe also suspected sometimes that Darren moved for no other reason than he was short on cash and the rent was due.

"Aren't you going to ask where I've moved to?"

"You aren't staying at Dad's?" Joe turned off the flame beneath the skillet. "'Not after today."

"So, where have you moved?"

"I leased an apartment in Sugarcreek today."

"Where?"

"It's upstairs over an old commercial building on Main Street."

Joe couldn't figure out why Darren seemed so pleased with himself. "I thought you were broke."

"I am," Darren said cheerfully.

Joe's heart sank. His brother never took his situation in life seriously. He slid Bobby's sandwich onto a plate decorated with cartoon figures. "Do you have any plans? I really can't help you this time, Darren. I honestly don't have any money to give you these days."

"That's okay," Darren said. "I thought I'd go into business with you instead."

"Me?"

"Yep. Hey, you think you could make one of those grilled-cheese sandwiches for me? It looks good."

Joe handed the one he'd just made to his brother and began buttering a fresh one for his son.

"What do you mean, go into business with me? That's crazy talk."

"Actually, I thought I'd be the one funding *you* this time. At least for a little while."

"Get serious, Darren. What are you talking about?" Joe didn't know what was coming next, but he was certain he wouldn't like it.

Darren polished off the grilled cheese in four bites, wiped his hands and mouth on the paper napkin Joe handed him, and then took out his cell phone and pulled up a photograph, which he showed Joe.

"I rented this," Darren said. "It's so close you can walk to it, and I'll be living there."

With spatula in hand, Joe glanced at the photo. To his astonishment, it was a picture of a storefront in downtown Sugarcreek where a small restaurant had once operated. It had stood empty for months.

"You rented this?" Joe asked. "Why? And with *what*?"

"I sold my Lamborghini."

"You sold your car? What are you driving?" Joe asked.

"I'll walk until we get on our feet."

Darren without a nice car was unimaginable. His brother always managed to drive an impressive vehicle even when he was flat broke.

"I have a great name for the place," Darren said. "We'll call it 'Miracle Micah's Home Plate'!"

"First of all, please drop the 'Miracle Micah.' Around here, I'm Joe. What on earth have you done, Darren?"

"My car bought us six months of rent and all the used restaurant equipment the old owner left behind," Darren said. "Ta-da! Joe's Home Plate! Don't you remember our last discussion? Mom's recipes? Joe's Home Run Burger. Joe's Slider. Joe's Fastball? We had it all planned out. The only thing we needed was money, and I found some. The upstairs apartment was part of the deal. You know, I've always wanted to be the kind of business owner who lived above the shop."

"You've always wanted to be the kind of business owner who made millions of dollars without having to work for it," Joe said.

"Well, yes," Darren agreed. "But next to that, living above the shop sounds like a lot of fun."

"You actually sold your car?" Joe said. "To rent a restaurant?"

"Yes."

"But you loved that car."

"Yes," Darren said, "but I love you more."

Joe stood still at the stove, watching the second grilled cheese fry. His little brother had been the bane of his life when he was a teenager—the polar opposite of himself. Clumsy. No athletic ability. A bit of a momma's boy. He'd followed Joe around like a puppy for most of his young life. Joe had not minded giving Darren the occasional infusion of money in the past because it kept Darren out of his hair. Now his brother was wanting to—what? Go into business together? Run a *restaurant* together?

"This is crazy," Joe said. "I know how to fry a decent hamburger, but I don't know anything about running a restaurant, and neither do you. Can you get your money back?"

"Look," Darren said, "I know I'm not as smart as you, and I know I haven't been a big success in business…yet. But this is a good idea. I can feel it deep down in my bones. I've got it all figured out. You can display your trophies and awards and put up old photos of yourself, and I'll take care of advertisements, and…"

"But we need to actually manage to *cook* something that people will want to eat!"

"That's the easy part," Darren said. "First of all, this place is dying for a good burger. Even the tourists who come here must get tired of eating mashed potatoes and noodles after a while. The location is perfect—all those people walking around and looking at the World's Largest Cuckoo Clock? We're almost right across the street from it, Micah. We can rig a fan to blow the smell of frying meat and onions across Main Street, and they'll follow their noses."

"Let me say this again," Joe said. "We know nothing about running a restaurant. We'd have to hire staff. How would we pay them?"

"We've got me and you," Darren said. "Rachel would pitch in when she could. I bet Lydia would provide the desserts. Customers would crowd in just for her pies alone. You've got family, Micah. And friends. You told me once that that was the genius behind so many of the business successes of the Amish—they can depend on their families and friends to help out. Won't you at least give it a try?"

Darren's voice had become choked with emotion as he tried to convince him of the merit of this ridiculous idea.

"Joe's Home Plate." Joe had to admit, the name had a nice ring.

"Just think about it," Darren said. "What do you have to lose? It's my money we're gambling with for a change. Who knows? Maybe after all the deals I've had go bad, it's time for something to actually work out for me. I'd like to at least try."

"Bobby!" Joe slid the second grilled-cheese sandwich onto a plate and sat it on the table. "Come eat your lunch!"

Darren watched him carefully, waiting for an answer.

The idea had been running through Joe's mind ever since that first night Darren brought it up. And even though he knew it was crazy, he had continued to think about it.

"I should have my head examined," Joe said. "And I know I'm going to regret this…but I'll give it a try. You'd just better not run out on me when things get tough. Running a restaurant is hard work."

"I won't run out on you!" Darren jumped up, grabbed his brother by the arms, and began dancing him around the kitchen.

Bobby's eyes grew wide when he came into the kitchen and saw his uncle's excitement. "What are you doing with my daddy, Uncle Darren?"

"Let go." Joe disengaged himself. "You're scaring my son."

"We're going to have a family business, Bobby!" Darren whooped. "It's finally going to happen. I've dreamed of something like this forever. I'm finally going to get to work with my brother!"

"Um…can I have a peanut-butter sandwich?"

Chapter Thirty-Five

Carl named his dog *Shadow* because he had found him hiding in the shadows. It took a week for Shadow to come close enough to sniff Carl's hand and another week before the dog allowed him to caress his head. In the meantime, Carl purchased dog food and treats and hurried through his janitorial duties just so he could spend time with his new friend.

Having a dog to nurture gave greater meaning to his days. The weather was warm and would continue to be. In late June, he didn't have to worry about Shadow getting cold for a while. The church had window wells to give the basement sunshine during the day, and when he saw that Shadow liked sleeping in the window well that shed light into his own janitor's closet/bedroom, he knew he was making progress. The dog was choosing to be near him.

That next day, Carl retrieved an old, soft blanket that had been in the Lost and Found since before he came to the church, so he was pretty certain no one wanted it. He spread it out in the window well to soften Shadow's nights and give the dog a place to nestle.

He wanted to bring Shadow into the church building with him and often considered doing so, but he wasn't sure the dog *or* the congregation was quite ready for that yet.

The decision maker was the night a lightning storm broke so viciously that even in the basement, Carl felt the building shake from the violent crack of thunder. A few moments later he heard scratching and whining at the back door. When he opened it, Shadow was standing there dripping from the rain and trembling all over, begging with his eyes to be let in.

Unfortunately, Shadow smelled like what he was—a dirty, wet dog—and that was not a smell Carl wanted in the building. "You can come in," Carl told him, "but you'll have to have a bath if you want to spend the night in here."

Shadow slowly wagged his tail, and Carl took that as an indication that the dog was willing. He used dish soap and the janitor's sink to bathe the dog. Shadow stood very still and quiet, as though he were enjoying having gentle hands massage the warm suds into his short brown fur. It made Carl happy when Shadow closed his eyes, as if to say, "That feels sooo good!"

After toweling the dog off, Carl brought a cushioned rubber mat from the kitchen, laid it on the floor beside his bed, and savored the feeling of having a friend beside him to enjoy the comfort of the little TV he'd recently picked up at Goodwill. In the middle of the night, he discovered that Shadow was smart enough to be naturally housebroken. The dog woke him, whining, and stood at the door, waiting to be let out. After quickly taking care of business, the dog hurried back as though concerned that Carl might change his mind and not let him back inside.

Carl decided to purchase a collar and take his new dog to the vet soon. Even though he didn't make a lot of money, his needs and wants were few. He'd saved enough that he thought he could afford to at least get Shadow checked out and his doggie shots brought up-to-date.

Spending money on this neglected animal, with money he himself had earned, gave Carl a warm feeling. He was building a life for himself one step at a time. Having a good dog back in his life felt wonderful. The best thing about his new freedom was that he would not have to give up Shadow to anyone. This time, all the training, love, and care would be for as long as the dog or he lived.

Unless he made a mistake, of course—something his parole officer would warrant demanded a trip back to prison. There were so many rules to follow on the outside—but now that Carl had Shadow depending on him, he had an extra reason not to break any of those rules.

Chapter Thirty-Six

"Boo!" Anna said, as she came through the door of the police station carrying a cat.

Rachel acted startled and then put her hand over her heart. "Oh, Anna! You scared me!"

After Anna enjoyed a giggle over Rachel's fright, she turned solemn. "Gray Cat is sick."

The cat did look listless and ill, but Rachel was more concerned with the fact that Anna had apparently walked the mile into town while carrying it. Her cheeks were flushed and her breathing was heavy.

"Does Bertha or Lydia know you're here?"

"They are asleep."

Rachel glanced at her watch. It was nearly two o'clock. Her three aunts usually did lay down for a short nap in the afternoon. Worry over the sick kitty had probably kept Anna up. The other two would be waking soon and wondering where Anna was.

She turned to Ed, who was working on vacation schedules for the five active Sugarcreek police officers. "Do you mind?"

"Go ahead," Ed said. "Things are pretty quiet today. I'll call Bertha and let her know Anna is with you."

"Gray Cat wants to see Doctor Peggy," Anna announced.

"Of course she does." Rachel gathered her keys. "We can do that."

"And Gray Cat wants to get ice cream." Anna's face was hopeful.

"We'll see. It depends on how long it takes." Rachel glanced at Ed. "I'm still on duty. I don't want to be gone too long."

Anna and her cat climbed into the backseat of the squad car. As usual, Rachel had to remind her to buckle her seat belt. Buggies didn't have seat belts, and wearing them didn't come automatically to Anna or to the rest of the Amish.

Then they headed to Millersburg. There was a woman veterinarian there who had a special relationship with Anna. They were chronologically the same age, and had played together as children while Peggy was being fostered by Amish cousins. Anna trusted Doctor Peggy, who was always patient with Anna's questions and the best at soothing her fears. She would also understand the need to work the cat into the appointments already scheduled that day. Anna did not understand the necessity to wait for an appointment when it came to her pets. If one of her beloved animals was sick, she wanted them tended to immediately.

The waiting room was torture for Anna when they arrived. They had to wait, and the longer they waited, the more nervous Anna became. She fidgeted, questioned Rachel at least a dozen times about how much longer it would be, and made everyone in the waiting room nervous for her because of her great concern.

Rachel was worried too. The cat seemed more and more listless as it lay on Anna's lap. She hoped it didn't have one of those feline diseases where the vet would have to put it down. She didn't want to be alone with Anna on the way home if that were the case. When Anna cried, it was with her whole heart.

While Rachel flipped through a magazine, trying to find pictures that would engage Anna, she was marginally aware that a man had come in with a dog. She glanced up and admired the healthy-looking animal. It was dark brown with some hints of gold in its fur, well-muscled, and young. The owner's back was toward her and she did not pay any attention to him until she heard him state his name to the receptionist.

"Carl Bateman," the man said. "I'm here for my dog, Shadow."

The receptionist asked him a question, but Rachel didn't catch it. Her mind had begun whirling and tumbling at the mere sound of his voice.

"No, just a checkup," Carl answered the receptionist. "I've only had him a short time and he needs his shots. There's nothing wrong."

That was a lie. There was something *very* wrong. Rachel was going to be forced to sit near the one person on earth she could not bear to be in the same room with.

It galled her that her father's murderer was walking around doing normal things like owning a dog and going to the vet. How incredibly unfair! Her feelings for the man who had beaten her and put her in the hospital in Akron was nothing compared to how she felt about Carl Bateman. After all, she had survived. Her father had not.

The floaty out-of-body feeling started again and she fought it down the best she could. She could not have another one of those stress-induced amnesia episodes. She just couldn't.

"Let's go," she whispered to Anna.

"Go?" Anna looked bewildered while she stroked the cat. "No! My kitty is sick."

Rachel wanted to grab the cat and Anna and run straight out the door. There were other vets in the area. Doctor Mike was getting his practice started over in Sugarcreek and people said he was good. One thing she knew: she couldn't sit here in the same room with this man much longer.

Why did he have to come here to live, anyway? There were plenty of places in Ohio where he could have lived and she would never have to see him again. Why did it have to be here?

"Seriously, Anna," Rachel whispered, "this is taking too long. Let's go back to Sugarcreek and see if we can get in to the vet there."

"But I like Doc Peggy," Anna whined a little too loudly. "I don't want to go."

Up to this point, Carl had apparently not noticed the fact that they were sitting there, but now he turned and seemed startled when he saw her.

She stared straight back at him. *Yeah, that's right, buddy. It's me.*

He nervously glanced around for a different seat, but the only one available was beside Anna.

Anna, who had never met a stranger.

As he lowered himself into the seat, the dog—the one he'd called Shadow—sat at attention in front of him. It didn't pull away or whine; it seemed completely at ease sitting there. Every now and then it would look up at its master with adoration.

"Your doggie is pretty," Anna said.

Carl said nothing. At least the man knew his place. There was no way she would tolerate him engaging in conversation with sweet Anna.

"Do you want to pet my kitty? She's not feeling so good."

More silence.

"My name is Anna," she continued. Such innocence. She had already asked everyone in the room their name and the name of their pet. Rachel hadn't minded until now. "What's yours?"

More silence. Carl certainly wasn't a chatterbox, but now it bothered her that he was completely ignoring Anna.

"His name is Carl." Rachel's voice was calm but laced with venom. "He's the man who killed your brother."

There was a common gasp around the room. Everyone looked at her and Carl with concern. No one knew quite what to do. People didn't say rude things like that in waiting rooms—at least not here in Amish and Mennonite Country.

Anna glanced at her, puzzled. Then she turned back toward Carl. "You killed my brother?"

"Yes," Carl said in a low voice, "I did."

"Are you sorry for it?" Anna asked.

"I'm very sorry," Carl said.

"That's all right, then," Anna said brightly. "Bertha says we must forgive people if they are sorry. Do you want to pet my kitty?"

"Anna..." Rachel was furious at him, exasperated with Anna, and embarrassed that this scenario was playing out in a room filled with strangers.

"Well," Anna turned toward her, "he *said* he was sorry!"

Rachel furiously flipped through her magazine without reading a word. It gave her someplace to focus her eyes. With all her heart, she wished Anna's stupid cat hadn't gotten sick and she hadn't been forced to sit in this stupid waiting room for half the day. She could not believe her bad luck in Carl Bateman showing up.

Leave it to Anna to strike up a conversation!

The time dragged on. No one in the waiting room spoke, even to one another. It was as though everyone was too embarrassed to speak. At least it was a small comfort that she didn't know any of them. On the other hand, she was wearing her Sugarcreek Police uniform, so if anyone wanted to find out who she was, it wouldn't be hard.

Anna's name was finally called. The cat had some sort of feline flu that Doc Peggy gave them meds for. It only took a few minutes, even with Anna chattering away with her old friend about her cat. When they left, Rachel caught a glimpse of Carl sitting on a stool in one of the examination rooms, his hand resting on his dog's head.

Their eyes locked for a second. She tried not to be affected by the sadness she saw in those eyes, because she didn't care if he was sad. His sadness couldn't touch the amount of sadness she'd experienced because of his actions.

Her bitterness at Carl combined with the slight nausea of pregnancy she'd been experiencing. It created so much bile to rise in her throat that she had to skitter off into the restroom to keep from accidently ruining the vet's shiny floor. As she fisted her hair into a ponytail and bent over the commode, all she could think about was how this was all Carl's fault.

Chapter Thirty-Seven

Carl had never been inside a civilian doctor's office. As a kid, it never occurred to his mother to take him. Before he was imprisoned, he hadn't bothered as an adult. As a prisoner, he got occasional checkups from the prison physician. He had, on the whole, always been remarkably healthy for a sixty-two-year-old man.

There had been a program on TV about how children who were exposed to a few germs in their childhood tended to develop a healthy immune system. He guessed that since he'd spent a large part of his life sleeping in the dirt with stray animals, he must have built up a walloping good immune system—if what the TV program said was true.

He had never been in a veterinarian's office either, and he wished he hadn't come now. Running into Rachel was hard. Trying to respond to Anna while Rachel listened and judged every word was harder. He wished he could have felt freer to talk with that gentle little soul about her sick pet.

He'd had a cellmate once who was similar to Rachel's aunt, with a child's mind inside an adult's body. Carl had always wondered how bad of an attorney the man's family had engaged for his cellmate to have ended up in prison with real criminals.

He'd tried to protect the guy when he could. It wasn't easy. Men with *slow* minds tended to become targets for men with *small* minds, and there were a lot of men in prison with small minds.

There was a soft knock on the door. A woman vet came bustling in and shook his hand.

"I'm Doctor Peggy Oglesby," she said. "People call me Doc Peggy."

"Hi. I'm Carl, and this is Shadow."

Her hair was cut short, probably for convenience. Her nails were also short and unpolished. She did not wear a white coat. Instead, she wore a plaid flannel shirt over a faded Ohio State T-shirt and work boots. Although the doctor had a large presence, she was actually a smallish woman who barely came up to his chin. He wondered how she managed to care for the larger animals.

"I apologize for the smell," she said. "A farmer friend had a cow in trouble this morning. I'm afraid I got into a bit of manure. Had to come straight here or people would have been sitting on each other's laps in the waiting room." Doc Peggy laughed, he smiled, and she stooped to take a good look at his dog. "Tell me about Shadow."

"I found him behind the Dumpster where I live. He was skin and bones. It took a while before I could get him to trust me."

"Well"—she fondled the dog's fur as she spoke—"he looks healthy and fit now. You've done a great job."

Shadow, happy with the attention, immediately put both paws on her shoulders and nearly knocked her over.

"Shadow! Sit!" Carl commanded. The dog sat. Head erect, it stared straight ahead at the wall.

The doctor perched on a small stool and regarded the dog with interest. "Did you teach him to obey like that?"

"Yes."

"What else can he do?"

Carl put Shadow through his small repertoire of tricks. The dog shook hands, rolled over, and played dead.

"He walks with a lead really well too," Carl offered.

"That's impressive," Doc Peggy told him. "When some of my patients come through the door, I often wonder who is master of whom. The pets frequently seem to be the ones in charge."

"He was easy to train," Carl said, "It didn't take long to teach him a few things."

"He looks like he's mostly German shepherd," she mused. "With some mountain cur thrown in, perhaps?"

"That's what I thought."

"Nice combination," she said. "You're going to have one loyal dog there. Let's get him up on the table where I can take a better look at him."

Carl gave a low whistle. Shadow minded him perfectly and leaped up onto the examining table.

"Seriously?" the doctor laughed. "Now you're just showing off."

"Maybe a little."

He liked this woman. She appeared to be in her late fifties, with faded blonde hair and kind blue eyes. No makeup, but she had dark circles beneath her eyes as though she could use a good night's sleep. She seemed compassionate but weary. The only jewelry she wore was a small silver tree hanging from a thin silver chain.

"Shadow looks perfectly fine to me. My technician will be in soon to take some blood and give him his shots. You be a good boy, fella." She gave Shadow a hug, and the dog surprised Carl by licking her face. "Funny thing about rescued animals," she said. "They often tend to be more loyal than others. It's as though somehow they realize what you've done for them and they never forget it."

"It's nothing compared to what they've done for me," Carl said under his breath, as she started to leave the room. She hesitated at the door then seemed to make up her mind about something.

"You aren't looking for a job, by any chance, are you?" Doc Peggy asked.

"Why?"

She shrugged. "Oh, it's just that I don't run across too many people who have the ability to take an abandoned animal and train them this well. It's obvious Shadow trusts you, and I could really use another technician."

Carl felt his heart begin to thud. A job? Working with animals? He couldn't be so lucky! Then the dreaded question came immediately—the question he knew would stop any possibility of a job with her.

"How did you learn to train dogs so well?"

He wanted to lie, but he couldn't. There would be forms to fill out, background checks made... There was no way this kind woman doctor would ever feel safe around him after she knew.

"I worked with the prisoner dog-training program," Carl said.

She didn't flinch. "What were you in for?"

"Murder." He stared at Shadow, waiting for her rejection.

"How long were you in?"

"Twenty years."

"I've heard about the prisoner dog program. They don't let just anyone participate."

"No, ma'am, they don't."

She pondered this information for a moment. "Where do you live?"

"The preacher down the street helped get me a job. I work as a janitor for his church, and I live there."

"Inside the Mennonite church?"

"Yes."

"I know that church, and I know the preacher. If things worked out, do you suppose George would let you come help me part-time?"

Carl felt a jolt of hope. "I'm sure he wouldn't mind. There's not enough work at the church to keep me all that busy, but...are you sure?"

"I'm really tired of hiring kids." Doc Peggy sighed. "Their schedules are so complicated that I end up feeling more like a social director than a boss. Problem is, they're all I can afford. I can only pay minimum wage. I know that isn't much, but it would be wonderful to have someone with real experience—someone who actually *knows* something. I don't suppose you'd be interested...?"

Interested? He'd already deep-cleaned the church enough that he hardly had work to fill a couple of hours a day. The idea of getting to work with dogs in a real veterinarian's office would be a dream come true. He could learn so much here.

A young male technician walked in.

"I have another patient waiting," the doctor said before she left, "but think it over. If you're interested, stop by the front desk and fill out an application before you leave. I can probably give you twenty hours a week."

Carl watched his dog being cared for by a kid so young, he still had blemishes on his face. He also wasn't very good at what he did. Shadow yelped and bit the air near the kid's hand when he gave him the shot.

And then he realized there was one other thing Doctor Oglesby needed to know before he applied for the job. She was in the hallway filling out a chart when he and Shadow left the examination room.

"I hate to say this," Carl said, "but I can't take the job."

"Oh?" She looked up from her clipboard. "Why not?"

"I had a drug problem before I went in."

"Do you have a drug problem now?"

"No. I kicked it a long time ago."

"Great. Come in on Monday and I'll have a lab coat ready for you."

"Just like that?"

"Unless there is a problem with your preacher or parole officer when I call them."

"No, they'll probably be fine with it."

"Leave their contact numbers with the office staff when you finish your application. I'll call both of them tonight, and I'll be sure to mention that we keep all our drugs safely locked up. I'm the only one who handles them."

"I appreciate what you're doing, ma'am," he said, "more than you'll ever know...but why are you willing to take a risk on an ex-con?"

"All the reasons I mentioned earlier." She hesitated. "And because I know what it feels like to be a rescue."

Chapter Thirty-Eight

"All it needs is a sign out front, some decorations, and a couple wait-resses before we're ready to go," Darren said.

"That's all, huh?" Joe said. "What about some recipes and a little experience with running a restaurant?"

"You don't need experience when you've eaten in as many restau-rants as I have," Darren said. "I know what works. I know what people want. Trust me, brother, this place is going to be a success."

"It's probably going to be a disaster," Joe said. "But since it's your money we're losing for a change, I'll give it a try and see how it goes. I don't have all that many options right now. I'd really rather not sell insurance if I can find a way to avoid it."

"Insurance?"

"Yeah. They seemed to think a former pro ballplayer would make a dandy salesman."

"Oh, Micah." Darren sighed. "You're in even worse shape than I realized."

The building was old but well-kept. It had been a restaurant once before, so the wooden booths were already in place. The kitchen had ovens and a couple of fry baskets, and Darren had made arrangements for a commercial refrigerator to be delivered.

"We'll need an oversized grill for the burgers," Darren said. "I'll scout around and see if I can find one that's not too used. By the way, it's not just my money that I'm putting into it. I'm putting in my heart and soul too. If it succeeds, it could make a real difference for our family. Please don't be negative."

Joe saw the need in his brother's eyes and felt his own attitude changing. Deep down he was excited by the idea, but he was afraid to hope that it might actually become a success. After all, most new businesses failed, didn't they?

"I'll help you run the restaurant, Daddy," Bobby said.

"Of course you will, buddy." Joe ruffled his son's hair. "You'll be a big help."

"I've already made some inquiries about supplies," Darren said. "I figure we'll keep things as local as possible. It'll cut down on shipping expenses, and we can advertise that the food we serve is locally produced. That seems to be a big thing to a lot of people these days."

"Sounds good to me," Joe said. He tried not to be surprised at how much thought Darren had already put into it.

His brother continued. "We can use local beef, we have tons of locally made cheeses around here, and the buns we'll use are baked fresh daily right here in Sugarcreek. Vegetables can be seasonal most months, and I'm thinking of Mom's potato salad as one of the side dishes."

"She did make excellent potato salad," Joe agreed. "Whenever we actually had refrigeration."

"There's a place near here that makes potato chips too. And of course, we have Lydia's pies. Those things would bring in customers even if we didn't have anything else to serve."

"What's in here?" Bobby wandered into an adjacent room.

"That's where the bar is," Darren said.

"What's a bar?" Bobby asked.

Darren looked to Joe for an explanation.

"It's where people go to drink and talk."

"I like to drink and talk!" Bobby said. "Can we have my favorite?"

"What's his favorite?" Darren asked.

"He had some homemade root beer at the Bulk Foods Store the other day and loved it. I think it actually had the name *sarsaparilla* on the old-fashioned labeling."

"Do they make that locally?"

"I think so."

"Hmm." Darren stared at the mirrored shelves behind the bar. "I have an idea."

"What is it?"

"I wonder what would happen if we brought in all sorts of boutique-type sodas from Mom-and-Pop-type factories. Old-fashioned ginger ale, sarsaparilla, crème sodas, whatever we could find. We could have Pepsi and Coke products too, of course, but think of all those different-colored sodas up there on the shelves with the mirroring behind them. Could be something to look into."

"Sounds like an old-fashioned soda counter," Joe said. "They already have that sort of thing at Lehman's up in Kidron."

"And look how successful Lehman's is," Darren said. "But that's a long way to drive for gourmet soda pop. I think people would love it. They could come through the door for a burger and end up having a handmade root-beer float to wash it down. Or a cucumber-flavored soda, if they wanted."

"Cucumber?"

"It's a thing," Darren said. "So is rhubarb and lavender. I've had them both. They're not bad."

"How on earth do you *know* these things?"

"My misspent youth," Darren said. "I've been in some very odd places, brother."

"Evidently." Joe looked up at the ceiling, which had several worrisome brown stains. "It's going to be a lot of work."

"When did you ever shy away from hard work?" Darren asked.

"No offense, but it wasn't me I was thinking about," Joe said. "I have to be honest with you. I'm afraid you'll get this started and then fade away."

"I don't have any place to fade to," Darren said. "I'm betting my last penny on this place, and it's obvious that I can't use you as my private ATM anymore. I have to make this work."

"I understand," Joe said. "But to me it feels like being a young ball-player again, and suddenly having to pitch for a major-league game with absolutely no experience."

"Well, then, you should feel right at home, Micah."

Chapter Thirty-Nine

Rachel safely delivered Anna and Gray Cat back to Lydia and Bertha. She had not stopped for ice cream. She had not been in the mood for ice cream after that scene in the vet's office. Anna, sensing Rachel's tension, mood had not asked.

Things were stiffly polite between her and Bertha when she dropped Anna off. She checked in with Ed, then went on patrol in her squad car.

It was a quiet day in Sugarcreek as she drove down Main Street, which meant she could let her mind wander. The problem was, her mind had been wandering the same tired path lately to the point that it had worn a groove so deep that it was hard for her to see out.

She and Joe were decent, good people. It really wasn't fair how much their lives had been impacted by two criminals. Henrietta had managed to devastate Joe financially, and having Carl nearby was turning Rachel into a person she didn't like much. Rachel was pretty sure it wasn't doing her marriage any good, either.

She could tell that Joe was getting annoyed by her obsession with Carl. He seemed to think she should simply get over it—to ignore the fact that her father's murderer was walking around free. But it was impossible for her to ignore it. Knowing she could run into Carl at any moment made her feel vulnerable, which was unacceptable. Every time she left her house, her nerves were on full alert. She was afraid to let go of her anger

At a time in her life when she had expected to be shopping for sweet baby things and worrying about nothing more than the best way to create a nursery in their small house...she couldn't stop obsessing over her father's killer.

It was easier for Joe. His nemesis, Henrietta, was tucked away in a psych ward at a prison in California. He didn't have to constantly wonder whether his homicidal former agent would suddenly appear the minute he stepped foot outside his house.

It bothered her that Joe wasn't as indignant as she was over Carl. For the first time, she wondered if it would be better for Joe to go ahead and take that job in Cleveland. Or Columbus. He could commute home on weekends. Other couples did it...although none she knew did it all that successfully.

As she drove through downtown Sugarcreek nursing her anger against Carl, her resentment toward Joe, and her hurt feelings by Bertha, she saw Joe and Bobby standing on the sidewalk behind a large delivery truck parked crookedly on Main Street. She stopped to investigate and saw that Darren was also there, directing delivery men to carry a commercial-sized refrigerator to an old storefront that had been empty for a couple of months.

Leaning against the side of the building was a large sign painted in red, white, and blue block letters. It said, "Joe's Home Plate."

She parked, got out, and was greeted by her husband and son. Darren seemed practically giddy as he followed the delivery men inside.

Bobby was jumping up and down with excitement as she approached. "Me and Daddy and Uncle Darren are making a restaurant!"

"Is that right?" Rachel smiled at Bobby then shot Joe a questioning look.

"Hi, sweetheart," Joe said cheerfully. "I'm glad you stopped. Apparently we are officially going into the restaurant business. Or we'll be in business as long as the money from the sale of Darren's car holds out."

"Why didn't you tell me about this?"

"I didn't know about it until this morning. Darren showed up and told me he'd sold his Lamborghini and rented this building for the next six months. He already had the sign made and had arranged to have a commercial refrigerator delivered today. My head is still whirling."

"The sale of his car is paying for all this?"

"That's what he says."

"So he sold it and invested the money in a restaurant that involves you without saying a word to you about it?"

"He did." Joe wore the biggest grin she'd seen on his face since he'd come back from L.A. Apparently he was not the least bit upset that his brother had done this thing without consulting them.

"I remember him talking about opening a restaurant the night he had dinner with us," she said. "But I had no idea he was truly serious about the idea."

"Me either." Joe put his arm around her as they stared at the storefront together. "I have to admit, I have a lot of reservations, but he's so excited about the idea that I'm kinda feeling it too…even though I think we should probably both have our heads examined."

"Uncle Darren wants Daddy to bring his trophies," Bobby announced. "All of them."

"For decoration," Joe added. "He's got this baseball theme going on."

"And Daddy says I can bring my trophies too," Bobby said. "Except I don't have any yet."

"I'm sure that will change," Rachel said.

"Yep." Bobby nodded his head in agreement, full of six-year-old self-confidence. "It probably will."

"Do you want to bring your trophies too?" Joe asked, teasing. "The ones for shooting?"

"No."

"Why?"

"Three reasons: Bertha, Lydia, and Anna."

"Those are good reasons."

"Yeah, I have enough issues with my aunts without displaying my sharpshooting awards."

"Didn't they know?"

"No. I was on the force in Akron at the time. I didn't mention it."

"The refrigerator is installed!" Darren walked outside, sweaty, disheveled, and with a big grin. "Whaddya think of my idea, Rachel?"

"I think you've taken a big gamble," she said, evenly.

"True, but wouldn't it be something if that gamble turned into a way to make a good living?"

"Daddy says I can help," Bobby said. "Ezra and his daddy sell vegetables. I can help my daddy at work just like Ezra does."

"It does seem to be the Amish way for the whole family to be involved in a business," Joe said.

"I think you and your brother might have been around my aunts for too long. You'll be trying to open another B & B here in Sugarcreek before I know it."

"Hey," Joe said, "this wasn't my idea."

"Do you suppose you could talk Lydia into making pies for it?" Darren asked.

"I don't know," Rachel said. "She has her hands pretty full with the inn."

"I'll go talk to her about it," Darren said. "Now, Micah, about the menu..."

"Can I talk to you in private, Joe?" Rachel asked.

"Sure. Darren, keep an eye on Bobby?"

"I don't like this," Rachel said, once she and Joe were sitting in his truck and no one could hear.

"I didn't like it either, at first," Joe said. "But the more Darren talked about it, the more it sounded like a good idea."

She tried to reason with him. "Joe, you aren't a businessman. You've already proven that to both of us. You can't cook more than a handful of items. I hate to say this, but I think you're making a huge mistake, getting hooked up with Darren."

The smile melted from Joe's face.

"What am I supposed to do, Rachel? Sit at home and let you support me? You don't want me making commercials. Neither of us want to move Bobby away from here. I can't play ball anymore. Apart from showing up from time to time at a convention to sign autographs, I don't have a whole lot of options. I've put in applications everywhere I can think of around here and I can't even get a call back from a lumber company. Everyone is thrilled to meet me, but they seem to think that my applying for a job is some sort of joke."

"I didn't realize you were so upset."

"How could you? You're so wrapped up in the fact that Carl Bateman is free, you hardly notice us. And even when you aren't talking about him, I know you're thinking about him because of the sour expression on your face."

"I have a right to be angry!"

"You do. But there are more important things for you to pay attention to than an old man who has served his time."

"I beg to disagree," Rachel said. "He did *not* serve his time. He served only twenty years. He was supposed to be in prison for life."

"I would expect that sort of reasoning out of a civilian, Rachel, but you know how the system works. You know people get out early all the time."

"I do know how the system works. I also know the system makes mistakes. Sometimes big ones."

"If it was anyone but Carl, you would hardly notice. This is all about letting go of the past. What you are doing is not healthy. You need to figure out a way to get over this, or…"

"Or what?"

"Or Bobby and I might have to go move into the daadi haus for a while, until you do."

"You're threatening to leave me?" She was aghast. "Because of a murderer?" "I'll do whatever I have to do," Joe said, "to protect my son."

"From me?" Rachel couldn't believe what she was hearing. "I *love* that child. He's my son too."

"Then get over yourself and act like it."

"Get out."

"It's my truck, Rachel."

She flung open the door, got out, and slammed it shut

He rolled down the window as she strode away. "I was on the fence about this restaurant business," he called. "But I've made my decision now. I'm going to give it my best shot…with or without you."

Chapter Forty

Joe was late in coming home, and since he had Bobby with him, Rachel was alone at the house for most of the evening. Unfortunately, she was also alone with her thoughts. They were not kind thoughts or conciliatory ones. All she could think about was that she and Joe had just had their first real argument since they'd gotten married, and it had been a doozy.

She blamed it all on Carl. If it weren't for him, she and Joe would still be happy together.

Had Joe actually threatened to leave her?

When she heard Joe's car pull up, Rachel made certain that she was busy doing something else. What? Dusting. She grabbed a rag from the closet and began to skim it over the nearest surface.

As Joe and Bobby came through the door, neither acknowledged the other. Bobby was subdued, looking from one parent to another and sensing that something was wrong.

"Time for bed, Bobby," Rachel said. "I'll run your bathwater."

"I'll take care of it," Joe said.

"All right."

For the first time since their marriage began, she did not help Joe tuck Bobby in after his bath. Being in the same room with Joe didn't seem like a good idea right now.

Forty-five minutes later, Joe came down the stairs. Having dusted everything she could in the small house, she was now energetically polishing the kitchen faucet.

"Excuse me," he said. She politely moved aside while he got a glass of water. The air was thick with unspoken words.

She could hardly believe Joe was being so cold to her. In the past, he'd always been so understanding and comforting. But if they were going to talk, he was going to have to initiate it—which he did.

"You didn't come up to tuck Bobby in," he said. "I know it's because you're hurt and mad, but he was upset about it. I think we'd better talk this out before we damage him further."

That was the second time he'd accused her of being a bad mother. Instead of hearing the concern in his voice, she was incensed by what she felt was an accusation. Being Rachel, she knew only one thing to do. Fight back.

"You threatened to leave me when I'm pregnant with your child. I never expected that out of you. What kind of man does that?"

"I wasn't threatening to leave you; I was telling you that I'll do whatever I have to—no matter how much it hurts me—to protect my son."

"From me?"

"From your anger. I love you, Rachel, but tonight Bobby asked me why you are mad at him. I tried to explain that you aren't mad at him; you're mad at someone else. He said he understood, but how can he? I'm not sure that I even understand. It feels like you're mad at me all the time too. Bertha tells me she's afraid to say anything to you for fear you'll blow up at *her*. Even Darren is feeling the tension."

"You've been discussing me with other people?"

"No, other people have been discussing you with me. They are worried about you. So am I, but I won't let you hurt my son with your inability to get over the fact that Carl is out of prison and there's nothing you can do about it. You're an adult. You can make your own decisions. I realize that what you went through as a child damaged you far beyond what I ever suspected, but I can't change that now. All I can do is try to make sure my son is okay. Bobby's a child. He needs to have a parental buffer between him and the world. That's what I intend to do. But I never dreamed I would have to be a buffer between him and you."

Rachel felt as if she were going to explode. "I need to get out of here," she said.

"Good idea," Joe shot back.

It surprised her that he didn't try to talk her into staying.

She drove around town trying to decide where to go. Under the circumstances, the sanctuary of her aunts' house did not feel like an option. She would probably get a lecture. Naomi had an extra room and was a good friend, but if she went there, she would probably hear some Amish platitude about not letting the sun go down on her wrath. With their money issues, a hotel was too expensive.

Finally, she went to the only place she was certain would welcome her. She had a key to the police station and there was a cot in the back room. With any luck, she could come in by the back door without the dispatcher noticing. Explaining why she was there was not something Rachel wanted to do right now.

Chapter Forty-One

When Rachel woke the next morning, she felt like a fool...not only because of the fight she'd had with Joe, but because Ed was standing there looking down at her.

"Rough night?" he said.

"I, um..."

"A fight with Joe?"

She nodded, embarrassed.

He put his hands on his hips and gave a sigh of frustration. "What am I going to do with you, Rachel?"

She scrambled off the cot, ran her fingers through her hair, encountered multiple tangles, and gave up.

"In case you're wondering"—Ed sat on the cot she'd vacated and crossed his legs—"you look like crap. Your eyes are all puffy. What did you do, cry yourself to sleep?"

She nodded.

"Go home, Rachel. Apologize to the man or throw dishes at him, I don't care. But work it out. Life's just too short."

Rachel went out the back way and managed to avoid seeing anyone else. Her internal alarm clock, which she'd always been able to depend upon, had failed her. It had certainly chosen a fabulous time. Ed was her *boss!* She was humiliated beyond words. With any luck, Joe would be gone when she crawled home looking like something the cat had dragged in.

But Joe and Bobby were sitting at the kitchen table, eating cereal, when she arrived. Bobby was adorable in his little SpongeBob underwear. Joe was wearing plaid pajama bottoms, and she conceded that he looked good in them. Her husband and son stared at her with astonishment on their faces.

"Are you okay, Rachel?" Bobby asked. "Did you fight some bad guys last night?"

Joe choked on his cereal.

"Not one word, Joe," she warned.

Joe sobered, rose, and went to the counter, pouring a cup of coffee. "You look like you need this," he said, handing it to her.

She sat down at the table and wrapped her hands around her favorite coffee mug, surprised that he'd picked the one she preferred. It was good to be home, even under the circumstances.

"No, Bobby, I didn't fight any bad guys while I was gone...but I did have a rough night." She glanced at Joe. "I feel a lot better this morning."

"Did your tummy hurt?" Bobby asked.

"A little."

"My tummy hurts sometimes."

"I know, sweetheart." Rachel's heart melted at the little boy's concern. "But I'm fine. I promise."

"Go get your clothes on, buddy," Joe said. "We've got a big day today at the restaurant. I'm going to let you help me scrape grease off an oven."

"Yay!" Bobby rushed up the stairs.

"He's easily entertained," Joe said.

Rachel stared down at her coffee cup, wondering what to say next. Apologies didn't come easy to her. When she looked up, Joe was studying her.

"What?" she said, shoving a strand of hair out of her face. "Is it *that* bad?"

"Actually, I was trying to figure out how a woman in a wrinkled uniform with puffy eyes and needing a hairbrush as badly as you do—could still be so gorgeous."

It was most definitely the right thing to say, and it broke the rest of the ice around her heart. "I'm sorry, Joe."

"I'm sorry too," he said. "I'll never threaten to leave you again. It's an empty threat anyway. I love you too much to leave. But—while you're working your way through this—try not to let your hatred of Carl affect your relationship with Bobby. Or with me."

"Of course," she said. "But do you understand why I'm struggling? Why I can't just pretend that nothing happened?"

"No one's expecting you to pretend. All we want is for you to act like *we're* not the enemy, because we aren't."

"I need to apologize to Bertha too, don't I?"

"Yes. That old woman loves you...but it might be a good idea to shower first. Where did you stay last night? I was worried, but I figured you could take care of yourself."

"The cot at the station. Ed found me sleeping there this morning."

"Ed found you?" Joe bit his lip. She could tell he was trying not to laugh. "So how did your police chief react?"

"I got a lecture. Then he told me to go home and give my husband a kiss."

"Ed said that?"

"No." She leaned toward him. "I just want to. I really am sorry, Joe. Let's not fight anymore."

He pulled her into his arms. "Sounds good to me."

Chapter Forty-Two

Even though Carl had been working for Doc Peggy for two weeks, he always made sure he never missed the ritual of morning coffee with George. It was nice having someone to talk to who was as pleased about his new job as he was. This morning, however, it was George who had some news for *him*.

"Brother Jones thinks you need a vehicle," George said. "He says his sister-in-law can't drive hers anymore and has gone into a nursing home. He thinks you might want it."

"How much?"

"She's giving it to you, if you want it and can afford the insurance."

Carl was surprised but cautious. He knew he was a bit of a project for the church congregation. He was grateful for their help, but even if the car was free, he didn't want to take on a piece of junk.

"Would it be rude if I asked to see it first?"

"Probably," George said. "But I could look it over for you and see if it's worth fooling with. I don't want you accepting something that would be better off sold as scrap metal. I'll go over right after I do my hospital visits."

A vehicle would be especially useful in teaching Shadow. He'd like to be able to drive far out into the country, where he could train his dog with a little more freedom. Shadow was showing signs of having an especially good nose. German shepherds were a great breed for search-and-rescue teams, but that was one kind of training he'd never done. When he mentioned the idea, Doc Peggy had ordered a couple of books for him. Being able to access woods and fields were a necessity in the training.

He'd been saving up, but it was going to take a long time to get enough for a dependable car. It would be wonderful if this one was roadworthy.

Carl waited anxiously until George came back that evening.

"It's a decent ride," George said. "A ten-year-old Dodge truck that belonged to her deceased husband. Only eighty thousand miles, with good tires. She maintained it and had the oil changed regularly."

A workable truck. That was better than anything Carl had hoped for.

"I don't have a driver's license."

"Well, that's easily fixed. You did drive once. Right?"

"Twenty years is a long time not to get behind the wheel."

"That needs to change." George handed Carl the keys to his old Ford. "Let's go. You can start practicing in the church parking lot."

Chapter Forty-Three

It had taken two days to scrape the caked-on grease from the industrial-sized stove. They had gotten the leftover restaurant appliances cheaply, but they were paying a heavy price in labor. The walls of the kitchen needed cleaned as well. And the ceiling. And the exhaust fan. There were wooden booths to sand and repaint. Tiled floors with years of ground-in dirt to scrub off.

He was exhausted and already struggling with a forbidding sense of failure. Who was he to think he could create food appealing enough for others to want to eat—let alone food they would be willing to pay good money for? Rachel was right. He was no businessman. The only thing in his life he'd ever been good at was playing ball.

"I'm tired, Daddy," Bobby said. "I want to go home."

His little boy had been playing with a couple of toy cars for over an hour, which was a long time for him to be so well-behaved. It was cruel to make him stay any longer.

"I'm sorry, buddy." Joe picked up Bobby and turned to Darren. "I need to leave. I think Bobby's had about as much as he can take of this today."

"Of course," Darren said. "I've got this. You go ahead."

As they drove home, Joe tried to pray for his wife and his marriage, but worries about the restaurant kept crowding in. The thing was turning into an even bigger and more overwhelming project than he had expected. In addition to trying to get the restaurant cleaned up, he'd spent most of last night trying to come up with the right blend of spices for a Vidalia onion sauce he wanted to use on one of his hamburgers. Several had been good, but nothing had been just right.

He was fighting fatigue, worry, and frustration. Opening night was a little over a month away—Darren's overly optimistic bright idea—and they'd already sunk advertising dollars and promotions into it. They'd gone too far to back out now—although he was starting to wish he'd never heard the words "Joe's Home Plate."

"Can we play Candy Land when we get home, Daddy?" Bobby asked.

"Probably not today," Joe said. "I've got to work on a recipe for the restaurant. There's not much time left before opening day. Maybe Rachel will play Candy Land with you."

"Can I have a peanut butter sandwich?" Bobby asked.

"Sure," Joe said, distracted by thoughts of sauce and supplies and Rachel. "I'll fix you one as soon as we get home."

There was paperwork he needed to complete tonight as well. He had to start getting ready for the upcoming school semester. It was the end of July, so a good bit of summer was left, but he needed to start getting his players into shape soon. His coaching job might not pay all that much, but he'd been building that team for two years now, he enjoyed building it, and he thought they might actually start winning a few games soon.

Joe's mind drifted to a million different things as he drove home. He did not notice that, in the backseat, Bobby had quietly begun to suck his thumb for the first time in two years.

***

Greta Johnson was probably only in her thirties, but unless one saw her up close, it would be easy to think she was pushing fifty. She wore baggy jeans, a gray T-shirt, and a gray cardigan. Her hair was stringy, she wore no makeup, and she didn't look people in the eyes when she was talking to them.

She had brought in a calico cat she called *Baby* to see Doc Peggy. Carl asked the basic question. "What seems to be the matter?"

"I can't put my finger on it," Greta said, staring hard at the wall. "She just seems to be 'off.' "

After a few more questions, he looked into the cat's ears, listened to her heart, palpitated the cat's stomach, noted his evaluation on the chart, and told Greta that the doctor would be in soon. Then he excused himself and handed the chart over to Doc Peggy in the hallway.

Peggy glanced at it. "Kittens?"

"Yes."

"Did you tell her?"

"No," he said. "That's your job."

And he went on to the next patient. There was no time to chat during clinic hours, but *after* hours was another matter.

In the late afternoon, once her patient visits were over and the staff had gone home, Doc Peggy liked to sit on the small couch in the break room, and allow herself to recuperate for a few minutes while she sipped a cup of green tea and ate a couple of oatmeal cookies. It was a little ritual she indulged in at the end of each day.

Once Carl discovered this, he made it his practice to have her favorite tea cup waiting for her, washed and dried and with a new tea bag in it. Then he would fill the electric teakettle with fresh water just before he left. The doctor worked so hard, and it made him feel good to do this small task for her.

After a couple of weeks, she had asked if he would stay for a few moments and discuss her concerns about one of her patients, an elderly dog so crippled with arthritis that it would be a kindness to put him out of his misery—except for the fact that he was loved by a very fragile, sick child.

"What would you do?" she had asked him. "What would you advise his owners?"

Carl didn't hesitate. "I know the dog. That child is his life. He is willing to endure the pain as long as he can give the child comfort."

She had looked at him quizzically. "How do you know what the dog is feeling?"

"I just do."

"Pour yourself a cup of tea, Carl," she had said. "I believe it would be helpful to discuss some of my other patients with you."

From that afternoon on they had fallen into the habit of reviewing the day's events after everyone else left, relaxing together in the break room, each with their cups of hot tea and her favorite brand of oatmeal cookies. Peggy always curled up on the couch with her shoes off. He always sat at the table several feet away. He cherished the ritual and was determined to make sure she always felt at ease with him.

That afternoon, as they went over their day, Peggy told him that Greta had been pleased about the probability of kittens.

"First time I've ever seen that woman smile." She dipped her cookie into her tea and took a small bite.

"You know her?"

"She's been in here before with the same cat, but yes, my daughter went to school with her."

"She seems like a lonely person," Carl said. "Any family besides her cat?"

"Actually, yes. She has a brother who recently moved home to live with her. I think he's been in and out of rehab several times. She told me she's pleased he's there but is worried he might relapse. They had a younger sister, Cynthia, who died a few years back."

"The poor woman couldn't even look at me."

"Greta's always been like that, even in high school. I have no idea why."

He poured more hot water into his cup. He hated the taste of the green tea but he was determined not to show it. Diluting it helped.

"How does she support herself?"

"She runs a small day-care center in her home," Peggy said. "My guess is that only the people who are desperate for cheap childcare employ her, but I don't think a child would actually be in danger there. People who are good with their animals usually treat their children well, and she is always quite concerned about Baby."

"A brother who just got out of rehab and lives in the same house as the children she's babysitting doesn't sound good."

"That makes me uncomfortable too, but there's nothing I can do about it."

Carl glanced at the clock and marveled inwardly at how quickly the day had flown. It had been an especially busy day. Each day in prison had felt like a week. Here, each week felt like a day.

"Can I ask you something personal?" Peggy sounded serious.

He stiffened. He had been expecting this. She was going to ask him about the murder he had committed or his life in prison—and he didn't want to talk about any of it. As much as humanly possible, he wanted to forget it. But this was Peggy asking, a woman to whom he would bare his soul if necessary.

"Of course."

"Why on earth do you keep drinking that tea when you obviously despise the taste?" And then she burst out laughing at the look of surprise on his face.

"Sorry," he said. "I didn't want to offend you."

"Pour that stuff down the sink, Carl! Bring in whatever kind of tea you want—or coffee or whatever. I don't care. Goodness! You're a free man."

He gratefully dumped the tea and then helped her lock up the office. It was time for him to rush back to the church to make certain everything was spic-and-span for the Wednesday night service.

Working with Peggy meant learning something new every day. During their late-afternoon discussions, she taught him a great deal more about animals. Seeing his eagerness to learn, she started lending him more books about animals. He had never been a reader, but he read the books Peggy loaned him. He observed closely when he assisted her during surgeries and memorized every movement and surgical tool.

Peggy said his ability to read animals was a rare gift. The more he worked with her, the more he believed that what she said was true. He could tell by a cat's body language what sort of problems might develop during an examination. He could tell by the droop or pitch of a dog's head whether it might be wise to wear the leather gloves or if the dog was a sweetheart and could be handled without them.

He found himself waking each morning with something he'd never felt in his entire life until now: eager anticipation of the day. He'd hurry and fulfill his few janitorial duties for the church and then jump into his truck and head over to the clinic. When he got there, he would put on the white assistant's coat that Peggy provided.

It didn't take long for Carl to learn exactly what to do and how to do it. As he became more skilled, the clients began to treat him not only with respect, but with deference. They asked questions and listened carefully to his answers.

He found himself instructing lonely, elderly women on how to cut back on calories and snacks for their overweight cats. Some actually did what he said and came back proudly to show him the weight their pets had lost.

He gave some of the children pointers on how to teach their dogs tricks and enjoyed their delight when they showed him what their animals had learned.

Some of the church members already had pets they brought to Doc Peggy, and when they saw Carl working there, they began to see him another light. Instead of "the ex-con janitor the church is helping out who lives in the basement," they saw him as a professional with training and knowledge that they did not have. Some started asking him advice about their pets after services. The awkwardness of his background and past began to disappear.

One day Carl caught a glimpse of himself in a store window, and for a moment he didn't recognize himself. He was standing taller, with his shoulders squared back. Strange how a job and a little self-confidence could make a man walk differently.

Although Doc Peggy took care of people's smaller house pets, she also dealt with farm animals as well. That meant sometimes she had to go out in the middle of the night to some farmer's barn. Often that barn was Amish, with no electric lights. Because Carl was always available and willing to help, he often accompanied her, sometimes if only to hold the large flashlight while she and the owner worked with the animal. He soon began to see why the good doctor had dark circles beneath her eyes—but each time he went with her, he learned something new.

It was the richest, best time of his life. He was drug- and alcohol-free. Had faith and conviction. Was making friends. Working hard at a job he loved but also enjoying his non-working hours because he had Shadow as a companion.

He'd even started a little bank account. With his history, it was hard to walk into a bank for the first time, but he did it. He kept reminding himself that he was there to put money in the bank, like a normal citizen. Even better, it was money he himself had earned with honest work.

He could afford a small apartment now, but his needs were so basic that it seemed unnecessary. A bed, a TV for a few programs at night, a kitchen, a bathroom…it was all there in the basement. The church building had actually begun to feel like a home to him. In the mornings, he often sat for a few moments in the silence of the sanctuary, watching the sun stream through the gleaming windows and giving thanks for this second chance—this resurrection of the soul.

He often contemplated how God had somehow managed to braid the bitter ends of his life together to create this new beginning for him. With all his heart, he wished he had not pulled the trigger that long-ago day, but he was in awe of the generosity of a God who had given him a good life in spite of his former actions and choices.

Neither Rachel nor Anna had been back to the clinic since he started working there, and he was grateful. Rachel's icy stare had the power to mentally put him right back inside the prison, where he was nothing but scum, instead of a contributing member of society.

He understood why she hated him, and he didn't blame her. But since he couldn't go back and change what he'd done, he was determined to try to stay out of her sight.

There was one problem with this plan. He wanted to visit Bertha to thank her for those letters she had written him…but to do so meant risking the possibility of running into Rachel.

He had not gone to see the old Amish woman before now because, well, he didn't feel worthy. Yes, he was out of prison, but for the past two-and-a-half months he felt like he carried it within him. Until he no longer felt worthless, he had not wanted to face the woman who helped save his sanity by sending letters of forgiveness and asking her cousin, George, to visit him.

Now, with a respectable job, a driver's license, and money in the bank, Carl thought he might be ready to go talk to her. He daydreamed about pulling up in front of her house in his shiny truck with his handsome dog beside him, wearing nice clothes, and showing Bertha the letters he'd saved.

She deserved to know what her forgiveness had meant to him. He looked forward to telling her that her great compassion had changed his life.

And next week, that exact thing would happen. George had talked with her about him, and she had said she would be happy to meet with him.

Carl hoped she was as kind in person as she had been in her letters. If this visit turned out well, it was going to mean everything to him. He knew and accepted the fact that he was a bad man, but with God's help, he was beginning to hope that maybe even a bad man could still do good things.

Chapter Forty-Four

Bertha was on the back porch leaning over the wringer washer when Rachel and Bobby arrived at Sugar Haus. It was a clear, hot, summer day—perfect for drying clothes—and Rachel was not surprised to find her aunt doing laundry.

Bertha held up a finger when they came up the steps, indicating that they should wait while she ran the last sheet through the wringer. The gasoline-powered motor of the old Maytag made it impossible to hold a conversation. Bobby watched fascinated, as the rubber wringer flattened and squashed wash water out of the sheet as the fabric snaked into a basket.

Bertha switched off the motor and said very formally, "It is so nice of you to come to visit."

Rachel heard the rebuke in Bertha's voice. "I don't want our difference of opinion about Carl Bateman to damage our relationship, Aunt Bertha. I came to apologize."

"I'm glad to hear that." Bertha wiped her wet hands on her apron. "Especially since he's coming to visit soon."

"*Excuse me?*"

"George called this morning to ask. Of course I said yes."

"You gave him permission to come *here*? To our *home*? Why?"

"Because he asked."

"I'm really struggling here, Aunt Bertha. It seems like everyone in

the county is fine with Carl Bateman except for me.

Bobby tugged at Rachel's hand. "Can I go play?"

"Of course you can." Rachel was so distracted by her aunt's revelation that she barely noticed Bobby as he ran off into the house. "What is that man trying to prove by asking to come here, Aunt Bertha?"

"He's not trying to prove anything." Bertha nested the laundry basket against her hip and started walking toward the clothesline as Rachel followed. "George says Carl just wants to thank me for the letters I wrote to him all those years."

"What? Wait." Rachel stopped and stared at Bertha. "*What* letters?"

"I wrote him twenty letters. One each year on the anniversary of my brother's death. Each one of them said that I forgave him."

"What on earth possessed you to do that?" Rachel cried.

"Keep your voice down." Bertha pulled a wet sheet from the laundry basket, shook it out, and hung it on the clothesline. "You don't want to upset Anna. You know how she gets when she hears people arguing. And we don't need to stress her heart."

Rachel lowered her voice. "Why didn't you tell me?"

"When?" Bertha asked. "When would have been the right time? You may find this hard to believe, Rachel, but my life does not entirely revolve around you. Forgiving Carl was something I had to do—for me. It had nothing to do with you."

"But how *could* you?" Rachel said.

"How could I *not*?" Bertha asked. "It is one of the main tenets of our religion. You Englisch might think you have the luxury of nursing grudges for life, but we Amish do not—at least not if we are truly striving to be God's people."

"And it was that easy for you? Because you are Amish you were able to forgive...just like that?" Rachel snapped her fingers.

Bertha rarely cried, but her eyes reddened at those words.

"No, I did not forgive 'just like that.' " Bertha mimicked Rachel by snapping her fingers as well. "I have struggled for twenty years to forgive the man. I have prayed long and hard about it. Each year it got a bit easier. Writing the words down and sending them to him made it a little easier. It felt as though I was mailing away a piece of anger each time. I was careful in writing those letters. I told him stories about Frank so he would know who my brother was besides a cop who had interrupted a bank robbery. I used the prettiest stationery I could find. I practiced exactly what I wanted to say on scrap paper before I recopied and sent it."

"You used your prettiest stationery." Rachel felt as if her heart would break at the thought of Bertha taking such pains. "I bought you some of that stationery. Why go to such an effort for someone like him?"

"It was an act of obedience on my part," Bertha said. "I was trying to obey God's command to forgive others as He had forgiven me. Jesus did not forgive people halfheartedly. I have a strong feeling that if Christ had written a personal letter telling me that He forgave me, it would not be on second-rate paper and it would be beautiful."

"Seriously?" Rachel was still angry. "What have you ever done to need forgiveness? If anyone has lived a perfect, godly life, it is you."

Bertha barked out a laugh of disbelief.

"It's true!" Rachel insisted. "Yes, I'm mad at you right now, but I've never known anyone who tries harder or does more."

"You have no idea who I am," Bertha said, bitterly. "Or what my struggles have been. Do you think I *wanted* to come back from my work in Haiti? Do you think I didn't rail against God for making me leave all that I loved there, even leaving the man I loved?"

"*You* were in *love*?" Rachel was so startled by this revelation that she forgot all about being upset.

"That slipped out." Bertha's cheeks reddened. "It is none of your business, Rachel. I did not mean to say that."

"No, wait a minute. You were in love? Who was it? What happened?"

"I have said enough. More than enough." Bertha's mouth was set.
"We will speak no more of this. Ever." She turned her back on Rachel,
reached into the clothespin holder, and found it empty. "These new
clothespins break so easily. They just don't last like the old ones did, but
I think I have a package of them in the house."

Rachel followed her aunt. She was not finished with their conversation—even if Bertha was trying to ignore her.

"But you said God forgave you," Rachel mused as Bertha rummaged
through a drawer in the front room. "Bertha, were you...*involved* with
this man?"

"It was all a long time ago," Bertha said. "I will not speak of it again
with you. Now, either help me find those clothespins or go away."

Rachel saw that she would get no more information from Bertha,
but her aunt's slip of the tongue had certainly given her something new
to think about. It had never occurred to her that Bertha had ever had a
life outside of being the matriarch of their family, except for the handful
of years she spent working at a Mennonite orphanage.

Still, the fact remained. Bertha had written letters to Carl, who was
now asking permission through George to come for a visit.

"Aunt Lydia is okay with this visit?"

"She has fought her own battle with forgiveness, but yes, she is prepared to welcome him into our home. George says Carl is doing won-
derfully well. He even has a job at Doc Peggy's veterinarian clinic in
addition to cleaning the church."

"That doesn't change the fact that I feel like you are betraying me by
allowing that man to come here, to this house."

"I'm sorry you feel that way, but this is not your house, Rachel. It
is mine, and he will be welcomed with the same love of Christ that we

extend to everyone."

"You're preaching at me now."

"Your own conscience is preaching at you. You should be concentrating on getting ready for your new baby instead of allowing so much bitterness to dwell in your heart."

It was impossible, of course, to win an argument with Bertha. In fact, Rachel could never remember having done so. The most she had ever achieved was a stalemate.

"But what if I *can't* forgive?"

"Then show some mercy. For your own sake as well as his. Just try to show the man a little mercy."

There was a small noise, like the rustling of a mouse, from the corner of the room, and that was when Rachel realized that Bobby was behind the couch. Had he heard what they were talking about? Did he understand the ramifications of what they were saying? She hoped not.

Bertha heard him too. "Come out from your hiding place, Bobby," she demanded. "A child should not be eavesdropping on adult conversation."

Bobby's head popped up. "I'm not ease-dropping," he said. "I'm playing with Gray Cat." He plopped the cat down on the couch and then climbed out after it, with his shoes on the couch cushions—which was not allowed.

Bertha was not amused. "We have guests who stay with us, Bobby," she admonished. "They do not want to sit in your footprints."

And that was the straw that broke the little boy's back. He began to wail.

Bertha looked at him in astonishment. "What on earth is wrong with the child?"

"I don't know," Rachel said, going over to comfort him. "I think he's overtired, maybe. It's been a long week. What's wrong, buddy?"

"You don't love me," the little boy sobbed. "Everybody wants me to go away."

"That's not true!" Bertha was completely shocked. "Everyone loves you."

"Daddy doesn't want me at the restaurant…he just says he does. He tells me to get down off the counters even when I'm trying to help. And Rachel's face looks like this all the time!" He made an angry face. "Even when I try really, really hard to be good."

"I'm not mad at you, Bobby. I'm never mad at you. I *love* you. You're the most important thing in the world to me, and your daddy is just worried about the restaurant being ready for opening day," Rachel tried to reassure him.

"I want my mommy," Bobby sobbed. "I want my *real* mommy."

Bertha cocked an eyebrow at her as though to say, *See what your inability to let go of the past has done?*

Joe had been right about what she was doing to Bobby. Rachel felt heartsick. She'd failed her precious son.

"I'm not mad at you, Bobby," she said again. "I'm mad at the man who took my daddy away when I wasn't much older than you. I'm sorry if I accidentally took it out on you."

"Henrietta took my mommy away, and I didn't take it out on *you*!" he accused.

He was absolutely right. He had been sweet and loving and giving, and she had been so preoccupied with her own life and job and pregnancy, not to mention her upset over Carl, that she had neglected the one person on earth who needed her the most.

"I'm so sorry, Bobby. You're right. I'll do better." She searched for an excuse a six-year-old might understand. "I–I've been very tired lately."

"Are you taking your vitamins?" Bertha asked, always the nurse.

"Yes, but this has nothing to do with vitamins," Rachel said. "I'm going home now, and I'm going to spend the rest of the evening paying attention to my son."

"I think that is an excellent idea," Bertha said.

"Can we play Candy Land now?" Bobby asked. "For real?"

"Absolutely for real."

He reached up and held her hand while they walked to the car. His instant forgiveness clutched at Rachel's heart.

It turned out that the emotional meltdown had taken a toll. After they arrived home, Bobby got tired after only two games of Candy Land.

"Which book do you want me to read?" Rachel asked him, after his teeth were brushed, pajamas put on, and prayers said.

"This one." Bobby picked a book from the shelf and handed it to her before climbing into bed. "This is my favorite."

The title was *I'll Love You Forever*, and it was the story of a little boy growing up and how his mother would love him forever no matter what he did or how he acted. A silly picture showed her climbing into his room after he became a grown man so she could check on him.

Rachel made up a tune to go with the repeated refrain of "I'll love you forever; I'll like you for always. As long as I'm living, my baby you'll be."

Even after singing and reading her way through the book, Bobby still wasn't asleep. He seemed worried.

"Will you love me forever?" he asked.

"As long as I'm living and beyond," she answered. "I'll never stop loving you, no matter what."

"Are you going to climb into my room at night on a ladder when I'm big?"

"Probably not, unless you need me to. But if you got lost or hurt or anything, there's nothing in this world that could keep me from coming to you."

He snuggled against her. "Even if I ran away and climbed way up on top of a mountain?"

"Are you planning to run away?"

"No."

"Good, because if you ever did, I'd find me some climbing gear and go looking for you on top of that mountain."

"What if I got in a big plane and went to Hawaii?"

Rachel knew that one of Bobby's friends had gone to Hawaii. "Then I'd buy a hula skirt and a plane ticket and come after you."

Bobby giggled. "What if I got on a big boat and sailed far away?"

"Then I'd hire me a big boat and sail far away to get you."

"What if some bad people came to steal me?"

"If bad people ever stole you away from us"—Rachel grew very solemn as the cop in her kicked in—"then Daddy and I wouldn't stop until we found you. If something like that ever happened, you must do anything you could to escape. Okay?"

" 'Kay." He burrowed into the covers and sighed with contentment. "I love you, Rachel."

"I love you too, sweetie. You're my boy."

Her throat choked up with emotion as she watched over the sleeping child in the bed. She coveted his love. How had she ever allowed this sweet little boy feel like she didn't care about him? How badly had her upset and distraction damaged their relationship…and what about Joe? Her husband was so busy trying to create a way to make an income for them that she barely saw him these days.

She heard the front door open quietly. Joe's weary footsteps made their way down the hall where she waited for him, still sitting on Bobby's bed.

"I think we might make the deadline," he said. "We still have to drive to Detroit to pick up a commercial grill Darren found online, but a few more hard days like this one and I think we'll be able to open on time. How's our son?"

"Bobby's fine," she said. "We played Candy Land and read books."

"Thank you, sweetheart. You're a good mom to him."

She followed Joe into their bedroom, where he slowly pulled off his shoes one at a time and left them on the floor instead of putting them away in the closet. For once, she didn't remind him. The poor man was exhausted, and after what she'd been through tonight, she didn't much care where his shoes landed. It only mattered that he was home.

"Anything important happen today?" he asked.

There were a million things she wanted to tell him about and discuss, but not now. He had already fallen back upon the pillow, on top of the covers, fully dressed except for his shoes, and was snoring.

Chapter Forty-Five

Carl expected to be nervous about his visit to Bertha, but instead he felt an unexpected calm as he got ready to go visit the woman who had changed his life.

Those letters. Those handwritten letters spread over twenty hard-bitten years. Not once had he written her back. Not once had he told her how much any of those letters had meant to him. He had tried many times, but he simply did not have the words. Nor did he feel worthy.

Perhaps George, her cousin, had conveyed to her what he knew of Carl's appreciation, but he doubted that even George knew the depth of his gratitude.

Carl kept expecting the letters to stop, but each year, like clockwork, on the anniversary of her brother's death, Bertha wrote of forgiveness. Each letter had been like a drink of cool water in the scorching desert of his life. The woman had meant what she said.

With two paying jobs, one quickly turning into a career, Carl had decided to shop for nicer clothing than the original hand-me-downs George had found. Those had been fine in the beginning, but he wanted to look his best when he met Bertha Troyer.

He had gone alone to shop for clothes. George was not exactly the best-dressed man he'd ever met. In fact, his mentor rarely seemed aware that he was wearing clothes at all. Carl had watched other people and seen how they were dressed and planned exactly what he wanted to buy.

A pair of sharply creased khakis, a dark blue polo, nicely polished dress shoes, and a good haircut was Carl's outfit of choice. The only full-length mirror in the church was the one in the women's bathroom, but since he cleaned it anyway, he felt comfortable in checking himself over there. Not a hair was out of place, nor was there a loose thread.

He'd lost about twenty pounds and shed the puffiness he'd gained while eating the cheap, carbohydrate-heavy prison food. He had worked outdoors with Shadow every day for weeks, and it showed in tanned, healthy skin and a trim body. He might be sixty-two, but he was fit and strong.

In his pocket was something he'd chosen with great care—a small pocket watch. Plain, of course, but beautifully made. George had assured him that although Amish women never wore jewelry, a nice pocket watch would be acceptable and appreciated. Carl was proud of the lovely satin-lined velvet box it came in, too. It seemed like such a small thing to do for Bertha as a thank-you, but at least it was something.

He also had a present for Anna, who had forgiven him so easily in the vet's office that day. He'd found it at Sol's in Berlin, which had interesting gifts. It had caught his eye because it was a piggy bank in the shape of a gray cat that looked almost exactly like the one Anna had offered to let him pet.

Carl decided to take Shadow with him as well. The dog was so well-behaved now that he went with him anywhere dogs were allowed. Besides that, he was proud of Shadow and wanted to show him off.

And last of all, he'd polished his truck until he could see himself in the surface.

"Let's go, boy!" he said to Shadow. "It's time."

And it *was* time. There were things he wanted and needed to say.

He just hoped that the little girl in the pink dress, who had grown into a cop with hard eyes, would not be there.

Chapter Forty-Six

Rachel was using part of the morning to clean out her car—a sharp, little red Mustang she adored—which was starting to feel a little inappropriate for a mom. Especially with a baby on the way. She hoped to shine it up, sell it, and purchase something more along the lines of a used minivan.

She was vacuuming the backseat, while Bobby helped by wiping down the dash, when she felt a flutter directly beneath her heart—as though a tiny butterfly had unfurled its wings. She leaned against the car with one hand on her stomach, savoring the feeling of new life within her. She was eighteen weeks along, and the pregnancy hormones had definitely taken over.

This worried her because she was developing a desire she had never before experienced—to stay home and forget this whole law-enforcement gig she'd chosen—at least for a while.

Instead of watching for potential crimes as she walked about town, she tended to catch herself admiring hair bows and children's books in the store windows. She tired more easily these days and found herself daydreaming about what color to paint the bedroom that the baby would share with Bobby.

But with convicted killers being set free by parole boards all the time, how *could* she relax her vigil? How *could* she lay down her gun and pretend that everything and everyone around her was okay?

She couldn't. That was the answer. While another woman might go to a park and coo over her newborn, she knew she would always have one eye watching for illicit drug activity and checking her perimeter to make certain no one was lurking in the shadows.

The instinct to be vigilant and protective of those she loved would never leave her, nor did Rachel want it to. But still, she wouldn't mind letting someone else shoulder the responsibility of keeping Sugarcreek safe for a while. It would be nice to relax and revel in the experience of preparing for the birth of their child.

For the first time, in spite of her brave words to Joe about living an ordinary life, she wished he were still the rich man he was when they got married.

"Can I go play with Ezra when we get finished?" Bobby asked.

"You played with Ezra yesterday," Rachel said. "I don't want you to wear out your welcome."

"Then can I go play with Aunt Anna?"

Rachel hesitated and thought it over. "I think that would be okay. Just don't expect her to play hide-and-seek or go for a long walk or anything."

"I won't," Bobby said. "Can I take Candy Land with me?"

"She'd probably like that."

The other thing on Rachel's list today, which she was looking forward to, was looking at paint samples. Getting to dream about the new baby and the redecorating she wanted to do—without having an impatient six-year-old tugging at her—sounded like a marvelous idea.

When they arrived at the Sugar Haus, Bertha, Anna, and Lydia were all headed over to the new Amish schoolhouse.

"What's going on?" Rachel said.

"Now that it's August, and school will be starting soon, the women from church are getting together today to get the new building ready for the scholars," Bertha said. "The desks are being delivered later and we need to make certain the floor is swept and mopped."

"And the windows need to be washed and polished," Lydia volunteered.

"I'm a duster!" Anna proudly held up her dust cloth. "I dust goot!"

"What were you planning to do today, Rachel?" Bertha asked.

"I had hoped to go to Keim Lumber and look at paint samples, but I can come help if you want me to."

"Naomi and several others will be here," Bertha said. "We'll probably have more hands than we need."

"Is Ezra coming?" Bobby asked.

Lydia smiled. "I believe so. Would you like to stay and help us?"

"Can I, Rachel?" he asked.

"Of course," Rachel said. "I'll be back in a couple of hours."

Bertha and Lydia exchanged glances. "Take your time," Bertha said. "Take all day, if you need. Bobby will be fine. Go shop for baby things after you get your paint."

"I'll probably just help Joe work on getting the restaurant ready—but thanks."

Rachel was walking back to her car when Bertha's words about baby things jogged a memory.

In a corner of her aunts' attic was a large cedar chest holding her own baby clothes that her mother had carefully stored away. The cedar chest had sustained some smoke damage from the fire that destroyed the original Sugar Haus, but the chest itself had not been burned. It would be a pleasant task to sort through it and see if anything was salvageable. With Bobby well entertained for the next few hours, she mounted the steps to the attic.

Two hours later, when she came back downstairs, Rachel had been through every piece of clothing and wanted to keep most of it. She had also had a good cry over never having known the mother who had lovingly wrapped every piece of baby clothing in tissue and laid dried lavender blossoms between each layer. She washed away her tears at the kitchen sink, but as she was drying her face, she heard the sound of a pickup truck stopping in front of the house. She pulled the curtain back to see who it was.

She might not have recognized the man had it not been for the German shepherd mix that jumped out of the cab and followed him up the path. Carl Bateman had changed since she'd seen him at the veterinarian clinic. Then, he'd been poorly dressed and slightly hunched, as though trying to protect himself from the world.

Today he walked with confidence, and his clothing was impeccable. He was also carrying a lovely floral gift bag.

And that dog was beautiful.

His truck was about ten years old but well-kept. Sunlight danced on the polished surface. If she hadn't known the type of man he was, she would have been impressed.

But she *did* know who he was, and Rachel resented the fact that he was here. It felt…sacrilegious. How could he have the gall to set foot on the farm where her father had lived his happy childhood?

Now she realized that Carl might be the reason for the uneasy glance Bertha and Lydia had exchanged right before they encouraged her to take her time in coming back for Bobby.

Had they known Carl was coming today? With a frustrated sigh, she walked out onto the porch. She was so tired of thinking about this man. He nearly tripped when he saw her. It was apparent that he was not expecting her to be there.

"What do you want?" she asked.

She was on the porch. He was on the ground. It made it possible for her to look down on him. It was the first time she had ever looked straight into his face, and she noticed a scar beneath his left eye. *Probably from a fight in prison.*

Although it was obvious that he had tried to clean up and dress nicely for this visit or confrontation or whatever he was trying to accomplish—beneath the nice clothes, he was still a rough-looking man.

"I was hoping to meet Bertha," he said.

"Why?"

"I wanted to thank her."

"For what?"

He hesitated a moment and then he dug into his pocket. "I wanted to thank her for these." He held up a small packet of letters.

"She told me all about them. Every year on the anniversary of my father's murder."

"Yes." He seemed resigned to her anger. "Your father's murder."

"It takes a lot of nerve for you to come here."

"Yes. It did take a lot of nerve." He didn't flinch. "It took every bit of nerve I had, but I wanted to finally thank her face-to-face."

"I'll give her the message." Rachel turned to go inside.

"When is your baby due?" he asked.

She whirled and placed a protective hand on her stomach. At four-and-a-half months, she was showing some, but not all that much yet. "How did you know?"

"George told me. I'm happy you will have a child. He says you have a good husband and a good marriage. I'm glad. I worried about you… afterward."

"You want me to believe that you actually cared about what you had done? Or felt remorse for it?" She felt herself starting to tremble.

"I'd give anything if I could go back and undo what I did."

"I don't buy it," she said. "Although it's remarkable how skilled ex-cons can become at manipulating other people's emotions. I'm sure you're a master at it." There was a porch column close by and she reached out to steady herself against it. "But you can't manipulate me. I know exactly who you are, and I deeply resent the fact that you are trying to worm your way into my aunts' lives. How dare you..."

"Rachel!" It was Bertha's voice.

Rachel had been so intent on what she was saying that she had not seen Bertha hurrying over from the school with Anna and Bobby. Her son had a half-eaten sandwich in his hand. Evidently someone had brought lunch and shared it with him.

"Bobby, go get in your mother's car," Bertha said.

"Can I pet the doggie first?" Bobby squatted down and offered Shadow the rest of his sandwich, which the dog delicately took from his hand. "What's his name?" he asked.

"Shadow," Carl said.

"That's a funny name. Why did you call him that?"

"Because I found him hiding in the shadows of a Dumpster. He was trying to find food. We've been friends ever since."

"Go get in the car," Rachel said. "Now."

Bobby, hearing the steel in Rachel's voice, did not hesitate any longer. They all stood frozen in place until Bobby closed the car door and they knew their voices would at least be muffled.

"You must be Carl. I am Bertha. You are welcome in my home. Lydia is still helping at the school, but she has some pastries waiting for us in the kitchen. I will make coffee and we will talk. Come. Your dog may stay on the porch. Rachel, you have said enough. Carl is my guest. I believe it would be best if you take Bobby home now."

Carl gave a command and the dog positioned itself near the door, where it appeared to stand guard.

Tears stung Rachel's eyes from frustration and embarrassment over Bertha's rebuke. Carl gave an apologetic shrug of his shoulders and followed Bertha onto the porch. Rachel choked back her emotions and tried to present a calm face to Bobby as she climbed into the car.

Unfortunately, the floaty feeling was suddenly back. Her heart hurt so badly that her mind apparently wanted to shut down again.

"Is everything okay?" the little boy asked.

With a great effort, Rachel fought the feeling away. She took several deep breaths and tried to find a pleasant subject to talk about. It was important for Bobby not to think she was upset or mad. The little guy was just too sensitive to allow him to know how she was feeling.

"Did you enjoy seeing the new schoolhouse today?" she asked.

"Uh-huh. I wish I could go to school there with Ezra," he said. "Can I?"

"Englisch children are not allowed." Rachel started the car. "Only little Amish boys and girls."

"I wish I were Amish." Bobby crossed his arms and pushed out his lower lip. "Then I could go too."

"But you wouldn't be able to watch cartoons anymore if you were Amish."

"I don't care."

Bobby's petulance did not last long. By the time they got to the restaurant, he was chattering about what he wanted for lunch and a tree swing his daddy had promised to build—once the restaurant was finished.

Innocent. Trusting. Loving. As forgiving of the people around him as Anna.

"He said he was sorry."

Rachel wished she could be like a child again. Even Jesus had talked about it and said people needed to change and become like little children in order to enter the kingdom of heaven.

But she could not. She just couldn't. Her innocence and trust had been stripped away on her eleventh birthday as she watched her father bleed out on the floor of the bank—put there by the same man who was no doubt enjoying one of Lydia's pastries right now.

"He said he was sorry."

"Sorry" was an easy word to say if one had everything to gain and nothing to lose by saying it. That was something Anna would never understand. Just like Anna would never understand that there was true evil in the world and sometimes that evil pretended to be good.

No matter how much Rachel wished she could make everyone happy by dropping her suspicions and resentment—she just couldn't.

Chapter Forty-Seven

It certainly hadn't been the reception he'd envisioned, once he saw that Rachel was there, but Carl was not surprised by the force of Bertha's will when she asked her niece to leave. Any woman who could have deliberately chosen to forgive the man who had killed her brother had to have a will of steel.

Anna was sitting in a rocking chair on the porch, smiling up at him. "Boo!" she said.

"You are supposed to act afraid," Bertha whispered. "It's Anna's little joke."

Carl tried to do a good imitation of acting startled, but he didn't think he was very convincing because Anna seemed disappointed until he handed her the gift bag.

"I hope you like this," he said.

Her eyes grew round when she reached in and drew the little ceramic bank out of the bag. "Ooh! Gray Cat!"

"I hope you like it."

"What a lovely gift," Bertha said. "Anna, perhaps you could go search for some pennies to put in it."

"Danke!" Anna hugged the ceramic cat to her chest as she trundled off the porch and into the house. They followed her inside.

"That means 'thank you,'" Bertha said as they entered the kitchen. She pulled the percolator from the back of the woodstove where it had been kept warm and poured two cups of coffee. Then she brought a cloth-covered plate from the counter and placed it on the kitchen table. She lifted the cloth away and revealed a platter of delicate-looking pastries.

That's when Carl noticed that although Bertha appeared calm, her hands were shaking.

"Please sit." She laid a cloth napkin in front of him. "Eat. There is creamer and sugar on the table."

Instead of reaching for a pastry, he carefully laid the small bundle of letters on the table. They were stained and worn. It was obvious that they had been read and handled many times.

"The letters," Bertha said.

"They saved my life."

"I'm glad. The first one was very hard to write."

"I can imagine," he said.

"Can you?"

"Maybe not. I've never had a brother."

"I was several years older than Frank. He was more like my own child than my brother. We did not fuss at each other like siblings. Instead, I helped raise him."

"As you helped raise his daughter."

"Yes." He saw her weave slightly as she stood at the stove and realized what a toll this meeting was taking on her.

He rose to his feet and pulled out a chair. "Please," he said, "sit down. I'm afraid this is too hard for you. I can leave if you'd like."

"No, it is not too hard," Bertha disagreed. "It is just that I have rehearsed what I wanted to say to you so many times in my mind, and now that you are here everything seems...unreal. I am tired and my mind isn't working as well as I would like. I'm afraid I won't get my words right."

"I feel much the same way."

Bertha reached out and caressed the small stack of letters, apparently deep in thought. It was as though she were reliving in her mind the sacrifice it had taken to write each one.

"I've had so many conversations with you in my head over the years," Carl said. "At first, I didn't allow myself to believe that you had forgiven me. I thought it was just a gesture or something you did to feel good about yourself. I never expected to get a second letter or a third. As the years went on and the letters mounted up, I began to allow myself to believe that you meant what you wrote."

"I have learned a great deal over the years," Bertha said. "One thing I learned is that forgiveness doesn't come in an instant. There were times when I would hear our little Rachel crying in her sleep or, worse, screaming from yet another nightmare about a 'bad man'..."

Carl winced. This was not easy to listen to, but then, he had not expected this meeting to be easy.

"There were times when I, an Amish woman raised to believe in total nonviolence, wished I could hurt you for what you had done to our family."

Carl nodded, accepting the truth of her words.

"Instead," he said, "you wrote me letters about your farm animals and guests and how your vegetable garden was doing...always ending with the words that you forgave me."

Bertha nodded. "And after a while I discovered that it was true. Looking back, I sometimes wonder if in those first years I was being obedient to God's teaching or if I simply grew weary of carrying around the burden of hate. Sometimes hate feels so heavy that it is just easier to lay it down and walk away. Like I said, I have found forgiveness to be an ongoing journey of faith. It does not come all at once."

"I am grateful you chose to make that journey."

"I'm not sure I had a choice. Had I carried that load of hatred, I doubt I would be alive today to see Rachel's child born."

"I brought you a gift," Carl said. "It feels like such a small thing to do, but you gave me so much over the years. I wanted to have something nice to give you when we met. George said it would be okay."

Bertha cocked her head to one side and smiled. "Like Anna, I am not opposed to gifts."

He took the small package out of his pocket and handed it to her. He had paid the clerk extra to wrap it in silver wrapping paper with a tiny red ribbon.

"It's very pretty." She turned it this way and that, admiring it. "I wonder what it could be?"

She carefully unwrapped his gift and then opened the velvet box. When she saw the gold pocket watch lying there, she grinned. "Exactly what I needed! My old one is not keeping good time anymore. We were late to church last Sunday because of it."

She admired the small object in her hand. "It is already set to keep time."

"I had the jeweler do that," he said. "I hoped you would like it."

It had cost him a month's wages.

"I like it very much," Bertha said. "And to my great surprise, I like you. I was prepared to forgive you, but I did not expect to like you. Now, you truly must eat some of Lydia's pastries or she will be upset. And while you eat, you must tell me about that good dog who did not try to follow you inside the house. How are you liking your new job at the clinic? Do you have any living relatives? How are things going with your parole officer? Do you like living inside a church? Your life has been so different than mine, and I have so many questions."

Thinking about it later, Carl realized how odd it was for an elderly Amish woman and a seasoned ex-con to find so much to discuss, but it appeared they had both been in each other's thoughts so often that they had many questions. Their conversation lasted much longer than either of them had expected.

Carl wanted to know more about Anna. He wanted to know about the fire and how they had lost their first B & B. The conversation went from the kitchen table to the porch swing, where he introduced Shadow to Bertha and showed off some of his tricks.

"This is a good skill you learned in prison," she said.

"It was the only good thing, but yes, I'm grateful for the training I got…and for George's friendship. It made all the difference."

"What man meant for evil, God turned into good," she said. "I've seen that happen so many times. You must come again to visit. I did not know if I would ever be able to say this—but now I can with a whole heart—you are welcome in our home, Carl Bateman."

Chapter Forty-Eight

"Aren't you going to church?" Joe asked.

"I don't think so," Rachel answered. "I went to the doctor yesterday afternoon with some mild cramps. She said it might be wise to take it easy for a day or two until they stopped."

"Why didn't you tell me last night?" He stood beside the bed with concern written on his face.

"You got home so late from working on the restaurant, and you were so tired. I didn't want to worry you unless I just had to."

"You're what, nineteen weeks now?"

Rachel nodded.

"Isn't the second trimester supposed to be the safest time in a pregnancy?"

"It is. The doctor also said that it is not unusual to have a little cramping as the baby grows and your body adjusts. The cramping stopped completely last night. I'm fine now. There's nothing I have to do today, so I'm just being extra cautious."

"Good." He sat down on the side of the bed beside her. "I was planning to leave right after early service to drive to Detroit to pick up that commercial grill Darren found on Craigslist. Do you want me to take Bobby with me?"

"He would hate being in the car that long. Would you mind taking him to Naomi's after the service? I called her last night and she's expecting him. She said they're hosting church today and he will be no bother with so many other children running around."

"Darren and I will drop him off on our way to Detroit."

"That would be helpful. Thank you. Darren is going with you?"

"Yes. He wanted to take a good look at that grill before we bought it."

Rachel pulled herself up against the headboard. "How are you going to pay for it? I thought you'd already nearly exhausted Darren's funds from the sale of the Lamborghini."

"I'll use my credit card."

"We're going into debt now for this venture?"

"I can't run a burger place without a good grill."

"I've been thinking about this for a while now." She pulled off her wedding and engagement rings and handed them to him. "I don't know what you paid for these, but if you want to sell them somewhere, I'd guess they would bring at least a few thousand to cover the grill and whatever other supplies you need."

"You're giving up your rings for the restaurant?" Joe said. "I can't ask you to do that."

Rachel's hands already felt freer. "I don't want to hurt your feelings, Joe, but we've been married long enough that I have to be honest about these rings. Grace might have wanted something like this, but I don't. I never did. I worry about losing something so valuable. I worry about catching them on something. I come from Plain people, and these rings embarrass me in front of my Amish friends."

"You've felt that way all this time?" Joe said.

"Yes. I'd much rather you turn them into cash you can use for the restaurant."

Joe looked down at the two rings he held in his hands.

"Don't you even want to keep the wedding band?"

"Frankly, no. It's encrusted with diamonds and you'll get more money if they're kept as a set. Bring me back what I really want, Joe—a plain, gold wedding band. The thinnest one you can find."

"If you're sure…"

"I'm very sure."

He rolled the rings around in the palm of his hand. "I'll probably only get half of what I paid, or less, but even that will make a huge difference." Leaning over, he kissed her. "Thank you, Rachel."

"Have a good trip, Joe."

"We will. You take care of yourself. Don't go anywhere and don't do anything. Just keep our baby safe."

In a few minutes, Bobby came in to say good-bye.

"I'm sorry you're sick," he said.

She brushed his hair off his forehead. "I'm not sick. I'm just being careful for the baby's sake."

"Daddy says the baby isn't done yet and needs to bake awhile longer."

"Kind of." It wasn't the analogy she would have chosen, but she supposed it would make sense to a six-year-old. "You have a good time with Ezra today. I'll miss you."

"I'll miss you too," he said.

"Bobby!" Joe called.

"Coming!" Bobby gave Rachel a kiss and hugged her neck. "I love you, Rachel."

"I love you too, son."

They had chosen to break the good news about the baby to Bobby earlier that week. She was glad they had waited. The little guy was so wound up and excited about having a brother or sister that she could already tell it was going to be a long four months of answering questions. In two days she was scheduled for an ultrasound to find out whether they would have a little girl or another boy.

As Bobby left the room, she noticed that he was in need of some new church clothes. His pants were a little too short and the long sleeves of his dress shirt were not quite long enough.

As she heard Joe's truck pulling out of the driveway, she reached for the notepad she kept by her side of the bed, wrote down "church clothes," and underscored it. Bobby was growing so fast.

It felt luxurious to be in bed, alone in her home, with plenty of time to daydream about the baby. She had some yogurt for breakfast then watched an old movie. She flipped through a parenting magazine and fixed a simple lunch of cheese and crackers. There were no more twinges or cramps, so she was pretty sure her body had gotten past whatever it was that had been going on inside her yesterday.

Actually, things were going pretty good. She was trying harder not to let Carl's existence affect her as much. Bertha was not happy with her right now, but she'd get over it eventually. Rachel knew she would because Bertha's forgiveness extended to her as well as others. And she and Joe were getting along pretty well too, although she still wasn't convinced that going into business with Darren was wise.

With the exception of Carl Bateman living only eighteen short miles away, her life was almost perfect.

There was a poem in one of Bobby's books about a little girl who was never satisfied. The recurring refrain was the little girl saying, "Almost perfect...but not quite." That refrain was running through Rachel's mind as she settled down for an afternoon nap. "Almost perfect..."

Perhaps if Carl made it through his mandatory year of living in Ohio, he'd move away and she could start feeling normal again. The fact that he lived so close dimmed the happiness she should be having.

With no responsibilities to tend to, she slept deep and hard until her cell rang.

Chapter Forty-Nine

"Rachel here." Years of police work had taught her how to come completely awake in an instant. She glanced at the clock. It was a little after five. She had been asleep for three hours.

"Rachel?" Naomi's voice was strained. "Do you have Bobby and Ezra with you?"

"No..." Fear clutched at Rachel's heart. "Don't you?"

"No. The church families left about a half hour ago. Luke was not feeling well, so he laid down. I was putting away some leftovers from lunch. Bobby and Ezra were playing in Ezra's pony cart, going up and down the driveway. I warned them not to go out into the road, but sometimes small boys do not listen well... I—I hoped you had come and gotten them for some reason."

"I would never take Ezra or Bobby without telling you first, Naomi." Rachel's hand started to tremble. She gripped the phone tighter.

"Could Joe have come and gotten them?"

"Joe is on his way to Detroit," Rachel answered. "He's probably already there by now. When did you first notice the boys were gone?"

"The pony brought the cart back empty a few minutes ago," Naomi said. "I saw it coming up the driveway without them."

"Could the boys just be playing in the barn or in one of the outbuildings?"

"I've been running everywhere, looking and calling for them, but I haven't heard an answer." Naomi's voice shook with fear. "Ezra would come to me if he heard me call. He would not pretend he did not hear me. My son is not that unkind, and neither is Bobby."

"I'll be right there." Rachel threw back the covers, threw on her clothes, and was out the door in under three minutes.

It was a fifteen-minute drive to Naomi and Luke's house. Rachel made it in ten. She kept telling herself that the two little boys would already be back at the house by the time she got there, with an explanation of how the pony had somehow gone home while they were someplace they shouldn't have been. There were some deep woods around Luke and Naomi's house, and boys loved to explore. Children also had no sense of time when they were playing.

She would have to be careful not to overreact if that was the situation. Bobby was energetic and curious but he was also kindhearted and would not knowingly frighten her or Naomi.

Joe would want to know, but she hated to scare him if this turned out to be nothing—which she was pretty sure it was. Nothing. It *had* to be nothing. Her mind shied away from anything else. Bobby and Ezra were fine. Of *course* they were fine. An empty pony cart did not mean anything. Children were often thoughtless, giving their parents unnecessary worries.

The moment Rachel drove in, she knew from the expression on Naomi's face that the boys had not shown up yet. Luke was standing on the porch, looking pale and supporting himself with the railing. She was disturbed by his changed appearance. She knew he was fighting leukemia, but he was sicker than she'd realized. He did not look strong enough to be out of bed.

"They are still gone?" Rachel slammed the door of the squad car and strode across Luke and Naomi's yard as she spoke.

"Yes," Luke answered. "We've looked everywhere."

"Did you go down to the creek?" Rachel asked. "If they were playing beside it, they might not hear your voice from here at the house. You know how little boys are once they start playing..."

"I've already checked the creek," Naomi said. "I've looked all over the house and barn. Luke called our bishop while you were on your way here. Samuel has begun to spread the word to our people. Many will be praying for our sons soon."

"How did you get hold of Samuel so quickly?"

"Samuel is a carpenter," Luke said. "He is allowed a basic cell phone for business calls, as are the other business owners in our church. This was decided at our last *Ordnung* meeting. Picture phones like the Englischers use are still forbidden, of course. One way or another, word will spread fast."

Rachel saw the pony and pony cart tied up at the hitching post near the Yoders' kitchen door. "Did you try to follow the wheel tracks?"

"I tried." Luke sounded as fatigued as he looked. "But many buggies have gone in and out of our road this morning. It is impossible. Church Sunday is not a good time to search for specific buggy tracks."

Rachel suddenly became aware of hoof beats and steel wheels spinning down the dry dirt road. She turned to look and saw a black open buggy coming faster than any sane Amish person would normally drive. The horse's head was low and it was running flat-out, its black coat glistening from sweat. The buggy almost tipped over as it swung into the driveway. Their young bishop, Samuel Yost, leaped out and came running toward the porch.

"The others are coming," he said. "My wife is calling those with telephones, and I sent the oldest Miller boy to get word to the rest. He has the fastest horse."

While Samuel questioned Naomi and Luke about the missing boys, Rachel called Joe.

"Hi, sweetheart!" His voice sounded happy and upbeat. "How is the most beautiful girl in the world doing today?"

"I'm at Naomi's and Luke's," she said. "We're having trouble finding Ezra and Bobby."

The cheerfulness fell from Joe's voice. "What do you mean, 'having trouble'?"

"They were driving Ezra's little pony cart and it came back to the house empty. Naomi's looked everywhere and called for the boys, but we haven't found them yet."

She heard Joe's ragged breathing as he tried to process what he had just heard.

"Have you looked in the outbuildings?"

"Naomi says she's looked everywhere."

There was another pause while Joe tried to absorb the terrifying news. "We're leaving. Now. I'll be there as soon as I can."

She knew that as upset as he was, he would take chances on the road as he tried to get home, things he wouldn't do under normal circumstances. "Please be careful."

Joe had already disconnected.

Nearly frantic with worry, she glanced up and saw a sight she would never forget for as long as she lived. A covered buggy had topped the rise and the horse was trotting toward the Yoder house—and a steady stream of buggies just like it were directly behind. Dozens of Amishmen on saddled horses were riding near the line of buggies. To have riders hunting on horseback for the children, in addition to those searching on foot, would be quite valuable, a conclusion to which she was certain the practical-thinking Amish had already arrived.

She tried to hold it together, to keep her panic in check and think calmly like the experienced cop she was, but as she watched these sober-faced Amish men and women, many still dressed in their black, formal church clothing, pouring into the driveway willing to help, tears of gratitude began rolling down her face, dripped off her chin and fell onto her shirt.

The physical and spiritual strength of her Amish neighbors was solidly behind her, and she was beyond grateful.

"Just tell us what to do," Peter Hochstetler said quietly beside her, pulling a clean, white handkerchief from a pocket inside his coat and handing it to her to mop up her tears. "We're ready."

***

Joe had been getting ready to help Darren load the commercial grill into the bed of his truck when Rachel's call rang in.

"Hold on," he told the phone while he took off his work gloves. The grill was used and needed a good cleaning as soon as they got it home, but it was functional and Darren had negotiated a good deal on it with the owner, who was closing down his restaurant. Craigslist could sometimes be very helpful. The owner, not so much. He kept telling them that new restaurants were doomed to failure.

Joe had dredged his phone out of his pocket and said hello, and then his world fell in.

His terror was so great that his brain couldn't entirely grasp the reality of what Rachel was saying. If he were still in LA, his first thought would be an abduction, but things like that didn't happen in Sugarcreek. Bobby was safe in Sugarcreek. Or at least Joe had thought he was.

This was probably nothing more than two little boys who had somehow gotten lost, he rationalized. There would be an explanation.

For now, all he knew was that he had to get back there. His son needed him, and his wife needed him too. Rachel might be a cop, but she was probably just as terrified.

"What's up?" Darren had been waiting and listening. "You look like you just saw a ghost."

"They can't find Bobby," Joe said. "We need to go."

Darren didn't hesitate. "I'll drive."

"Good. I don't trust myself right now."

As they pulled out of the parking lot of the old restaurant where they had purchased the grill, Joe was vaguely aware that his brother was trying to say something comforting, but he couldn't hear Darren over the roaring in his ears.

Chapter Fifty

Samuel, who knew all the people in his church by name and also the terrain of the area, took over forming and directing the various search parties. Rachel was grateful to give him the job. Everyone there was used to obeying their bishop. No one argued or questioned his judgment, just gave quick nods of affirmation as they received their assignments.

The people spread out, ready to search every dip and cranny of the fields and check behind every tree and clump of brush in the surrounding woods. Others were assigned to go over the outbuildings again and to leave nothing to chance. Naomi had been a terrified mother when she had run around opening doors and climbing into hay lofts. There was a chance she might have missed something.

Samuel instructed two of the younger women to do a thorough examination of Naomi's house and cellar. He told them to look beneath every bed, every staircase, and in every closet and trunk.

"Children like to play hide and seek," Samuel told the assembled group. "And sometimes if they think they might be in trouble for something, they can hide like quiet little mice."

Rachel wanted to believe that was all that had happened, but deep down she knew that although the bishop's words might be true for Ezra, they did not hold true for Bobby. The child simply couldn't sit still and be quiet for that long.

She wanted to start charging this way and that, frantically searching for her son, but there were already about a hundred men, women, and older teenagers doing exactly that, set on covering every inch of the surrounding countryside.

Was that another small cramp she felt?

It was probably nothing. She forced herself to calm down and think like the experienced cop she was. The first person she needed to call was Ed. His wisdom and advice would be invaluable in this situation. But when she called, his wife answered.

"Is Ed there, Sally?" Rachel said. "I really need to talk with him."

"Oh, I'm sorry, honey," she said. "Ed's up in Canada on a fishing trip. Don't you remember? I can't even get him on his cell phone. Is everything all right?"

"Not exactly," Rachel said, "but I can't talk right now. Thanks, Sally."

Her next call was to Nick. Sugarcreek was proud that it had been able to raise the funds to purchase that drug-sniffing dog. He was also skilled at finding lost people. The black Lab had already found one elderly Alzheimer's patient who had wandered off from a family picnic and gotten lost. There had been a write-up in *The Budget* about it.

When Nick answered, she told him what had happened and asked if he could bring Ranger out to try to track the children.

"I can't," Nick said.

She didn't understand. If there was ever a situation in which Ranger was meant to shine, it was this one. "Why not?"

"Ranger and I are at the vet's right now. Somebody tried to poison him."

"Are you serious?"

"Unfortunately, yes, I'm dead serious. I found some meat in his kennel that I hadn't put there. He must have realized something was wrong with it after a few bites, because he didn't eat all of it, but he got enough in him to do some damage. Doctor Mike opened up the clinic for us. He's pumping out Ranger's stomach right now."

Rachel was appalled. "Is he going to be okay?"

"I don't know," Nick said. "The doctor said the next twenty-four hours will tell us. Right now he's critical."

"Oh, Nick!" she said. "I'm so sorry."

"Not as sorry as the people who did this will be when I get hold of them," he said. "I love that dog."

"I know you do," Rachel said. "We all do."

"Hey, I gotta go, Rachel. It's Sunday and Doc doesn't have any staff in here today. He needs my help."

It seemed an odd coincidence that the only dog in the area with the training to help find the children was deliberately poisoned at the same time Bobby and Ezra went missing. The thought of what it might mean gave Rachel a chill.

Her two other local options were Kim, who would be little help, and the latest addition to their five-person force—a rookie with whom both she and Ed were unimpressed. She doubted he would do much except get in the way, and she didn't trust Kim not to put the whole thing on Facebook.

She knew there were three neighbors along this dirt road. They were farm people who lived much of their lives outdoors. There was a good chance that someone had seen the two little boys wandering off. Or— this thought was nearly more than she could face—perhaps they had seen an unfamiliar car or van.

"I'm going to go question the neighbors," she told Samuel. "Maybe one of them saw something."

"There is no need," Samuel said. "The neighbors on this road are all part of our church, and they are here. I've already asked them if they saw the boys. Most were inside their homes or in their barns doing chores. No one saw anything."

***

"If only I had not taken my eyes off the boys…," Naomi said. "I am so sorry."

"I would not have expected to have to watch them every minute, either." Rachel tried to comfort her friend in spite of wishing with all her heart that Naomi had not taken the time to put away the leftovers.

"I have trouble believing that our Ezra would leave our driveway when his mother told him not to," Luke said. "That is not like him."

"This is true." Naomi nodded. "He is an obedient child."

"It is probably your son's fault that they did not stay in the yard," Luke said. "I am sorry to have to say it, but I regret that we allowed your Bobby to be friends with our son. I was afraid that spending so much time with an Englisch child would not be good for Ezra, but Naomi's old friendship with you made her softhearted."

"Luke," Rachel said softly, "please don't blame Bobby for Ezra's disappearance."

"I do not blame your son; I blame you," Luke said. "If you had stayed at home where a mother belongs and raised your son yourself instead of bringing him over here so often, this would not have happened."

Rachel knew that Luke's words came from a place of fear and illness, but they stung no less. She looked at Naomi, hoping for support, but Naomi remained silent. Either she did not want to speak up and contradict her husband or she agreed with him.

It had never occurred to Rachel that either of them resented Bobby's boisterous presence in their lives—especially since she was paying them for watching him.

"I apologize, Luke," she said. "After we find the boys, I will not bring my son to visit again."

"Naomi," he said, "I need another pill. The pain is worse." Luke shuffled back inside with Naomi following.

Rachel could usually handle harsh words—she had heard plenty of them as a cop—but the combination of fear, mother guilt, her pregnancy, and Luke's accusations brought her tears dangerously close to the surface right when she could least afford to lose control.

On the far end of the porch, she saw that Samuel was trying to be the wise bishop he thought he should be. He sat on the porch swing with his head bowed, obviously praying, while men and women wearing black hats and bonnets dotted the countryside all around them, busily hunting for any sign of the boys.

Samuel finished his prayer and Rachel approached him.

"I'm grateful for all these people hunting for the boys," Rachel said, "and I'm thankful for your prayers...but I think it's time to stop assuming that the boys are simply lost. It's been more than enough time to search before calling the authorities. If this is an abduction, there are people much better trained than I am in dealing with it. I think we need to prepare for all possibilities."

"There are many bishops who would disagree with you," Samuel said. "We are slow to seek help outside of our own people."

"I am aware of that, Samuel."

"Are you also aware of the good reasons behind our reluctance?"

"Of course I am. Englisch people are fascinated with the Amish. The hint of an Amish child being lost or abducted will bring people out of the woodwork—and not necessarily in a good way."

"Then you understand why I hope to keep news of this situation confined within our church alone. Give my people a little more time to search."

"I'm sorry, Samuel, but I'll never forgive myself if I don't do everything within my power to find those children."

"There is much evil in the world these days," Samuel said. "Too many people like to prey on children who have unsuspecting parents."

At that moment, they heard a shout from far down the road. Samuel leaped to his feet. Rachel saw Peter running toward them with a small, black, flat-rimmed Amish hat in his hands.

"I found this in the ditch near the culvert." He handed the hat to her. "I think it might be Ezra's."

"Naomi!" Rachel yelled. "Peter found something."

Naomi came rushing out of the house. When she saw the hat, she grabbed it and clutched it to her as though it were her son instead of his hat that she clasped to her breast.

"I assume he was wearing this the last you saw him?" Rachel said.

"Either he or Bobby."

"Why would Bobby be wearing an Amish hat?"

"I did not tell you? Bobby spilled a glass of lemonade on himself during lunch. He was so sticky and miserable, I gave him a quick wash and dressed him in Ezra's spare clothes."

"And I'm guessing since he was dressed as Amish, he insisted on wearing a hat as well."

"Yes," Naomi said. "He seemed quite taken with himself, wearing Amish clothing. This is Ezra's old hat from last year. It's the one Bobby was wearing."

Rachel's stomach was in a knot. If someone had kidnapped Bobby and Ezra, she knew Bobby would resist. That was his nature. The hat could have been knocked off in some sort of scuffle. The discovery was especially ominous because she knew that if it had simply blown off his head while riding in the pony cart, he would have gone back and gotten it. That was also in his nature.

"What's this?" Naomi had discovered a note card stuck inside the hat. She brought it out, looked at it, and gasped, her eyes going wide.

"Let me see that." Rachel plucked the card out of her hand.

"What does it say?" Samuel asked.

"It is written in a heavy hand that no child could copy," Rachel said. "And it says, 'An eye for an eye.'"

Chapter Fifty-One

Naomi's cell phone, which was lying on a side table on the porch, began to ring. She looked at Rachel uncertainly.

"Go ahead and answer it," Rachel said.

Rachel hoped it was merely a relative or a friend who had heard about the children's disappearance. Then she saw the color drain from Naomi's face.

"Ezra!" Naomi cried. "Where *are* you?" Trembling, Naomi steadied herself by gripping the back of a chair. "Don't take the phone away. I want to talk to my son. Where is he? Who are you?"

Rachel's worst fears were confirmed.

Naomi paused for several heart-stopping seconds as she listened to a voice on the other end of the phone. "But we don't have that kind of money." Another long pause. "Yes, I understand."

Her hand dropped by her side and the phone slid to the floor. She stared at Rachel and Samuel as though in shock.

"Naomi?" Rachel said. "Talk to me."

Her friend continued to stare.

"Look at me!" Rachel gave her friend a shake. "Tell us who that was. What did they say?"

Naomi looked at her, and the terror Rachel saw there was so deep and wild that she took an involuntary step back.

"The man said he has both boys. He wants one million dollars apiece. If he doesn't get the money, he'll kill them. He said if we call in the police, he will kill them. If we call in the FBI, he will disappear and make our children disappear as well. He said we will never know where their bodies are buried unless we do everything he says."

Rachel went dizzy with fear, but then her fear was replaced with anger. If she could put her hands on that kidnapper right now, she would gladly tear him apart with her bare hands—pregnant or not.

"Doesn't he already know I'm a cop?" Rachel asked. "How did he expect me not to find out about this? I'm Bobby's mother!"

"Maybe Bobby didn't tell him," Naomi said. "He might think Bobby is Amish since they're dressed alike and Bobby's hair has grown nearly as long as Ezra's these past few weeks."

It's long because I didn't have time to cut it. Just like I didn't have time to buy new church clothes that fit him—or even notice that he needed new church clothes until this morning. The memory of his fragile-looking ankles and wrists sticking out of his too-short pants and too-short shirt felt like an accusation.

Such a good little boy with such a kind heart. He'd been so patient with all his parents' busyness. He had tried to fit his little life around the things they were doing. Why hadn't she paid more attention?

"If he doesn't know who the boys are," Rachel said, "how did this man know your phone number?"

"Ezra might have given it to him. When Luke got sick and the church allowed me to carry a cell phone, I had Ezra memorize the number. I thought he might need to know it."

Luke staggered out the door. "Who was that on your phone?"

Naomi told him.

He would have fallen had Naomi not been standing close enough to grab him.

"This day has been too hard," Naomi said. She guided her husband to a porch chair and tucked an afghan around him, which he immediately threw off.

"I feel so useless," Luke fretted. "Why would anyone think we have money? We don't even own this farm. We're barely able to pay the rent on it."

"Did the caller say anything else?" Rachel asked.

"When I told him we don't have that kind of money, he laughed and said we should make our bishop draw it from the helping fund the bishops are in charge of, the Amish Helping Fund."

"That's strange. It must be someone who knows at least a little about the Amish culture, to know that fund exists," Rachel said. "What did he sound like?"

"He had a gravelly voice, like someone who has smoked too many cigarettes."

"Did you hear any background noise?" Rachel asked.

"Now that you mention it, I did hear something strange," Naomi mused. "A silly voice saying silly Englisch words over and over."

"Could you make out any of them?"

"Yes, but they didn't make any sense. Something about a sponge and pants?" Naomi said. "I don't think I heard it right."

"SpongeBob SquarePants?"

"Yes, that's right," Naomi said. "Is that important?"

"It's a kids' TV show. Wherever the boys are, it sounds like they are watching cartoons."

"A home or a hotel," Samuel said. "They've settled in somewhere. The boys have been gone, what? About an hour?"

"Maybe a little longer," Rachel said. "We don't know how long they were missing before Naomi noticed."

"So," Samuel said, "figuring sixty miles per hour, probably less on these roads, and deducting the time it would take to get the boys inside and the TV turned on…they are probably within forty miles of here. Maybe a lot less."

"Asking about the Amish Helping Fund bothers me," Rachel said. "Most outsiders don't know about that. Also, there is the 'eye for an eye' note. Are there any particularly disgruntled ex-Amish people you can think of who might do something like this? Someone who would like to get back at the church?"

"There are some ex-Amish who have a dislike for the church, but kidnapping? Our people wouldn't do this," Samuel said. "Even those who have left us. They might complain about the rules, but they would never do something this evil. Not our people."

"I have to get the FBI involved," Rachel said. "They have the training and the tools to deal with this. I don't."

"No!" Naomi said. "They will kill them if we do. You did not hear the man's voice. I did. He meant what he said."

"I agree with my wife," Luke said. "No police of any kind. It is too big of a risk."

"Let me call the bishops who are in charge of the Helping Fund," Samuel suggested. "Perhaps they will give us the money to ransom the children."

***

Joe had heard horror stories about the roads in Michigan, and he now knew why. They'd bounced over plenty of potholes as they neared Detroit. Now the highway was packed with cars and families making their way south after spending a long weekend at the tourist spots north of Detroit. Everyone was trying to get home in time to get up for work on Monday morning.

"I can't go any faster," Darren apologized.

"I know," Joe fretted. "But why did every person on the face of the planet have to decide to head the direction we're going? I should be with my wife, helping to hunt for my son."

"Uh-oh," Darren said.

"What?"

"Roadwork." Darren nodded at a sign they were passing as they neared Toledo. "They're going to force us down to one lane up ahead."

It was not Joe's intention for his fist to put a dent in the dash of his truck, but his body seemed to have developed a mind of its own.

"Breaking your hand isn't going to help find Bobby," Darren observed.

"No, but it makes me feel better."

Chapter Fifty-Two

....

"I won't wear that." Bobby stuck out his lower lip and crossed his arms over his chest. "You can't make me."

"I thought Amish kids would be easy," the man who had grabbed them said to the dark-haired woman. "I thought they'd do anything we told them to."

The man's name was Junior and the dark-haired woman's name was Greta. Junior was big. Even bigger than Daddy, although Bobby was pretty sure Daddy could still beat him up. Junior had a shaved head, a lot of muscles, some interesting tattoos of pretty girls, and a loud voice. Greta was small and talked like a mouse. They were brother and sister, and Bobby was pretty sure they didn't like each other very much right now.

"They're usually very obedient," she said. "At least the ones I've known are. The other little boy didn't make a peep when I cut his hair and put Englisch clothes on him."

"Well, this one is defective," Junior said. He raised his hand as though to strike him. "I bet I can make him obey, though."

"Don't!" She inserted herself between Junior and Bobby. "I said I'd help you get the money and I will, but you promised you wouldn't hurt the kids. They haven't done anything wrong."

Junior lowered his fist. "Do you think they'll come through with the money?"

"Two little Amish boys?" she said. "Of course they will."

"And they won't call the cops?"

"The Amish don't want anything to do with the police. You know that. You're the one who used to run with them when you were a kid. The church takes care of everything."

Bobby was not happy. First these people dragged him and Ezra out of the pony cart right after they'd finally gotten finished with church and lunch and were starting to have some real fun. Then they called Ezra's mommy and tried to scare her.

Something had made him wait to give his real name or Rachel's or his daddy's phone numbers. He had good reason to hold back information. He still remembered how his daddy had changed his name when they were running from the reporters after his mommy died. He had a feeling that it would not be smart to let Junior know who his daddy was.

If he hadn't been so little, he could have fought Junior. Instead, he told a lie. He told them the wrong name and said his mom and dad didn't have a telephone. Lying was wrong, but he had a feeling he needed to protect the information of who he belonged to, for now.

They were too stupid to realize he wasn't an Amish boy, and he liked knowing he had a secret from them. It made him feel like he had at least a little bit of control over what happened to him and Ezra.

"Now, sweetheart," the woman cajoled, "just put this nice little shirt on. We need for you to look Englisch for a while."

He glanced over at his friend. Ezra looked scared and funny in Englisch clothes and the bad haircut Greta had given him with her scissors.

"I'm Amish. I don't want to wear Englisch clothes!" Bobby was so frustrated that he started shouting.

"You little brat," Junior said. "You'll wear the clothes or I'll know the reason why. Greta, make the kid pipe down. Someone might hear."

"People are used to hearing children yell around here. I babysit for

people, remember?"

"Where are those kids today?"

"I told the parents I was going on vacation," she said. "If this works out, we might be able to go on vacation permanently."

"I wish we'd picked a different kid," Junior grumbled. "It would have been a lot easier."

"Hey, this whole thing was your idea. You wanted to get back at Luke for what he did to us, remember? Picking some random kid wouldn't have worked."

She struggled to remove Bobby's suspenders.

At that, he set up a scream so loud and shrill that Junior and Ezra covered their ears.

"Now that you have that out of your system," Greta said sternly, "we're going to put a T-shirt on you."

"It has a nice picture of Donald Duck on it," Junior offered.

"This kid doesn't know who Donald Duck is," Greta said. From the sound of her voice, it was obvious that her nerves were getting a little frayed, and Bobby was glad. "He's Amish. They don't let their kids watch TV."

Bobby knew very well who Donald Duck was. Sometimes he and his daddy talked to each other in silly Donald Duck voices. Daddy could do it better than him, but he was getting pretty good at it too. Still, he had a feeling it might be best to keep that bit of information from them also.

As the woman tried to maneuver the colorful T-shirt over his head, he set up another howl. Bobby wasn't happy. And he was hungry. And he didn't like these people or the smell of their house. He wanted his daddy and Rachel and he wanted a peanut butter sandwich. Right now. And he did *not* want to wear this T-shirt. Ezra's mommy had given him the Amish clothes to wear. She had made them herself, just like she did all of Ezra's clothes. They smelled like her, and that smell was comforting, and he had no intention of taking them off.

As he fought and twisted and screamed over not wearing the T-shirt, Ezra, who had been standing there wide-eyed, had finally had enough. He began to cry.

"Now we got one brat screaming and the other one bawling," Junior said. "I thought you knew how to deal with kids."

"If you think you can do a better job, you're welcome to try." Greta sat back with a sigh of frustration. Bobby immediately pulled the Donald Duck T-shirt up over his head and threw it onto the floor.

"What am I supposed to do with him?" Junior said.

"Make him change his clothes," she said. "My nerves are shot. I'm going for a walk. I'll take the good one with me. You worry about the brat."

"Okay...," Junior said doubtfully. "What if someone sees him with you?"

"That's why I wanted them to wear Englisch clothes. People are going to be looking for two little Amish boys, not Englisch."

"I'll make this one behave."

"Just remember, if something goes wrong, the better shape these kids are in, the easier the cops will go on us," she said. "Don't leave any marks on him."

"You've always been too soft," Junior said.

Greta grabbed Ezra's hand. "Come on."

Ezra worriedly looked back over his shoulder at Bobby as Greta pulled him outside and closed the door. Bobby had felt relatively safe as long as Greta was there, but with Junior he wasn't sure how far the man would go, and he didn't want to find out.

When Junior turned back around to deal with him, Bobby was already dressed in the Donald Duck T-shirt and stiff blue jeans that were too big for him, and he was sitting on the couch with his short legs sticking straight out, obediently watching television.

"That's more like it!" Junior growled. "You'd better not get off that couch until Greta gets back if you know what's good for you."

Bobby knew what was good for him. He stared at SpongeBob and didn't move. For the first time in his life he was thoroughly sick of television.

Chapter Fifty-Three

Carl had discovered a great place to take Shadow for a walk. It was an old railroad bed that had been converted to a hiking trail. The trailhead was not too far from the old part of town, just over the hill from the historic Hotel Millersburg. He loved taking Shadow for long walks there. It was a beautiful trail and went on for miles in either direction.

If he turned left on the trail, he could walk all the way to Killbuck if he wanted to, passing Walmart, which had an access place in the back of the parking lot.

If he turned right at the Millersburg trailhead, he could walk all the way to Holmesville, or even the rest of the way to Fredericksburg, although he had never attempted to hike that far yet. He doubted that having the freedom to take long, uninterrupted walks without looking at razor wire and having to watch his back every second would ever grow old.

Peggy closed her office on Sundays, so after he'd put the hymnbooks and Bibles away after services and straightened the church auditorium, he was completely free to take Shadow for a long walk.

The trail was paved, and bicyclists as well as hikers and runners used it. Every now and then a horse and buggy would trot by, the riders enjoying a drive with no threat of being run over by cars, which were strictly forbidden. It was an amazing place, and Carl was grateful to have discovered it.

A woman in a gray sweater walked toward them from one of the small side paths that intersected the larger trail. She was gripping a child's hand. Her head was down, and long hair covered her face. The child had a bad haircut and ill-fitting clothes, and he looked at Carl with frightened eyes.

Carl did not like the look on the child's face, but he did not know what to do about it. After all, he didn't know the reason behind the fright. Perhaps the child had been chastised for some infraction of his mother's rules.

She was so deep in thought that she didn't see him until she was almost upon him. When she glanced up, she looked vaguely familiar to him, but he couldn't place her. He nodded to be polite, but she turned and disappeared down the side path, pulling the child behind her.

There was a slight breeze then and Shadow sniffed the air, whined, and tugged at the leash. He looked back at Carl as though trying to tell him that they needed to go investigate that situation.

"None of our business, boy," Carl said. "Let's keep going."

Shadow kept looking back over his shoulder at the child, as though puzzled about something. It was odd behavior for his dog, but there was nothing he could do about it. It wasn't as though he was on easy speaking terms with anyone in law enforcement. Going up to a Millersburg cop and saying that he and his dog had a funny feeling about a child could be easily misunderstood.

When a man was still this fresh out of prison, it was wise to fly beneath cop radar even if he was doing nothing wrong.

Chapter Fifty-Four

"This is bad for us," Bobby said. "We aren't supposed to watch programs like this. They are too violent. My daddy says so."

"Shut up, kid," Junior said, peering around him. Big Time Wrestling was on, and the sweaty men wrestled and grunted and pounded each other. "Just sit still and watch TV like your friend."

"He isn't supposed to be watching this either," Bobby insisted. "You should turn it off and play games with us or read us a book."

"You have got to be kidding." Junior actually chuckled. "Greta can play games with you when she gets up from her nap—if she wants to. You gave her a headache."

"And all you've done is feed us potato chips and pop," Bobby continued to complain. "My stomach hurts. I want a peanut-butter sandwich and so does Ezra."

Ezra glanced at him in surprise when he heard his name but then turned his attention back to the television. The child was mesmerized. He had never seen such a spectacle.

"My daddy and mommy are going to be so mad at you for doing this," Bobby said. "Just you wait."

"Yeah?" Junior laughed. "And what are your parents going to do? Pray for me? That's a real threat there."

For a moment, Bobby was tempted to tell Junior what he knew—that Rachel would be looking everywhere to find him and she wouldn't give up until she did. He wanted to tell this mean man that Rachel carried a gun and was so good with it that Daddy had found trophies up in the attic. But something told him that it was best if he continued to pretend to be Amish. It probably wasn't a good idea to tell Junior that his mommy was a cop and his daddy was big and strong and famous.

Instead, he went to the door and tried the knob. "I'm going home."

"Oh, you are, are you?" Junior said.

Bobby rattled the doorknob again.

"It's dark outside. There's nothing out there except trees," Junior said. "You wouldn't be able to find your way home even if I let you go."

"I'd rather be lost than here with you!" Bobby said.

"Not when a coyote decides to eat you," Junior said. "They have big teeth and yellow eyes, and they're out there just waiting for a juicy little boy to try to escape."

That gave Bobby pause. He was pretty sure Junior was just trying to scare him, but he didn't think it would be wise to test it. There *were* coyotes in the area. He had heard Aunt Bertha and Aunt Lydia talking about them.

"How long do we have to stay here?" Bobby plopped himself back down in front of the television and crossed his arms.

"Until some nice Amish people bring us a whole lot of money. Then I plan to never see your face again, or his." Junior said. "Hey, I gotta go to the can. You rug rats better still be sitting here when I get back."

Bobby could feel tears welling up in his eyes but kept his head turned away so Junior wouldn't see them. He didn't want Junior to think he was a baby.

After Junior left the room, Bobby wiped his tears away and went back to the door. He tried again to get out, only this time he tried really hard. He remembered Rachel telling him that if someone ever managed to steal him, his job was to try to escape and not give up.

"You need to be good," Ezra said in Pennsylvania Dutch. "You should not be a bad boy and talk back to him like that. You should be more respectful. If we do what they say, I think they will let us go."

"I don't want to be respectful," Bobby said. "I want to get out of here."

"You heard Junior. There are coyotes out there. They will eat you."

"Junior is a coyote." Bobby gave up on the locked door, gave it a kick, and then started working on opening one of the windows. It was stuck, and he wasn't strong enough to unstick it. "He's a bad man. I'd rather get eaten by a coyote than stay here with him."

"He'll come back and catch you trying to get out the window," Ezra said. "You need to get back here and sit down quick."

Junior walked back into the room and heard the two little boys talking to each other in Pennsylvania Deutsch. "What are you two saying? Get away from that window! Come back here and sit down before I swat your behind."

Bobby obeyed. He came back and sat, but he let Junior know he wasn't happy by glaring at him over his shoulder every now and then as he watched the two sweaty men wrestle and fight.

"I want to watch cartoons," he said.

"Well, I don't."

"Well, I do."

"Are you sure you're Amish?" Junior narrowed his eyes at him.

Bobby rattled off a string of Pennsylvania Deutsch, telling Junior that he was nothing but an old, ugly, stinky coyote. Ezra giggled.

Junior narrowed his eyes at Bobby. "What did you say?"

"I told Ezra a joke."

Greta came through the doorway, rubbing her eyes. "Your turn," she said. "I'll keep watch for a while."

"Good," Junior said. "This kid is giving *me* a headache now."

"We're not supposed to watch things like this," Bobby said. "And I want a peanut-butter-and-jelly sandwich. Ezra wants one too, don't you?"

"Well, it's obvious he's scared to death of us," Junior said. "Obedient Amish child, my foot! This one is as bad as any Englisch kid I've ever seen."

"Calm down." Greta changed the channel and a blue train engine took over the screen. "I've got some peanut butter."

"We don't have to do this, you know," Junior said. "We don't have to feed them or listen to this one's mouth. I could tie them up, put duct tape on their mouths, have some peace and quiet, and get some sleep. Tomorrow is going to be a long day and we need to be sharp in order to do the exchange."

"I'm not going to starve these kids or tie them up." She put her hands on her hips. "A little TV time won't do these kids any harm, and tomorrow night they'll go back to their parents. No harm, no foul. Just you and me and enough money to live on for the rest of our lives."

"Their church better come through with the money."

"Trust me, they'll come through with it. And they won't hardly miss it."

She left for a few minutes and came back with peanut-butter-and-jelly sandwiches for both children.

"Danke," Ezra said politely.

"You used red jelly." Bobby couldn't help himself. He was unhappy and needed to complain. "I only like purple jelly."

"That's all I have," she said. "And you're lucky to get that."

"I don't like red jelly." He threw the sandwich onto the floor. "And I don't like you."

She rolled her eyes at Junior. "You're the one who decided to grab this one. Thanks a lot."

"How was I to know?" Junior shrugged. "They all look alike to me. All I wanted to do was take Luke Yoder's kid. How was I to know he'd have a friend with him?"

"I'm beginning to wish we'd never started this. Setting hay bales on fire and letting cattle loose is one thing. Kidnapping is another."

"Messing with those people was fun. They deserve it after what they did to our sister."

"Well, there is definitely something defective with this one. I've never seen an Amish child act like this."

"Go get some duct tape," Junior said.

"Go cool off. We get the money and we hand over the children—in as good a shape as we got them. Period. Now pick that sandwich up!" she said to Bobby. "And I don't want to hear another word from you."

Silently, and with every movement screaming rebellion, Bobby picked up the sandwich and threw it into the overflowing trash can. He would rather go hungry than give these people the satisfaction of seeing him eat it.

He sat back down on the floor close beside Ezra.

"Please don't make them any angrier," Ezra whispered in their private language. "I'm afraid of what they will do to us."

"Don't worry. Rachel will find us."

"How do you know? Maybe she can't."

"Because she said she would. And if Rachel says she will, I know she will, because she always keeps her word."

"Just be a good boy," Ezra warned. "If we're nice, I think they'll let us go when they get the money."

Bobby didn't answer. He had absolutely no intention of being a good boy.

Chapter Fifty-Five

Samuel called off the search party, but few Amish people went home. Instead, most of the men waited in the yard and on the porch, ready to help in any way they could. Some of the women quietly brought out the leftovers that Naomi had been putting away when the boys were taken.

Those neighbors closest to the Yoders' went home and brought back loaves of bread to slice for sandwiches and anything else they had that could be easily eaten. Fresh coffee was made. Dishes were washed and set out to be used again and again.

Their mere presence was a source of comfort. The sound of the quiet murmuring of concern enveloped Rachel and helped keep her from screaming in her frustration and fear.

And then her cell phone rang and everyone's heads turned her way.

"Rachel!" Bertha's voice came over her cell phone loud and clear. "Why did you not tell us that Bobby is missing!"

"I've had my hands full," Rachel said. "How did you find out?"

"The Amish grapevine, of course!" Bertha said. "And in all this time you could not make one short phone call to us?"

"I didn't want to worry you."

"Ach! That is like those foolish people who do not pray because they do not want to bother the Lord with their troubles. I will call a driver and we will be right over."

"No, Aunt Bertha, you know how Anna is about Bobby. I don't think knowing he might be in danger would be good for her heart."

"You are right. I have another idea. Carl Bateman told me last week that he has begun training that smart dog of his for search-and-rescue. It was Doctor Peggy's idea. Perhaps he should bring Shadow and see if he can track the boys."

"That wouldn't do any good, I'm afraid."

"And why is that?"

"They've been kidnapped. Stolen out of Ezra's pony cart and carried away in some sort of vehicle."

"How do you know this?"

"The kidnapper called. He wants one million dollars for each boy."

"They want a million dollars for our Bobby? Will you and Joe give it to them?"

"Joe and I don't have it, Aunt Bertha. Not even close."

"Nor do Luke and Naomi."

"I know," Rachel said. "But right now I would do anything to get Bobby back."

"Then we will sell the farm. We have been offered more than that for it in the past. Perhaps Luke and Naomi's people can find the money to ransom Ezra."

In spite of the turmoil and terror she was going through, Rachel's heart melted at the old woman's words. That place meant the world to Bertha, but not more to her than Bobby. Bertha would rather go home-less than risk the life of that little boy, and so would she. Rachel's annoy-ance with Bertha over those yearly letters to Carl seemed childish right now.

"Don't do anything yet..."

"The bishops want to talk with you," Samuel said, interrupting.

"I have to go, Aunt Bertha," Rachel said. "I'll call you when I know more."

Samuel took her to the back bedroom where the bishops had been meeting privately. Luke was there, along with Naomi.

"We've decided that we cannot afford to give the kidnappers the money," the oldest bishop said. "Even though there are many millions of dollars in the fund."

Rachel was stunned. The bishop was Reuben Miller. In addition to being a trustee of the fund, he also happened to be Naomi's father...and Ezra's grandfather.

"But the money is there!" Naomi said. "What do you mean, you can't afford to do this, *Daett*?"

"If we give it to the kidnappers, word will get out," Reuben said. "If other *Englisch* people find out how easily we gave in to the kidnapper's demands, it would be open season on all of our Amish children. None of them would ever be safe again."

"But Ezra is your grandchild," Naomi pleaded. "The man said he would kill the children if we didn't pay."

"We will continue to pray that he will not," the bishop said. "But we cannot save two lives at the expense of all the other lives we are responsible for. I am Ezra's grandfather and my heart is breaking, but I must make decisions that are best for all, not just for my own family."

Rachel knew that these were not empty words. In the Amish mindset, an individual's needs were important but never more important than the needs of their community.

"I'm calling in the FBI," Rachel said. "I've waited long enough."

"You can't," Naomi insisted. "You know what the kidnapper said would happen to our children if we got the authorities involved."

"The FBI have teams that are specialists in abduction. The nearest office is in Cleveland. It is only an hour and a half away. I can have a team here in two or three hours."

"And you have new information to give these specialists?" Reuben

Miller asked. "Something that will help them find the children?"

"Not yet."

"I think even the FBI must find a thread to tug on before they can start the unraveling."

"Of course."

"They will need to ask many questions of many people. I am thinking that FBI agents will not blend well into our community. They will drive government cars. They will be noticed, and quickly. Word spreads fast."

Which would put the children at greater risk.

"Please, Rachel," Naomi begged, "the kidnapper said he would know if we called in the police. You can't do this."

"I have to do what I think is best for my son."

"Even if it puts *my* son in danger?"

"You seem to think these people will keep their word, Naomi," Rachel said. "They are criminals. They will say anything. Apart from the slim hope we have if we gave into their demands for money—which we can't do—our only chance is to find them before the deadline. I don't have the resources to do that by myself. I have to call in help."

"And once again, our people will be on the front page of every newspaper and on all the TV and radio stations," Reuben said. "There will be newspeople from all over the world camped on our doorsteps, much like our Nickle Mine Amish friends had to deal with. How will that help our children? The kidnapper might feel that with so much attention, he has no option but to kill them as he threatened to do. We must keep Englisch out of this at all costs."

"But," Samuel's voice was strained, "maybe if we *did* have the money to give them...maybe they *would* keep their word. Those children..."

"We must not fight among ourselves," Reuben said sternly. "We will continue to pray and ask for the Lord's wisdom and intervention. He is our greatest hope. Let us bow our heads as we pray for the children's deliverance."

Everyone bowed their heads in prayer, but Rachel's mind was whirling. She desperately needed to *do* something. But what was the wisest course of action? If she *did* call the FBI and the kidnapper found out and did what he threatened to do, she would never forgive herself. If she *didn't* call the FBI and things went bad, she would never forgive herself either.

A small cramp hit. Not a bad one, though. She ignored it and allowed her mind to keep circling the things they knew so far.

The cell phone that the kidnapper had called from was a disposable one that couldn't be traced. They were probably still in the vicinity—at least close enough to come get the ransom money. Apparently no one had seen anything or anyone on the road. Whoever had taken the children had at least a general knowledge of the Amish culture. Perhaps he was a local. The kidnapper had not yet called her, which either meant that Bobby had chosen not to give them the number, or...wasn't able to.

Her knees nearly buckled at the thought, but she forced herself to stay upright.

There was a scripture that kept running through her mind, the one where Jesus said it was better for a person to have a millstone tied to his neck and thrown into a lake than to hurt a child. She and Jesus definitely saw eye to eye on that issue!

Reuben cleared his throat, a signal that the group's silent prayer was over. Daniel Hershberger, the other trustee of the fund, spoke up.

"During prayer, I thought of something else. If we were to pay the ransom but allowed no outsiders to know what happened, it might not become general knowledge after all. The kidnapper could not advertise what he's done for fear of being caught. I think it might be our best chance of preserving the boys' lives without endangering our other children."

"I do not agree with this way of thinking," Reuben said. "We cannot, as a people, justify paying criminals for their crimes."

"Daett!" Naomi cried. "Why are you being so stubborn? This is my son!"

"And my beloved grandson." Reuben was holding himself so rigidly, it looked as if he might break apart at any moment. "But as a bishop, I must do what I think is best. People know we are a nonviolent people, but we must not appear so weak-willed that we will give in to every ransom request an Englischer makes of us. If we were to do that, no Amish man, woman, or child would be safe from this kind of evil."

***

Naomi ran from the room and Luke followed slowly. Bishop Reuben watched his daughter depart with a look of great grief on his face.

With nothing more to say, Rachel left the room as well. As a cop, she knew that Reuben had made a good decision. As a mother, she wanted to toss the two million dollars at the kidnapper and take the children and run.

"I wish I had a photograph of our son," Rachel heard Naomi murmuring inside the kitchen doorway. "Just in case we never see him again."

"And you think this would give you comfort?" Luke said. "I do not see that the Englisch, who have many photos, grieve any less because of it."

Rachel overheard this and went into the kitchen. "You don't have any photos of Ezra?"

"Luke feels strongly about obeying our church's rule against photographs," Naomi said. "And I have honored his wishes."

"I think I have one," Rachel said. "I took it one day when they were playing outside. I honestly didn't even think about the restrictions. They were just two little boys having fun, and I wanted to remember that day."

"Can I see it?" Naomi asked eagerly.

Rachel took out her cell phone and scrolled through the photos until she found the one she was looking for. "Here."

Naomi stared longingly at her son's face. "I'm so glad you have this. I will have a picture of him in case we never get the boys back."

"We'll get them back," Rachel said. "When they call back to give you instructions for the drop-off, don't tell them we can't get the money. Tell them we are working on it."

"Won't that be a lie?" Naomi said.

Rachel thought of Bertha's offer to sell their farm for the ransom money. "Not entirely. The important thing is to find out exactly where the meeting place is and when they want us there. Then I'll scout it out and begin to prepare."

She went out to her car, climbed in, and punched the phone number for the FBI. Regardless of what Naomi, Luke, and the bishops thought, she knew it was past time to call in the cavalry. She could not do this alone.

***

Carl was giving Shadow a bath in the large metal tub used to dump dirty mop water. Shadow had enjoyed his walk on the trail a little too much. He had discovered a raccoon carcass before Carl realized what he was into.

His dog seemed almost human at times, practically able to read Carl's thoughts and anticipate his needs. Other times Shadow was all dog, and being all dog meant rolling in things that left most humans holding their nose and shaking their head in bewilderment. Why would anything want to smell like a rotting animal? Shadow definitely needed a bath before he could sleep in Carl's room tonight.

Shadow was unrepentant. He stood in the soapy water with a goofy grin on his face, happily allowing Carl to hose him down in the janitor's tub.

Carl was still troubled by the expression on the face of the child who had been with that woman in the gray sweater. It kept nagging him, but he kept reminding himself that there was nothing he could do about it.

He lifted Shadow, dripping, out of the tub and then stood back with a towel in front of him like a shield while the dog shook his fur and water flew around the room.

"Feel better now, Shadow?" George said as he walked into the room.

"Oh, hi, George," Carl said. "My dog did something dumb. Why do they think it's a good idea to roll in dead, smelly things?"

George shrugged. "I don't know. Why do people roll around in dead, smelly things?"

"They don't." Carl was puzzled. "Do they?"

"If you spent much time on my side of the desk while people told me their secrets, it would seem that way."

"What's up?" Carl knelt down and started rubbing Shadow's fur with the towel. "You usually don't come around this late—especially on a Sunday after you've worked all day."

"I got a call from Bertha," George said. "She has terrible news."

"Is Anna okay?" Carl asked. "I know they've all been worried about her health."

"It isn't Anna. It's Rachel's son, Bobby. He and a little Amish friend have been kidnapped. They're being held for two million dollars' ransom."

Carl stopped rubbing Shadow's fur and stood up. "What did you say?" He couldn't believe his ears.

"You heard me right. Bobby and a friend have been kidnapped and are being held for ransom. Bertha thought you and Shadow might be able to help since you've been training him for search and rescue. She just found out that the Sugarcreek police dog was poisoned by someone—probably the kidnapper—and is still fighting for his life."

"You know I would do anything for Bertha, but I've only been training Shadow for a few weeks. It takes at least a year to train a search-and-rescue dog. He's smart, but I don't think Shadow is even close to being able to do that effectively."

"That's what I was afraid of," George said. "I'll go tell her."

"Wait—did you say there was another child with Bobby?" Carl asked.

"Ezra Yoder. Bobby's best friend."

"What does he look like?"

"I don't think I've ever seen him."

"Would anyone have a picture?"

"Probably not. The child is Amish...but I can call Rachel and find out."

"If so, I'd really like to take a look at it," Carl said. "I noticed something on the trail late this afternoon and I'm still uneasy about it. It might not have anything to do with this, but I'd feel better if I could take a look at the face of that child."

"I'll call her right now," George said. "Bertha gave me Rachel's cell phone number a few minutes ago just in case you could help."

Carl let Shadow's bathwater drain out of the tub while he waited for George to finish.

A few moments later George handed him his cell phone, and Carl stared into the happier face of the child he had seen on the trail. The child was wearing Amish clothing in the photograph and his hair was longer, but Carl had spent the past twenty years reading faces for his own survival, and he was absolutely certain it was the same child.

"Tell Rachel I need to talk to her," Carl said.

Chapter Fifty-Six

"I could walk home faster than we're going," Joe complained.

"Someone in a body cast using a walker could get home faster than we're going," Darren said.

They were creeping along a few inches at a time, sitting completely still more often than not. They had only managed to travel about a mile in the past half hour. Horns honked for no apparent reason except the drivers' frustrations.

"I wish we could find a side road and get out of this mess," Darren said.

"Do you see what I see?" Joe said.

A woman driver had exited her sedan, and with both the front door and the back door propped open for a modicum of privacy, she was relieving herself in the middle of the highway. After adjusting her clothing, she closed the rear door and climbed back into her car.

"She's pregnant," Joe said. "No wonder. It was hard on Grace when she was pregnant. She had to go about every fifteen minutes."

"How are things between you and Rachel?"

"Why do you ask?"

"I don't know. Things have felt a little strained when I'm at your place. Is she annoyed with me for getting you involved in the restaurant?"

"Probably, but the main issue at home is her obsession with her dad's killer. One of Rachel's greatest qualities is her ability to hyperfocus when she needs to. It's also a weakness because if something is bothering her, she can't just shrug it off and go on with her life. She and Bertha are barely speaking these days because Bertha had the audacity to forgive the man and write to him."

"Sounds tough."

"And since Rachel went through that weird stress-amnesia thing where she didn't even recognize me, I keep wondering whether it will happen again if she's under enough pressure. The last thing she needed was to have to face this kidnapping thing by herself."

"I've been praying for those two little boys while I've been driving."

"You have?" Joe was surprised. Faith was not Darren's strong suit.

"Yes, I have. Dad's teachings didn't fall on entirely deaf ears. I love my nephew, and I don't want anything to happen to him."

"Thank you," Joe said. "Now if only we could get off this road!"

"We might be in luck." Darren sat up straighter. "There's a sign way up ahead pointing to what I think might be an alternate route. I see other cars getting off there. Check your GPS to make certain, and I'll start trying to worm my way over."

***

"Where are you, Joe?" Rachel asked as she sped toward Millersburg to meet with—of all people—Carl Bateman. "How soon do you think you're going to get here?"

"We got stuck in one of the longest traffic jams I've ever experienced, and that's coming from a man who lived in LA. We're finally making decent time now, so if nothing else happens, I should be there soon. Is there any word on Bobby? Did you call the FBI yet?"

"I did. Naomi and Luke were fighting me on it. They think if we bring in outsiders, this thing will go public and it will get the children killed. Right now I'm checking out a new lead. If it turns out to be nothing, I'll be glad for any help the FBI can give me."

"What's the new lead?"

"Carl Bateman thinks he saw Ezra dressed in Englisch clothes and walking beside some woman while he had Shadow on the Holmes County Trail this afternoon."

"How would Carl know what Ezra looks like?"

"I had a picture in my cell phone and sent it to George. Carl says he's positive it's the same child."

"Do you believe him?"

"Of course not. I don't believe a word that man says. But I have to check on it. I have nothing else. The thing that bothers me is that it seems awfully coincidental that *Carl* just happened to see a child who resembles Ezra."

"We don't exactly live in a metropolitan area, Rachel," Joe said. "It's rare for us *not* to see people we know every time we go out. You've run into Carl twice now by accident. Why would it be impossible for Carl to have seen Ezra?"

"Call me paranoid, but I'm wondering if this might be a setup. Maybe Carl was in on the kidnapping."

"But why would he kidnap Bobby? He's been working with that vet, building a life, making friends… Why on earth would he risk going back to jail when he has all that?"

"I hope you're right."

"Be careful, Rachel. I'll be there soon."

She knew from experience that she was close to the end of her phone service. For some weird reason, she always had cell service in Sugarcreek, but somewhere between Walnut Creek and Berlin her phone always stopped getting a signal.

"I have to hang up now, Joe. I'm going to lose service soon."

He didn't respond, and she realized she was talking into a dead phone.

***

Bertha was grateful not to have guests right now. Finding out Bobby was missing had been harder on her than anyone knew. Her spirit moaned with anguish. Not knowing what was happening to Bobby, not knowing if he was being hurt or hungry and scared…she didn't think she could stand it if anything happened to that child.

Everyone thought she was strong, but her carefully guarded secret was that she was not at all strong. She was just more determined than most to hide her pain and heartache.

Tonight she was not strong enough to pretend strength that she did not have anymore. She needed to take refuge, emotional and physical. Her favorite choice, like Anna's, was their old barn. It had been a friend to her since childhood. It was as though it had sheltered so many animals for so long that it had become a sort of living thing that wrapped its arms around her and gave her sanctuary when her heart was troubled.

Eli's sons had stacked several bales of hay in her barn. She seated herself on one now.

She often came out here for solace. Bertha was frequently sad, although she hid it well. Her life had been useful and productive, but it had not been happy. And her lack of happiness was not something she allowed herself to dwell upon.

Happiness was simply not something Amish people thought to pursue. Obedience, faithfulness, personal discipline, honesty, hard work—yes. These were Amish attributes, the things they tried to instill in their children. Happiness was seen as a by-product of all these virtues, not a goal in and of itself.

All her life Bertha had tried to live up to those biblical standards, but the by-product of happiness still eluded her. She knew the reason, of course. It was her deepest secret. No one had ever known.

To her abiding shame, she had once allowed herself to fall in love with another woman's husband.

In those days Bertha had been quite beautiful.

His wife was not.

He was a good man, but she could tell that he was sorely tempted. So was she.

She supposed that in today's self-centered culture of the Englisch, there would have been little thought about the devastation a love affair might cause. A divorce would have probably followed. Their happiness would have superseded all other considerations. It seemed as though in recent years, individual happiness had become society's most sacred cow.

But Bertha had been raised in a different culture and a different time. Rather than destroy his family, not to mention her own soul, she fled.

She had never cared for another man. Instead, she had poured her life into good works and other people. Perhaps it had made her a more brittle person, but she had done the best she could. She found as she grew older that she did not regret the lack of a husband in her life as much as she regretted not having had a houseful of children.

Now, faced with the possibility of losing the child she loved above all others, she did not think she could bear it. It made her want to hurt the people who had done such a thing to those two innocent children.

Maybe there was such evil in the world that the Englisch were right to create tools to combat it after all. Maybe she had been too hard on Rachel for her choice of a job.

Bertha shook her head. What was she thinking? She had lived a lifetime believing and participating in a life of nonviolence. Jesus had said to turn the other cheek. She had believed she could do so...until it came to protecting Bobby.

Looking at the hay scattered beneath her feet, she tried to allow the peaceful feeling she always got in this barn to infuse her soul—but it did not come. In fact, she wasn't sure she would ever feel anything close to peace again unless Bobby and Ezra came back unharmed.

She knew that she needed to pray like she had never prayed before—a powerful prayer that would wake the heavens and draw God's attention.

Staring up into the hand-hewn timbers of the old barn, she tried. She really did try. But the only words that came were a heart-wrenching, "Lord, please have mercy!"

After that, she broke down crying. The old woman whom everyone thought so strong was helpless in the face of this evil, and all she could do was cry.

Chapter Fifty-Seven

Rachel pulled into the dark church parking lot in Millersburg. George and Carl were waiting outside for her with Shadow. Seeing Carl made her stomach churn yet again. She was grateful for George's presence.

She did not waste time with pleasantries. "Tell me everything," she said. "Do it quickly, but leave nothing out."

Carl told her every detail, quickly and concisely. Had he been any other civilian, she might have been impressed.

"That's an awful lot for someone to take in so quickly and to remember with such detail," Rachel said.

"When you've spent twenty years in prison trying to stay alive, you develop the ability to read details about people fast because it can save your life."

"Right," she said. "I'd like to search the church before we go."

"Why?" George said. "I thought you'd want to get on the trail as soon as you got here."

"It's because she wants to check to make sure I don't have the children hidden away in the church," Carl said.

"Why would she think that?" George was genuinely puzzled, but Carl was not.

"She thinks I might have done something to them out of spite."

"Rachel!" George sounded genuinely shocked.

"She's right," Carl said. "There are people twisted enough to do something like that. The fact that I'm the one who saw Ezra feels too easy. A good cop would ask to search the church."

"Coincidences are often God's way of making things happen," George said.

"May I look inside, or will I have to get a search warrant?" Rachel said.

"Goodness!" George unlocked the church door and held it open for her. "No, you don't have to get a search warrant."

Rachel had been inside the building a couple of times before—the last time being when she had confronted Carl. The first thing she noticed now about the church was the smell. The musty odor that clung to most old churches, including this one, was gone. Instead, it smelled clean. The floors shone. The oak pews gleamed. Hints of lemon and beeswax were in the air.

None of the inside doors were locked. She opened one that said Janitor's Closet and was surprised to see a neatly made cot, a handful of clothes hanging on hooks, and at least a dozen books on dogs and animal care on top of a shelf beside a small TV. One straight-backed chair served as a bedside table where an alarm clock sat. It was clean and Spartan. Not what she had expected.

It was not a particularly large church, so it did not take her long to search. Once she finished, she was convinced that there was no place Carl could have hidden the children. She had, however, taken the opportunity to use the restroom. There had been another small cramp as she did so. She ignored it. Willed it away. There was no other choice.

"I had to make sure," she said as she emerged from the building and rejoined the men. "If your dog is ready, let's go."

"You realize he's not completely trained for this yet," Carl warned. "If he doesn't find anything, I'll at least try to point out where the woman was walking. I hope that will be enough."

"It's better than nothing," Rachel said. "Which is what I have right now."

"Do you have that piece of Ezra's clothing I asked you to bring?"

"Naomi gave me these." She handed him two small black socks. "He wore them all day yesterday."

Carl took the socks, gave Shadow a sniff, and then walked ahead of them with the dog on the leash. Rachel switched on her flashlight and illuminated the path.

"The place where we saw the woman was a mile or two down the trail," Carl said.

"Were there other people on the trail?" George asked.

"A few. Not many. I nodded when I saw her and kept going, but I couldn't get that kid's scared face out of my mind. When I looked back, they had disappeared."

Rachel was trying hard to continue to hate this man, but his concern for those children seemed so real that she was finding it difficult. Besides, at the moment she was a whole lot less interested in worrying about her own twenty-year-old emotional wounds than in saving her son's life.

"I've been thinking ever since I heard about the kidnapping," Carl said as they walked. "Dogs have the ability to remember smells for a long time. When I first went to Bertha's, Bobby gave Shadow part of his sandwich. He petted and made over Shadow until Rachel told him to go sit in the car."

"I remember. He did spend time with your dog," Rachel said. "Why does Shadow have his nose in the air? I thought tracking dogs were supposed to keep their noses close to the ground."

"There's a difference between tracking and air-scenting," Carl explained. "Dogs who are trained to track tend to stay ground-oriented, but German shepherds are natural air-scenters. Humans shed about forty thousand dead skin cells per minute. Each cell carries vapor and bacteria that represents the unique scent of a person. I'm thinking some of Bobby's scent lingered on Ezra. My theory is that the reason Shadow kept looking back at the woman and child was because he caught Bobby's scent but knew Bobby wasn't there. He was trying to figure out why that little boy had Bobby's smell on him."

***

"Have you seen Anna?" Lydia asked as Bertha came in from the barn.

"No," Bertha said. "Have you looked in her room?"

"Yes," Lydia said. "Anna overheard some of your conversation with Rachel. After you left, Anna started pestering me to tell her where Bobby was. She was getting more and more insistent, so I finally told her as much as I thought she could comprehend. She acted like she understood and went up to her room. I knew she was upset, so I made some hot chocolate and took it to her. But by the time I got there, she was gone. I thought maybe she'd decided to find you."

"How much do you think she really understood about the kidnapping?"

"I don't know, but I'm afraid that Anna can't deal with something like this. I hope she didn't try to go look for him herself."

"It's dark outside and Anna doesn't like the dark," Bertha said. "Remember, when Anna is upset, sometimes she hides. We probably just need to look in her favorite hiding places."

Chapter Fifty-Eight

The darker it got outside, the more fidgety Bobby became. He did not know why his dad and Rachel had not come to get him yet, but he was tired of sitting in this living room that smelled like mildew and cat. He was tired of Junior and Greta. And he was getting a little bit tired of Ezra, who thought if he did everything just the way Junior and Greta told him to, everything would be okay.

Bobby was beginning to regret his temper tantrum over the peanut-butter sandwich. After he threw it into the garbage, nothing else had been offered to them.

Bobby sat very still beside Ezra and pretended to watch the silly television shopping program that Greta was watching. He hoped that if he didn't bother her, maybe she would go to sleep. Grown-ups did that sometimes—doze in front of the TV. Junior was already snoring in the bed in the next room.

He could hardly wait for Greta to fall asleep too, because he kept thinking about something he had seen.

The front door he had tried to open was locked, and he didn't know how to unlock it. All he knew was that when he twisted the handle, it wouldn't open. He was pretty sure the back door would be locked too, although they had not let him wander that far out of sight. He might be able to get out through one of the windows, but not without making a lot of noise, and even then he wasn't sure he could do it. But in the little bathroom off the kitchen, he had seen something that gave him hope.

There was one window in that bathroom. It was high and small, but it was cranked open. It was covered with a screen, but Bobby thought he could get past the screen. If the drop outside wasn't too much, he might be able to leave.

The idea of escaping was almost as scary as staying. As it grew darker he was getting more and more afraid to escape, because he didn't know what was outside that bathroom window. He thought there might be bad things out there—but he definitely *knew* there were bad things in here!

When Greta made him go throw the sandwich from the floor into the garbage, he had done so. Fortunately, she had also left the small peanut butter knife laying on the counter. With her and Junior paying attention to the television or their plans, he managed to put the knife in his pants pocket. It was not a long knife, but a short stubby one like what Rachel placed beside the butter dish.

The knife might be helpful in getting that bathroom screen off. Or it might not. All he knew was that he wanted to get out of there and it might be a handy tool.

He would have no chance of escaping if Greta or Junior were awake, but he had seen Greta's head nodding and thought she might go to sleep for real before long. If he was patient, there might be a chance.

Bobby curled up into a ball on the floor as far away from the couch as he could get without making her suspicious and then pretended to go to sleep. If she ever really fell asleep, he would climb on top of the bathroom sink and try to crawl out the little open window. He was pretty sure the bathroom door had a lock, and he would use it. That should give him a little bit of time if they woke up and came looking for him.

***

Lydia and Bertha were growing frantic. They had worn themselves out searching every corner of the barn, the sheds, the nearby pasture, the attic, every room, every closet, under every bed, and the culvert beneath the driveway. Bertha even went to Cousin Eli's house next door, and he joined in the search. They had to face the facts. Anna was gone.

Bertha considered calling Rachel, but she didn't know that Rachel could do much under the circumstances. Then Lydia hurried out to where Bertha and Eli were standing on the porch, discussing what to do next.

"I was just in Anna's room again."

"And?" Bertha asked.

"Her little Gray Cat bank is gone!"

***

When Bobby awoke, he was angry at himself for falling asleep. He wished he knew what time it was, but he could not tell time yet. He had been practicing with Bertha recently, but he still hadn't mastered it. He did know that it was late, because Greta had fallen asleep on the couch and pulled a cover over herself. Her mouth was hanging open and making a "pup-pup-pup" sound. Junior was still snoring in the next room. Ezra was asleep too. The TV was still on and some woman was talking about jewelry and trying to convince people to buy a big, fancy ring that Bobby thought was ugly.

If he was going to try to go out that little bathroom window, now was the time. He was frightened but utterly determined. He sat up slowly and waited to see whether anyone noticed. Ezra stirred beside him. Bobby didn't know if it would be a good thing or a bad thing if his friend woke up. He wasn't sure Ezra would be happy with his plan. His fear was that Ezra might try to stop him.

There had been a couple of times in the past when Ezra had told on him to Naomi, when Bobby had been getting into some small mischief he didn't think was all that bad. Ezra was his friend, but he didn't trust him not to go tattling to Greta.

Bobby laid back down and pretended to go to sleep. He waited to make sure Ezra was deeply asleep again and then he began to creep a few inches at a time across the carpet. Greta stirred a couple of times and Bobby immediately lay in perfect stillness.

It took all he had in him to go slowly, when what he wanted to do was get up and run toward the bathroom and try to claw his way out the window as fast as he could—but he knew if he didn't move slowly he might wake someone up, and that was something he could not afford to do.

As Bobby inched his way across the carpet, he went over his plan in his mind…just like Daddy said he always did before a big game. When he finally made it to the bathroom, he would lock the door behind him, climb up on the sink, try to punch out that window screen…

As he lay on the floor, almost afraid to breathe, staring through the kitchen table legs, he saw something that he had not noticed earlier. There, at the bottom of the door that led outside from the kitchen, was a tiny door covered with some sort of black material. It was big enough for maybe a cat or a small dog to come through. He knew exactly what it was because Aunt Anna's Gray Cat had one.

If he could squeeze through it, he wouldn't have to climb out the scary window or make any noise going into the bathroom and locking the door. If he could squeeze through, he could go get help. Maybe he could find Rachel and Daddy and they would come and take care of these bad people—although he hoped they didn't hurt Greta. She had been nicer to them than her brother.

He carefully wiggled toward the little door. The linoleum kitchen floor was a lot easier to slide on than the dirty carpet. He was careful not to let his sneakers squeak as he pushed himself along.

Chapter Fifty-Nine

"What's a gray cat bank?" Eli asked.

"It's a piggy bank, except it's a shaped like a cat instead of a pig," Lydia explained. "Carl bought it for Anna. She's been putting stray change in it ever since. She loves going into the rooms after guests have left, hoping to find a dropped penny or two."

"Do you think she took it with her?" Bertha asked. "It had a good bit of change the last time she showed it to me. It can't be all that light."

"She must have overheard us talking about the ransom money and whether the bishops would decide to provide it," Lydia said.

"Anna can't grasp the concept of money values," Bertha explained to Eli. "She doesn't know the difference in value between a penny and a quarter and a hundred-dollar bill."

"But she likes to count things," Lydia added. "Yesterday she took all the money out of her bank and told me she had two hundred monies."

"So, to Anna," Eli said, "a piggy bank filled with pennies could seem as valuable as a million dollars."

"She went to ransom Bobby!" Bertha exclaimed. "But where?"

"Anna is a special child of God," Eli said. "He will look after her. He will not allow any harm to come to her."

"This has been an awful day," Bertha said, wringing her hands. "Bobby kidnapped, Anna missing... If only daylight would come."

As Rachel and George followed Carl and Shadow, she wondered if they were going on a wild-goose chase. Could this ex-prisoner possibly hold the key to finding Bobby? She'd been a cop for way too long to get her hopes up.

On the other hand, as a cop she'd seen a few incredible strokes of luck lead to important captures. It would be incredibly lucky if Carl had happened upon Ezra earlier in the day. Of course, Bertha would attribute it to God's mercy rather than luck, and Rachel was okay with that too. She didn't care who or what got the credit as long as she got her son back.

Carl was right about one thing: someone who survived twenty years as a prisoner had well-honed instincts about people. Some got practically psychic in their ability to read people's facial expressions and body language. When it was a matter of life or death, one got really good at it or one got dead.

It could be that Carl was that good. Or he could be leading her on for spite or even just for the fun of it. She figured one outcome was about as possible as the other. She didn't trust him, but she had no choice. They had to check this out.

Up ahead Shadow was eager, pulling at the leash as though wanting to drag Carl down the trail. The man held firmly to the leash—well in control. Working two jobs must be agreeing with him. For a man in his sixties, he was in good shape. Without her gun, she would be no match for him and that dog if Carl tried to harm her.

Her heart ached to hold her son again. She wondered whether he was remembering the night when she had promised Bobby that if he ever ran away or got lost, she would find him If he was on the highest mountain, she would come for him. If he swam the deepest ocean, she would get a boat and go to him.

He had giggled and tried to come up with impossible situations, but she had meant it. She would do anything to get him back. Even if it meant following her father's killer down a dark path. If she didn't do everything she could and something happened to Bobby that she could have prevented, she would never forgive herself.

***

Bobby had no idea whether he could wiggle his way through that cat door. He was growing so fast that he had little sense of what size his body was. He thought he could do it, but he wasn't sure. The faint rustles his small body made as he shoved his head and shoulders through—one arm at a time—did not awaken his captors, although Greta's very fat cat did come in from the bedroom to investigate the person invading its personal doorway. Bobby heard it hop off the bed and then felt it stepping over his legs as he struggled to squirm through the hole.

Half in and half out, Bobby was terrified to hear the cat give a harsh meow. It sounded loud enough to awaken the household, and the fear gave him added strength to pull and push his way through. It would take a few seconds for Greta and her brother to wake up and get to the door to unlock it. That delay would give him time to run, and Bobby intended to run very fast.

The moment he felt his body clear the pet door, he jumped to his feet and ran. He did not wait to hear whether anyone was coming after him. He just ran and ran and ran, over the long grass and into the woods, until he tripped over a log and lay quiet, catching his breath, listening. He did not hear Greta or Junior coming after him yet. All he heard were his own gasps as he tried to suck in enough air to keep running, and then he ran some more even though the woods were very dark and very frightening.

He tried not to think about what things might be out in the woods that might want to eat him.

Finally, when Bobby could run no more, he slowed to a walk. The minute he did, something soft flew past him, brushing his legs, and he stifled a scream. Then it came back and began to twine around his legs, and he realized it was Greta's cat. At first Bobby was annoyed that it had followed him, but then he decided he was happy to have something following along that wouldn't try to eat him.

The next thing he had to do was get help. Before, when he and his first mommy had gone shopping in the city, she'd taught him that if he ever got lost or separated from her, he was supposed to talk to the first police officer he could find. She had worked with him until he memorized his name and phone number.

Thinking about his mommy brought tears to his eyes. He missed her so much, although he loved Rachel too. His daddy had told him that was okay, that it wasn't wrong to love Rachel and still love Mommy too. Then Daddy told him a secret—he felt the same way as Bobby. That made Bobby feel a lot better. If Daddy did something or felt something or said something, he knew it was right.

He wished Daddy were here now. Or Mommy. But most of all, he wished Rachel were here. Rachel carried a gun and arrested bad guys and put them in jail. That's what Bobby needed now, not someone to teach him his name or make him memorize his phone number. He didn't even need a daddy who could pitch and hit and catch a ball better than anyone in the world. He needed Rachel because he knew where some bad people were, and he wanted very much for her to put them in jail.

He had no idea where to find Rachel or which way to walk, except to continue going far, far away from the house where they had been keeping him. That house was a dangerous place.

Then he heard a bark and grew afraid again. When he had lived in LA, there had been a mean dog next door. He had seen that dog kill a baby rabbit with its big teeth. The dog he was hearing could be mean. He dropped to the ground again, behind a tree. He would be very still and hope the dog hadn't already heard him or smelled him.

301

Chapter Sixty

"I can't tell you exactly where it was now that it's dark," Carl said. "All I can say is that it was about a mile from the Millersburg trailhead when I saw the woman and child.

Suddenly the dog started dancing on his hind legs, pawing the air and barking.

Carl knelt and gave Shadow another whiff of one of Ezra's socks. "You got something, boy? You smell Ezra?" He unsnapped the leash and Shadow took off running into the woods.

"He definitely got wind of something," George said.

"Do you think it could be one of the boys?" Rachel was afraid to hope and yet started hoping in spite of herself.

"Maybe," Carl said as they headed into the woods right behind the dog. "Or it might be a rabbit. Or a female dog. Or someone's leftover sandwich. Shadow has good instincts. In time he might become a gifted tracker. But I can't guarantee him yet."

"He's better than nothing," she said.

"Wait a minute." Carl held still and put his hand behind his ear like her grandfather used to do. "Do you hear something?"

They all grew quiet and listened. Then she heard a faint sound—like a child trying hard not to cry but failing.

"Come on!" She plunged farther into the woods, crashing through the underbrush toward the sound.

"Don't you come any closer," Rachel heard a child say. "I have a knife!"

The voice was small, and it was filled with tears. It quivered slightly on the word "knife." And then there he stood—her brave son, shivering in the night air with a tear-streaked face, but with legs planted in a fighter's stance and a small butter knife clutched in his fist. He stared defiantly into the beam of her flashlight.

Bobby was safe.

She handed the flashlight to George, dropped to her knees, and held out her arms. "Oh, my child."

He blinked a couple of times before realizing that the person behind the flashlight beam had been Rachel. He dropped his little knife and ran into her arms. Now that he no longer had to stand his ground, he began sobbing with relief while he clung to her for dear life.

"I knew you'd come!" His voice was muffled with his face pressed against her neck. "I told Ezra you'd come for me. No matter what, you would come for me. I told him!"

"Where is Ezra?" Rachel asked.

"Back at the house," Bobby said. "They were all asleep when I left."

"Is he okay?"

"Yes. He wanted to go home, but he kinda liked watching TV."

Rachel felt her throat close up with gratitude. Both boys were unharmed—so far. One thing she had to avoid was the kidnappers turning Ezra into a hostage.

"Good boy!" Carl was ruffling Shadow's fur and giving him treats. "Good job!"

"Can I pet him?" Bobby asked.

"Sure thing."

Bobby gave Shadow a hug, and the dog licked his face. When Bobby let go, Shadow danced around all of them, happy about finding the child.

Rachel felt a little like dancing herself, but there was still work to be done and no time to waste.

"Tell me everything you can remember about the people who took you."

"I tried to fight them. I knew you and Daddy would want me to. But they were too big."

"I'm proud of you. Who are they?"

"Junior is big and he's not nice. I don't like him. Greta is his sister. She's not nice either, but she wouldn't let him hurt us. Greta had to take a nap because she has nerve problems, and Junior said I give her a headache."

Rachel choked back a laugh. She could relate. "What else? Think hard."

"They had a sister named Cynthia, but she died and now they're mad at Luke and all the other people at his church."

"Anything else you can remember?"

He frowned, concentrating. "Greta said they were going to move far away and she would never have to take care of other people's kids again."

Something pinged in the back of Rachel's mind. "Greta takes care of children?"

"Yeah. I guess so. She had toys and stuff there, but they were baby toys. I didn't want to play with them."

"Tell me about the house."

When Bobby finished describing the living situation, Rachel realized that she knew the exact farmhouse where the children had been kept, and she knew Greta.

"I delivered a warning to Greta two months ago," Rachel told George and Carl. "I was getting some complaints from parents. When I checked, there were definite violations of her in-home child-care facility. Greta didn't make the improvements that were needed and we had to shut her down. No wonder she was trying to raise some quick cash. I know exactly where this woman lives." She put her hands on Bobby's shoulders. "Do you think Ezra is in any danger right now?"

"Greta and Junior were asleep." Bobby was rubbing his own eyes. Now that he had abdicated his safety to Rachel, his exhaustion over the ordeal was apparent. "But if they wake up and find out I'm gone, they'll be really mad."

Rachel debated. "George," she said, "would you take Bobby back to the church?"

"If that's what you want me to do."

"I don't want to go with George," Bobby said. "I want to stay with you."

"Bobby," she said, "I need to get Ezra out of there, and I want to make sure you're safe while I do. Go back to the church with George and wait for me there, please. Okay?"

"Okay."

"Did you notice whether Junior or Greta have a gun?"

"A toy one," Bobby said.

"How do you know it was a toy?" she asked.

"Because he teased us with it. He acted like he was going to shoot Greta's cat, but when he pulled the trigger, it was just a black squirt gun. I told Ezra not to be afraid of it."

That was the information she needed. She was armed. It sounded like the kidnappers probably weren't. These two weren't professionals. Greta was nothing more than a woman who had tried to make some under-the-table cash by taking care of children and had done so badly. It was the brother who was the threat.

Rachel was trained for this. The kidnappers were not. It would probably be enough.

Carl stood there, waiting. He'd put Shadow back on the leash, which was wound around his wrist. "Tell me what you want me to do," he said.

"I don't want to involve a civilian in this, and I have to move fast. If Junior or Greta wake up and find Bobby missing, there might be repercussions. I need to get Ezra out of there, but I don't want to have to protect you too. Let's see if Shadow can find the way there, but then wait. I don't want you getting involved."

***

Lights came up the driveway as a pickup truck drove to the house. An Englisch neighbor helped Anna get down out of the truck.

"Yoo-hoo!" Anna called as Lydia and Bertha scrambled off the porch to go to her. "I'm home!"

Anna's clothing was dirty and disheveled, and there was straw clinging to her clothing. Her white prayer kapp sat askew on her head, but she clung tightly to the cat-shaped piggy bank in her hands.

"Where have you been?" Bertha was so distraught, she hardly knew whether to hug Anna or give her a shake. "You nearly frightened us out of our wits."

"She was in my barn tonight when I went out to check on one of my cows that I've been treating for mastitis," the man said. "I'm Rob Maddock. I run a dairy farm over near Ragersville."

"She walked all the way to Ragersville?" Bertha asked.

"It's only a few miles by the back roads," he said. "When I asked her where she was from, she said she lived with Lydia and Bertha. My wife bought a quilt from Lydia several years ago and remembered seeing Anna here. We thought about feeding her first, but we decided you were probably worried, so I brought her straight here."

"You have been very kind," Bertha said. "Thank you so much for bringing our sister back to us."

"She was no problem," he said. "Just gave me a little start when I walked into the barn and she rose up from a pile of straw and said, 'Boo!'"

"That's Anna's little joke," Bertha explained. "She's done that since she was a girl. We've never figured out why. I apologize for her scaring you."

"I fought in Korea," the elderly farmer said. "Finding an Amish woman in my barn wasn't scary, just a bit surprising."

Lydia went into the house and came out carrying a fresh loaf of homemade bread from the kitchen. "For your breakfast," she said to him gratefully.

"Thank you, ma'am," he said, taking the bread. Then he climbed back into his truck and headed home.

"What on earth were you thinking?" Bertha scolded Anna. "Why did you go away like that?"

"The bad people wanted money for Bobby. I have lots." She handed the piggy bank to Bertha. "But I couldn't find anybody to give it to."

Chapter Sixty-One

Neither Rachel nor Carl made small talk as Shadow led them the way Bobby had come. As they walked, Rachel checked her gun, making sure every chamber was loaded.

"I did not know your father," Carl said, "but I think any man would be proud to have you as a daughter."

There were several sharp retorts Rachel could have and would have made had he not just found her son.

"Thanks," she said. "I think we should be getting close. It can't be much farther if a six-year-old was able to walk it. Turn off your flashlight. I don't want them to look out the window and see lights coming."

With the flashlight off, she could see a faint house light up ahead. "Stay here," she instructed. "I'm going to see if I can tell from the outside where Ezra is located."

"Then what?"

"Then I'll call in the Millersburg police for backup and go after him."

***

The old farmhouse was so isolated that the inhabitants were apparently not in the habit of pulling the blinds. Lights were blazing from within the house, and it was easy to find a vantage point to see in. Ezra and Greta were in the living room.

Greta had her hands on her hips and was yelling at Ezra. The old windows were single-paned, and Rachel could hear most of the words. Greta was browbeating Ezra for Bobby's escape.

Ezra was cowering against a wall. Being yelled at was not something that happened in Naomi and Luke's house. Seeing that sweet child's fear infuriated Rachel.

It would be another hour before she could begin to expect the FBI. Still watching the house, she drew her cell phone out of her pocket and started to dial 911—until someone grabbed her by the shoulder and spun her around.

It was a large man, and he appeared very angry.

"Where did *you* come from?"

"You're Junior," she said.

"Yeah. And this is private property. Who are you, and what are you doing here?"

He was outside, Ezra was inside, and she had stupidly waited too long to call the Millersburg police. She took one step back and pulled her gun from where it nestled against the small of her back, training it on him. "Turn around and put your hands against that tree."

"Why?"

"Because the child who escaped is my son, and the little boy inside is my best friend's son."

"Huh! I *thought* there was something wrong with him. Never saw an Amish kid act that way."

"Turn around and put your hands against the tree."

"So you're the kid's mommy." Junior did not turn around, and he did not put his hands on the tree. "I'll bet you never even shot that thing before. What is it, your boyfriend's gun?"

At that moment, his sister came out onto the porch, firmly holding Ezra by his suspenders. "What's going on out here?"

"Greta," Rachel said, "bring Ezra over to me."

Before Greta could answer or comply, Rachel was hit by a cramp. It was mild and she could still function, but she bit her lip, trying to conceal the pain.

Unfortunately, Junior had heard her small gasp. "Something wrong?"

"Nothing's wrong," she said.

She didn't say anything else because she felt another cramp coming on. Dear God! Why now? Unless she was mistaken, something was going terribly wrong.

A sly grin crept over the man's face. "Not feeling so good, are we?"

"I'm fine."

And at that point, a cramp hit that was so severe, no matter how hard Rachel tried to fight, that it doubled her over where she stood, panting, with her hands on her knees. The gun dangled from one hand as she gasped for breath.

Junior approached her. She weakly waved the gun in his general direction. "Stay away."

Suddenly he was all business. "Get the rope, Greta."

"You'll never get away with this." Rachel was finally able to stand up straight. She took a deep breath, brought the gun back up—and then another cramp hit and she doubled again. What was going on with her body?

"You can hardly hold your head up, let alone shoot me. Hate to tell you this, but you aren't much of a threat."

A harder cramp hit, knocking the breath right out of her. Rachel grew dizzy from the pain. Never had she felt so vulnerable or so useless. Junior came over and plucked the weapon right out of her hand, and there wasn't one thing she could do to stop him.

Now, not only was she unable to save Ezra, but she was unable to save even herself. There was a heaviness in her abdomen she had never felt, and the worst pain she'd ever experienced kept ripping through her body.

"Tie her up," Junior growled at Greta. "We've got to get out of here. I don't know where that other kid is. He might bring somebody here."

"Please," Rachel gasped. "Please don't."

If they tied her up, she was afraid she would die from whatever was happening to her body and her unborn child.

"Sorry, sweetie." Greta approached her with a length of rope. "But he gets real mad if I don't do what he says."

"Don't do it," Rachel said. "Please. I'm pregnant!"

"I gotta," Greta said, beginning the process. "Like I said, he gets mad."

Rachel tried to fight as the other woman began to tie her hands, but the cramps were coming on hard and strong now and she could no longer stand up. Her knees buckled.

"Now hold still, honey. Don't make this difficult."

"I need a doctor," Rachel said. "Call an ambulance. Please, Greta. I won't press charges about the abduction and you won't face jail time if you'll just call an ambulance for me. Whatever you do, don't tie me up."

Before Greta could completely immobilize her, Rachel heard a voice.

"Leave her alone."

Rachel vaguely heard a gruff male voice through the blue-like pain she was experiencing. After she got through the next cramp, Rachel glanced up and saw Carl standing over her.

"And who are you, old man? Her grandfather?" Frustration and anger laced Junior's voice.

"Me? I'm the man who murdered her father." Carl stood with his fists clenched. "And I'm only going to warn you once...leave this woman alone. She's been through enough."

Rachel heard the sheer fury in Carl's voice as he shielded her from

Junior and Greta with his own body.

"*You* are warning *me*?" Junior, a big man in the prime of his life, started laughing. "What could you possibly do to me?"

Rachel, lay on the ground, her body convulsing. She bit the inside of her cheek until it bled as she tried to keep from screaming out in pain and fear.

She could hear Ezra sobbing, calling her name, begging Junior not to hurt her.

Then she heard a low whistle, and suddenly a heavy body exploded out of the woods and flew past her. She felt a moment of hope as she saw Carl's dog running as silently as his name and as deadly as a bullet, straight at Junior.

"Don't!" Carl yelled, as Junior raised the gun.

But then the Glock fired and caught the beautiful dog in midflight as he leaped. Shadow yelped in pain and fell to the ground. Carl roared with anger and went after Junior, who stood his ground with the gun now pointed at Carl.

That was when she knew that her father's killer was going to die, and in spite of her own fear and pain, she suddenly and desperately wanted him to live.

Chapter Sixty-Two

Darren skidded into the parking lot. The lights were on in the church. Joe jumped out of the car before it came to a full stop, ran up the church steps, and pounded on the door.

George opened it.

"Where's Rachel?" Joe said. "She said she was coming here. I haven't heard from her since."

"Are you Joe?"

"Yes."

"We found Bobby. Your son managed to escape. He's asleep in my office."

"My boy escaped?" Joe said. "Oh, thank God! Is he hurt in any way?"

"He was dirty, scared, and hungry when we got him, but he's not hurt."

"Where's Rachel?"

"She was planning to check out the house where Bobby was held. Ezra's still there."

"Is she alone, or did she call for backup?"

"Carl and his dog are with her. I don't know if she called anyone else."

"Show me where they are."

"Okay, but I don't want to leave the boy alone."

"Darren! Come here and stay with Bobby," Joe called as he strode across the parking lot. "George, get into the truck."

"It's only a couple of blocks to the trail," George volunteered, as he did what Joe said. "We could easily..."

His speech was cut short as Joe pressed the gas pedal and George's head was thrown back against the headrest.

"I know where the trail is," Joe said between gritted teeth. "And I don't intend to walk."

Joe swerved around the concrete barriers at the trailhead and drove straight onto the wide trail. He knew there was a rule against motorized vehicles on the trail, but right now Joe didn't care. He had a sick feeling in the pit of his stomach, and it kept getting stronger. His child was safe, praise God, but he had to get to Rachel. Something was wrong and he had to get to Rachel.

"Tell me when to stop," Joe said.

George looked out the passenger window for a few moments and then suddenly pointed to a gnarled oak tree on the right. "There! I remember that tree."

Joe stopped the truck and cut the lights. Then he and George got out of the truck and quietly and quickly made their way into the woods. The moon illuminated their path as George led him in the direction that Carl and Rachel had gone.

After a few moments, George knelt down and whispered, "There it is."

Joe dropped to his knees beside George and took in the scene. Directly in front of them was a farmhouse—and for a moment, Joe couldn't accept what he was seeing. Then it came became crystal-clear. The figure writhing on the ground was Rachel. Carl stood in front of her, talking to a man who was holding a gun. Ezra was crying and trying to get away from a woman who was holding him.

They heard a low whistle just as Joe started to charge in, but George held him back. "Look!"

A large, dark brown dog burst out of the woods and ran straight at the man who was holding a gun on Carl. There was a gun blast, and the dog crumpled mid-leap.

Joe's fingers dug deep into the dirt as he watched that courageous dog collapse.

***

In prison, in order to survive, Carl kept his anger carefully bottled up. He knew how to protect himself if necessary, but he didn't pick fights. He didn't make friends, and he tried not to make enemies—but in the depths of all that carefulness, his anger simmered.

When he got out, he kept the fires of his anger carefully stuffed deep, deep down as he tried to stitch together what shreds of life he still had left. He spoke softly and kindly to the patients who came to Doc Peggy's clinic. He made sure to have patience with the bumbling young staff members Peggy hired. He held back sharp words when he saw gum wrappers carelessly tossed onto the carpeted floor of the church auditorium he carefully maintained. If he was going to stay out of prison, it was imperative that he never, ever let his anger show.

Until now.

Now, with his beloved dog bleeding out on the ground, he no longer cared about restraining his volatile emotions. The rage Carl felt came out with a primal scream, and he charged Junior.

Junior raised the gun and pointed it at him.

Carl didn't care.

Then suddenly Junior's face took on a look of great surprise. His eyes rolled back in his head, the gun fell out of his hand, and he crumbled to the ground.

Carl stumbled to a stop, confused. Then he recognized a famous baseball player striding out of the woods and rubbing his right shoulder. Carl glanced down at Junior, lying unconscious on the ground, and understood. A rock the size of a fist lay before him.

"Good throw, Micah!" Then Carl remembered why he was angry, and he began searching frantically for the bullet wound in his dog, trying to stop the bleeding. "Good boy, Shadow. You are such a good boy! We'll get you to Doctor Peggy. She'll take care of you."

Meanwhile, Joe knelt and lifted Rachel into a sitting position. "Talk to me. Tell me what to do."

"I think I'm losing our baby, Joe," she said. "Call an ambulance."

"I already called 911," George said beside them.

A faint ambulance siren doubled and grew stronger. Suddenly two ambulances and three police cars pulled into the driveway.

"The bullet penetrated Shadow's chest area," Carl fretted. "I need to get him to the clinic. If I can get him to Peggy, she might be able to save him."

EMTs approached the group, bringing a gurney.

"This is my wife," Joe said. "She's nearly five months pregnant. She thinks she's losing the baby. Please be careful."

As he helped them put her onto the gurney, Rachel seemed to fixate on Shadow and Carl.

"Is Shadow alive?" she asked, peering over Joe's shoulder.

"So far, but Carl needs to get him to the clinic."

"Take him in the other ambulance."

"Of course," the EMT said. "We'll get the unconscious gentleman into the second ambulance just as soon as we take care of you."

"Not the man, the dog," Rachel said. "Get Shadow to Doctor Peggy Oglesby's clinic."

"We can't do that, ma'am. It isn't allowed."

"My wife is Officer Rachel Mattias from the Sugarcreek Police," Joe said. "If she says to transport the dog to the animal clinic, you'd probably better listen to her."

"That dog is a valuable asset." Rachel stopped speaking and panted for a moment as another spasm hit and passed. "I'll take responsibility."

Carl was surprised but grateful when they loaded Shadow into the ambulance.

"Where's Ezra?" Rachel asked as they rolled her away.

"George is with him. They are talking with one of the cops," Carl said. "Greta took off on foot when Joe knocked out Junior. It won't take them long to chase her down."

As Carl and his dog were being driven away from the scene, he saw Junior sit up and shake his head as though to clear it, and then the Millersburg Police helped him to his feet and cuffed him.

Chapter Sixty-Three

Two days later, Naomi drove her buggy over to Rachel's. When Rachel opened the door to the knock, she saw that Naomi was carrying a large bag.

"I heard you were out of the hospital," Naomi said. "Are you feeling better?"

Rachel shrugged. She was no longer in pain, but better? Not really.

"I brought you something." Naomi pulled a pot out of the bag. "It is your favorite—my chicken noodle soup. It is still warm. May I put it in the kitchen?"

"Of course."

Rachel did not follow her friend into the kitchen. Luke's words the night of the kidnapping about her and her son still stung. She hoped Naomi did not intend to stay long.

"Thank you," Rachel said, when Naomi finished her small errand and came back into the living room. "I'm sure Joe and Bobby will appreciate it."

Rachel did not offer Naomi a seat. There was a stiff politeness between them. The easy friendship they had once enjoyed was gone.

"How is Bobby?" Naomi asked.

"He's fine. How is Ezra?"

"He misses Bobby."

Rachel said nothing. Bobby would not be going to their home. He was not wanted.

Naomi sighed. "Luke said bitter and angry things the night the boys were stolen. I know he hurt you, but he was speaking from pain and weakness and frustration over his inability to protect our son. He needed to blame someone for what had happened, and harsh words came out of his mouth."

"He was just saying what he felt, Naomi," Rachel said. "I don't blame him for that."

"I want you to know that Bobby has never been a bad influence on our Ezra. Ever. Quite the opposite. Luke's illness has been hard on our son. It has turned him into a worried child, much too quiet and careful—except when Bobby comes over. Your son is boisterous and bright and he takes Ezra's mind off his father's illness. When Bobby is there, Ezra plays like a little boy *should* play."

"I wish you would have said all that at the time," Rachel said. "It was hard to hear my son criticized at a time when I didn't know if I would ever see him again."

"You have lived among us long enough to know that a good Amish wife never criticizes or corrects her husband in front of others, Rachel."

"True."

"Luke asked me to tell you that he is sorry and to thank you for all you did. He also wanted me to ask whether Bobby could come over soon to play with Ezra."

Rachel had nothing to say to that. Apologies were all well and good, but Luke had meant what he said that terrible night. She had no intention of allowing Bobby to go there anytime soon.

"Ezra speaks of nothing else except how brave your son was. And how unafraid Bobby was in standing up to the man and woman who took them. He will be devastated if he cannot have his friend come to play."

"I'm just not comfortable with it, Naomi. I'm sorry."

"I understand." Naomi reached into the bag she had brought and pulled out an old quilt. "Do you remember this?"

"It's the one your grandmother made for you before you were born."

"Do you remember when we got the mumps at the same time?" Naomi said. "Bertha offered to nurse both of us through it. My mother had a houseful of children and didn't argue. When my mother packed my things, she put my favorite quilt in as well. You and I lay in the bed together beneath that quilt. We were feverish and miserable, but your aunt took good care of us."

"Bertha was a wonderful nurse." Rachel wished Naomi would make her point and go. She had been through too much the past few days.

"When we started getting better," Naomi continued, "you said it was because of the quilt. You said my grandmother had made a magic quilt that could heal people."

Rachel smiled. That was a lifetime ago, when she and Naomi were little girls and as close as sisters.

"It has been mended many times," Naomi continued. She stroked the faded blue-and-white fabric she held in her arms. "As battered as it is, it is still my favorite. When I am ill or sad, I curl up beneath it and pretend that it is a medicinal quilt. I pretend that it can heal people's bodies and minds. It's a childish thing for a grown woman to do, of course. I've never told anybody else."

Rachel reached over and fingered the old quilt stitched so carefully by Naomi's loving grandmother. "Your grandmother put a lot of love into this quilt. I'm sure that alone gives it some healing qualities."

"I'm so glad you said that. Here." She placed the folded quilt in Rachel's arms. "I want you to have it. It is a gift."

"I can't take this."

"Please. I was praying it might heal our friendship."

Rachel held the quilt against her heart that ached so badly. "I lost the baby, Naomi."

"I know." Tears threatened to spill from her friend's kind blue eyes. "I am so sorry. I came here hoping it would help you to talk about it."

"Let's sit," Rachel said. "I'm really glad you're here."

Rachel went over to the couch, put her stocking feet on the coffee table, and pulled the quilt over her. It did feel comforting.

Naomi seemed unsure of where to sit.

Rachel lifted one side of the quilt. "I'll share."

"Oh! I would very much like to share!" Naomi came over, sat close to Rachel, and pulled part of the quilt over herself. Then she toed off her shoes and put her stocking feet on the coffee table beside Rachel's.

"Joe and I are going to have a funeral for the baby tomorrow," Rachel said. "It hurts so badly, Naomi."

"And all this pain and loss because of Luke's behavior when he was young and foolish, and the bad things that came of it. I'm so sorry, Rachel."

"I know," Rachel said. "So am I."

With their shoulders touching and the old, soft quilt pulled up to their chins, the healing between the women began.

Chapter Sixty-Four

Joe enjoyed hearing the laughter and the camaraderie on opening night. It didn't feel as much like work as like a good party with people that he cared about.

It tickled him to look over his shoulder and see Lydia smiling and enjoying people while they sampled her pies, as she stood there in her little Amish dress, bonnet, and sensible black tennis shoes—with her new oversized baseball jersey overtop. Darren had had her name printed in block letters on the back above Joe's old team number. Joe hadn't expected her to be such a good sport about it, but the older woman still had some surprises about her.

His son was strutting around in his own miniature baseball uniform. Darren had special-ordered it for him just for opening night, along with blue-and-white jerseys in the colors of the LA Dodgers for the others. Rachel was wearing her jersey as well and looked adorable in it as she bussed tables. Across the front of all the jerseys read "Joe's Home Plate," and Joe's number 73 was displayed on the back.

It was crowded in the restaurant not only because it was opening night, but because they'd tried to make room for people to enjoy lots of samples. Small meatballs made up of five different recipes Joe had developed for his hamburgers, along with various sauces to dip them in, were set out. People could choose their favorite combination that way. There were small plastic cups of potato salad and baked beans, and Aunt Lydia was distributing tiny slices of her pies.

Even Anna had a job. Concentrating hard, she placed a small plastic fork beside each slice of pie Lydia handed out.

To Joe's astonishment, his brother's idea of opening Joe's Home Plate maybe wasn't such a bad idea. All he knew for sure was that he and Darren would work hard to make it a success.

The last few weeks, as he and Darren fought to get all the equipment they needed and learned the ins and outs of opening a new restaurant, their relationship had deepened. His kid brother was actually turning out to be a pretty good businessman. He had never expected to be proud of his brother, given Darren's track record, but tonight had been an eye-opener.

Darren presided over the boutique soda "bar," giving out samples like he was offering fine wines. At one point, Joe heard laughter and Darren saying, "This one is a presumptuous little soda with overtures of green apple. I believe the vintage is about two weeks ago."

Lydia's pies, displayed in an old-fashioned circular display case left over from the original restaurant, were a huge hit. She was in her element. Joe watched her trying to accept all the compliments with admirable Amish humility—but her eyes sparkled with each "Danke" she uttered. He thought she was adorable.

Guys from the Garaway baseball team were working the tables, while Joe and an experienced short-order cook Darren had enticed were busy filling orders and flipping burgers.

The place was still a little rough around the edges, but intentionally so. They wanted a restaurant where people could feel at home—and the focus was on the food, not the decor.

The menu was short, but the food was stellar. They'd made sure the produce was as local as possible. Sugarcreek's Sweetwater Farm had provided all the vegetables. The condiments had been carefully selected as an organic assortment purchased from the Swiss Village Bulk Foods, which was a short walk from the restaurant. And the baked beans were as addictive as they could possibly get them—not from cans, but from navy beans soaked overnight and then seasoned with real bacon, sugar, and ketchup before baking two hours in the large ovens.

The eggs the restaurant used were from a local farmer who truly allowed his chickens to range free, which meant the yokes were nearly orange from all the nutrients the chickens ingested, and the chilled egg-infused potato salad was a darker yellow than those made with commercial-type grocery-store eggs. People were already commenting on the extra flavor. Once Joe and Darren perfected the potato-salad recipe, they'd pasted the recipe to the kitchen wall.

The buns were baked just down the street, so new that a fresh-bread smell permeated the place. There were three different cheeses to choose from for those who wanted a cheeseburger—cheddar, pepper Jack, and Swiss—all from local, award-winning suppliers. It had been no trick to find a local farmer who had grass-fed Angus beef to sell.

Then there were the three large-screen televisions replaying baseball games from the past—everything from grainy, black-and-white clips of early players to some of Joe's shutout games. The restaurant would show contemporary games during baseball season.

One of their biggest challenges, as far as Joe could see, was going to be keeping Bobby from sampling too many of the sodas. The different colors were just too tempting, and the child definitely didn't need any more sugar in him. He was already about as hyper as a little boy could get. Bobby was currently having the time of his life bragging about how he'd helped his uncle and daddy set up "his" new restaurant.

As Joe flipped burgers over the grill, he could hardly believe the happy sound of diners enjoying conversation and good food. This was his place, with his family helping. He had no idea if he could make a living with this, but if tonight was any indication, they just might.

During a short lull, he took a moment to go behind the bar, throw one arm over his brother's shoulder, and give him a one-armed hug.

"You did good, bro," he said. "Thank you."

The look of gratitude and happiness that Darren gave him was worth all the worry and work they had gone through to make this happen.

One of the things that Joe was proudest of, the thing that had nearly broken his heart when Darren had insisted on it, was a small sign in the window that said: "If You Are Hungry but Have No Money, You Can Still Eat. Ask to See the Manager. No Questions Asked."

"Why?" he'd asked his brother.

"Because once, when I was hungry and had no money, I saw a restaurant that had this same sign in their window. I went in. They fed me and I never forgot it. That meal and the way the manager treated me made all the difference. I had a bit of good luck after that, and whenever I was back in that city, I would make sure to eat there and leave a big tip to make up for it. I always told myself that if I were ever in the same position, I would do the same."

It hurt to think that his brother had gone hungry from lack of money. "I never realized you were that desperate," Joe had responded quietly.

"More than once," Darren had said. "I appreciate the help you gave me through the years, though. It'll be nice to help you for a change. I'm really enjoying working with you."

"Me too, bro." And Joe meant it. Creating this business together had also created a real relationship with his brother—someone he now realized he'd never known—a man who had lived in his older brother's shadow for too long while trying to find his own way.

As the brothers now stood with their arms around each another's shoulders, just savoring the feel of the moment, Joe's eyes feasted on the sight of Rachel and Bobby working in this restaurant he and Darren had created. He couldn't get enough of looking at them or of thanking God over and over that they were safe. He prayed daily that he and Rachel could have more children. Losing the baby had been hard on her. It had been hard on him too. It was not easy to lose a child. Explaining it to Bobby had been heart-wrenching, but the little guy had dealt with it better than expected.

Joe had learned something this week, the most important lesson of his life. If a man's family was healthy and safe, he didn't have any problems. Everything else—absolutely *everything*—was just window dressing.

Chapter Sixty-Five

Carl wanted good things for Rachel and her family and hoped the restaurant's opening night would be a success. Darren and Joe had promoted it so heavily that everyone in the area was aware that tonight was the big night.

So, Carl had showered, shaved, slicked back his thinning hair, and put on his best blue shirt and khaki pants to make this visit. It felt strange not having Shadow with him, but his good dog was past the crisis and on the mend. One of the technicians at the clinic had offered to stay with Shadow while Carl came tonight, and he was grateful. He didn't want his dog to be alone.

Now he watched from across the street, periodically hearing laughter and snippets of conversation and wondering if it would all stop when he walked into the room.

Carl didn't care if he got a meal; he just wanted an excuse to check on Rachel and make sure she was okay. He knew she'd miscarried the baby after the ambulance had whisked her off. A woman like Rachel would have to be devastated about losing a child. With the childhood he had survived, he was impressed with any mother who would fight to care for her child.

The little girl in the pink dress who had faced him over her daddy's body had grown up into a ferociously protective mom. He knew it was a strange connection they had, but Carl felt almost paternal in his pride of her.

George said he was certain Carl would be welcome at the restaurant tonight, but he wasn't so sure George was right. To go in or not to go in, that was the question. If he went in, would the roses he'd brought be appropriate? Probably not. After twenty years in prison, how could he know what was appropriate and what wasn't?

It was late September, and although the weather was still warm, there was the scent of fall in the air. He rolled down the windows of his truck and sat there, trying to screw up the courage to go in. The place was going to be quite a hit, judging from the people coming and going. Every time the door opened, music and laughter floated out. People were surely having fun in there.

Carl had a recent fantasy he allowed himself to indulge in every now and then. He would never dare mention it to anyone, but as he sat on the outside of the restaurant looking in, he revisited it.

In his fantasy, he wasn't a childless ex-con. Instead, his life had taken an entirely different turn. Instead of killing Frank Troyer, he had married a nice, pretty woman—maybe someone like Peggy—and they were living a respectable life surrounded by friends and family. They had a daughter who was a lot like Rachel, a young woman who was courageous and smart but also compassionate.

There was a house that sat up on a rise on Main Street in Sugarcreek that he'd always liked. It looked sturdy and strong, and it had a symmetry that appealed to him. Carl imagined living in that house with his wife. It would be a Sunday afternoon. A beautiful day. They were sitting on the front porch, relaxing, and waving at friends as they walked by on the sidewalk. A roast was in the oven, cooking, as they waited for their daughter and her husband and their children to come by for supper.

He wondered what it would be like to have a son-in-law like Joe to talk baseball with after supper. He'd buy one of those large-screen TVs so they could watch games together. Maybe he would have a little grand-child on his knee. He would have to be careful not to yell at the team if he were holding a grandchild. He would never want to scare the child.

Or maybe he and this make-believe baseball-loving son-in-law could go to a real game sometime. That would really be something.

None of this was possible, of course. But it was nice to think about.

Two other people came out of Joe's Home Plate and the music and laughter drifted out again. The front window was large, and it was easy to watch all the hustle and bustle inside.

Typical of Carl to be on the outside looking in, while wondering what a normal life would feel like.

He had talked to Peggy about whether to come tonight. She had strongly urged him to do so. What if they had an opening night and no one showed up? she'd said. They would appreciate him making the effort. Take flowers, she'd said. What was the worst that could happen?

Carl had stopped at the florist's to purchase the flowers. He glanced at the bouquet of red roses now lying on the seat beside him. He'd heard that red roses were important to people.

Peggy was usually right about things. He trusted her judgment. But as he sat there trying to make himself get out of the truck and go in, he simply couldn't do it. Especially not carrying a dozen red roses. What sort of a fool would he look like? It wasn't as though he were a family friend or anything like that.

He didn't expect Rachel to throw him out anymore. Not after they had found Bobby together. What would probably happen from now on was a polite distance. That was okay. It was much better than the way it had been when he was constantly worried that he might run into her.

Carl heard the escalation of music and laughter again and noticed that someone else had come out. One person. Alone. Instead of walking off to a car, the person sat down on the bench outside the restaurant. It took him a moment, but then he realized that it was Rachel.

She wrapped her arms around herself as though she were cold, except it was too warm out for her to be cold. Then he noticed that she was rocking back and forth as though troubled. He waited for Joe or someone else to arrive to comfort her, but those inside must not have known she'd slipped out.

He screwed up his courage, got out of the truck, and approached her.

"Carl," she said, and she smiled at him.

She smiled not just with her mouth, but also with her eyes. Instead of her Sugarcreek Police uniform, she was wearing an oversized baseball jersey. She looked so much smaller without the uniform.

"Is there anything I can do for you, Rachel?"

"How is your dog?" she asked.

"Doc Peggy had to fight hard to save his life, but Shadow is going to be fine."

"That was really something, when he went after Junior. You're a really good dog trainer."

"Shadow is a really smart dog." He hesitated a moment. "Do you mind if I sit down?"

She had been sitting in the center of the bench. Now she scooted over to make room for him.

"Whatever happened to the kidnappers?" Carl said. "I haven't seen anything about it on the news."

"Luke and Naomi wanted to try to keep it quiet. So far we've been able to, but in the meantime I found out some things about Junior's motives."

"Besides the ransom?"

"It goes further than that." She brought her knees up to her chin and wrapped her arms around her legs. "Ezra's dad, Luke Yoder, was one of those Amish teenagers who thought the grass was greener on the other side of the fence. There wasn't much the Englisch world had to offer that he didn't get into. He and Junior became buddies. That's how Luke met Junior and Greta's younger sister. Cynthia liked to party, and Luke was happy to oblige. Sometimes wayward Amish kids scare themselves back into the church, and that's what happened to Luke. He saw that Cynthia was on a downward spiral and knew he had to get away from her before it was too late."

"My guess is that she didn't appreciate him leaving."

"Nope. She was a pretty unstable person. When she couldn't get him back, she overdosed. No one could determine whether it was deliberate or accidental. In the meantime, Luke had joined the church and was courting Naomi. I was away at the police academy and wasn't around very much."

"But that was several years ago. Why now?"

"Junior took it hard. He was the one who had introduced his little sister to drugs. He went out west and did everything from working on oil rigs to panhandling. Was in and out of rehab several times too. Finally, he came to the conclusion that he wasn't the one to blame for his sister's death—it was the Amish, and Luke in particular.

"What you probably don't know is that the local Amish have been getting harassed a lot recently. Fences cut, livestock getting loose, hay bales set on fire, that sort of thing. It was Junior all along. He even tried to poison Sugarcreek's canine officer, Ranger, that night to keep him from being able to track them. The dog survived, but it was an ugly thing to do. Everything Junior did was working up a head of steam for the big moment when he—to put it in his words—'made Luke find out what it feels like to lose someone.' Of course the idea of all that ransom money didn't hurt either."

Carl took a moment to absorb the news. "A man who would kidnap a child and poison a dog…"

"I know. Not to mention the fact that he was planning on tying me up and leaving me to die. He's a real peach of a fellow."

"What about Greta?"

"She'll do time, but not as much as Junior," Rachel said. "Weird woman. She was a whole lot more concerned about her cat, Baby, having kittens without her than any trauma she and her brother would cause the boys and their families."

"Baby?"

"That's what she called her cat. Why?"

"I remember her now. Baby is a patient of Peggy's. I *thought* Greta looked familiar."

"If you hadn't picked up on the fact that Ezra was frightened, and if you hadn't told George about what you had seen, and if you hadn't been there when I got in trouble..." Rachel choked up. "I owe you my life and the life of my son."

"I was glad to help."

"Did you hear that I lost the baby?" Rachel said, in a small voice.

"I did," he answered. "I'm sorry."

"Joe and I chose to have a small funeral, just the three of us, the aunts, and George. It helped a little."

Carl chose not to mention that they were not the only ones at that funeral. He and Shadow had also respectfully attended...from a distance.

"At the hospital, one of the nurses told me that if I had stayed home and in bed that day, I might have been able to save it."

"Maybe the nurse was wrong."

"Maybe." There was so much pain in her voice.

"You had no choice, Rachel. You had no choice but to go save your son and his friend."

"True, but it would have been nice if Junior had picked a more convenient time!"

"What's with these criminals anyway?" Carl joked.

"That's right." She gave a half laugh then sobered. "Do you know what I kept thinking while we were hunting for Bobby and I thought I might never see him again?"

"No."

"I kept thinking what a terrible mother I had been for not really wanting to play Candy Land with him, when he loved it so."

"I'm guessing you've played it a lot since you got him back?"

"Oh, yes. Many times. And I really hate that game."

"But you love your son."

"I do," she said.

Carl thought of the nights when his own mother had locked him out of the house, of not knowing whether he would be alive or dead the next morning. He remembered being hungry and afraid. In his world, a parent not playing Candy Land was pretty unimportant. He considered telling Rachel this but decided against it.

Instead, all he said was, "Bobby is lucky to have you for a mom."

Rachel's next comment was unexpected. "Do you like Peggy?"

"She's a fine person."

"I think she likes you. As in *likes* you."

He was pleased. "Seriously?"

"She came tonight. She's all dressed up, and she seems nervous. There's an extra seat beside her—and she told me she was saving it for you if you came."

"I doubt she'd be interested in a broken-down ex-con like me."

"Maybe. Maybe not. She's a good person, Carl, and she's been through a lot. Be kind to her."

"I can't imagine not being kind to her."

They sat in silence awhile, each deep in their own thoughts.

The door opened and Bertha stuck her head out. Carl was surprised to see her wearing a baseball jersey over her Amish dress.

"Rachel? Are you all right? I could use some help clearing tables." She squinted. "Who is that you are talking to?"

"It's Carl, Aunt Bertha."

"Ach," the old woman said. "Will wonders never cease? But you have talked long enough. You need to come get something to eat, Carl," she said, "before Joe runs out of food." And at that, she shut the door.

"She's right, you should come in," Rachel said as she stood.

"I'd rather go back home," he said. "It is enough to have gotten a chance to talk with you."

"No," Rachel said, shaking her head. "Doc Peggy has been saving that seat far too long as it is."

"I brought flowers for you to celebrate opening night. They're wilting in the truck. Do you want me to get them, or would you rather I not?"

"Of course I want the flowers."

He brought them to her. One dozen red roses, and they weren't wilted in the least.

"Perfect," she said. "Now, you wait out here for a couple minutes. Please don't leave."

He was genuinely surprised that it mattered to her if he stayed. "Okay."

"Promise?"

"I promise."

He waited on the bench for a few minutes before she came out.

"You'll like what I've done with your roses," she said. "We were missing something important for our grand opening. Come and see."

Against his better judgment, he followed her inside where all the music and laughter was. Where there was warmth and good friends enjoying themselves. Where he did not belong and never had.

As they came inside, someone turned off the music. Rachel stood on top of a bench and called for everyone's attention.

"Everyone in town knows what happened in the bank across the street twenty years ago. A drifter by the name of Carl Bateman shot and killed my father. Six weeks ago, that same man put his own life in danger to save my life and the lives of my son and his friend, Ezra. I want everyone to know that, regardless of what might have happened in the past, this is Carl Bateman. He is a *good* man…and he is my *friend!*"

Carl was stunned. He had never imagined anything like this.

He felt a small tug at his shirtsleeve and glanced down to see Bobby standing beside him.

In as loud of a voice as Bobby could muster, he said, "And he's *my* friend too!"

The room burst into applause. And as the applause swelled around him, Carl's eyes sought Peggy's. She was smiling, with tears streaming down her face, and he knew at that moment he would never be on the outside looking in again.

"We wondered when you'd finally get around to showing up!" George shouted as the applause died down. Everyone laughed and resettled.

Rachel pointed around at the tables—all twelve of which were decorated with a single red rose. "I forgot to order flowers. Thanks for helping out. Now let's get you something to eat. Joe makes a really good burger."

As Rachel led him to the table where a place had been laid beside Peggy, Bertha reached out to Carl. He paused and grabbed her hand, and they looked into each other's eyes with so many words unspoken. Words that did not need to be said. She knew, and he knew, that the forgiveness she had fought so hard to achieve over the years had been the key that ultimately led to this great healing.

The End

Author's Note

Sugarcreek, Ohio is a very real town. I go there often and I try to portray it as accurately as possible because some of my readers enjoy traveling and exploring the settings of my books. Therefore, I need to let you know that one of the eating establishment I write about, Joe's Home Plate, does not exist. It is, however, based upon Bags Sports Pub situated right on Sugarcreek's Main Street, not far from the enormous outdoor Cuckoo Clock.

Bags Sports Pub is locally owned and they do have great burgers. I once asked the owner where he had studied his craft. His answer was, "In my mom's kitchen." (Gotta love a guy who admits to learning how to cook from his mom.) Bags Sports Pub does not have a bar that displays gourmet soda pop, but if you walk a few blocks over to Sugarcreek Village Bulk Foods, you might find the locally-made sarsaparilla that Bobby loves.

Right behind Sugarcreek Village Bulk Foods is Sugarcreek Village Inn, which is one of my favorite places to stay in Amish country, and an excellent value. I especially enjoy sitting outside on the huge veranda watching the Amish buggies trot by. If you like the idea of sleeping in a remodeled train car, they have those, too.

The sign in Joe's Home Plate that says, "If you are hungry but don't have any money, you can still eat," came from a sign I saw at a locally owned BBQ place named Rowdy's in Jackson, Ohio—which is near my home—and is not far from a relatively new settlement of Amish.

The bakery I mention in the story is also situated on Main Street. The owner, Esther, is an Amish woman who definitely knows her way around pastries. I think even Lydia would approve—if Rachel could ever talk her into trying one of Esther's doughnuts.

-Serena

Love's *Journey*™

in Sugarcreek

Love
Rekindled

Love Rekindled - Sample

Keturah Hochstetler struggled to keep her eyes open as her buggy swayed down the unpaved township road. It was nearly two o'clock in the morning and she was bone tired. The dark December sky drizzled rain against the buggy's thin roof and she shivered inside her coat.

It would be nice to have a warm blanket right now, or heated bricks to put at her feet, but even though she was cold on the outside, she felt the warmth of contentment in her heart. The birth had gone well. That's all that mattered. At sixty-seven she had less stamina than in her twenties, but bringing babies safely into the world was her greatest joy—a holy profession.

The buggy gave a lurch as the buggy wheels hit a bump and jarred her wide awake again. The uneven tracks carved into the road by hundreds of iron-shod buggy wheels made for a bumpy ride. Because of that, the Englisch vehicles tended to avoid these back dirt roads and she was grateful.

The birthing she had attended tonight was especially gratifying. It had been a long labor. First babies were often reluctant to come out into the world, but the young mother had done well. The baby, a healthy little boy, had such strong lungs that his cries set the porch dogs to howling in sympathy. She and the grandmother laughed together at his indignation over having to leave his cozy spot beneath his mother's heart. Had he waited a few hours longer to make his appearance, he would have been a Christmas baby.

The older women in the extended family, wise in the ways of babies and new mothers, would take over now. She was free to think about her own family and the Christmas celebration they would have today.

She had prepared as much of the food ahead as possible. Her daughters-in-law would bring the rest. Soon their home would be filled with love and laughter. Unlike the Englisch, they did not spoil their grandchildren with gifts—only one small wooden toy each for the little ones. Her husband, Ivan, had made the toys in his shop and he was as eager as a child himself, waiting to see the grandchildren unwrap their presents. It had been a mild winter so far, but snow was finally predicted and Ivan was still holding onto the hope that by evening he could take the whole family for a sleigh ride.

She could hardly wait to give her husband the gift she had bought for him. The handle of his old straight razor had broken recently. Instead of buying a new one, he had taped it back together and continued to use it to trim the beard away from his mouth. It worked fine, he said. Then last week when they had visited Lehman's store, she noticed him lingering over the new straight razors in the display case, but he had walked away. No wonder. They were shockingly expensive, but she didn't care. Ivan had few wants. It wasn't often that she had the pleasure of finding the perfect gift for him.

While Ivan was engaged in conversation with a clerk in the hardware department, she managed to slip away to the razor display. With her midwife money, she quickly purchased the best straight razor they had. It was made in France and had a lovely cow bone handle. It cost over two hundred dollars, but it was worth it for something he would use so often. It was now hidden away in the bottom of her birthing bag, the one place she knew Ivan would never look. He was going to be so surprised.

The light from the lantern on the back of her buggy swung back and forth, and the sound of the rain and the rhythmic beat of Brownie's hoofs flinging dirt against the undercarriage combined to create a sort of hypnotic lullaby. Only two more miles to go before she could climb into her warm, cozy bed.

Her head nodded and the reins grew slack in her hands. It was not the first time her good horse had taken her home while she dozed.

The sound of a vehicle startled her wide-awake again. Somewhere up ahead a car was coming and it was very loud. She didn't know much about cars, but she knew the sound of a bad muffler.

Careful not to slip into the ditch, she guided Brownie to the far right side of the road, making certain to leave enough room for the car to get past them. Also, up ahead was a dangerously steep curve. She slowed Brownie down so they could stay back, far out of the way until the car got safely around it.

It sounded like the driver was going too fast for these rain-slicked roads, but what did she know? She was used to driving at the top speed of ten miles per hour.

The sound of a crash startled her.

"Whoa." She pulled back on the reins, bringing Brownie to a complete stop so she could listen. A car horn was blaring on and on, but the sound of a bad muffler had stopped.

She was neither a doctor nor a nurse, but during her years as a midwife and as the mother of sons who were not always careful, she had learned a great deal about the human body and what to do to stop bleeding or deal with broken bones. She even knew CPR. The fire department in Sugarcreek had sponsored a free class she had attended.

She hesitated only long enough to draw a deep breath before yelling "Giddyup!" and slapping the reins on Brownie's rump. The old horse was so startled, he broke into a gallop.

As they turned the curve, she saw that an old, blue sedan had collided head on with a large oak tree that stood in the elbow of the bend.

The windshield was partially knocked out and the car's front end was crumbled. The car horn continued to blare.

Brownie pranced nervously as she tried to calm him. As soon as he was steady, she grabbed her flashlight, stepped out of the buggy, and carefully approached the wreck.

Blood was splattered all over the windshield. Her knees grew weak at the sight, but she mustered her courage and walked closer.

There appeared to be no one in the car except the driver who was slumped against the door. Keturah played her flashlight over the side of the driver's face which was pressed against the window. It was a young woman, possibly a teenager, with short, blonde hair, wearing multiple earrings that sparkled against the light.

She wondered why this girl had chosen to disobey the Englisch law. If she had been wearing a seatbelt, she would not have hit the windshield.

"Are you okay?" Keturah knocked on the side window.

The girl stirred, opened her eyes, and looked around blankly.

Keturah tried the door, but it was locked.

"Can you get out?"

The girl fumbled with the door, managed to open it, and nearly fell out sideways. Keturah caught her and helped her to the ground. Her heart dropped when she saw the girl's hugely rounded belly. Unless she missed her guess, and she rarely did, the girl was about eight months pregnant. The seat belt had probably grown uncomfortable against her swollen stomach.

There appeared to be a large gash in the right side of her head. It was hard to tell because of all the blood. Keturah knew that even minor head wounds bled profusely, so she was hoping it wasn't as bad as it appeared.

The girl was agitated and grappled at Keturah's coat. "Don't let him take my baby," she said. "Please..."

She lost consciousness and fell back against the ground.

Keturah hunted for a pulse. There was none.

She had never had to use her firehouse CPR training, but she laid the flashlight on the ground, placed the palms of her shaking hands on the girl's sternum and began to push rhythmically.

Two minutes later, she still could not find a pulse. A surge of panic hit as she made calculations. A baby could only survive for about seven minutes in the womb once a mother had died.

"Come on, come on." Keturah said, as she resumed chest compressions. "Please breathe."

If nothing else, she knew she was forcing the mother's blood to carry residual oxygen still in her lungs to the baby which might keep it alive a little longer.

The cold drizzle that had accompanied her here began to turn nastier. A wind blew up, showering her and the girl with wet, dead leaves. She prayed for strength and endurance in her fight to keep the mother and baby alive. Her coat and clothing became soaked with rain. The car horn blared on and on—nerve wracking but perhaps the only hope of help. The sound might cause someone close by to investigate.

There was a strong smell that clung to the girl's clothes—a food smell. It reminded her of a niece who had once been employed frying dough-nuts at a bakery. Eventually, the niece quit the job because the family objected to the constant scent of vegetable grease that clung to her hair and clothing.

The rain had washed much of the blood away from the girl's face and hair. Keturah could see the wound clearer now and she nearly recoiled from the severity of it. Unless God sent a miracle, this girl was never going to breathe on her own again.

Now the burning question became—what about the baby?

Although she possessed much knowledge about the herbs and tinctures midwifes had passed down over the centuries, it did not keep her from embracing newer technologies. A small Doppler fetal monitoring device was back in the buggy. It was the only way to find out if the baby still lived.

She had fervently prayed for God to send help—but as each second ticked away, it had become apparent that the only help He had seen fit to send to this pregnant girl and her child was herself, a tired Amish midwife. Her aging knees cried out in pain as she rose and ran to the buggy where she kept her bag filled with supplies.

The rain increased as she slipped on the wet leaves and fell in her hurry to get the birthing bag. As her knee hit the ground, she cried out from the sharp pain, but immediately scrambled back up and limped to the buggy where she unhooked the battery-operated lantern hanging on the back. It would give her better light than the small flashlight. Then she grabbed her birthing bag and rushed back to the mother.

Squatting, she sat the lantern down near the girl. Then she reached into her bag for the tube of ultrasound gel, shoved the denim jacket aside, pushed the girl's black t-shirt up and smeared some gel on her belly. Then she fumbled for her Doppler monitor and began to search for the baby's heartbeat.

There. She could hear it. The baby lived, and the heart beat was relatively strong. The irony was not lost on her that she was allowed to own such a technically advanced instrument, but not allowed to carry a cell phone.

If there was one thing the Amish leadership took seriously—and they took many things seriously—it was trying to be a good example for the young. She understood their church leaders' fear that owning cell phones would be too much of a temptation to their young people. She had heard that many evil things could be accessed on those picture phones— unspeakable things. But oh, what she wouldn't give for a way to call an ambulance right now.

343

The thought struck that this Englisch girl might have one. Practically all the young ones she had seen walking down the streets of Sugarcreek had such devices in their hand. Quickly, she searched the girl's pockets. Nothing there. She checked inside the car. There was nothing there either, not even a purse.

She quickly began the compressions again, regretting the few seconds she had taken to search. Those precious seconds had been wasted. Had she even found a phone, she wasn't certain she could figure out how to use it.

The CPR instructor had taught them how to do mouth-to-mouth resuscitation but warned them that it was no longer advised. Especially if one was working on a stranger. It had to do with the possibility of contracting life-threatening diseases.

With the seven minute clock ticking down in her head, Keturah decided to ignore the instructor's warnings. She bent over the girl, pinched her nose shut, and began to force her own breath into the girl's lungs while she prayed that someone would hear that car horn and come to their rescue.

Once again, she stopped and listened for the baby's heartbeat. It was there, but it was growing fainter.

"Du nett schtauva, bobli," she said. "Please don't die, baby."

Sick to her stomach with fear and worry, Keturah made one of the hardest decisions of her life.

With tears of grief streaming down her face, she held her hands out palms up, and allowed the rain to cleanse them of blood and gel before she reached into her birthing bag for the sturdy surgical scissors she always used to cut umbilical cords. They were such a clumsy tool to use for a C-section but it was all she had.

Then she remembered Ivan's gift. She dug deep into the bottom of the bag and pulled out the slim box that held the bone-handled blade. The well-honed straight razor was as sharp as any doctor's scalpel.

"I am so sorry," Keturah said to the dead girl. "But I have to do this."

Biting her lip with concentration, she tried to shield the girl's body the best she could with her own as she opened the razor and drew it across the girl's abdomen.

"Lord help me," she said, as she exposed the thin membrane in which the baby lay.

About the Author

Serena B. Miller decided to get serious about writing fiction while she was working as a court reporter in Detroit and found herself developing an overwhelming desire to compose a happy ending for every transcript she typed. She and her minister-carpenter husband live in a southern Ohio farming community, in an 1830s log cabin that has been in her family for five generations. Serena was delighted when an Amish community formed not far from her home, and she has enjoyed getting to know these hard-working people. When she isn't canning tomatoes, splitting firewood, shooing deer out of the blueberry bushes, or feeding grown sons who drop by daily to see if she's cooked anything good, she helps out at her church and sings at the drop of a hat. She also falls in love with all her characters and writes as many happy endings for them as she can.

www.serenabmiller.com

More books by
Serena B. Miller

LOVE'S JOURNEY SERIES:

Love's Journey in Sugarcreek: The Sugar Haus Inn - Book I
(Formerly : Love Finds You in Sugarcreek, Ohio)
Love's Journey in Sugarcreek: Rachel's Rescue - Book II
Love's Journey in Sugarcreek: Love Rekindled - Book III

THE UNCOMMON GRACE SERIES (*AMISH*):

An Uncommon Grace - Book I
Hidden Mercies - Book II
Fearless Hope - Book III

MICHIGAN NORTHWOODS SERIES (*HISTORICAL*):

The Measure of Katie Calloway - Book I
Under a Blackberry Moon - Book II
A Promise to Love - Book III

SUSPENSE:

A Way of Escape

COZY MYSTERY:

The Accidental Adventures of Doreen Sizemore

NON-FICTION:

More Than Happy: The Wisdom of Amish Parenting

VISIT SERENABMILLER.COM TO SIGN UP FOR
SERENA'S NEWSLETTER AND TO CONNECT WITH SERENA.

Made in the USA
Columbia, SC
01 November 2019

82449093R00209